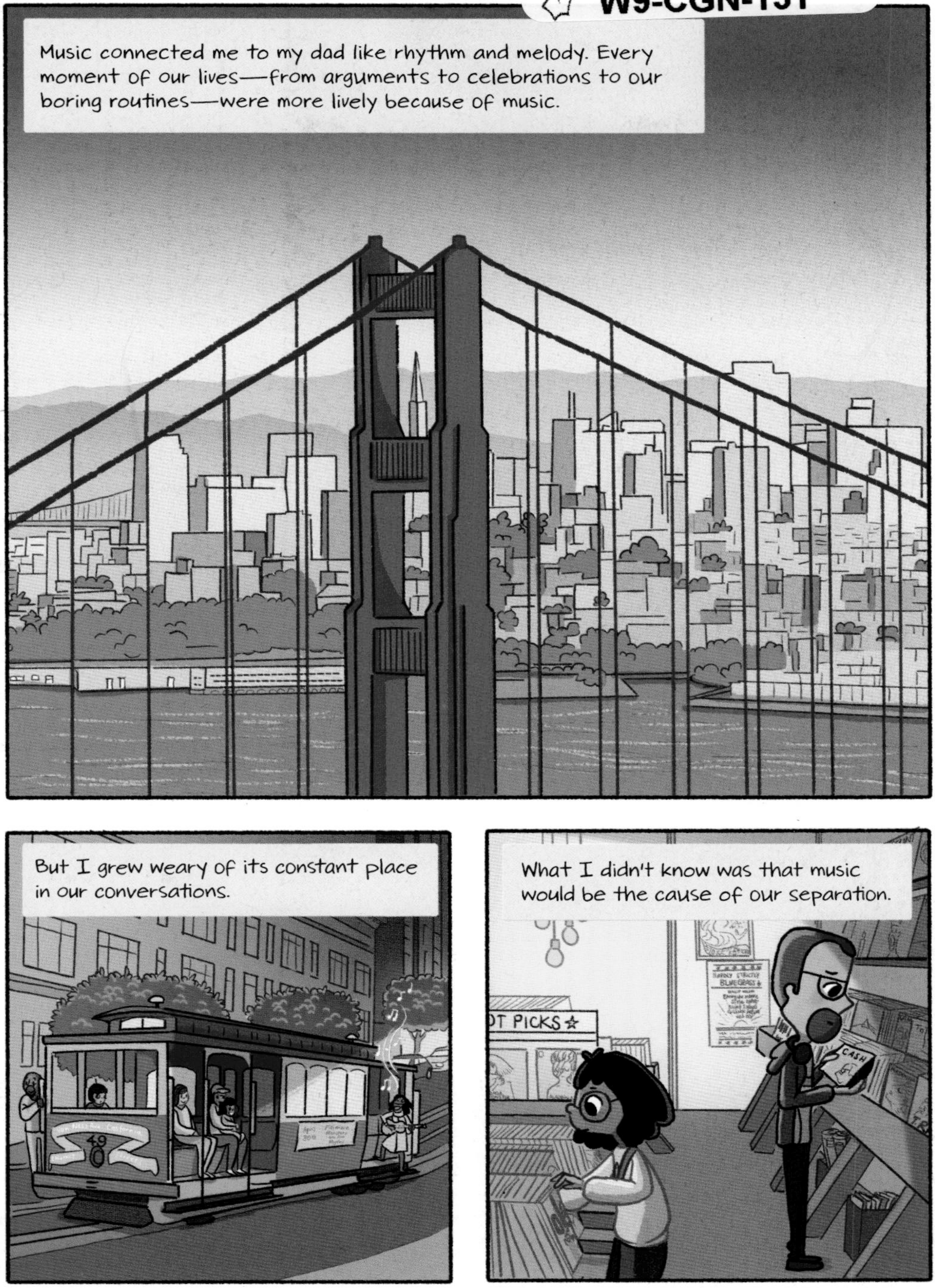
Music connected me to my dad like rhythm and melody. Every moment of our lives—from arguments to celebrations to our boring routines—were more lively because of music.
But I grew weary of its constant place in our conversations.
What I didn't know was that music would be the cause of our separation.
CASH

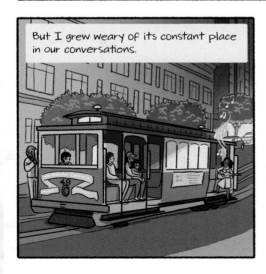

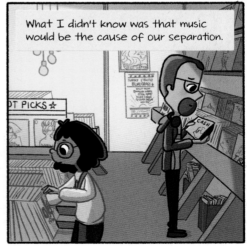

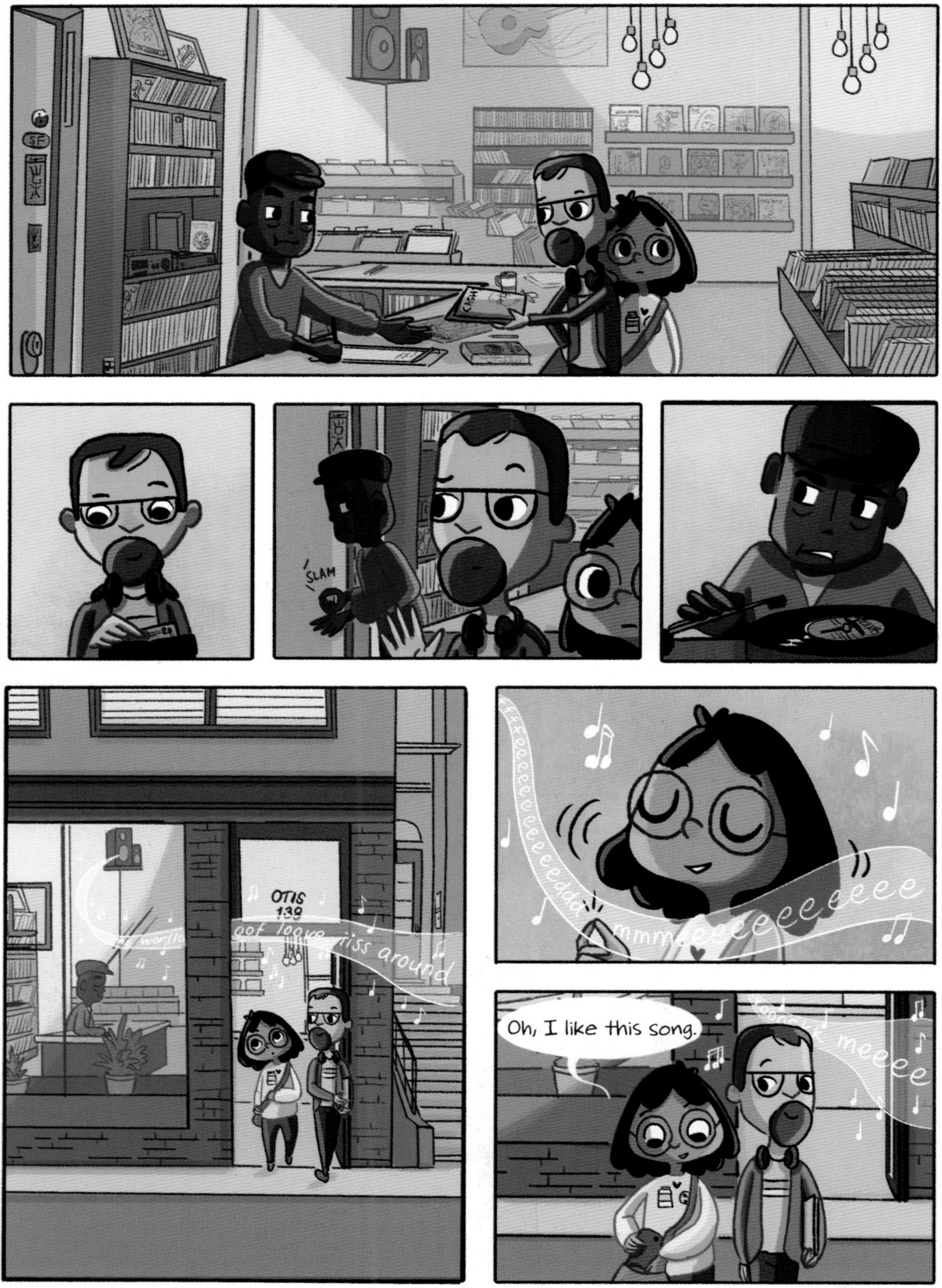
SLAM
OTIS
138
Oh, I like this song.

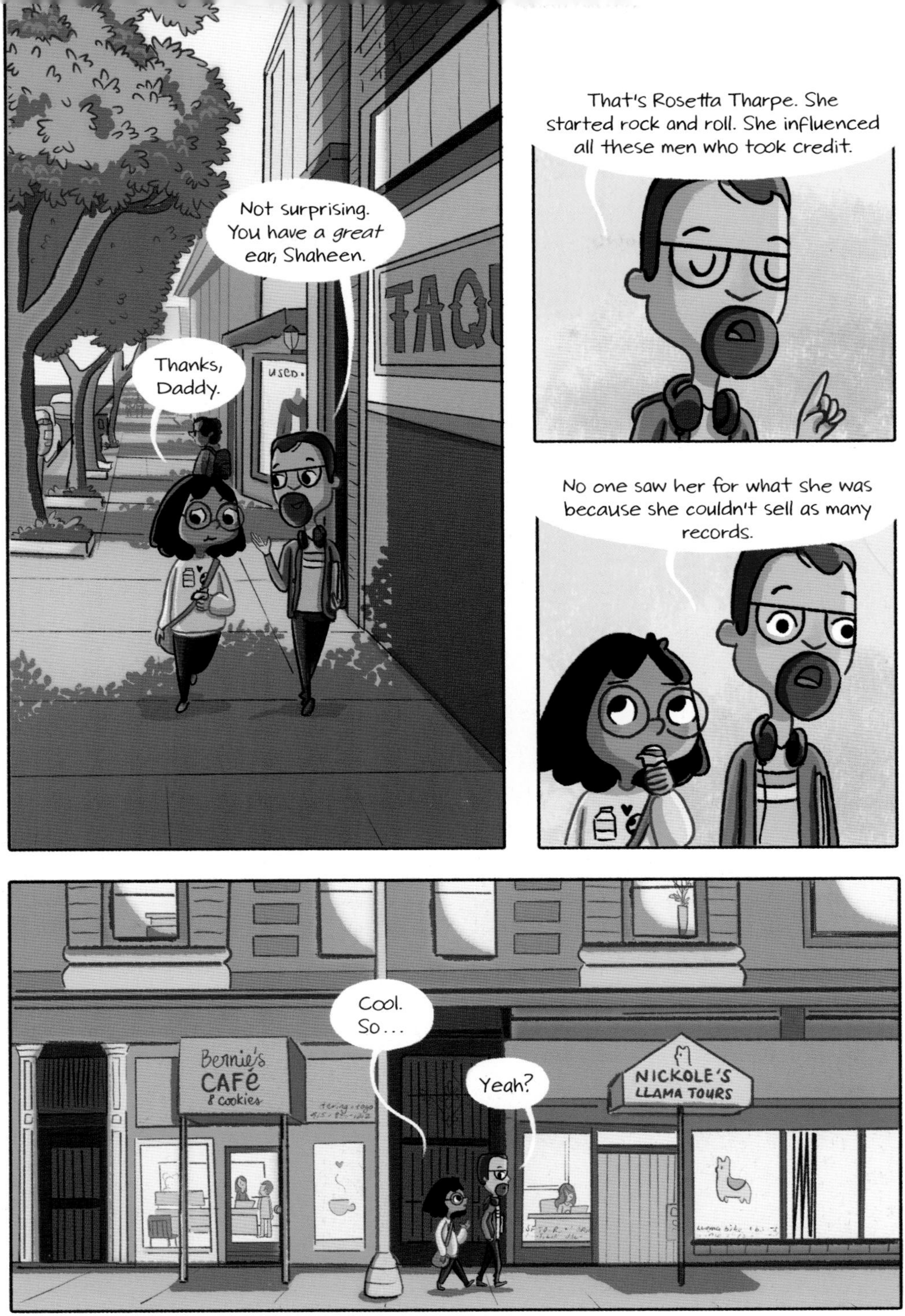
Not surprising. You have a *great* ear, Shaheen.
Thanks, Daddy.
TAQ
USED
That's Rosetta Tharpe. She started rock and roll. She influenced all these men who took credit.
No one saw her for what she was because she couldn't sell as many records.
Bernie's CAFÉ & cookies
Cool. So...
Yeah?
NICKOLE'S LLAMA TOURS

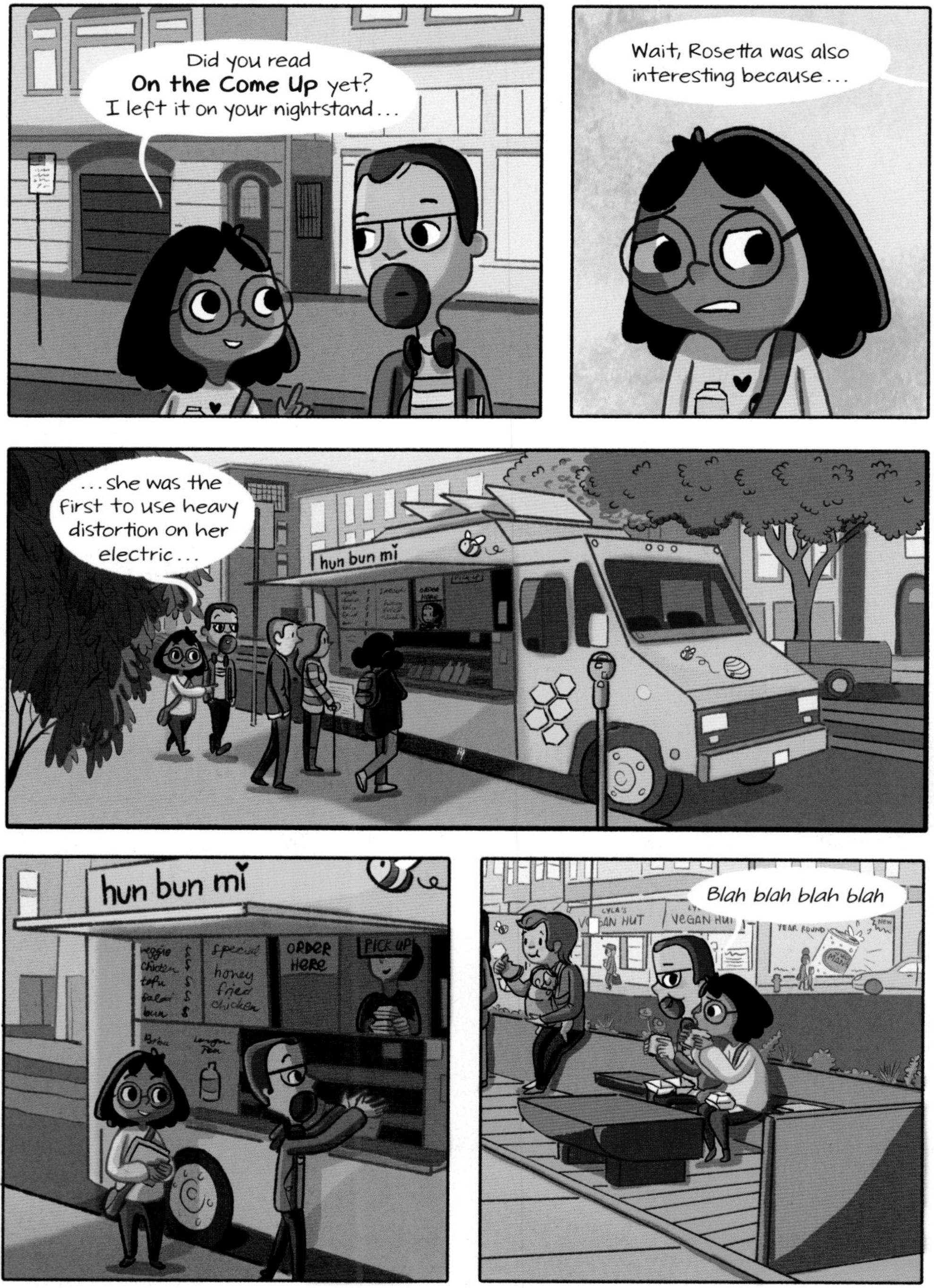
Did you read **On the Come Up** yet? I left it on your nightstand...
Wait, Rosetta was also interesting because...
...she was the first to use heavy distortion on her electric...
hun bun mi
hun bun mi
veggie chicken tofu salad bun
special honey fried chicken
ORDER HERE
PICK UP
Blah blah blah blah
VEGAN HUT
VEGAN HUT
YEAR ROUND

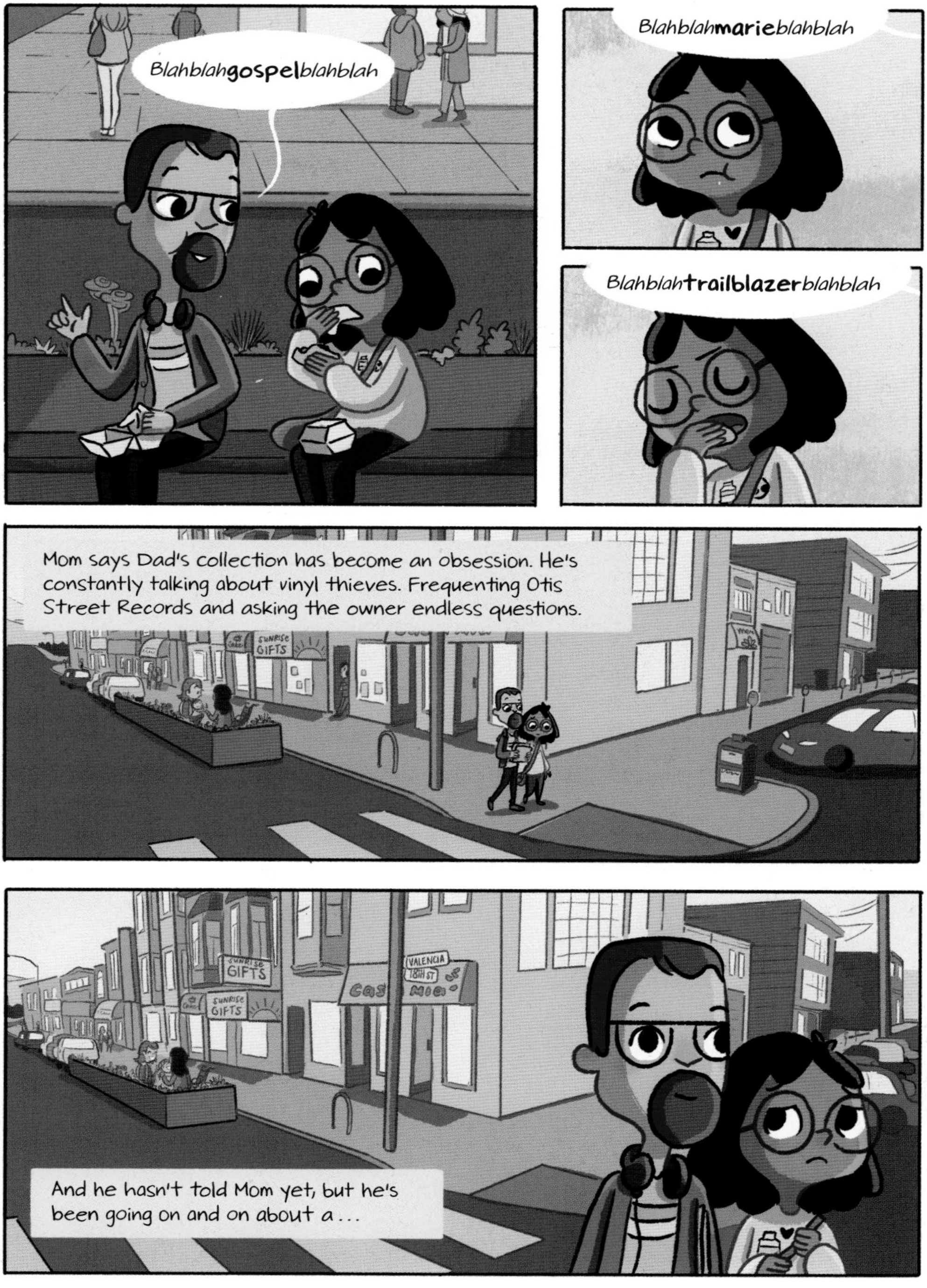
Blahblahgospelblahblah
Blahblahmarieblahblah
Blahblahtrailblazerblahblah
Mom says Dad's collection has become an obsession. He's constantly talking about vinyl thieves. Frequenting Otis Street Records and asking the owner endless questions.
SUNRISE GIFTS
SUNRISE GIFTS
SUNRISE GIFTS
VALENCIA
18TH ST
And he hasn't told Mom yet, but he's been going on and on about a . . .

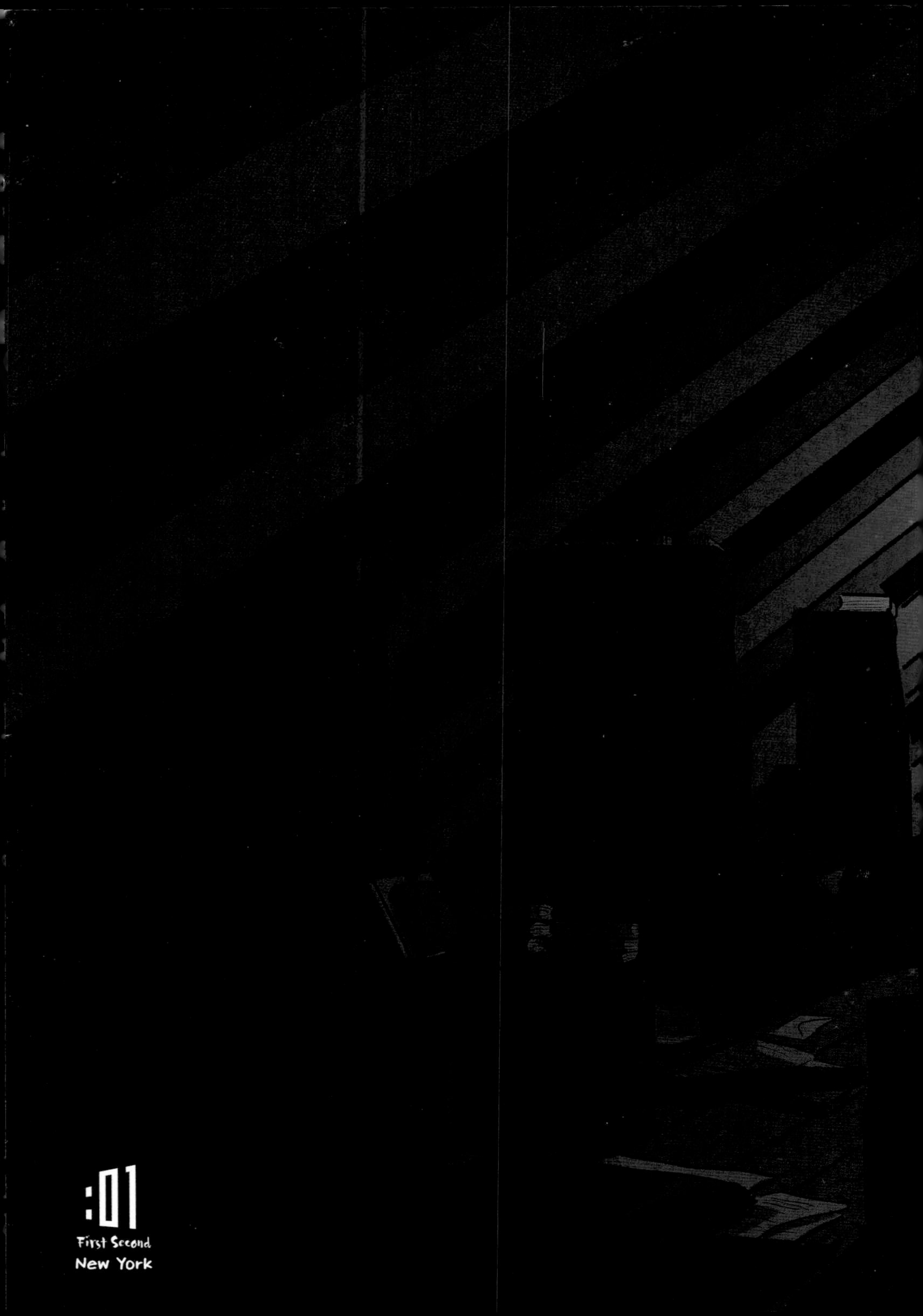

:01
First Second
New York

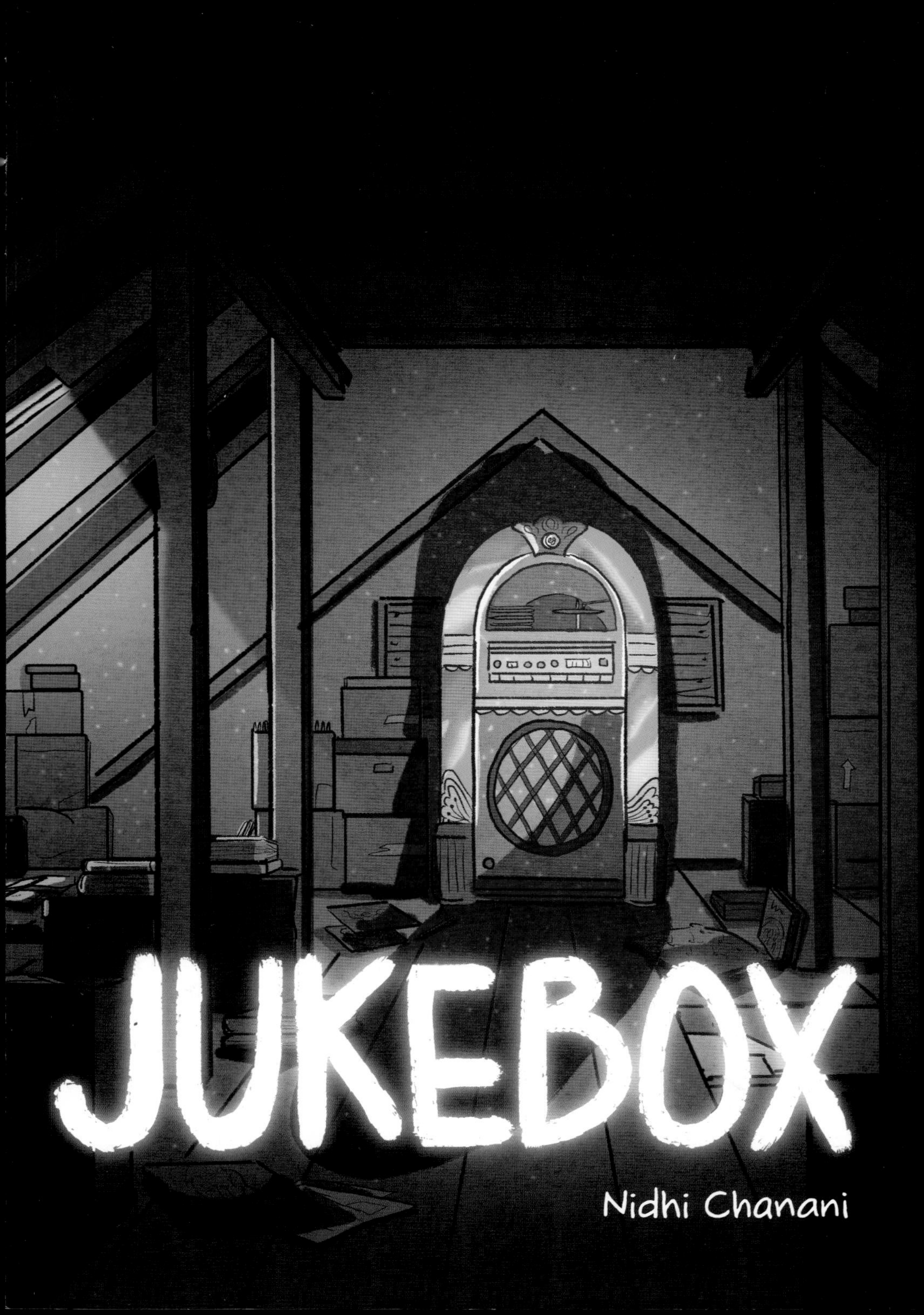
JUKEBOX
Nidhi Chanani

For Joe Giordano
and the music that brings
you back to us

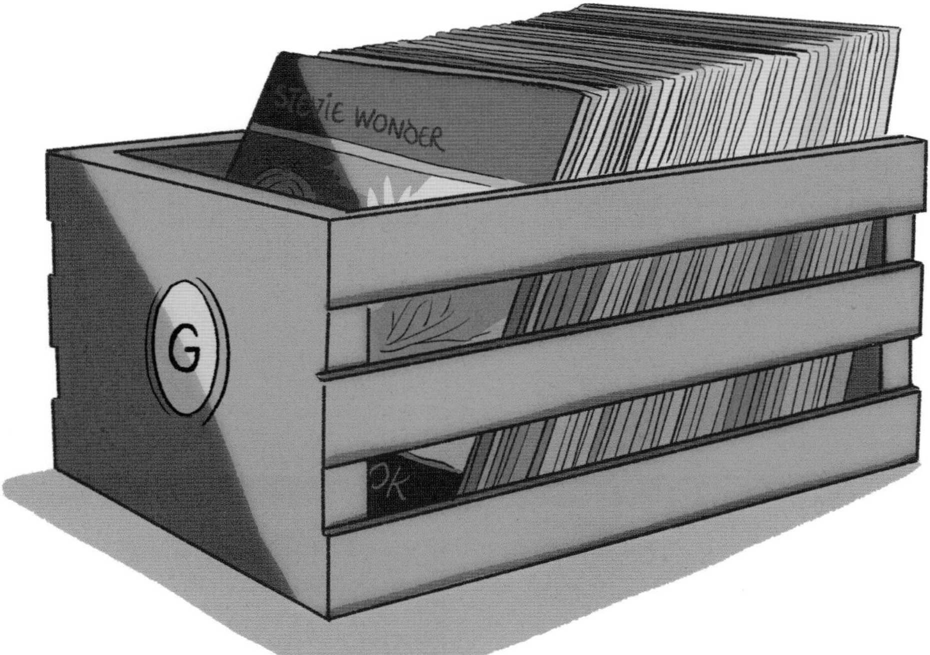

STEVIE WONDER
G

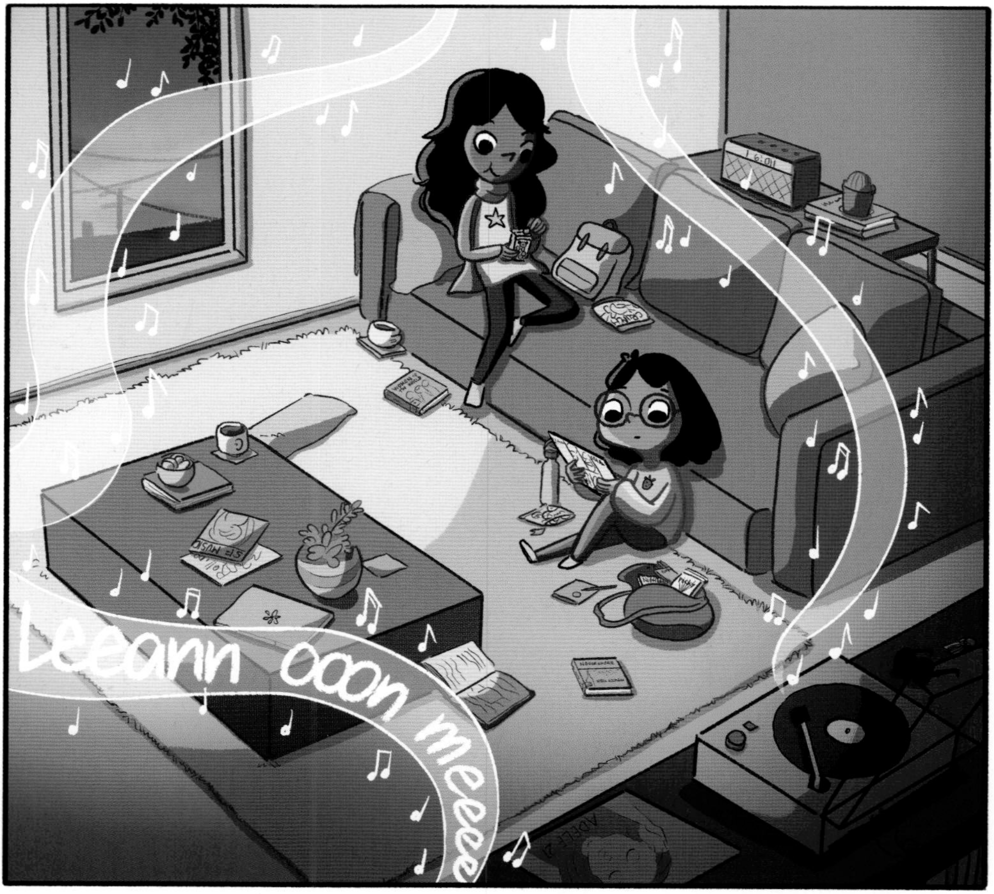
Leeann ooon meeee

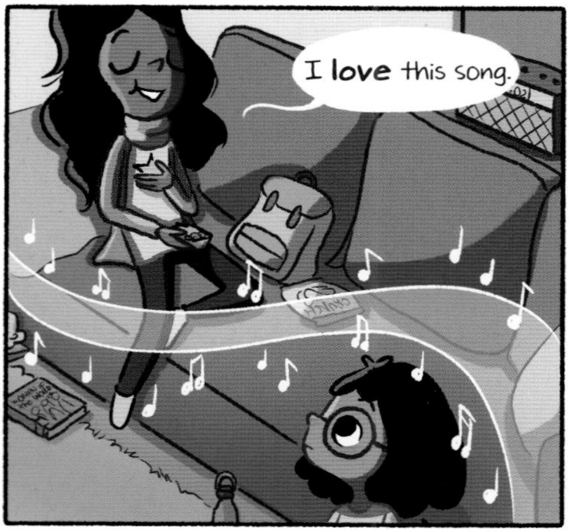
I love this song.

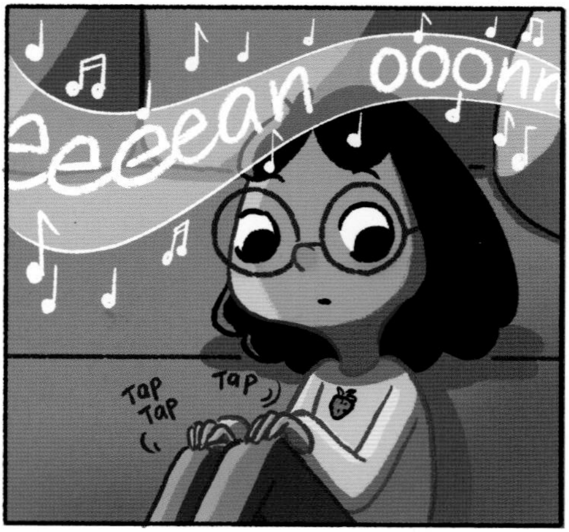
eeeean ooonn
Tap Tap
Tap

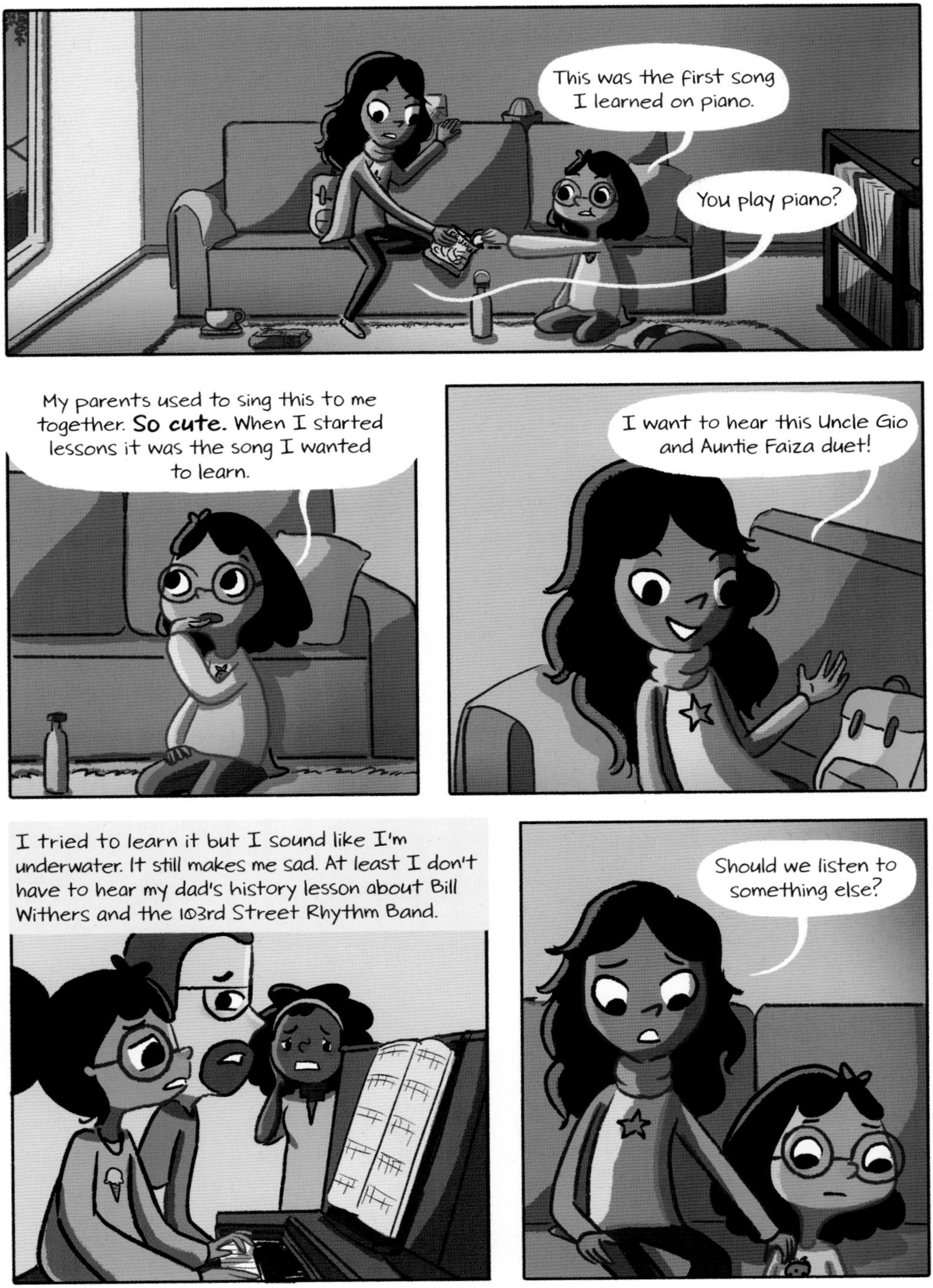
This was the first song I learned on piano.
You play piano?
My parents used to sing this to me together. **So cute.** When I started lessons it was the song I wanted to learn.
I want to hear this Uncle Gio and Auntie Faiza duet!
I tried to learn it but I sound like I'm underwater. It still makes me sad. At least I don't have to hear my dad's history lesson about Bill Withers and the 103rd Street Rhythm Band.
Should we listen to something else?

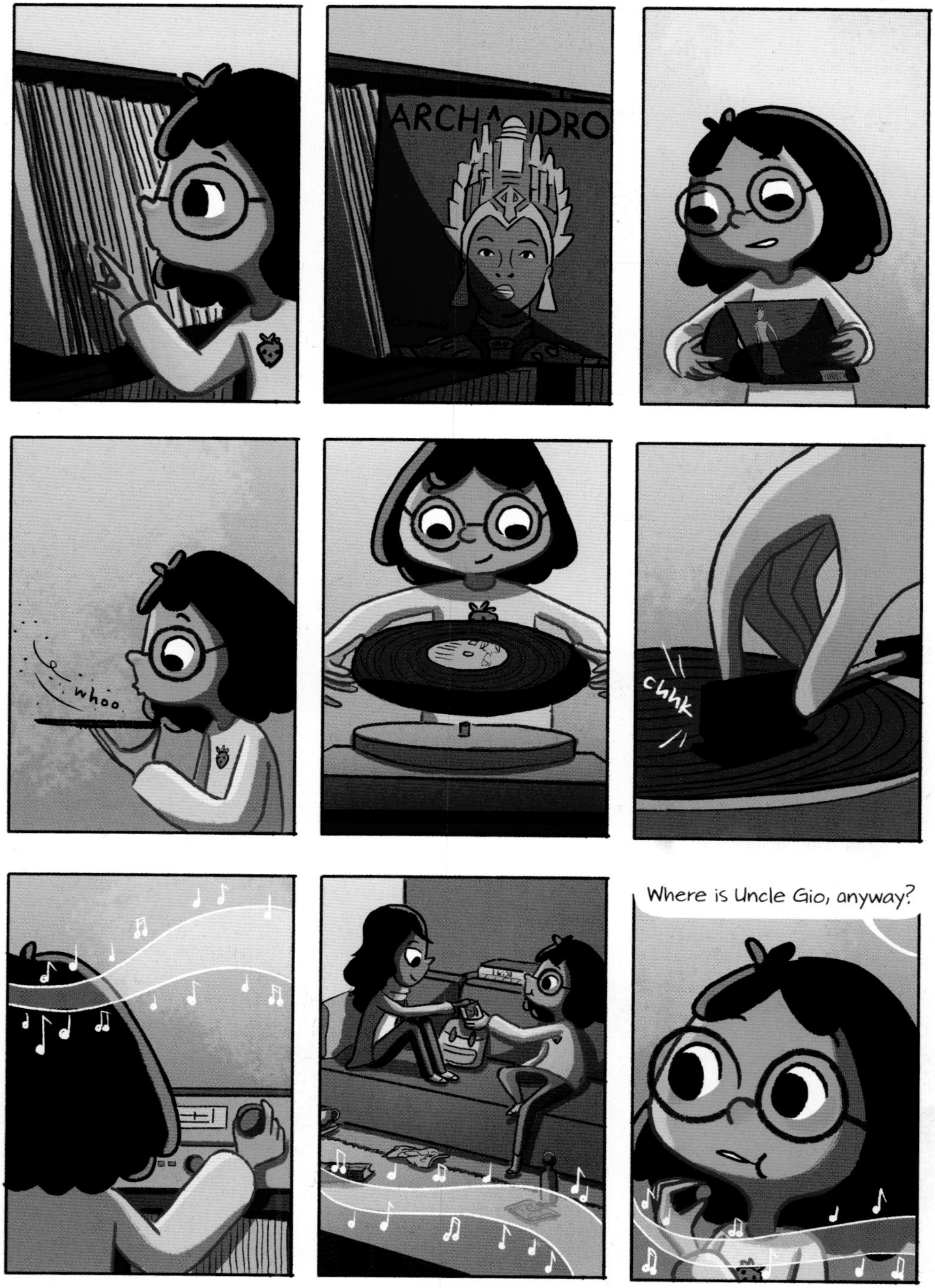
whoo
chhk
Where is Uncle Gio, anyway?

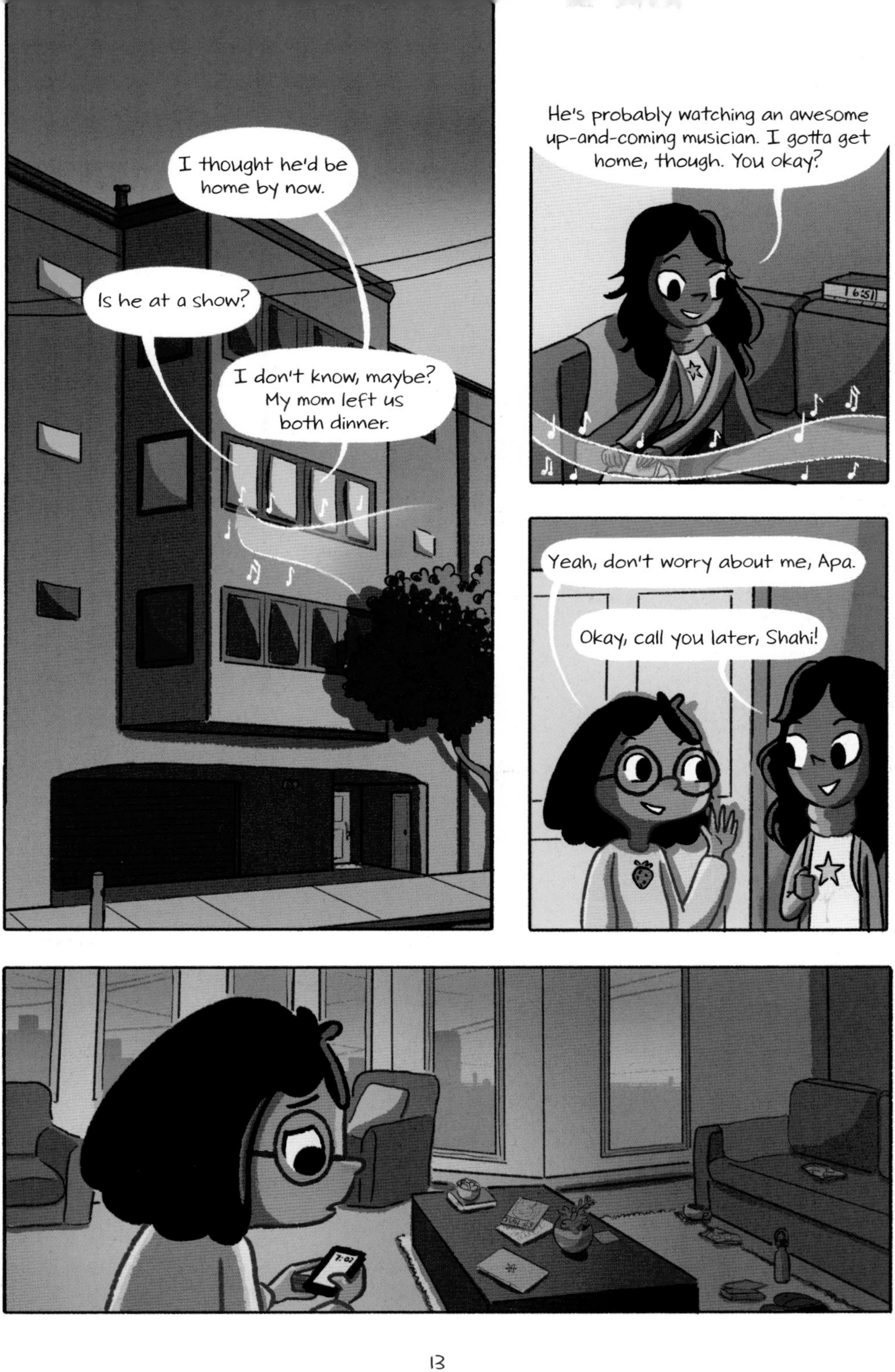
I thought he'd be home by now.
Is he at a show?
I don't know, maybe? My mom left us both dinner.
He's probably watching an awesome up-and-coming musician. I gotta get home, though. You okay?
Yeah, don't worry about me, Apa.
Okay, call you later, Shahi!

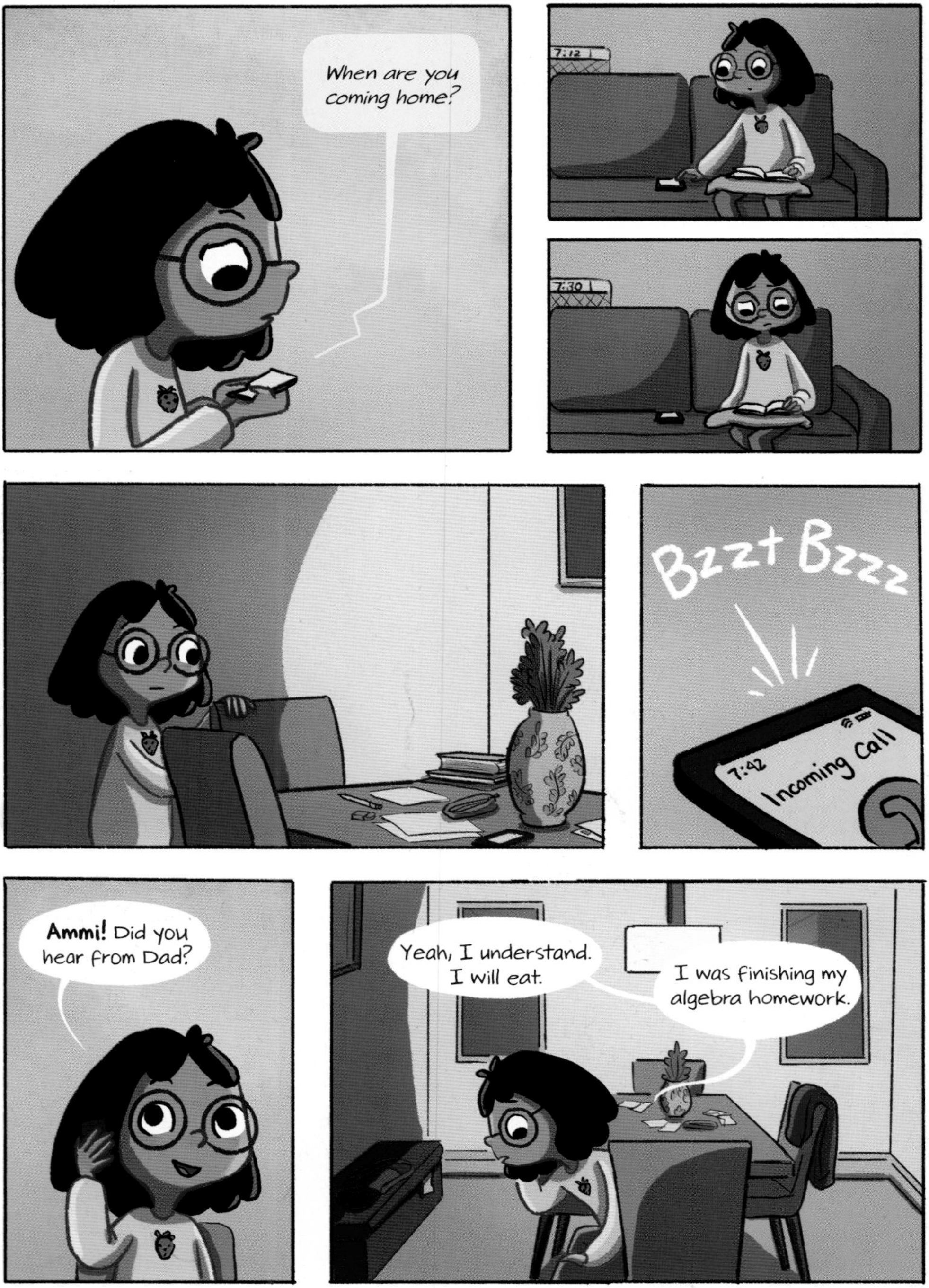
When are you coming home?
7:12
7:30
Bzzt Bzzz
7:42
Incoming Call
Ammi! Did you hear from Dad?
Yeah, I understand. I will eat.
I was finishing my algebra homework.

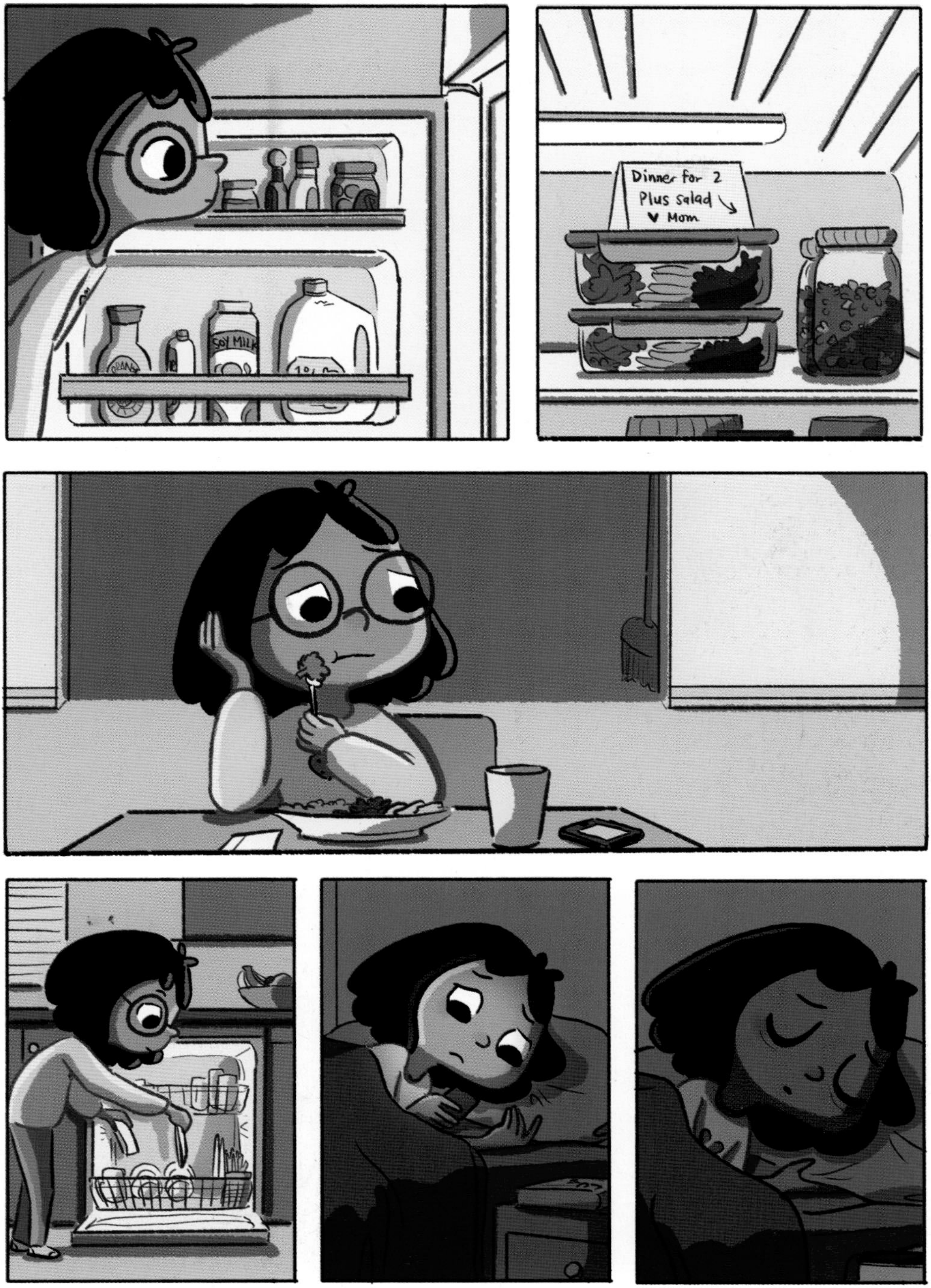

SOY MILK
Dinner for 2
Plus salad
♥ Mom

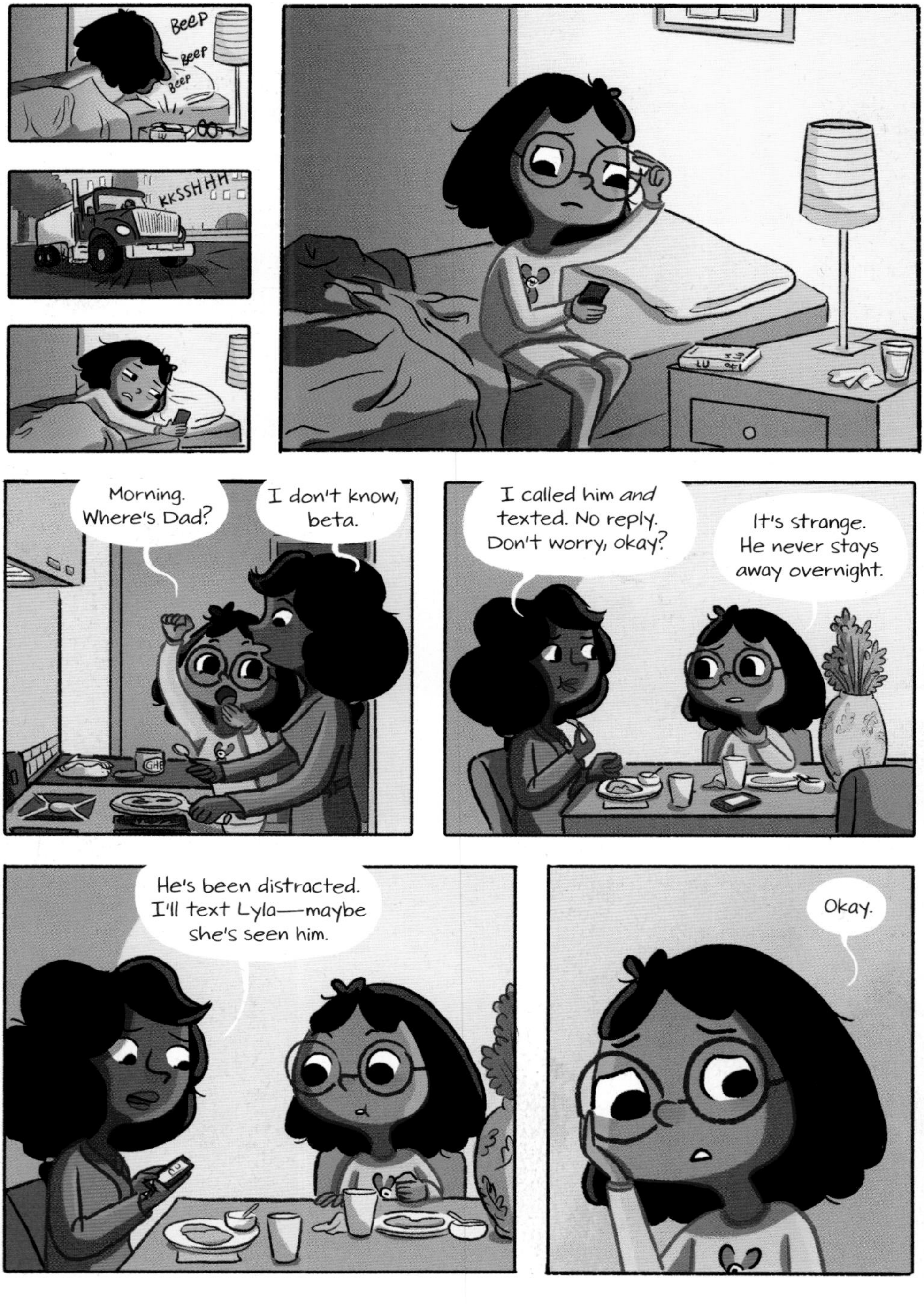
Beep
Beep
Beep
KKSSHHH
Morning. Where's Dad?
I don't know, beta.
I called him *and* texted. No reply. Don't worry, okay?
It's strange. He never stays away overnight.
He's been distracted. I'll text Lyla—maybe she's seen him.
Okay.

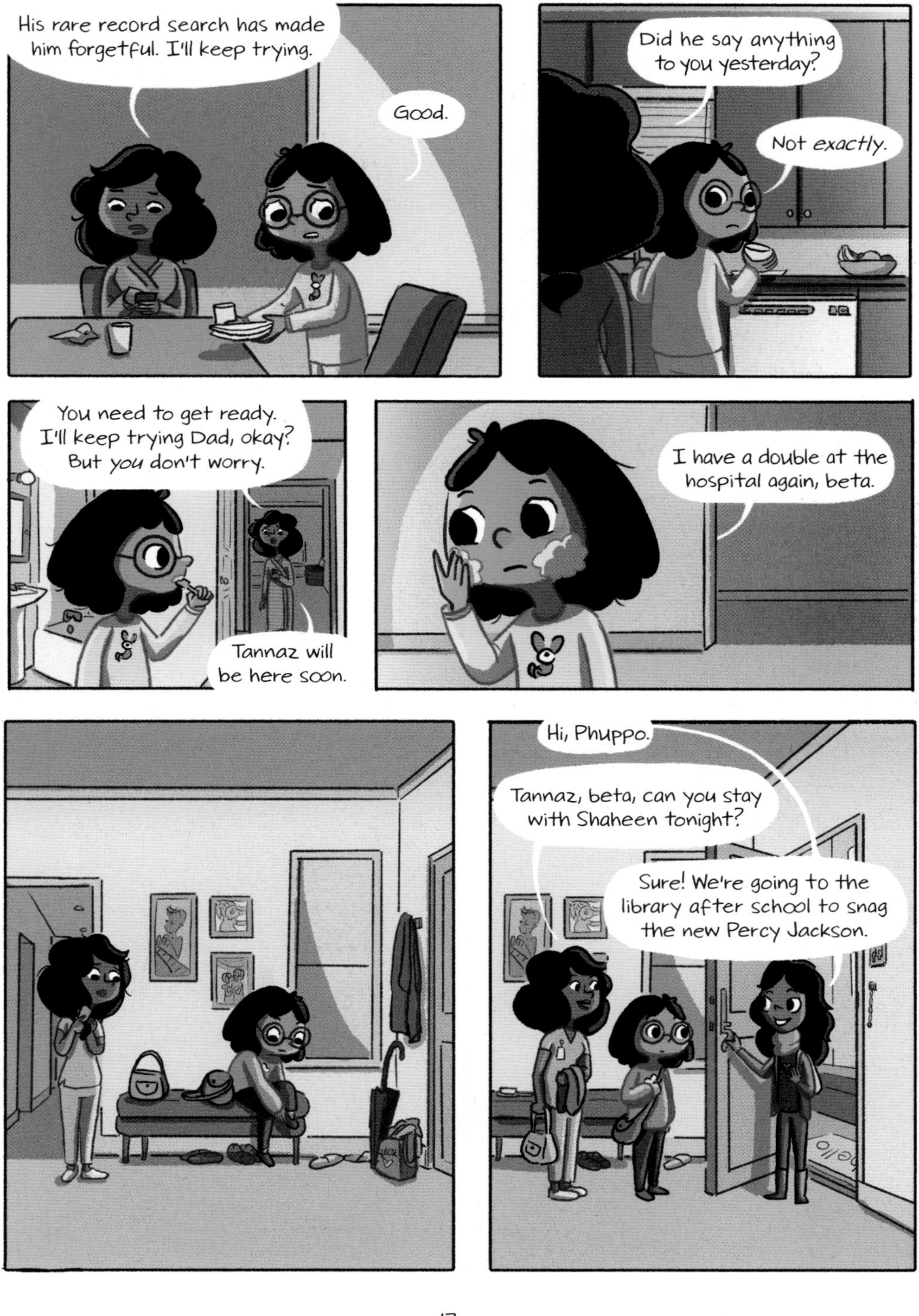
His rare record search has made him forgetful. I'll keep trying.
Good.
Did he say anything to you yesterday?
Not *exactly*.
You need to get ready. I'll keep trying Dad, okay? But *you* don't worry.
Tannaz will be here soon.
I have a double at the hospital again, beta.
Hi, Phuppo.
Tannaz, beta, can you stay with Shaheen tonight?
Sure! We're going to the library after school to snag the new Percy Jackson.

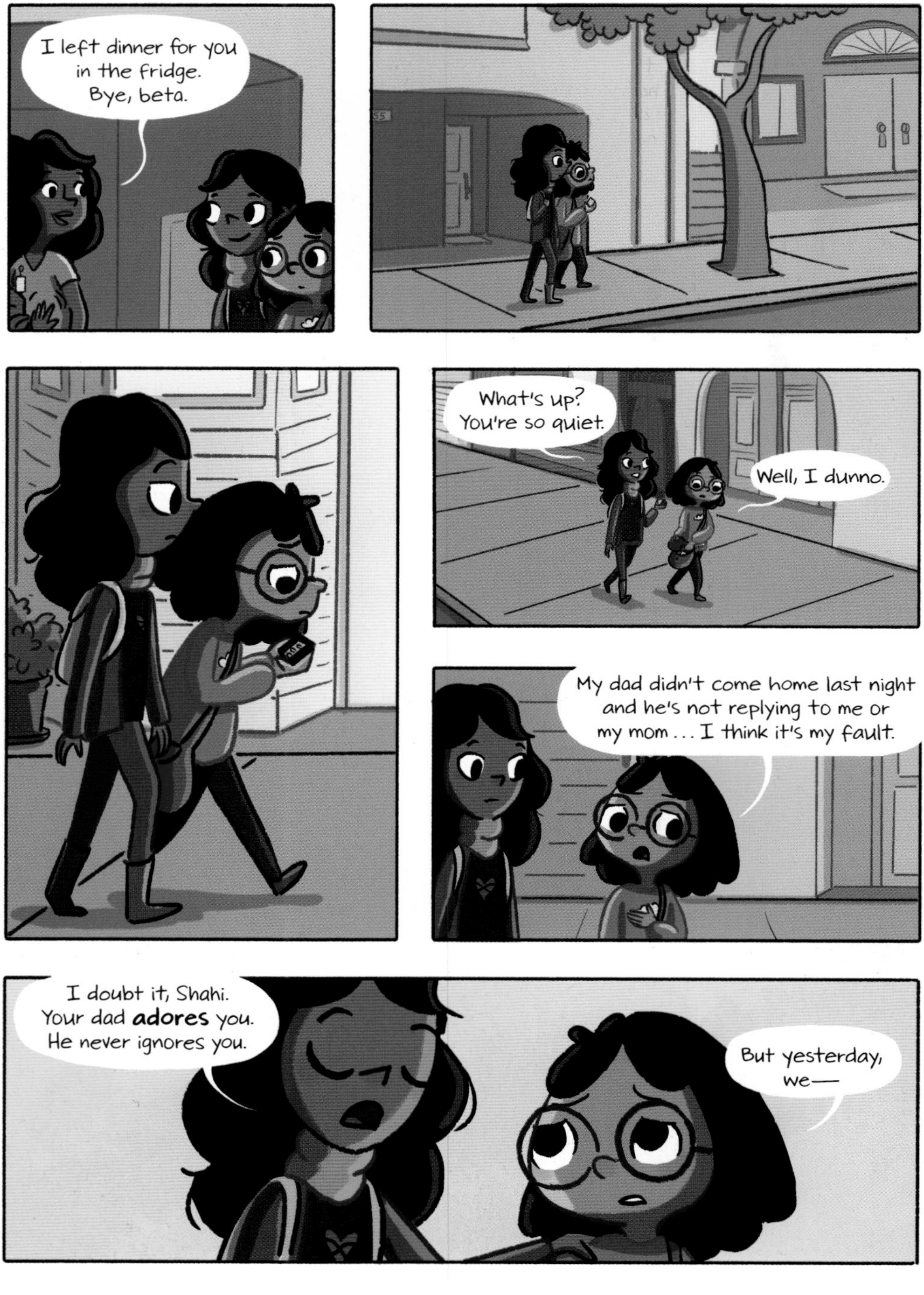
I left dinner for you in the fridge. Bye, beta.
What's up? You're so quiet.
Well, I dunno.
My dad didn't come home last night and he's not replying to me or my mom . . . I think it's my fault.
I doubt it, Shahi. Your dad **adores** you. He never ignores you.
But yesterday, we—

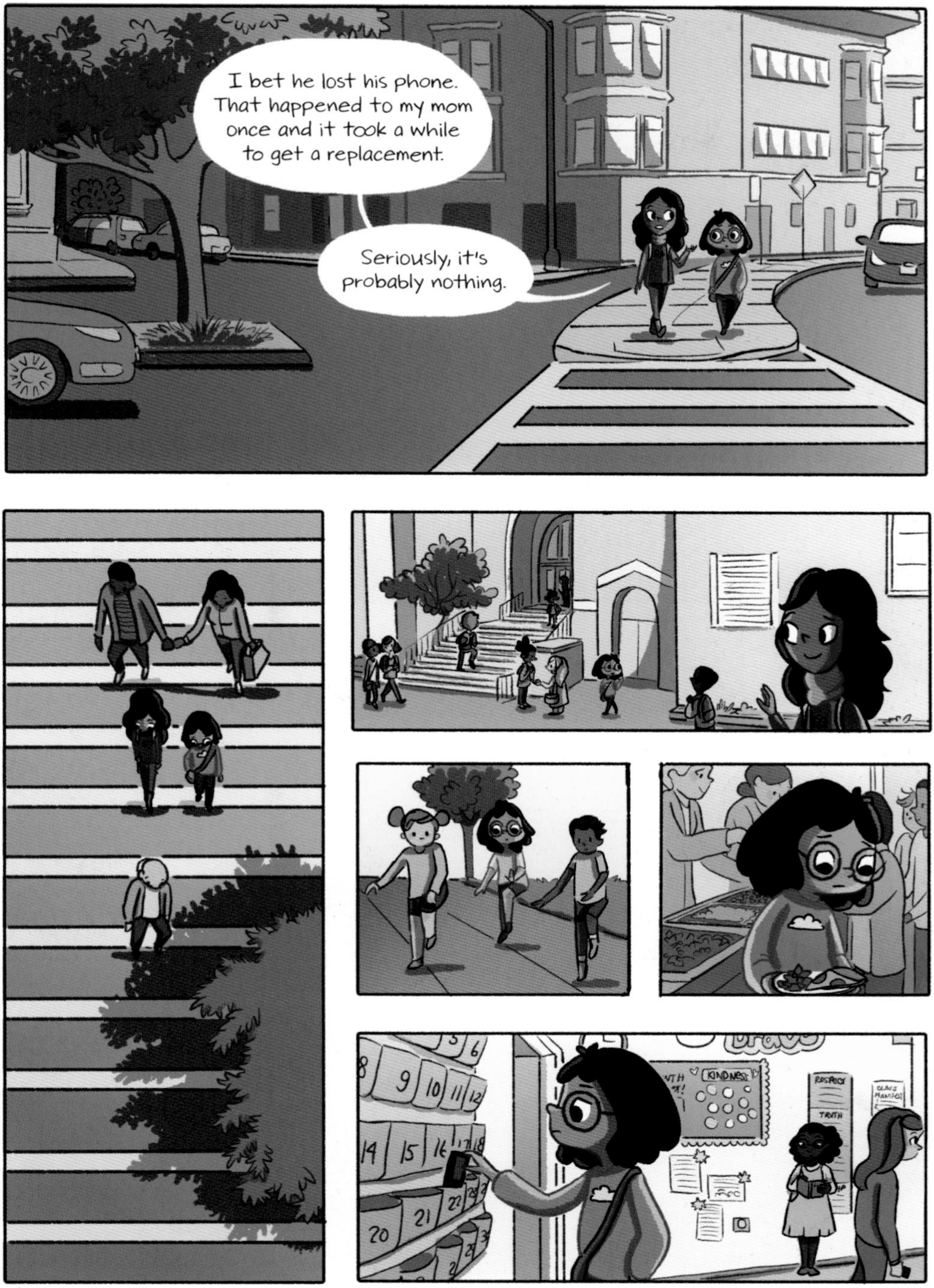
I bet he lost his phone. That happened to my mom once and it took a while to get a replacement.
Seriously, it's probably nothing.
KINDNESS
TRUTH

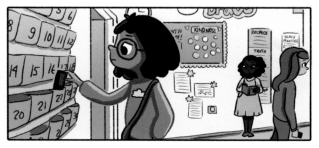

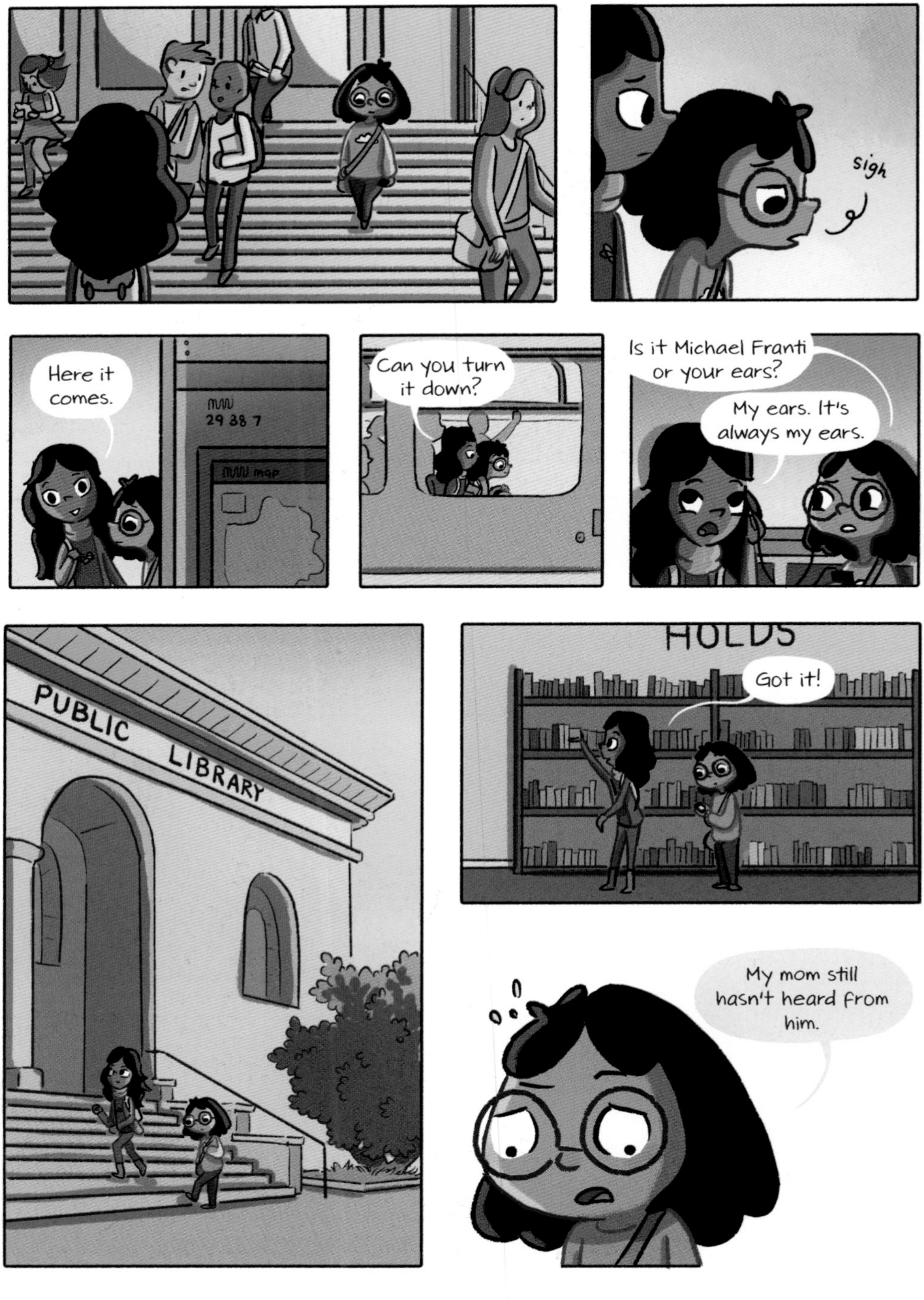
sigh
Here it comes.
29 38 7
map
Can you turn it down?
Is it Michael Franti or your ears?
My ears. It's always my ears.
PUBLIC LIBRARY
HOLDS
Got it!
My mom still hasn't heard from him.

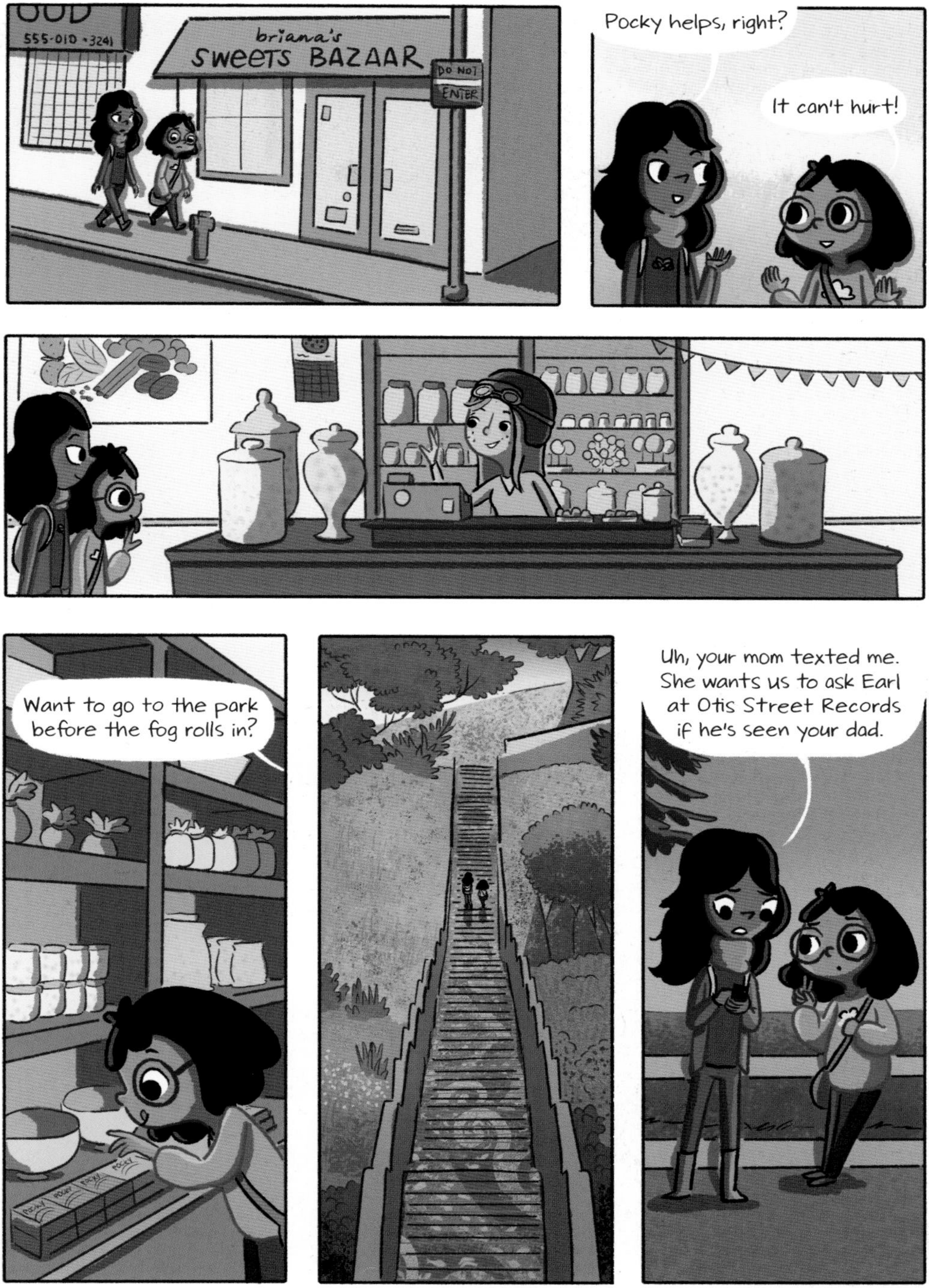

555-010-3241
briana's SWEETS BAZAAR
DO NOT ENTER
Pocky helps, right?
It can't hurt!
Want to go to the park before the fog rolls in?
POCKY
Uh, your mom texted me. She wants us to ask Earl at Otis Street Records if he's seen your dad.

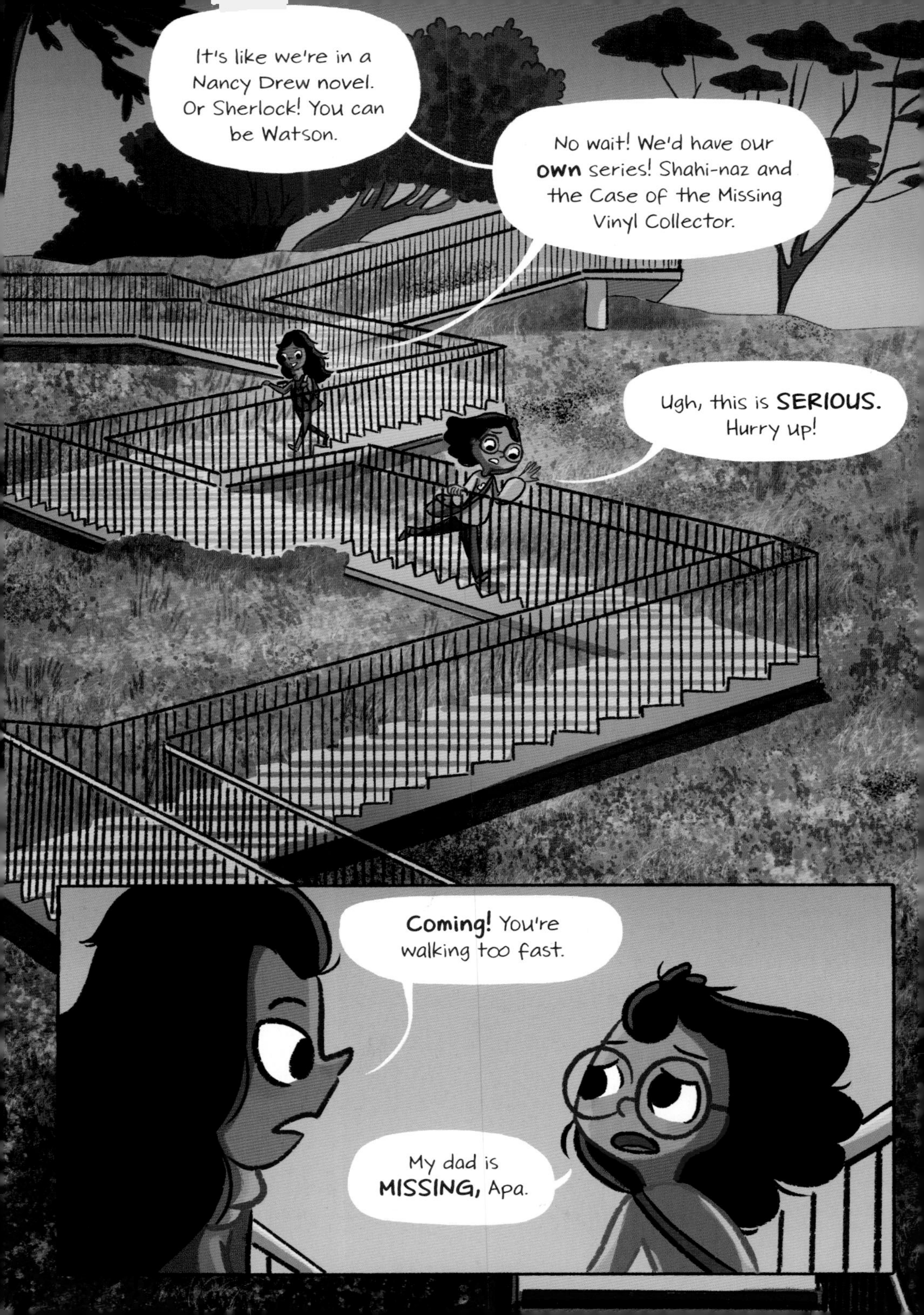
It's like we're in a Nancy Drew novel. Or Sherlock! You can be Watson.
No wait! We'd have our **OWN** series! Shahi-naz and the Case of the Missing Vinyl Collector.
Ugh, this is **SERIOUS.** Hurry up!
Coming! You're walking too fast.
My dad is **MISSING,** Apa.

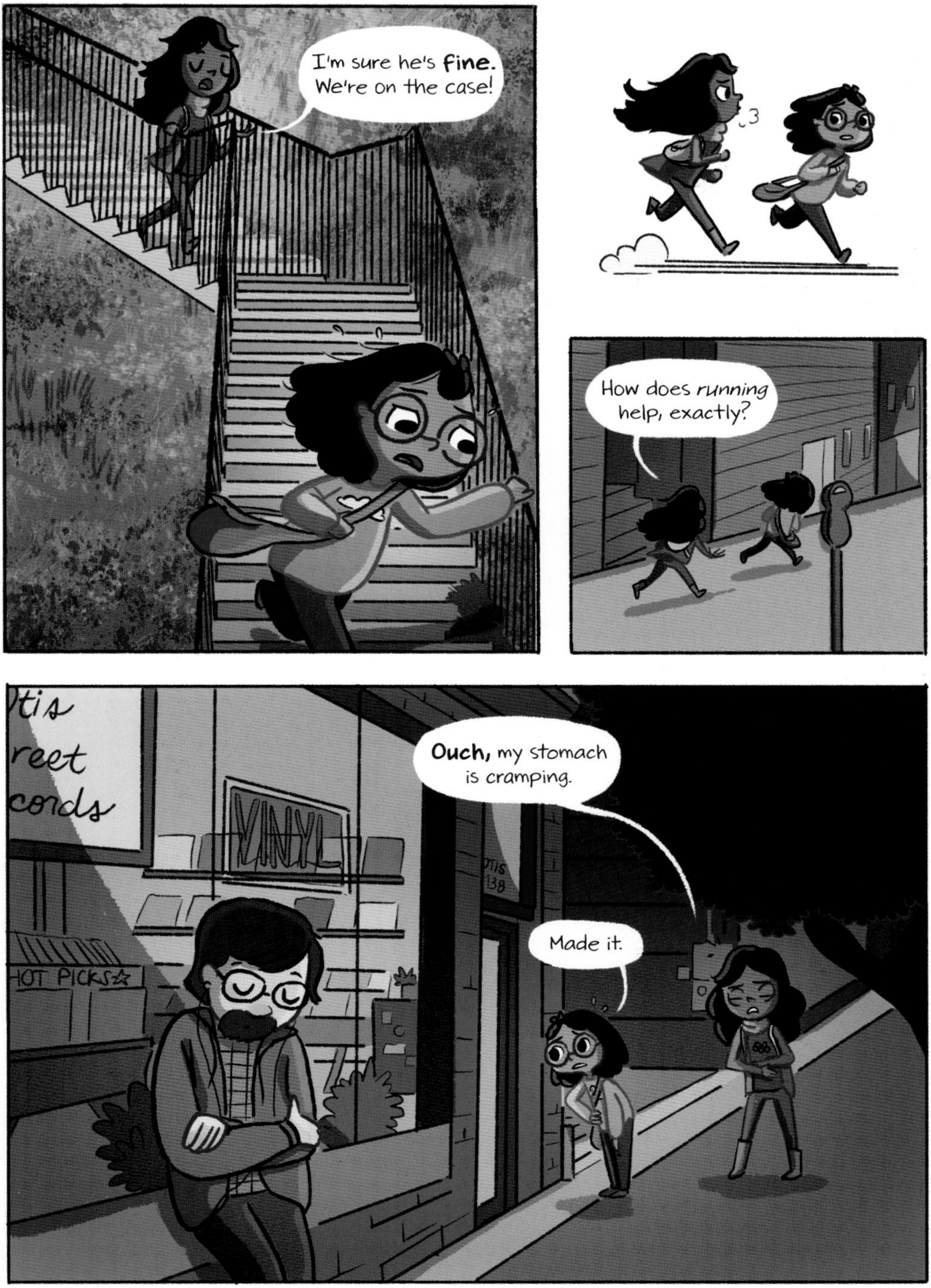
I'm sure he's **fine.** We're on the case!
How does *running* help, exactly?
Otis
Street
Records
VINYL
HOT PICKS☆
OTIS
138
Ouch, my stomach is cramping.
Made it.

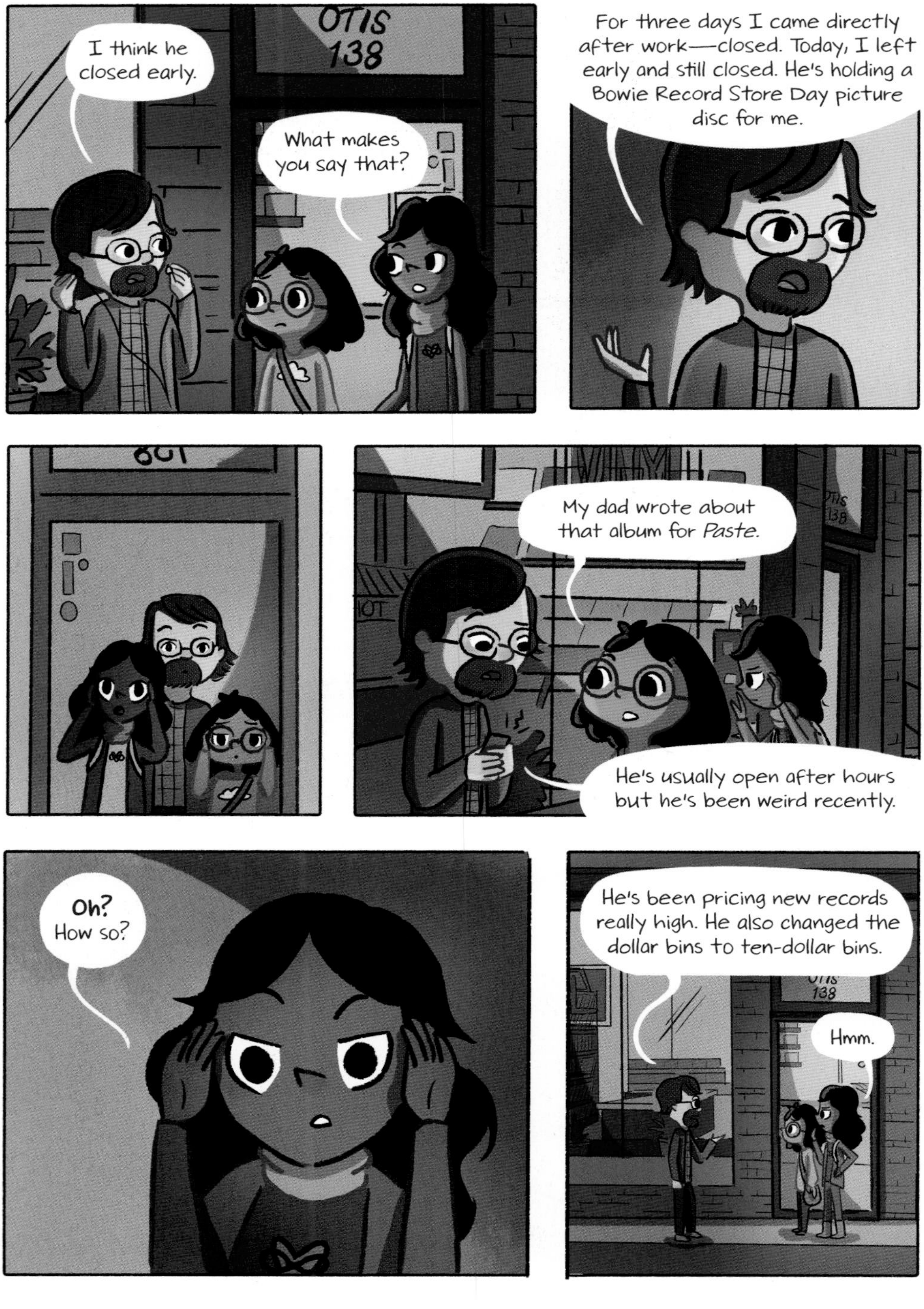
OTIS 138
I think he closed early.
What makes you say that?
For three days I came directly after work—closed. Today, I left early and still closed. He's holding a Bowie Record Store Day picture disc for me.
My dad wrote about that album for *Paste*.
He's usually open after hours but he's been weird recently.
Oh? How so?
He's been pricing new records really high. He also changed the dollar bins to ten-dollar bins.
Hmm.

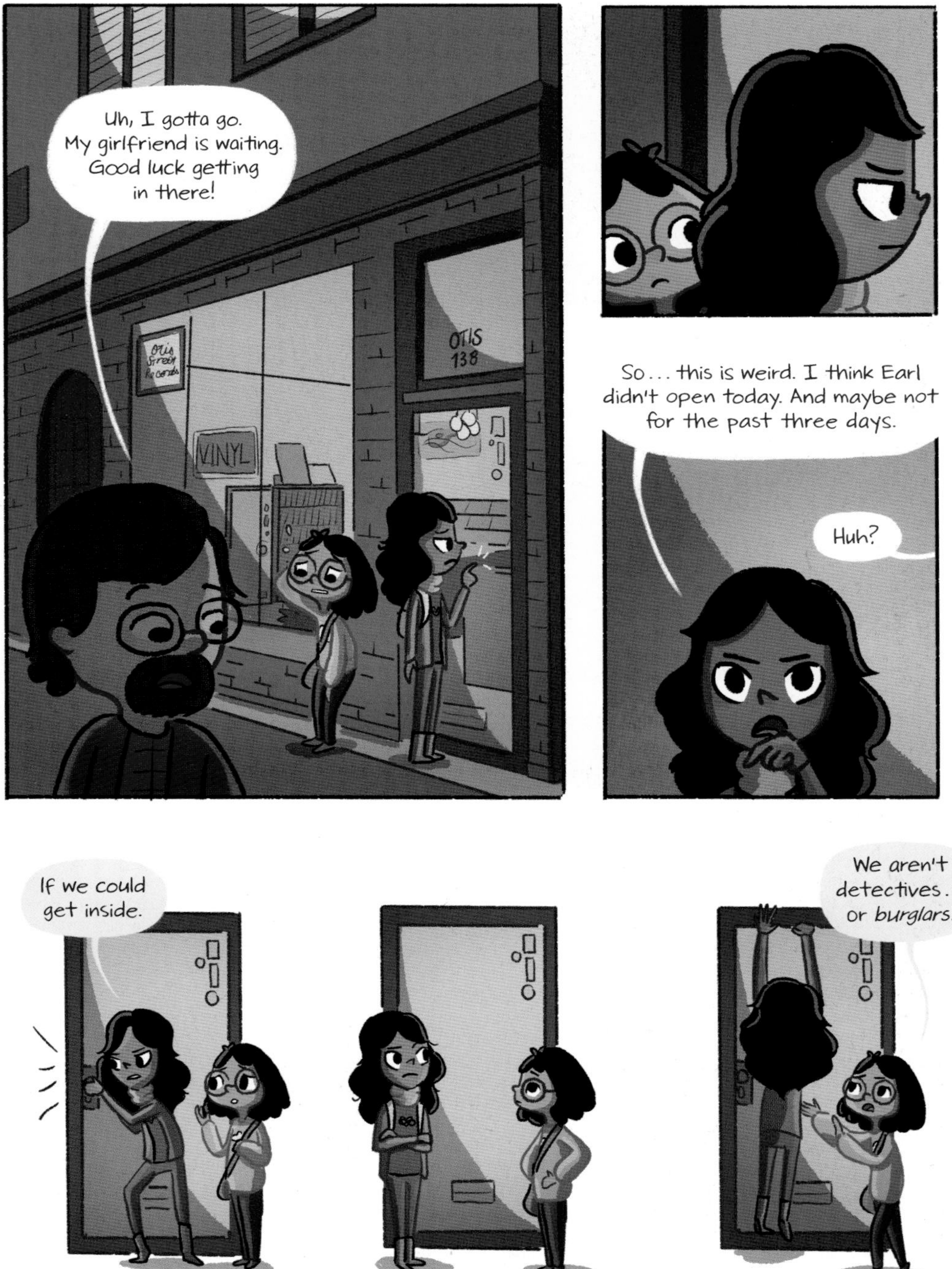
Uh, I gotta go. My girlfriend is waiting. Good luck getting in there!
OTIS 138
VINYL
So... this is weird. I think Earl didn't open today. And maybe not for the past three days.
Huh?
If we could get inside.
We aren't detectives... or *burglars*.

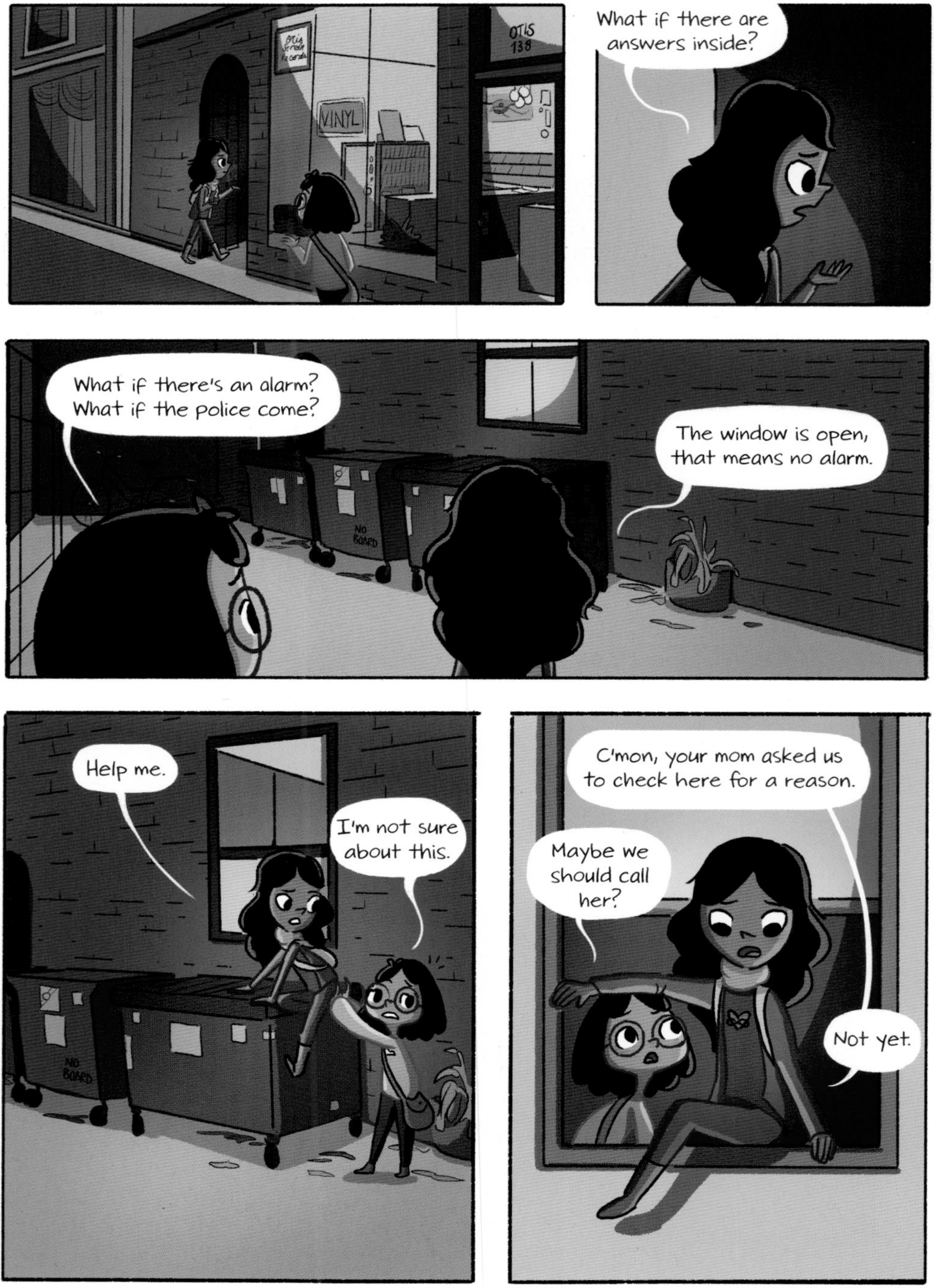
VINYL
OTIS 138
What if there are answers inside?
What if there's an alarm? What if the police come?
The window is open, that means no alarm.
NO BOARD
Help me.
I'm not sure about this.
NO BOARD
C'mon, your mom asked us to check here for a reason.
Maybe we should call her?
Not yet.

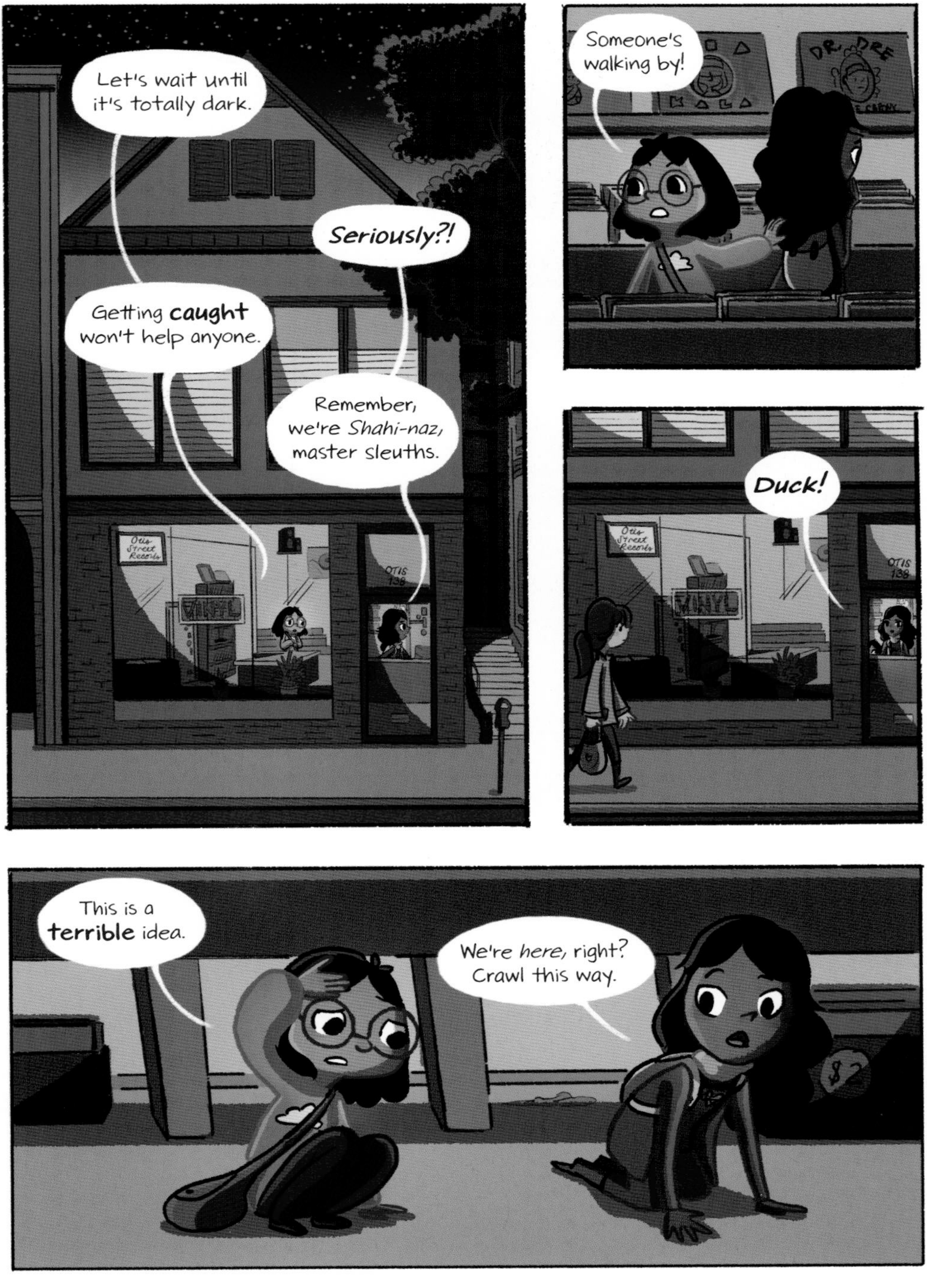
Let's wait until it's totally dark.
Seriously?!
Getting **caught** won't help anyone.
Remember, we're *Shahi-naz*, master sleuths.
Otis Street Records
VINYL
OTIS 138
Someone's walking by!
DR. DRE
Duck!
This is a **terrible** idea.
We're *here*, right? Crawl this way.

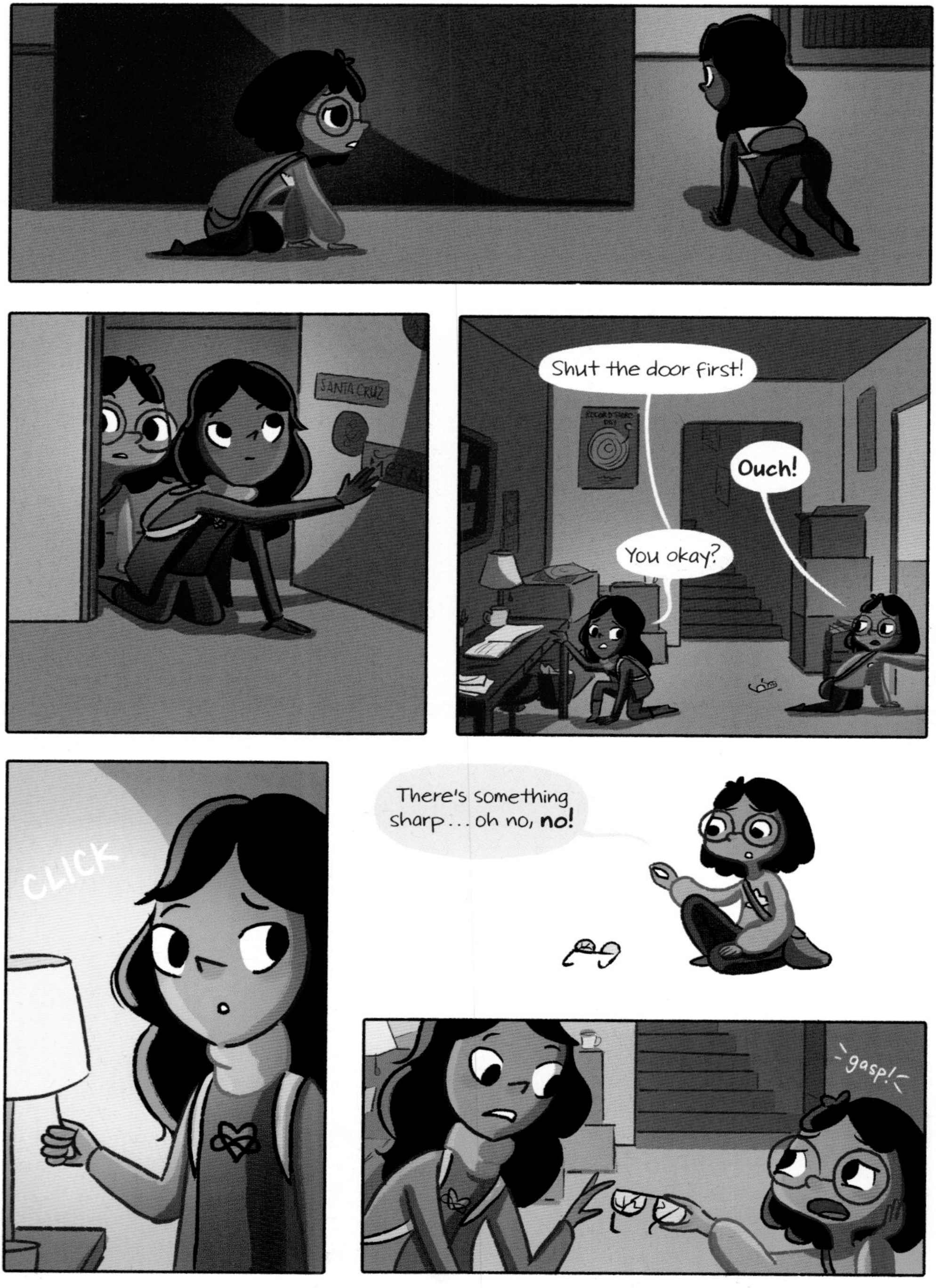
Shut the door first!
Ouch!
You okay?
CLICK
There's something sharp... oh no, **no!**
gasp!

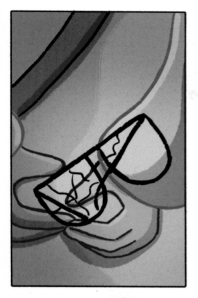

You're sure they're your dad's?

What's upstairs? We should check.

Yes! Earl doesn't wear glasses.

This is more thriller than mystery now.

I don't like it.

Should we call my mom?

I'm not opposed to it.

But what if your dad needs us now?

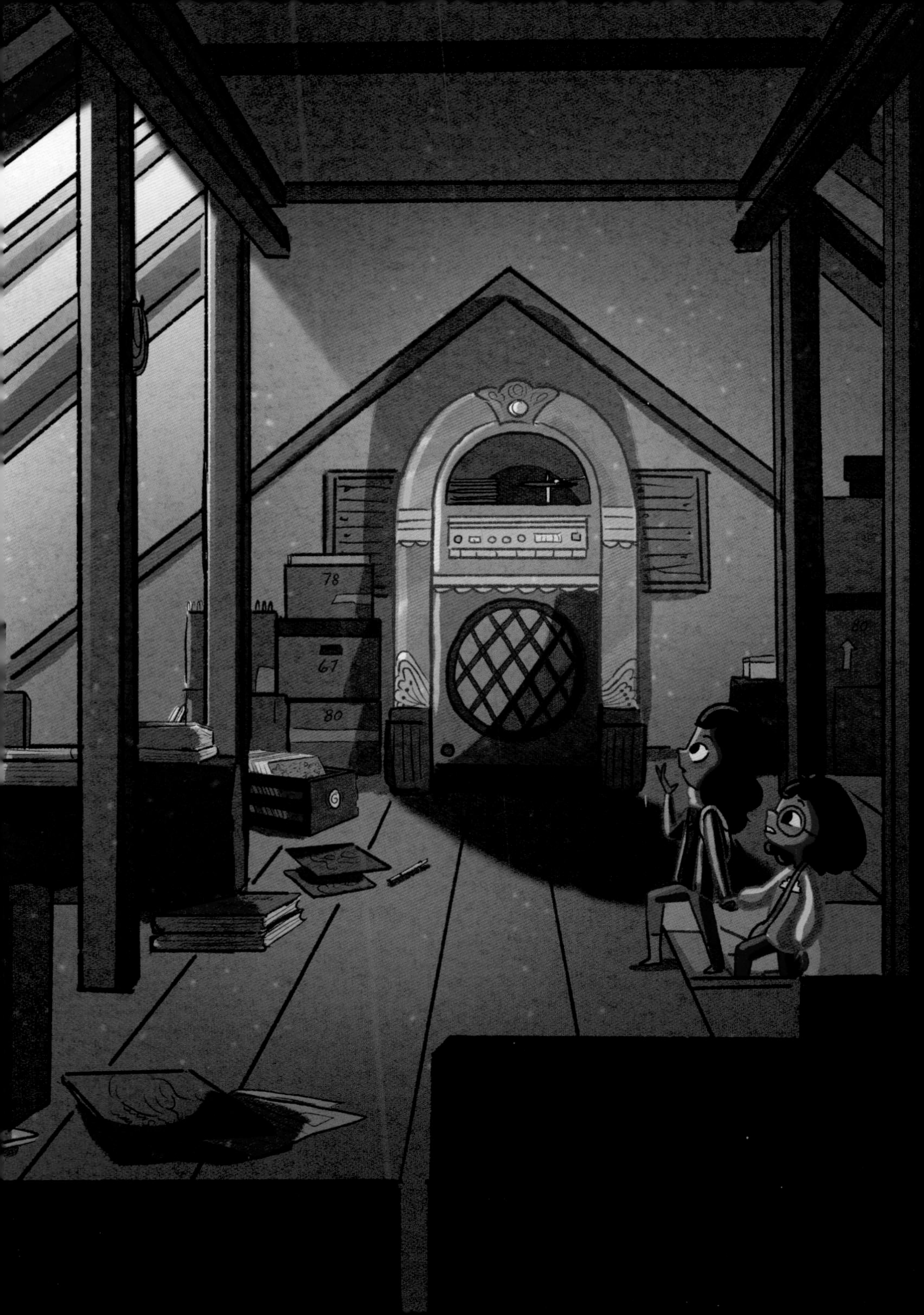
78
67
80

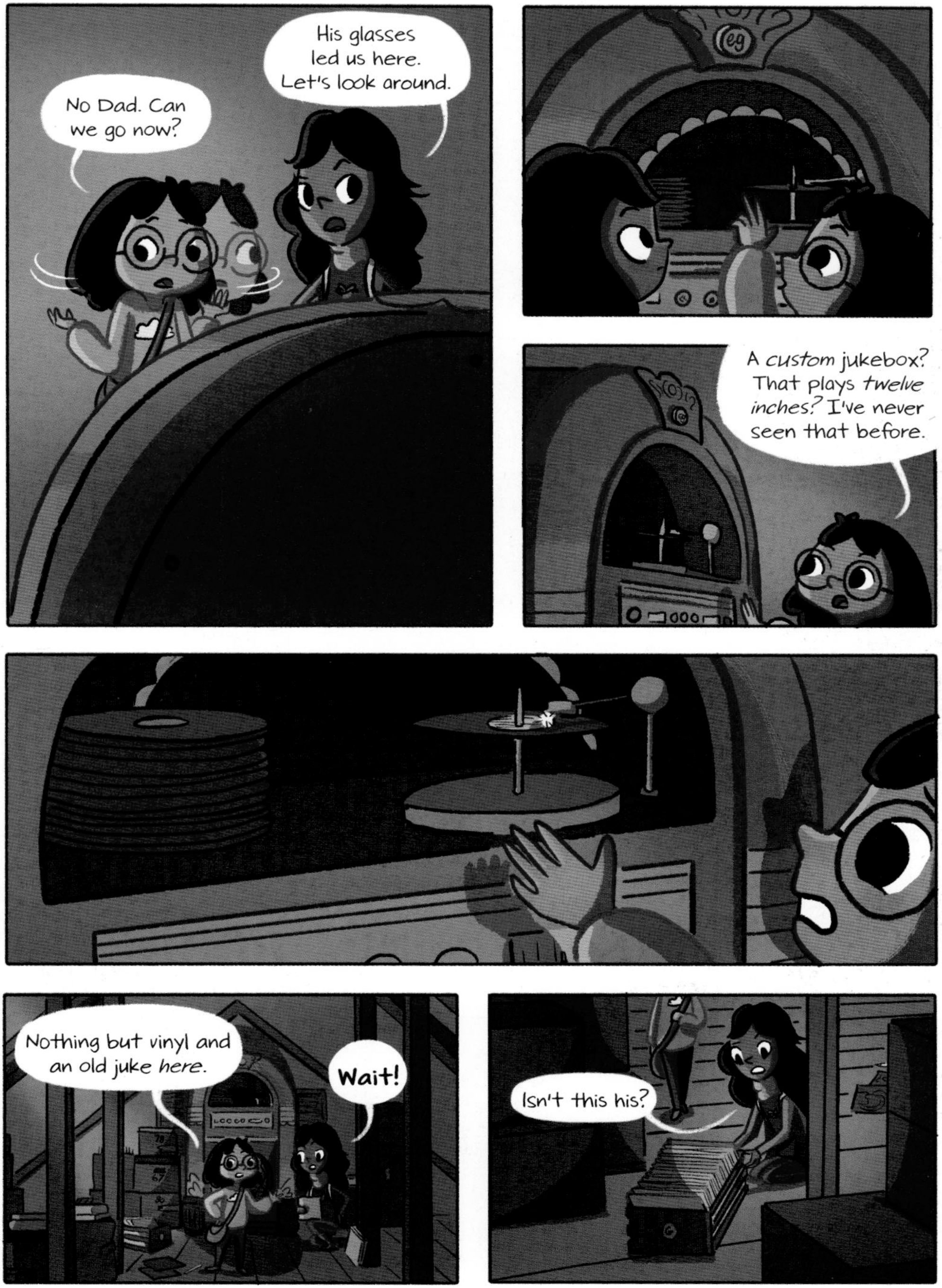

No Dad. Can we go now?
His glasses led us here. Let's look around.
A *custom* jukebox? That plays *twelve inches?* I've never seen that before.
Nothing but vinyl and an old juke *here*.
Wait!
Isn't this his?

Yeah. It's the deluxe, engraved record crate I bought him for Father's Day.

I'm not sure he liked it. I think he would've preferred records.

What's in there?

Albums from various artists. Nothing specific.

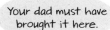

Why's it *here?*

Your dad must have brought it here.

He never sells to Earl. He always sells on Spin Friends because he likes the community.

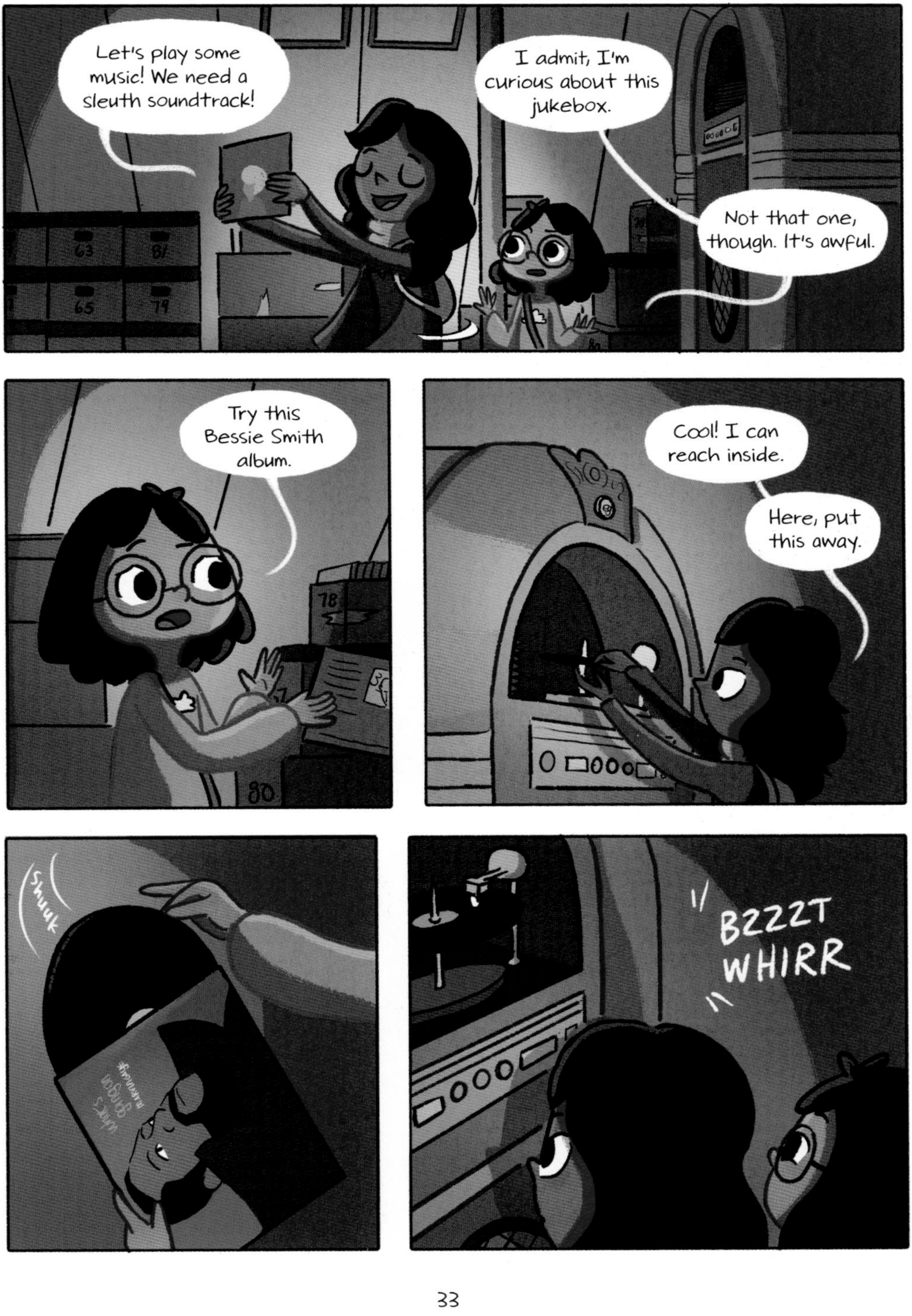
Let's play some music! We need a sleuth soundtrack!
I admit, I'm curious about this jukebox.
Not that one, though. It's awful.
Try this Bessie Smith album.
Cool! I can reach inside.
Here, put this away.
Shuuk
BZZZT
WHIRR

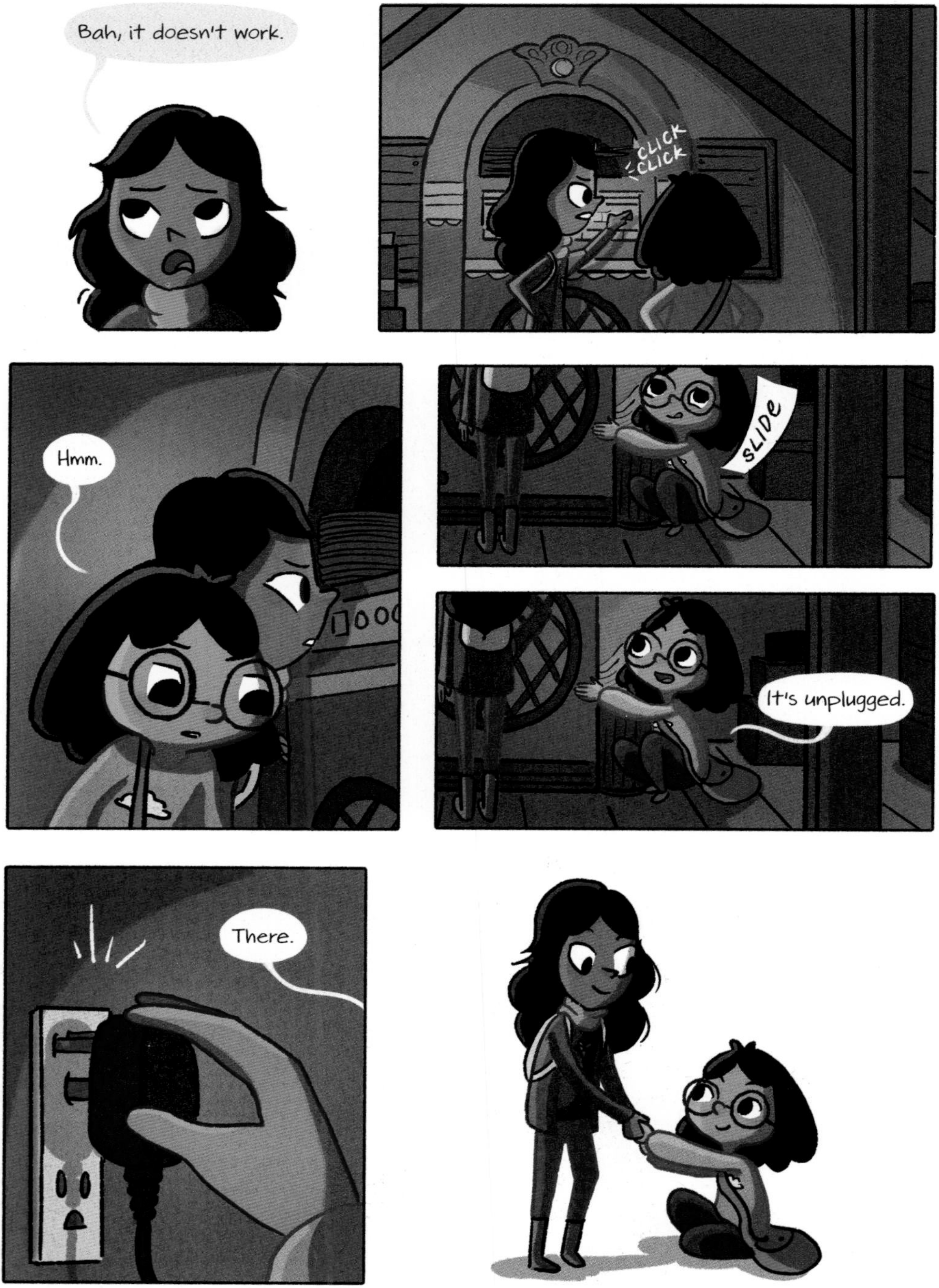
Bah, it doesn't work.
CLICK
CLICK
Hmm.
SLIDE
It's unplugged.
There.

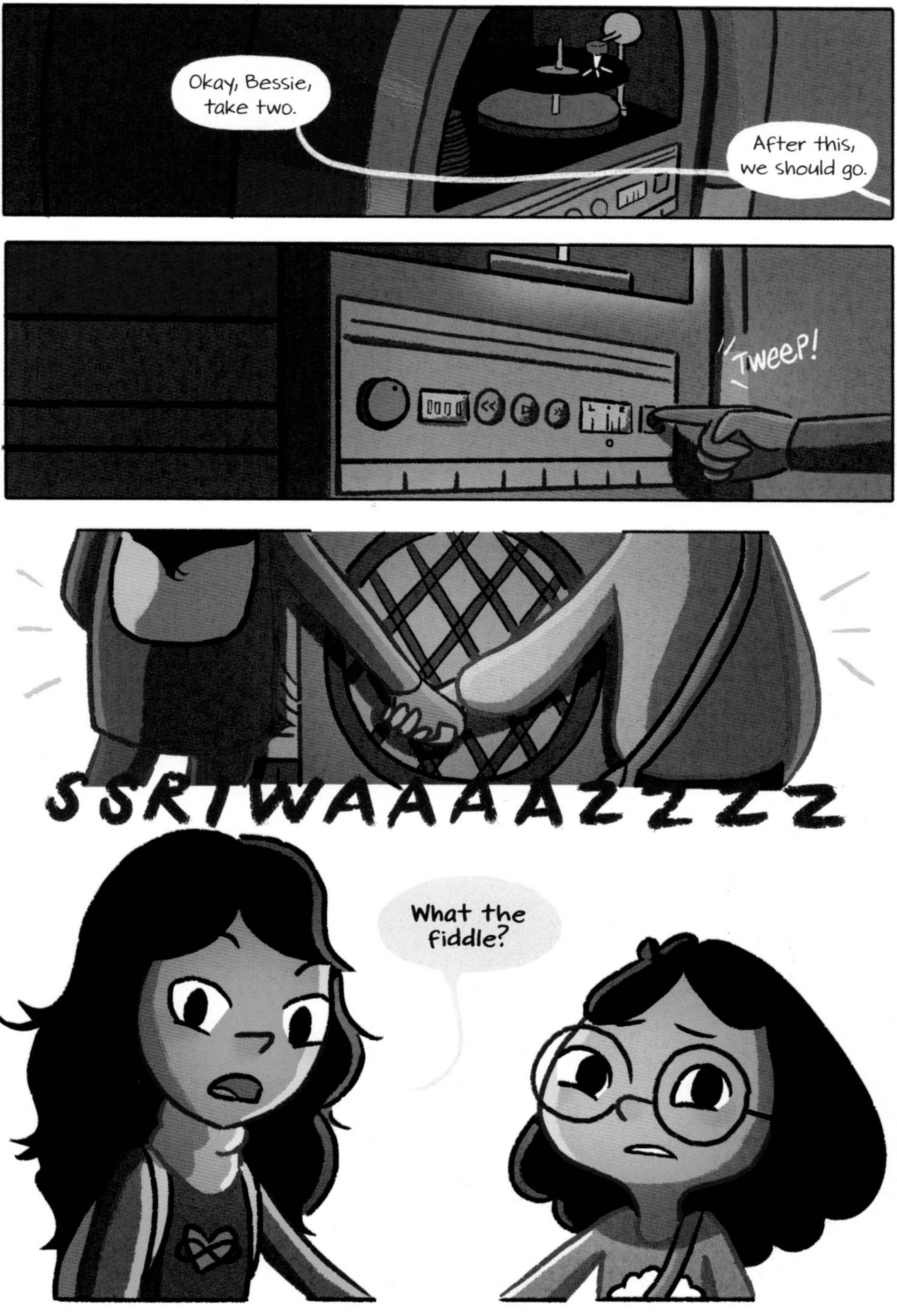
Okay, Bessie, take two.
After this, we should go.
TWEEP!
SSRIWAAAAAZZZZZ
What the fiddle?

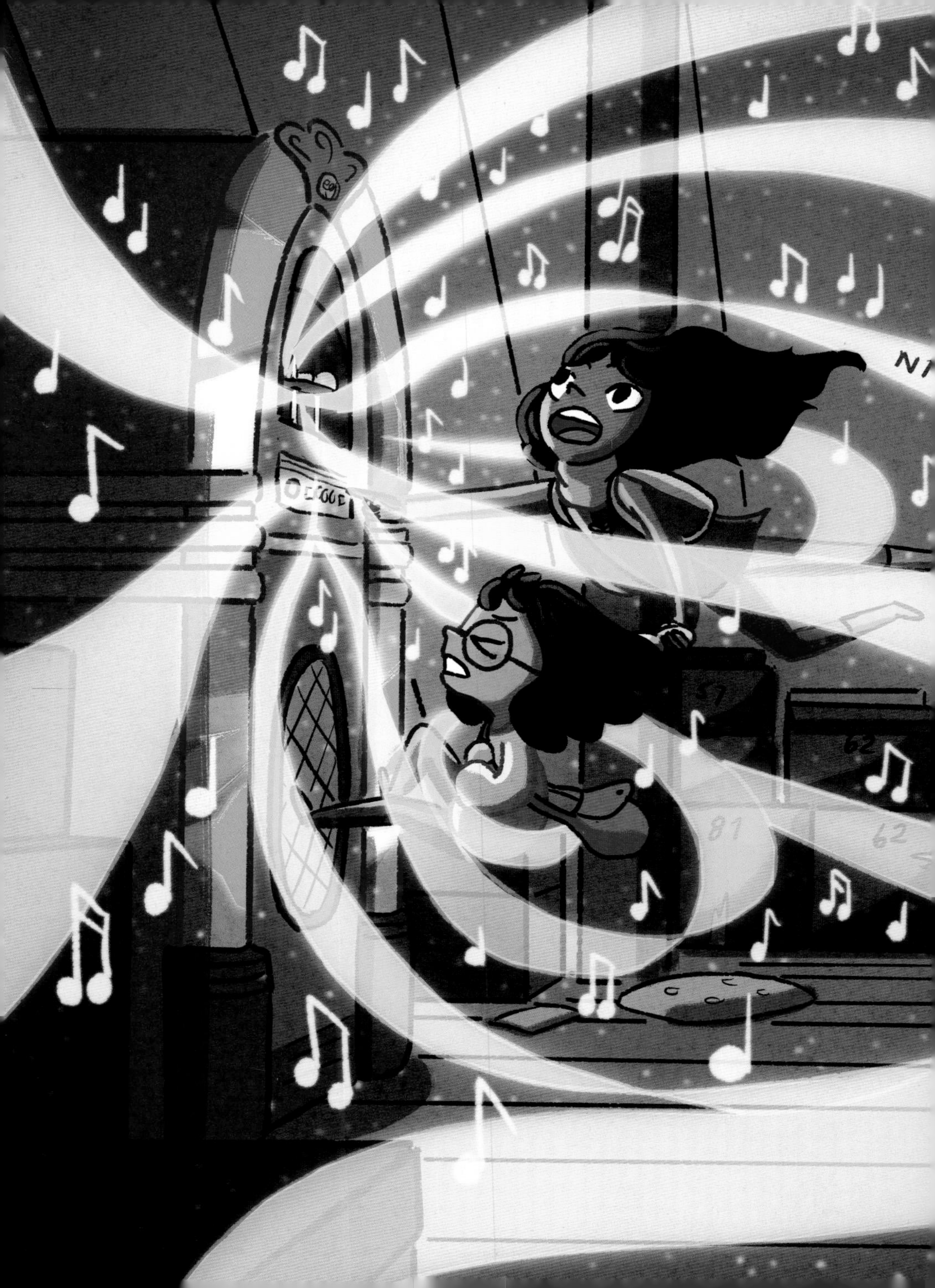
57
62
81
62

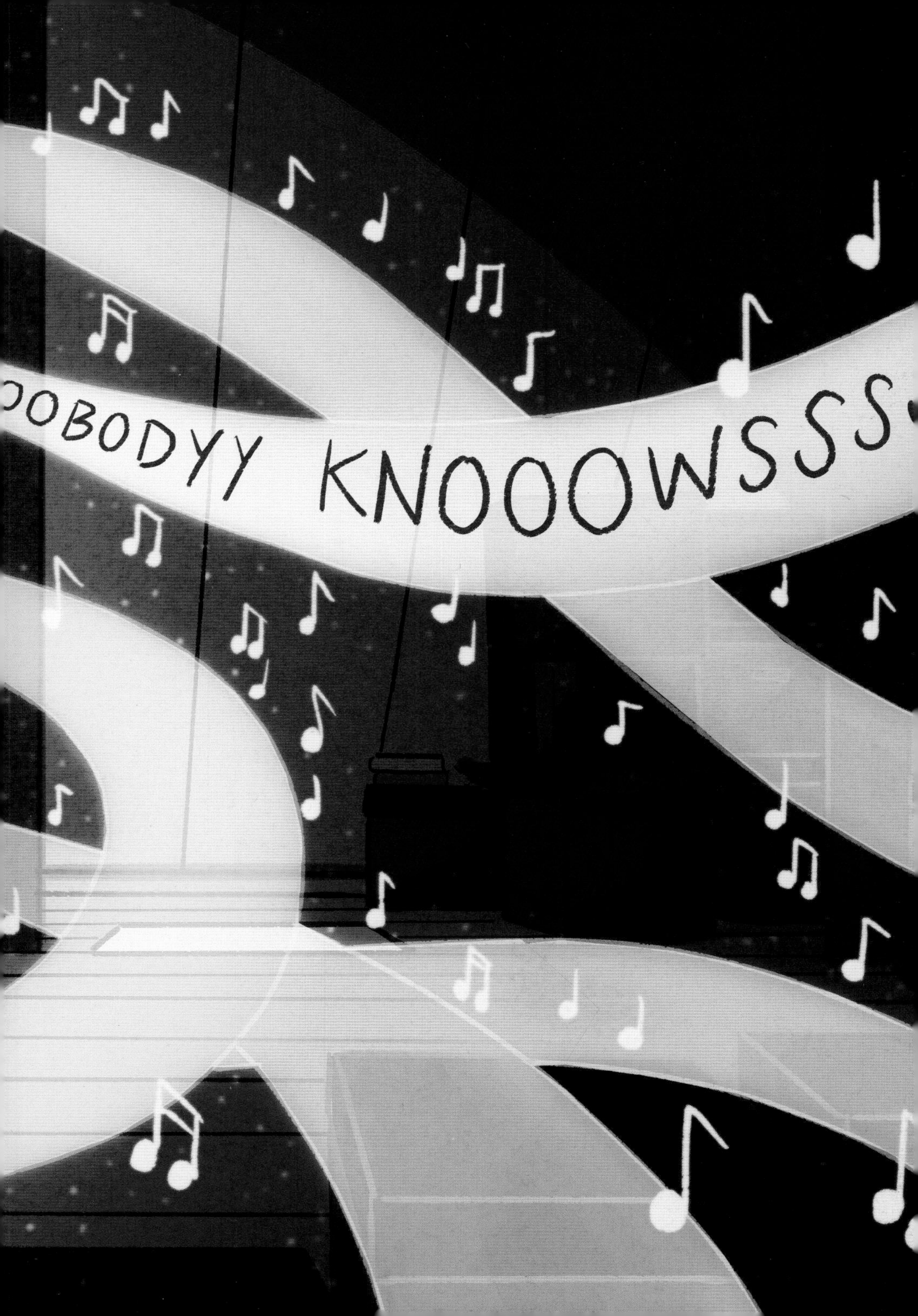
OOBODYY KNOOOOWSSS.

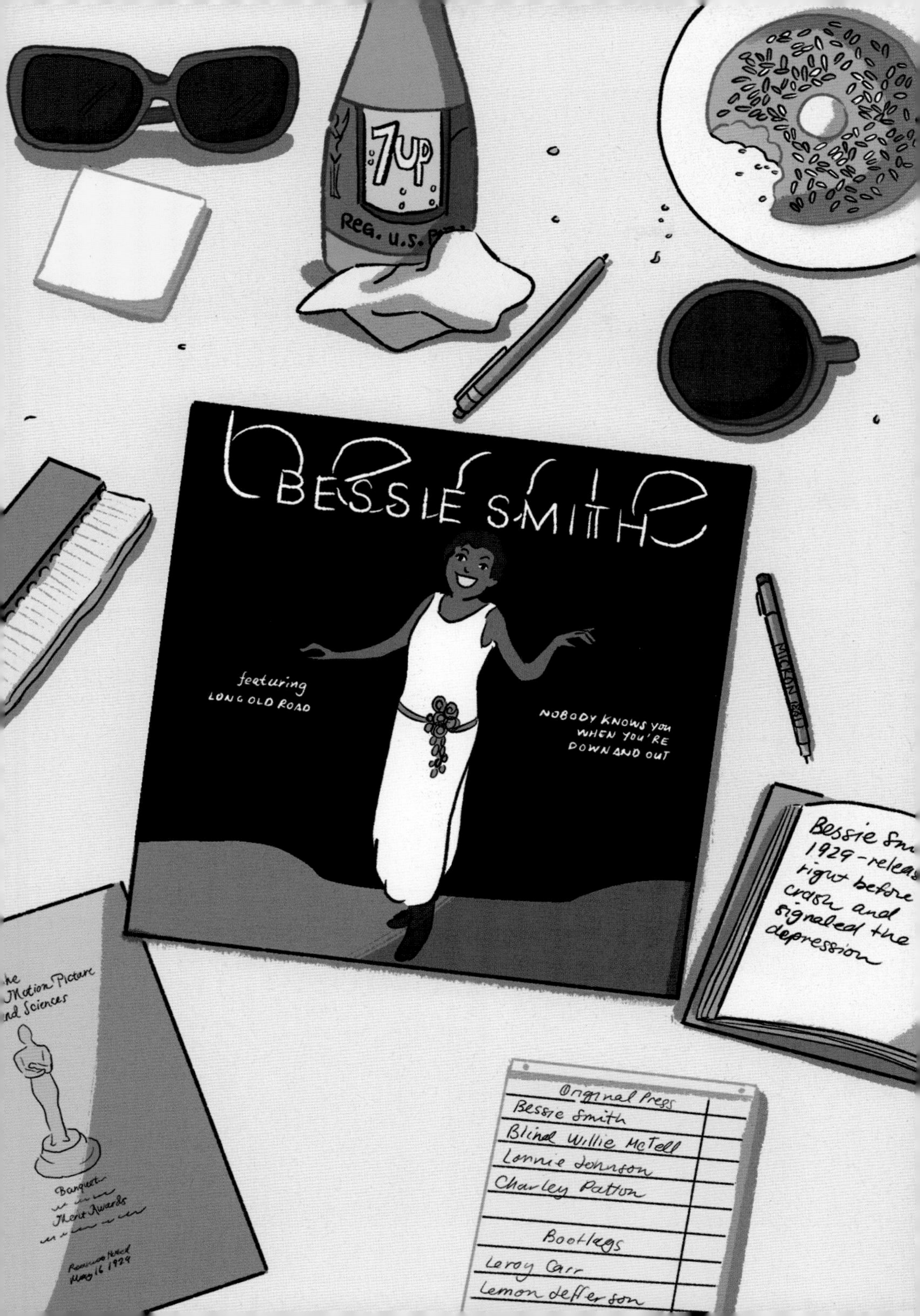
7UP
REG. U.S. PAT.
bessie
BESSIE SMITH
featuring
LONG OLD ROAD
NOBODY KNOWS YOU WHEN YOU'RE DOWN AND OUT
MICRON
Original Press
Bessie Smith
Blind Willie McTell
Lonnie Johnson
Charley Patton
Bootlegs
Leroy Carr
Lemon Jefferson
Banquet
Merit Awards

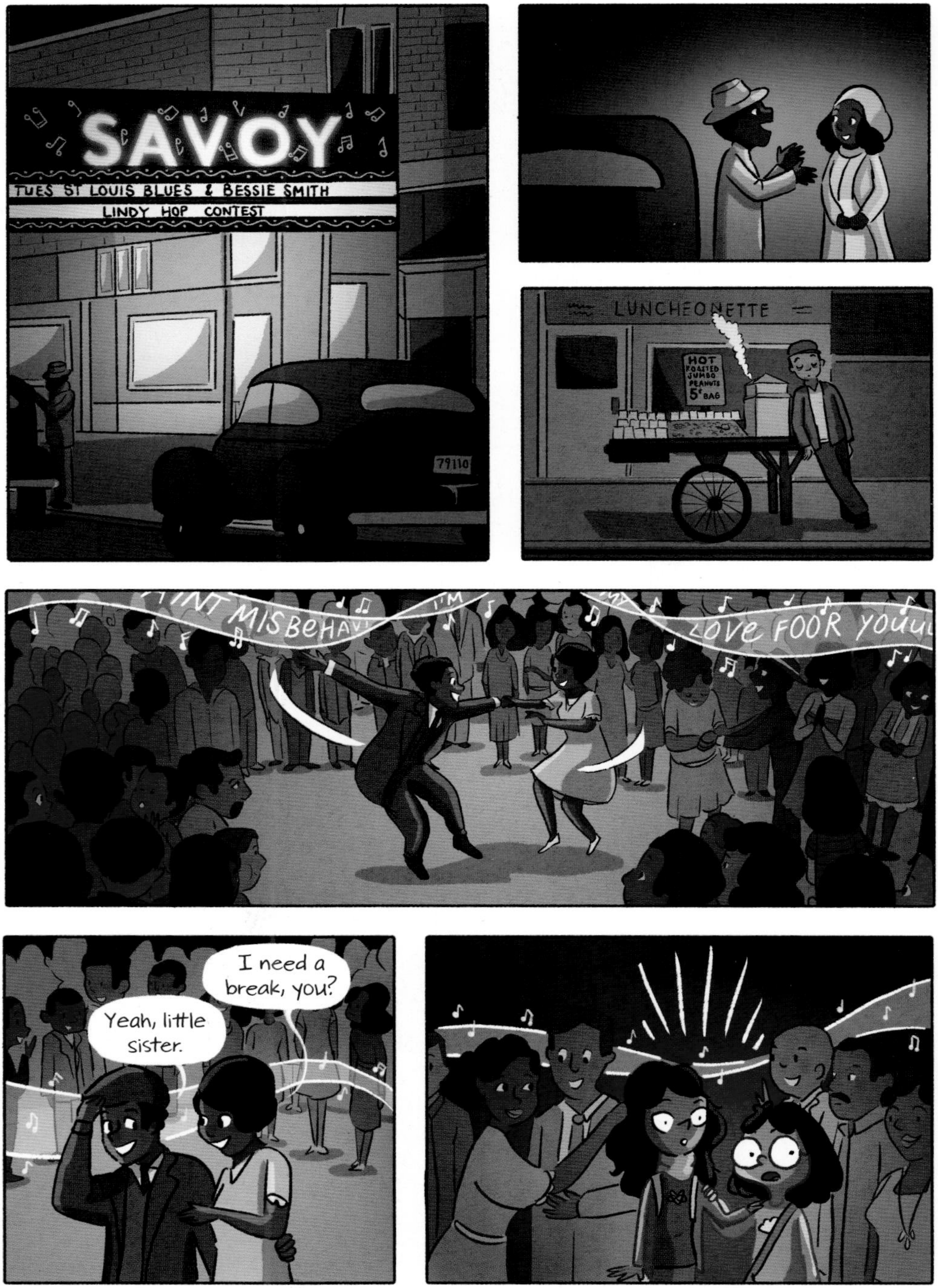
SAVOY
TUES ST LOUIS BLUES & BESSIE SMITH
LINDY HOP CONTEST
79110
LUNCHEONETTE
HOT ROASTED JUMBO PEANUTS 5¢ BAG
I need a break, you?
Yeah, little sister.

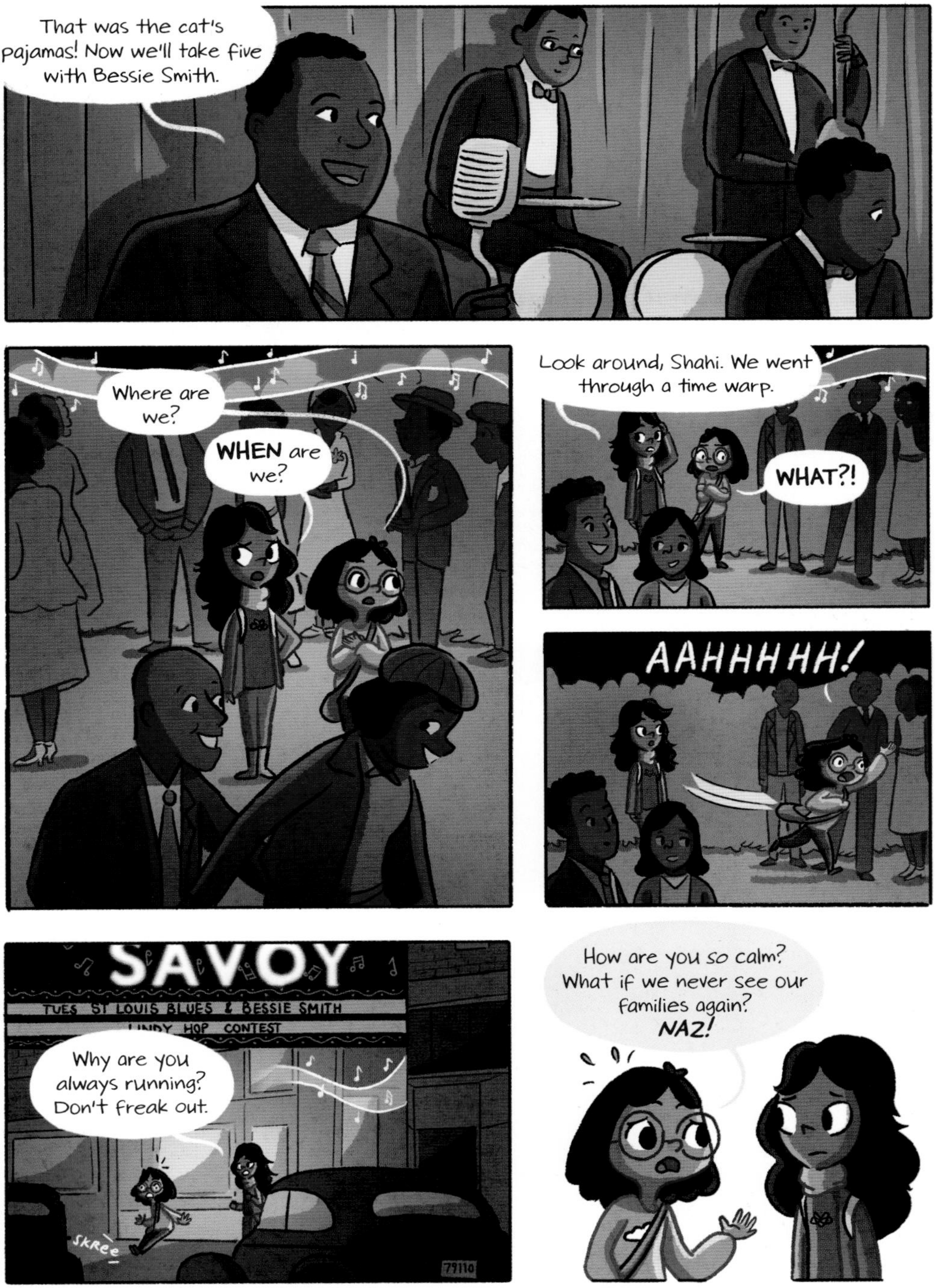
That was the cat's pajamas! Now we'll take five with Bessie Smith.
Where are we?
WHEN are we?
Look around, Shahi. We went through a time warp.
WHAT?!
AAHHHHH!
SAVOY
TUES ST LOUIS BLUES & BESSIE SMITH
LINDY HOP CONTEST
Why are you always running? Don't freak out.
SKREE
79110
How are you so calm? What if we never see our families again? NAZ!

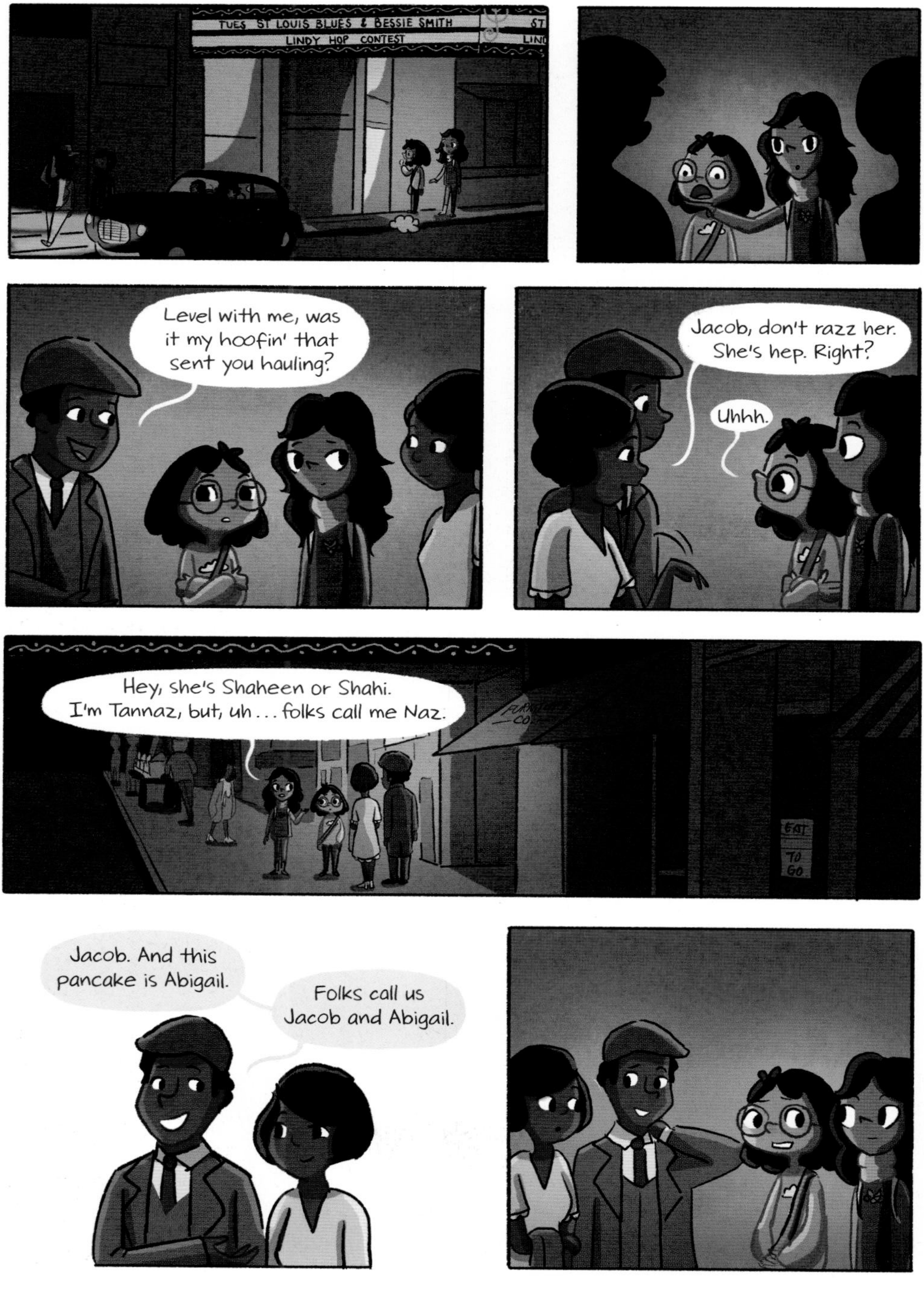
TUES ST LOUIS BLUES & BESSIE SMITH
LINDY HOP CONTEST
Level with me, was it my hoofin' that sent you hauling?
Jacob, don't razz her. She's hep. Right?
Uhhh.
Hey, she's Shaheen or Shahi. I'm Tannaz, but, uh . . . folks call me Naz.
EAT
TO GO
Jacob. And this pancake is Abigail.
Folks call us Jacob and Abigail.

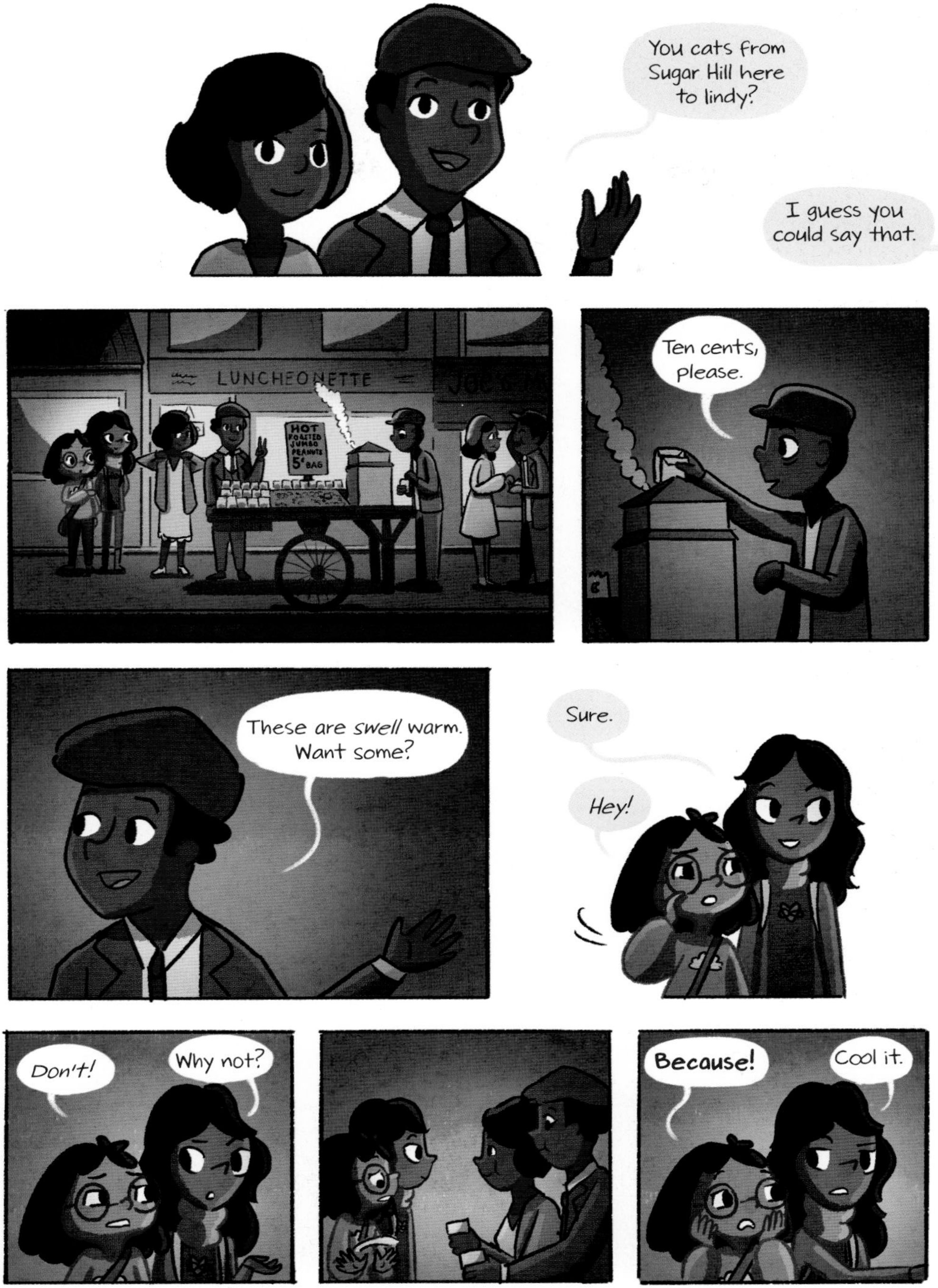
You cats from Sugar Hill here to lindy?
I guess you could say that.
LUNCHEONETTE
HOT ROASTED JUMBO PEANUTS 5¢ BAG
Ten cents, please.
These are *swell* warm. Want some?
Sure.
Hey!
Don't!
Why not?
Because!
Cool it.

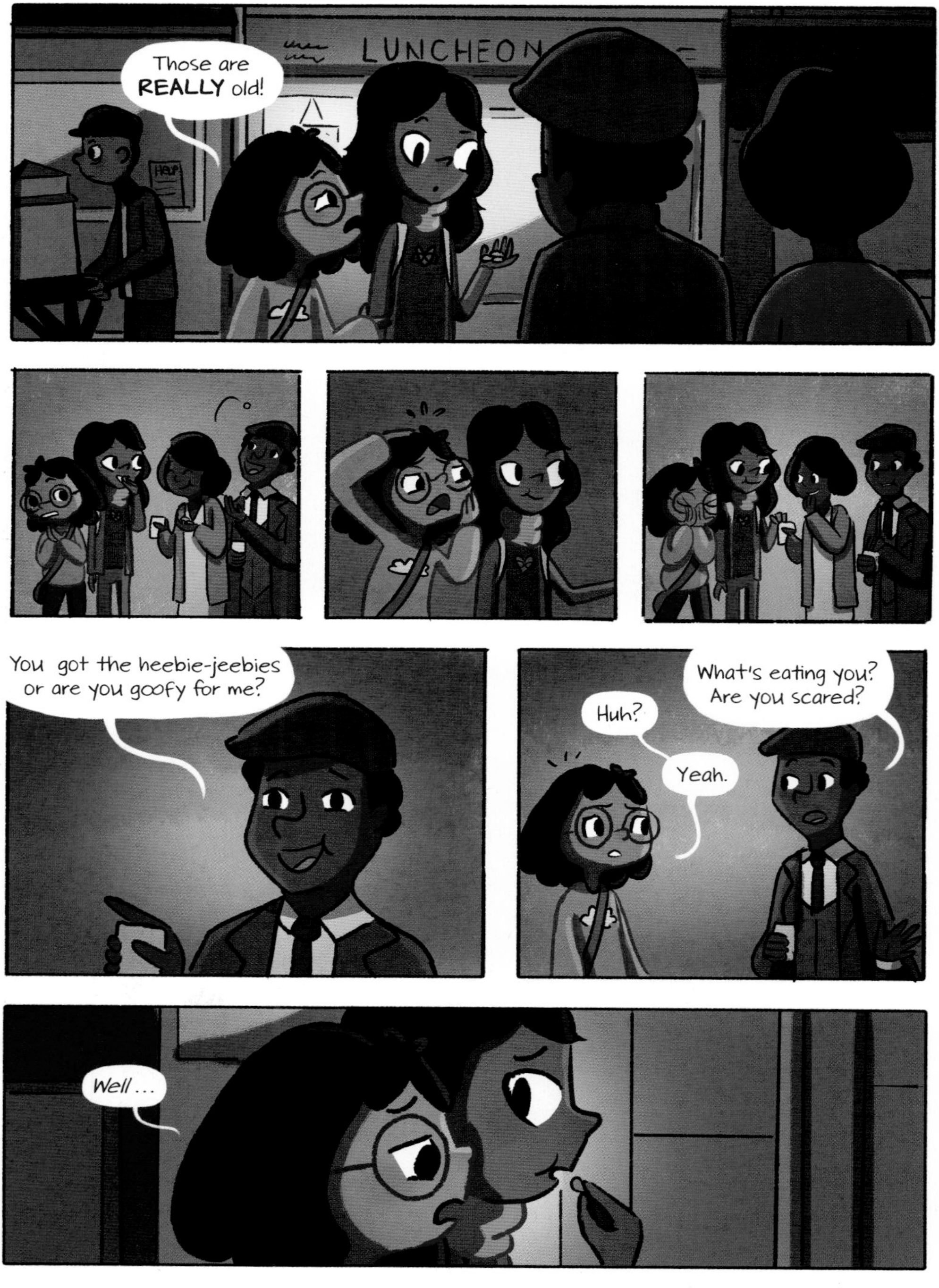

LUNCHEON
Those are **REALLY** old!
You got the heebie-jeebies or are you goofy for me?
What's eating you? Are you scared?
Huh?
Yeah.
Well...

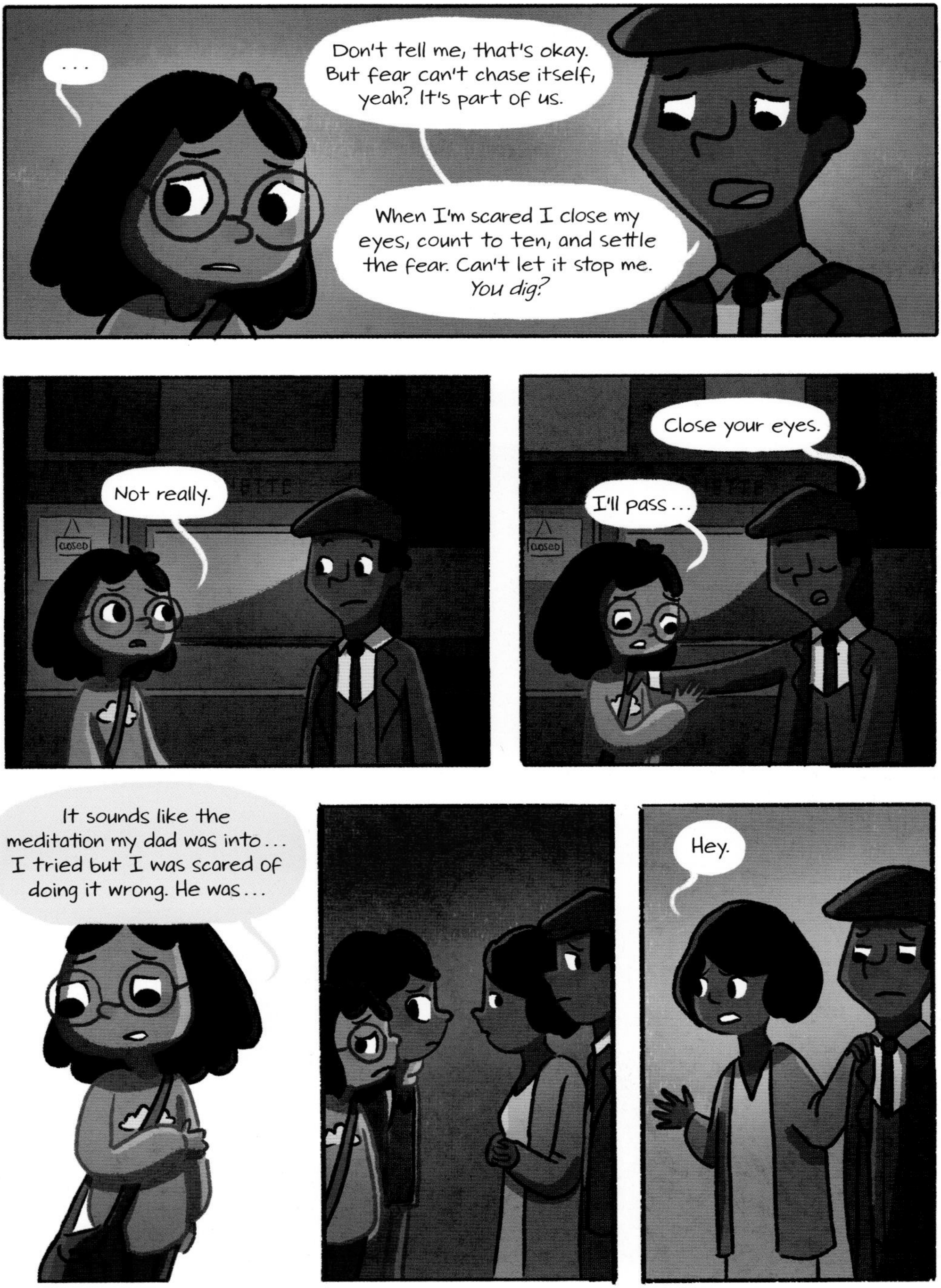

. . .
Don't tell me, that's okay. But fear can't chase itself, yeah? It's part of us.
When I'm scared I close my eyes, count to ten, and settle the fear. Can't let it stop me. *You dig?*
Not really.
Close your eyes.
I'll pass . . .
It sounds like the meditation my dad was into . . . I tried but I was scared of doing it wrong. He was . . .
Hey.

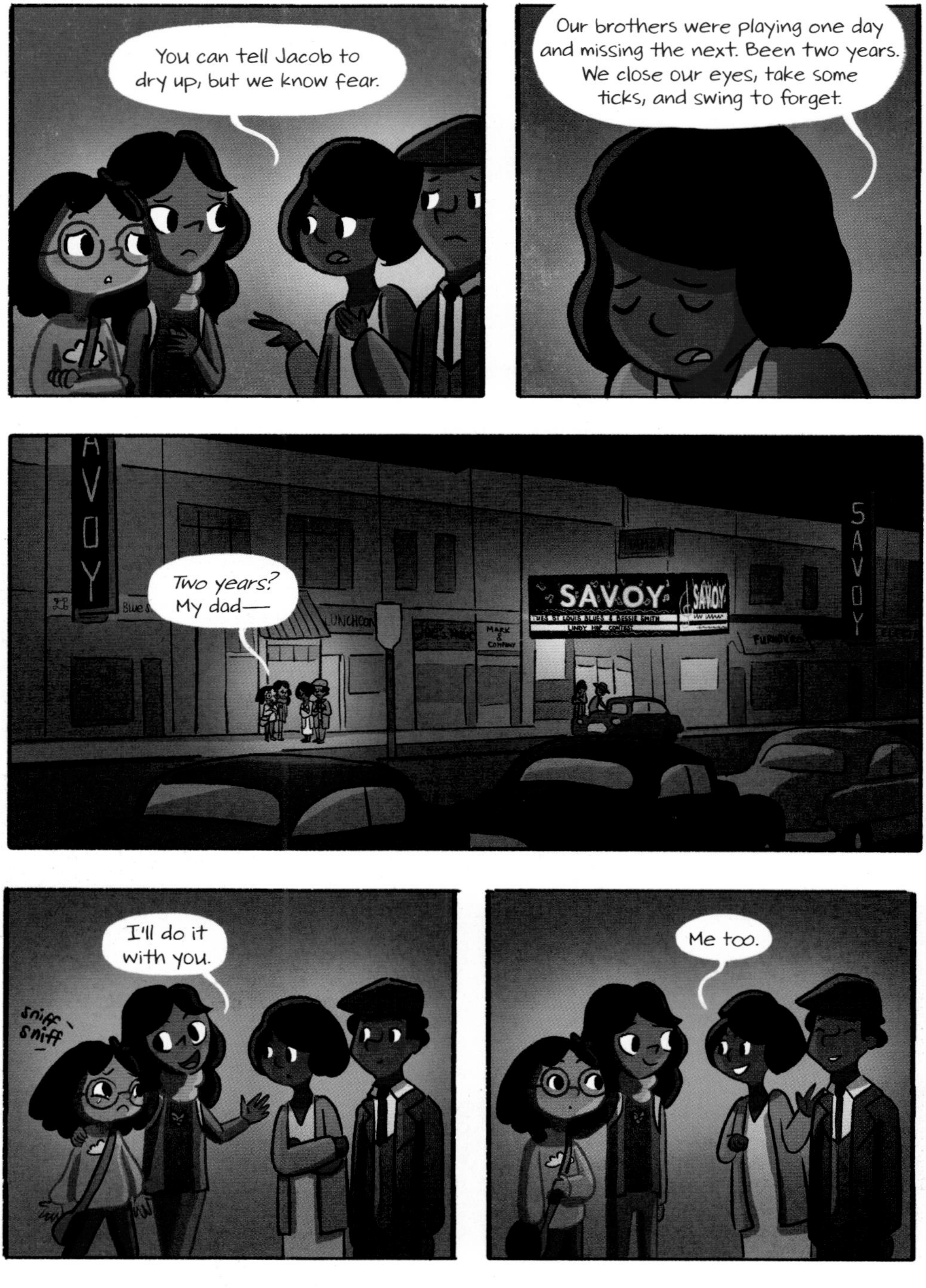
You can tell Jacob to dry up, but we know fear.
Our brothers were playing one day and missing the next. Been two years. We close our eyes, take some ticks, and swing to forget.
SAVOY
SAVOY
Two years? My dad—
SAVOY
LINDY HOP CONTEST
MARK & COMPANY
SAVOY
I'll do it with you.
sniff sniff
Me too.

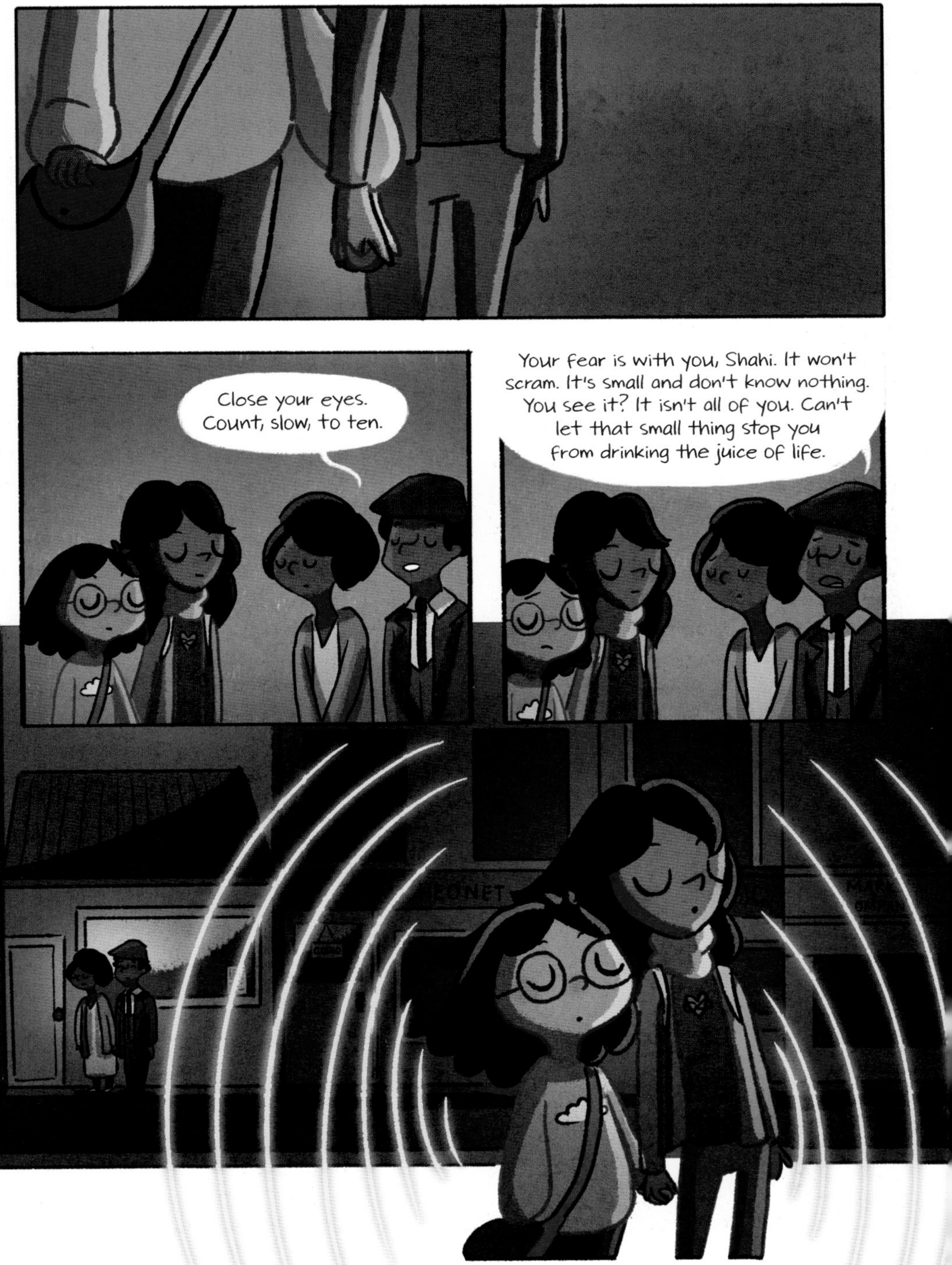
Close your eyes. Count, slow, to ten.
Your fear is with you, Shahi. It won't scram. It's small and don't know nothing. You see it? It isn't all of you. Can't let that small thing stop you from drinking the juice of life.

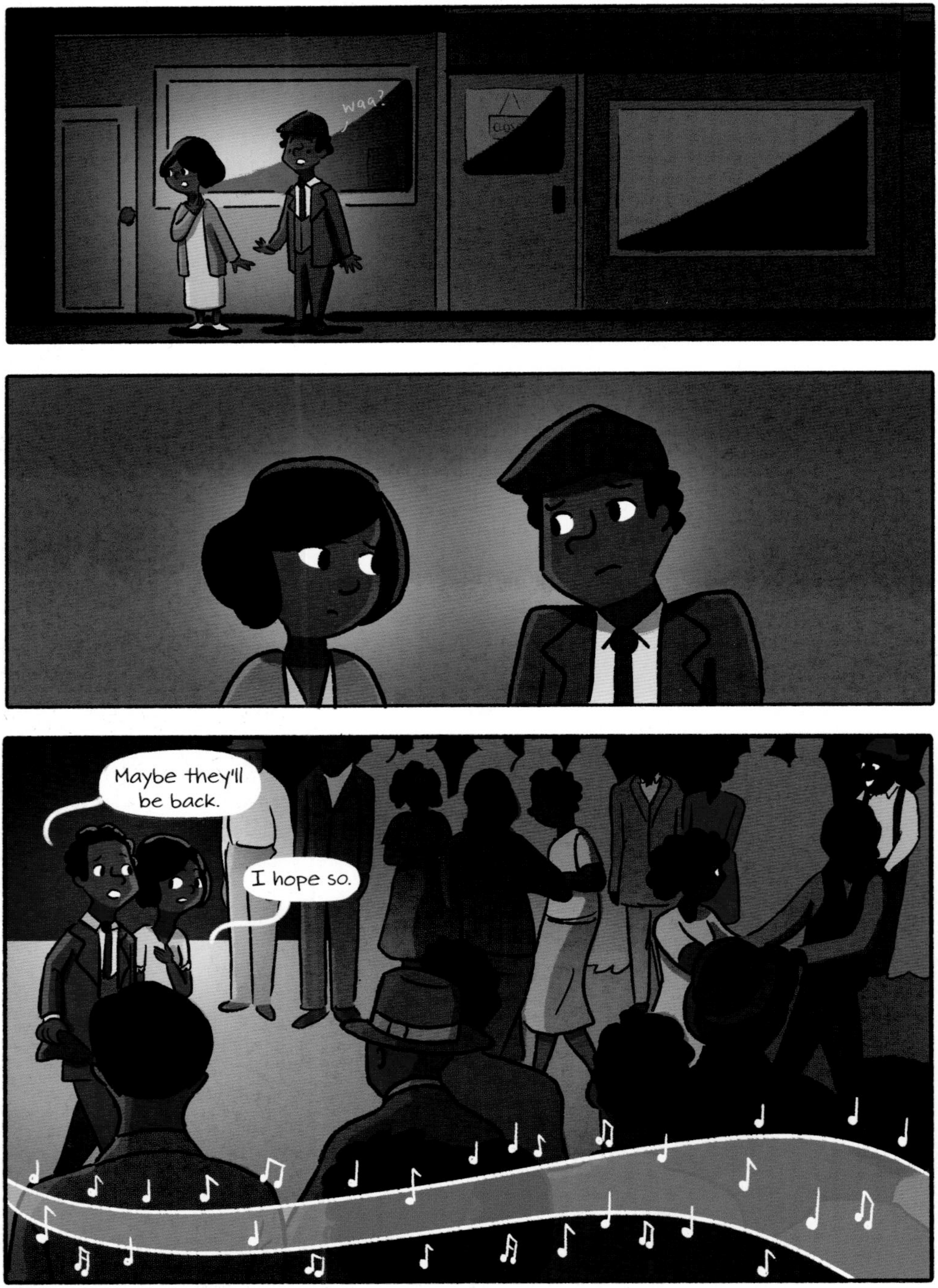
waa?
Maybe they'll be back.
I hope so.

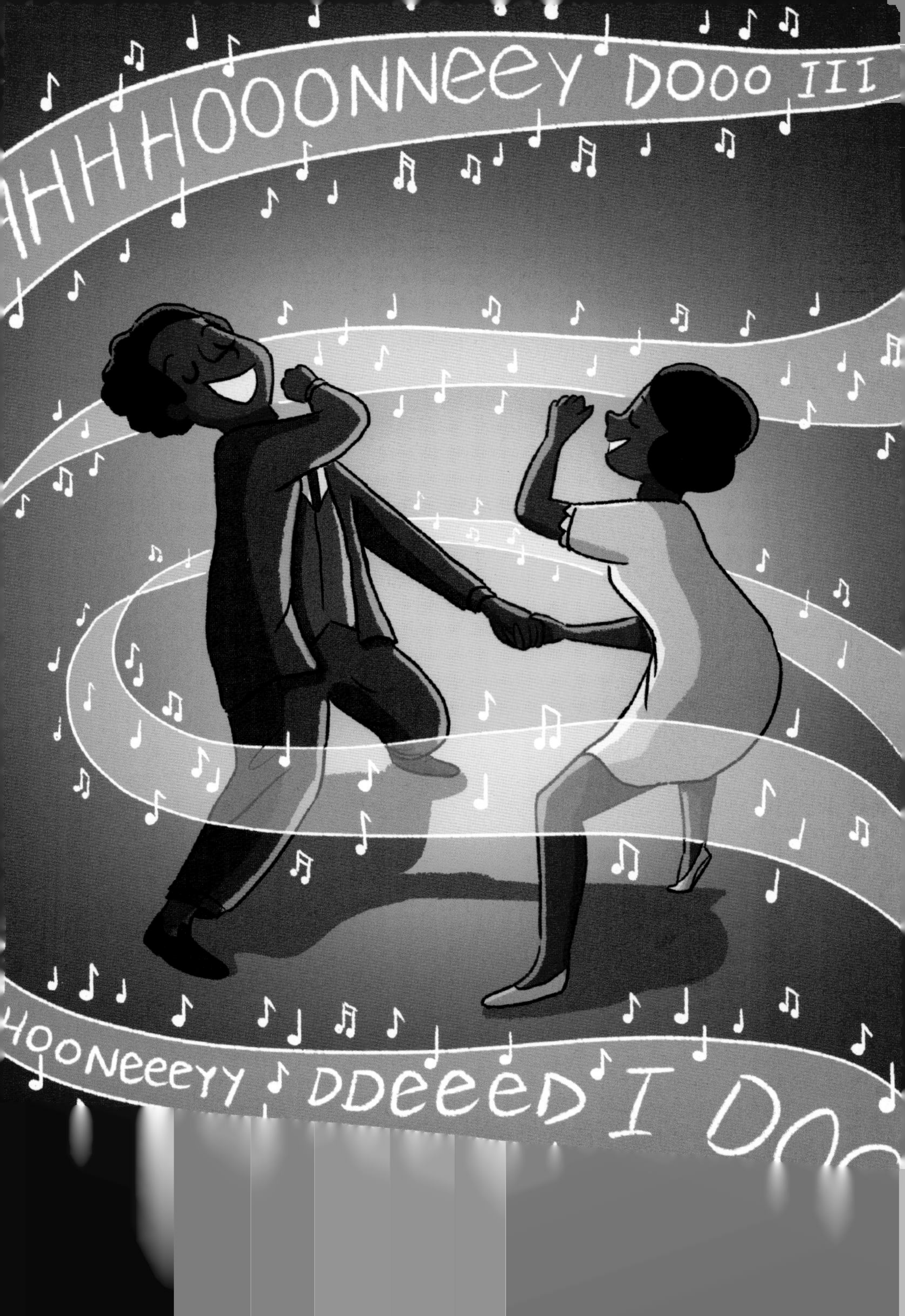

HHHOOOONNeeY DOOO III
HOONeeeYY DDeeeD I DO

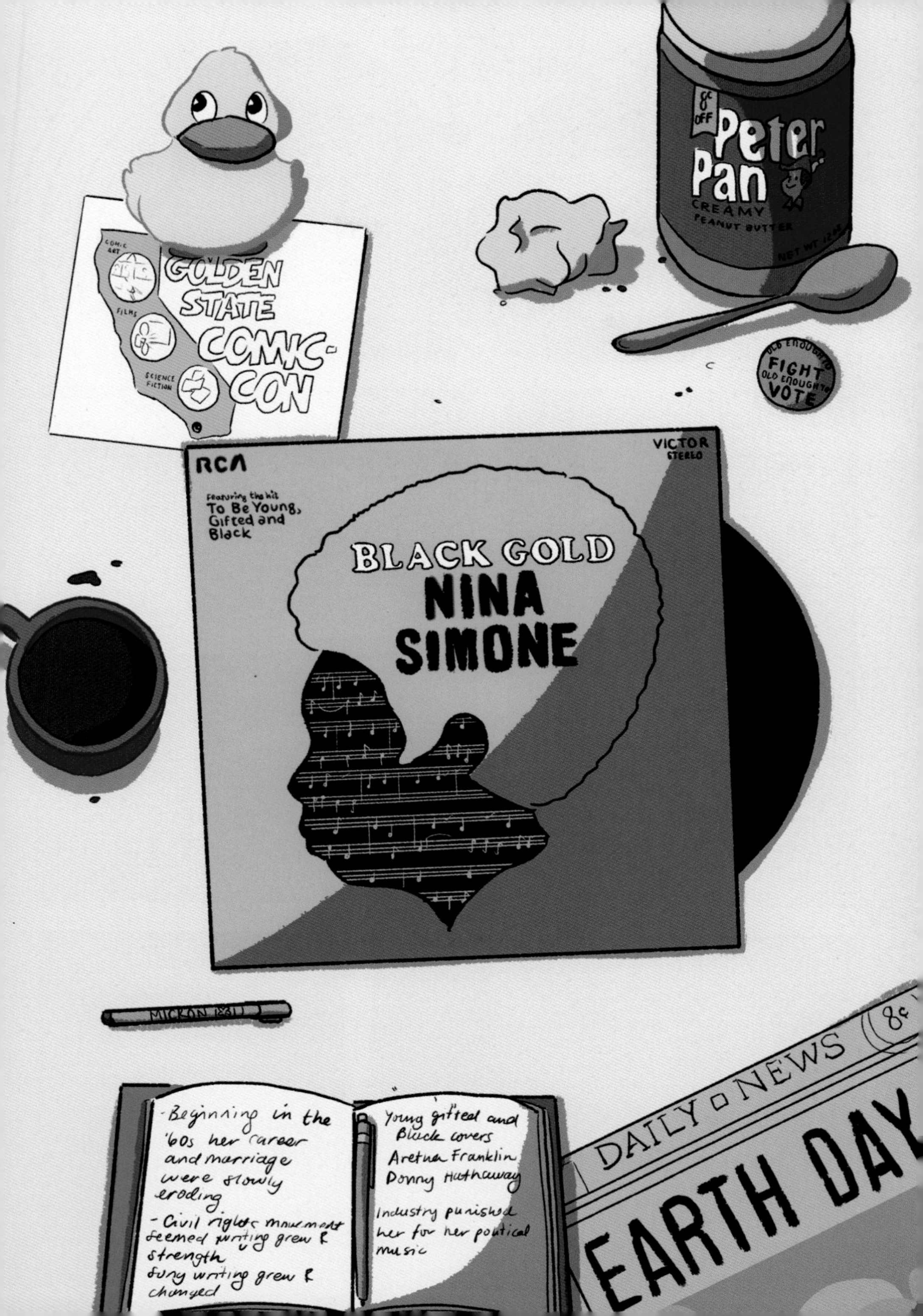
8¢ OFF
Peter Pan
CREAMY
PEANUT BUTTER
GOLDEN STATE COMIC-CON
COMIC ART
FILMS
SCIENCE FICTION
OLD ENOUGH TO FIGHT OLD ENOUGH TO VOTE
RCA
VICTOR STEREO
Featuring the hit To Be Young, Gifted and Black
BLACK GOLD
NINA SIMONE
MICRON
DAILY NEWS
8¢
EARTH DAY
-Beginning in the '60s her career and marriage were slowly eroding.
-Civil rights movement seemed writing grew & strength
Song writing grew & changed
Young gifted and Black covers
Aretha Franklin
Donny Hathaway
Industry punished her for her political music

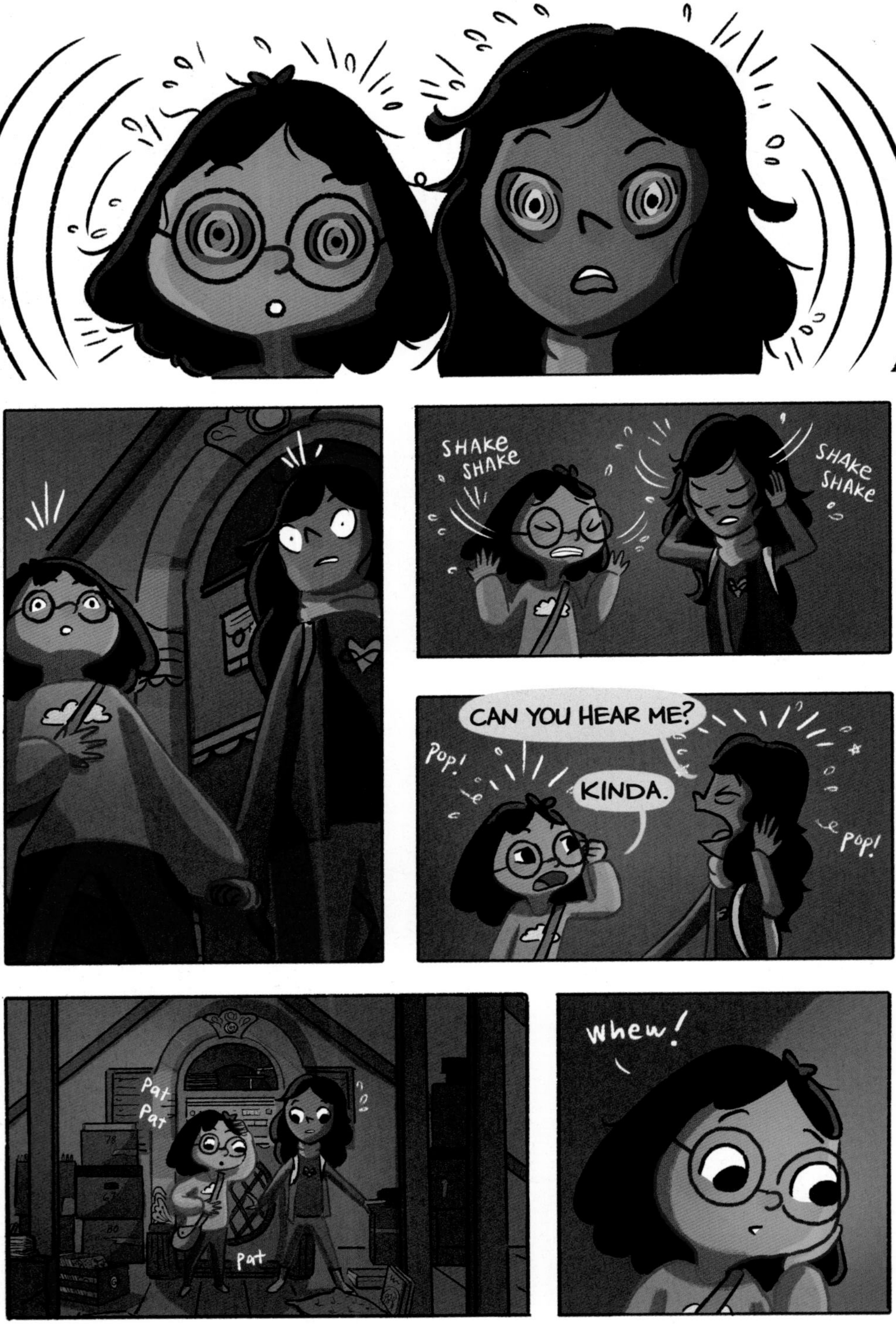
SHAKE SHAKE
SHAKE SHAKE
CAN YOU HEAR ME?
KINDA.
Pop!
Pop!
Pat
Pat
Pat
Whew!

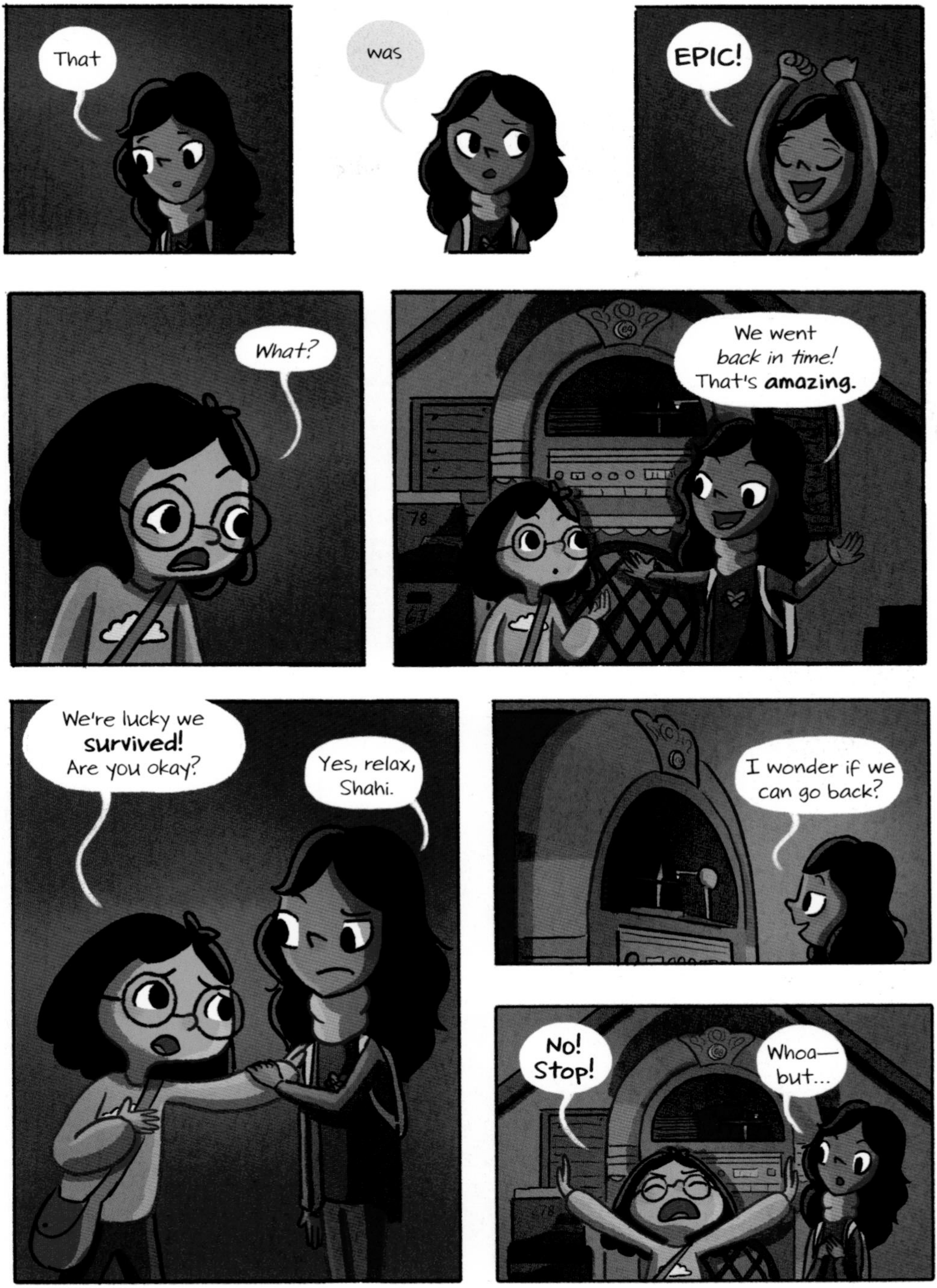
That
was
EPIC!
What?
We went back in time! That's **amazing.**
We're lucky we **survived!** Are you okay?
Yes, relax, Shahi.
I wonder if we can go back?
No! Stop!
Whoa—but...

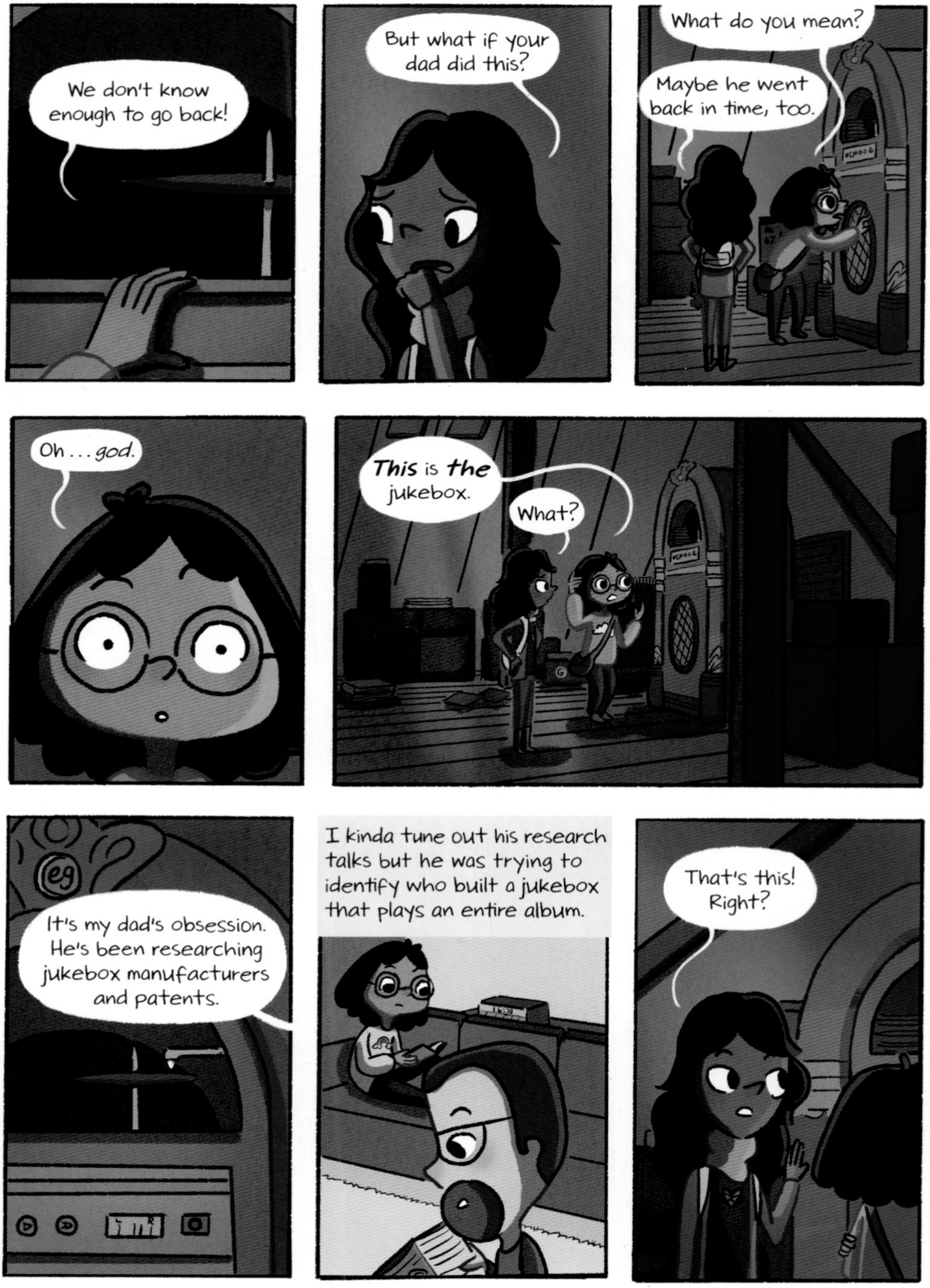
We don't know enough to go back!
But what if your dad did this?
What do you mean?
Maybe he went back in time, too.
Oh . . . god.
This is **the** jukebox.
What?
It's my dad's obsession. He's been researching jukebox manufacturers and patents.
I kinda tune out his research talks but he was trying to identify who built a jukebox that plays an entire album.
That's this! Right?

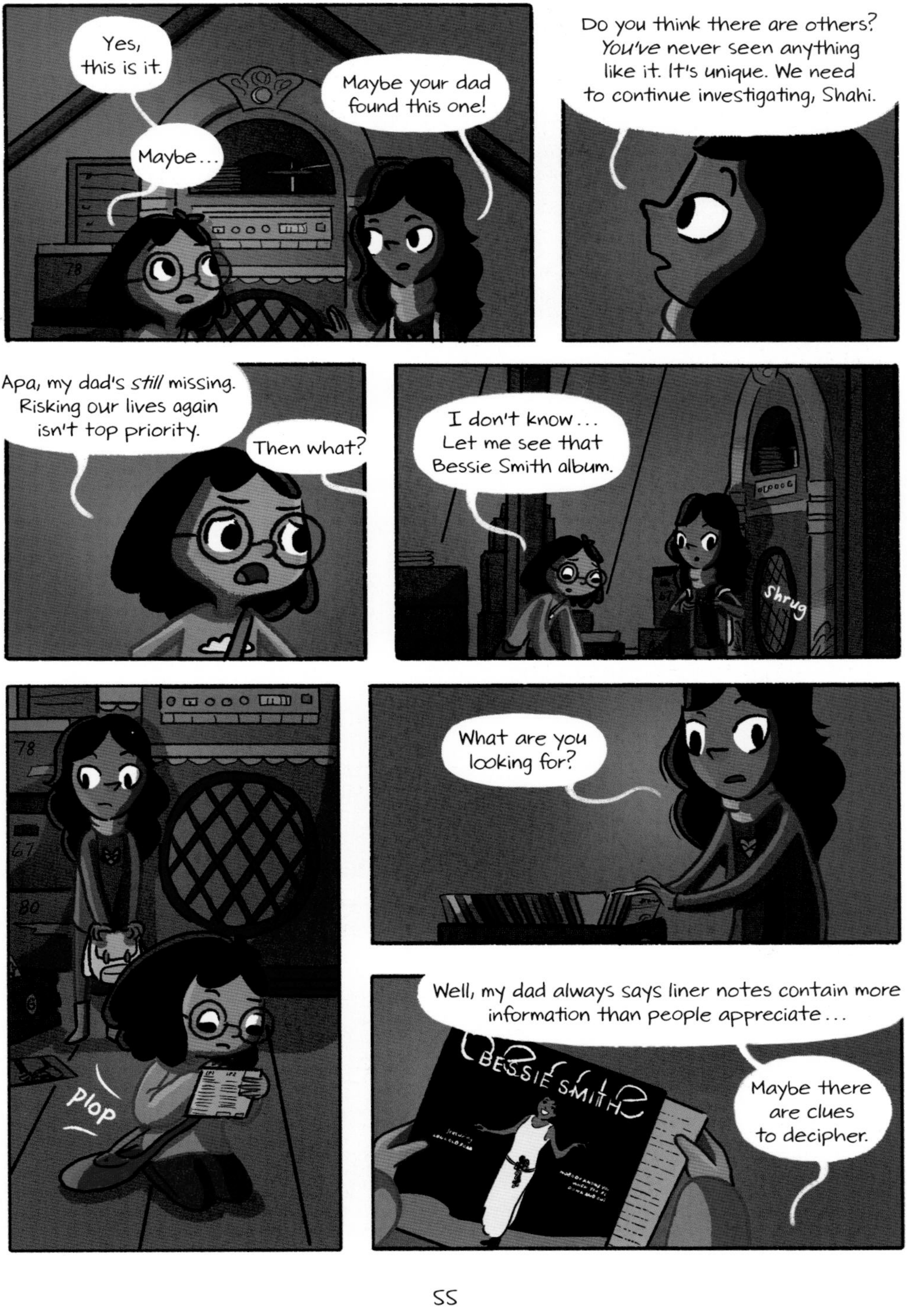
Yes, this is it.
Maybe...
Maybe your dad found this one!
Do you think there are others? *You've* never seen anything like it. It's unique. We need to continue investigating, Shahi.
Apa, my dad's *still* missing. Risking our lives again isn't top priority.
Then what?
I don't know... Let me see that Bessie Smith album.
Shrug
What are you looking for?
Plop
Well, my dad always says liner notes contain more information than people appreciate...
BESSIE SMITH
Maybe there are clues to decipher.

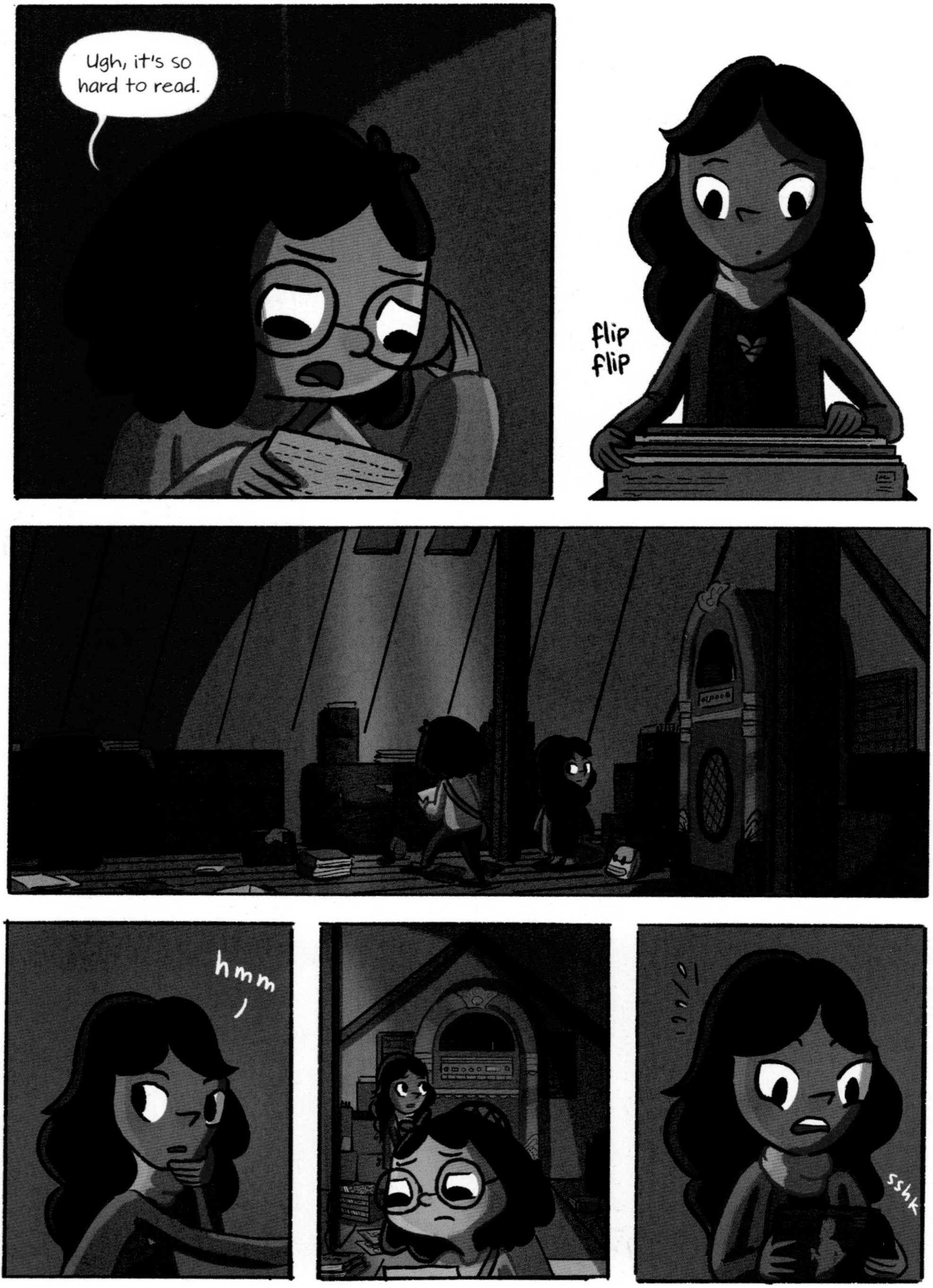
Ugh, it's so hard to read.
flip flip
hmm
sshk

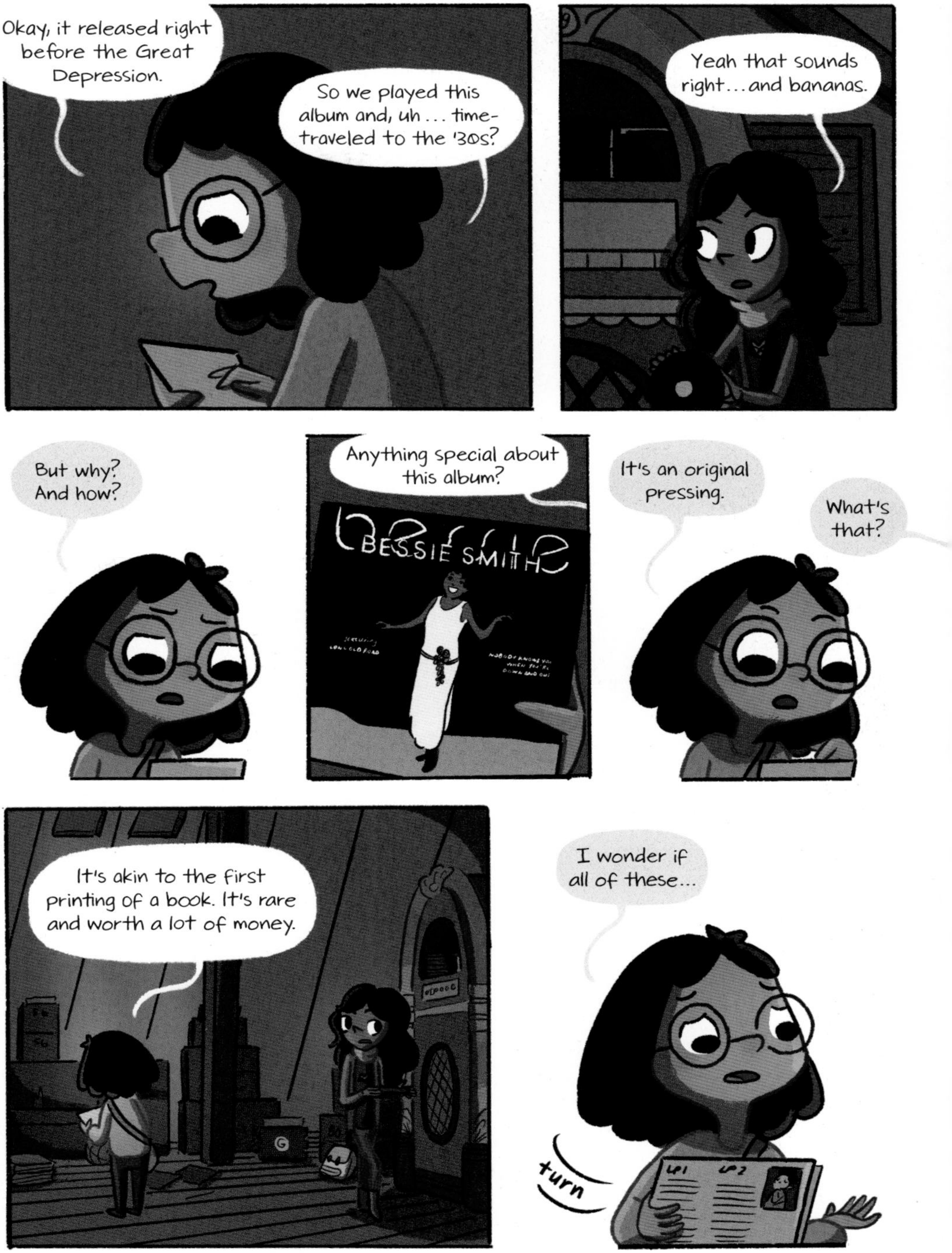
Okay, it released right before the Great Depression.
So we played this album and, uh . . . time-traveled to the '30s?
Yeah that sounds right . . . and bananas.
But why? And how?
Anything special about this album?
BESSIE SMITH
It's an original pressing.
What's that?
It's akin to the first printing of a book. It's rare and worth a lot of money.
I wonder if all of these . . .
turn

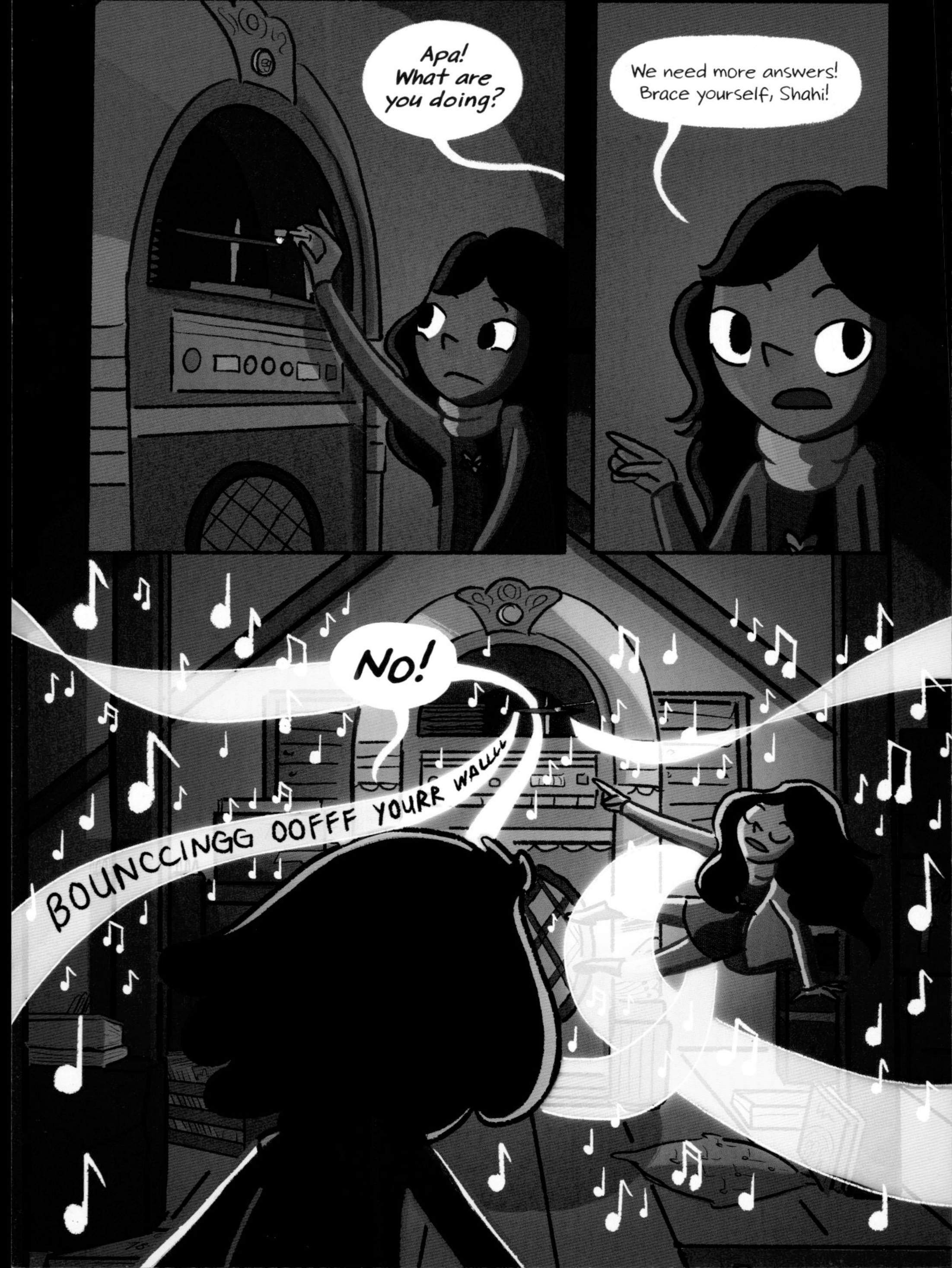
Apa! What are you doing?
We need more answers! Brace yourself, Shahi!
No!
BOUNCCINGG OOFFF YOURR WALLL

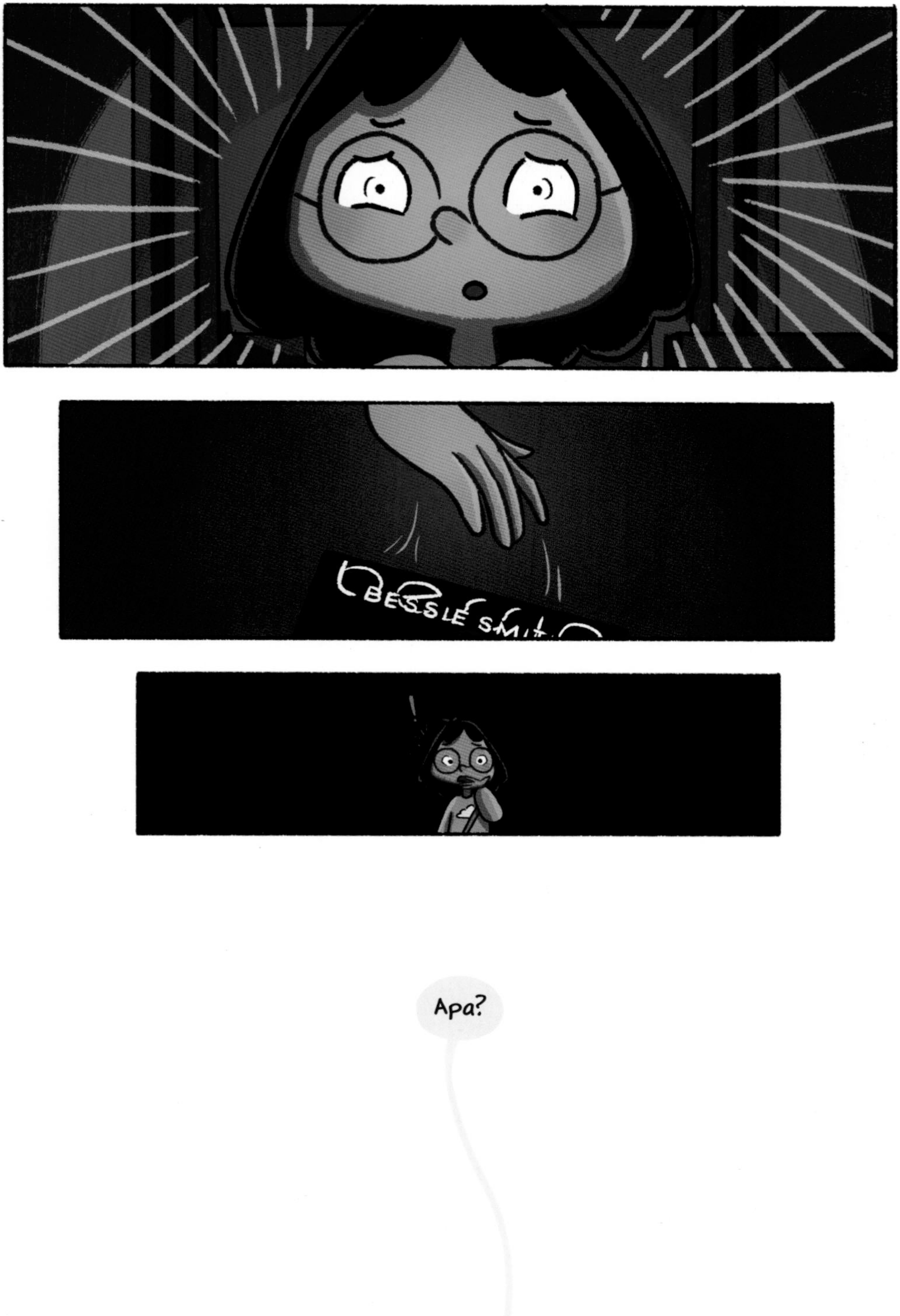
Apa?

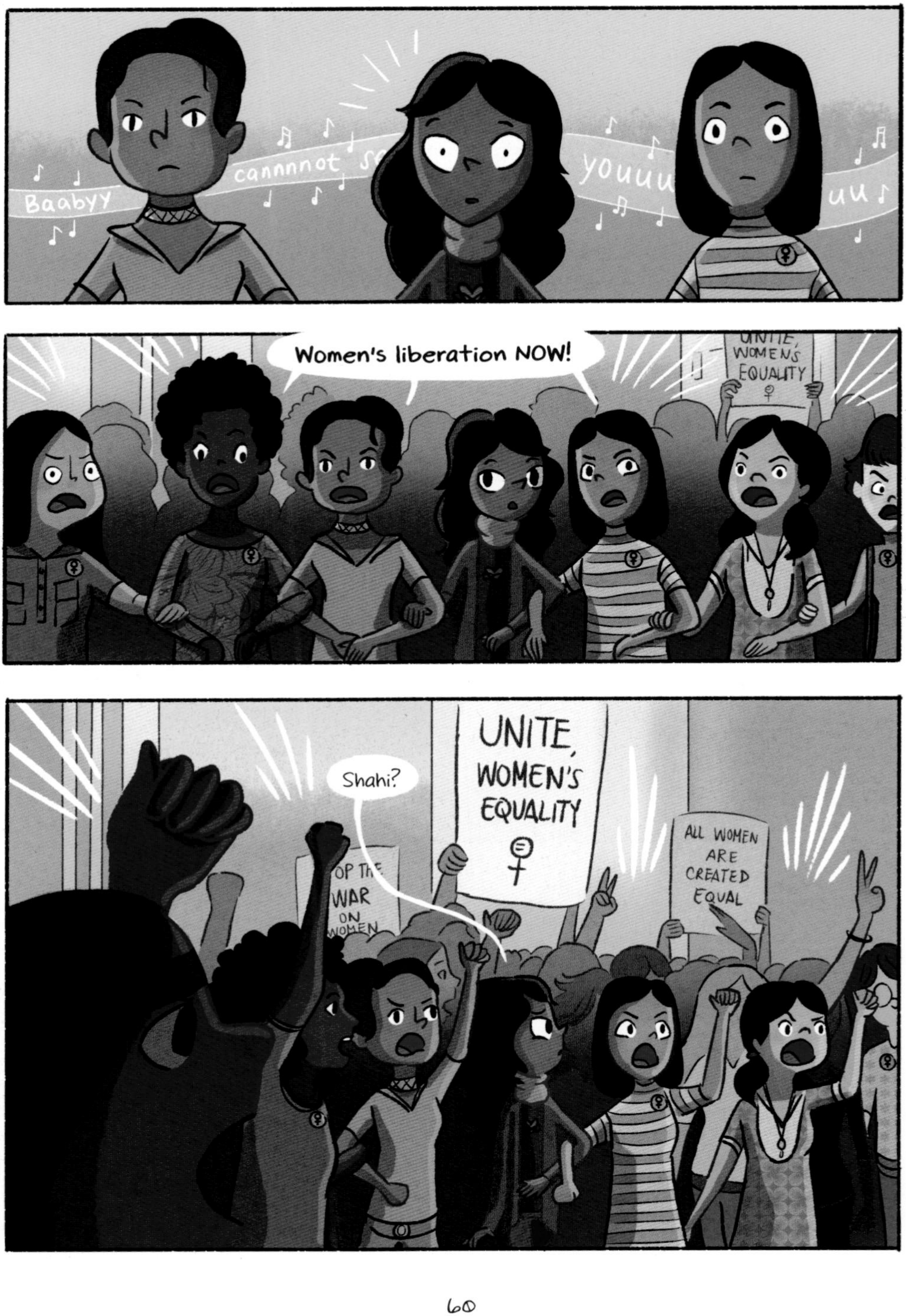
Baabyy
cannnnot se
youuu
uu
Women's liberation NOW!
UNITE, WOMEN'S EQUALITY
Shahi?
UNITE, WOMEN'S EQUALITY
OP THE WAR ON WOMEN
ALL WOMEN ARE CREATED EQUAL

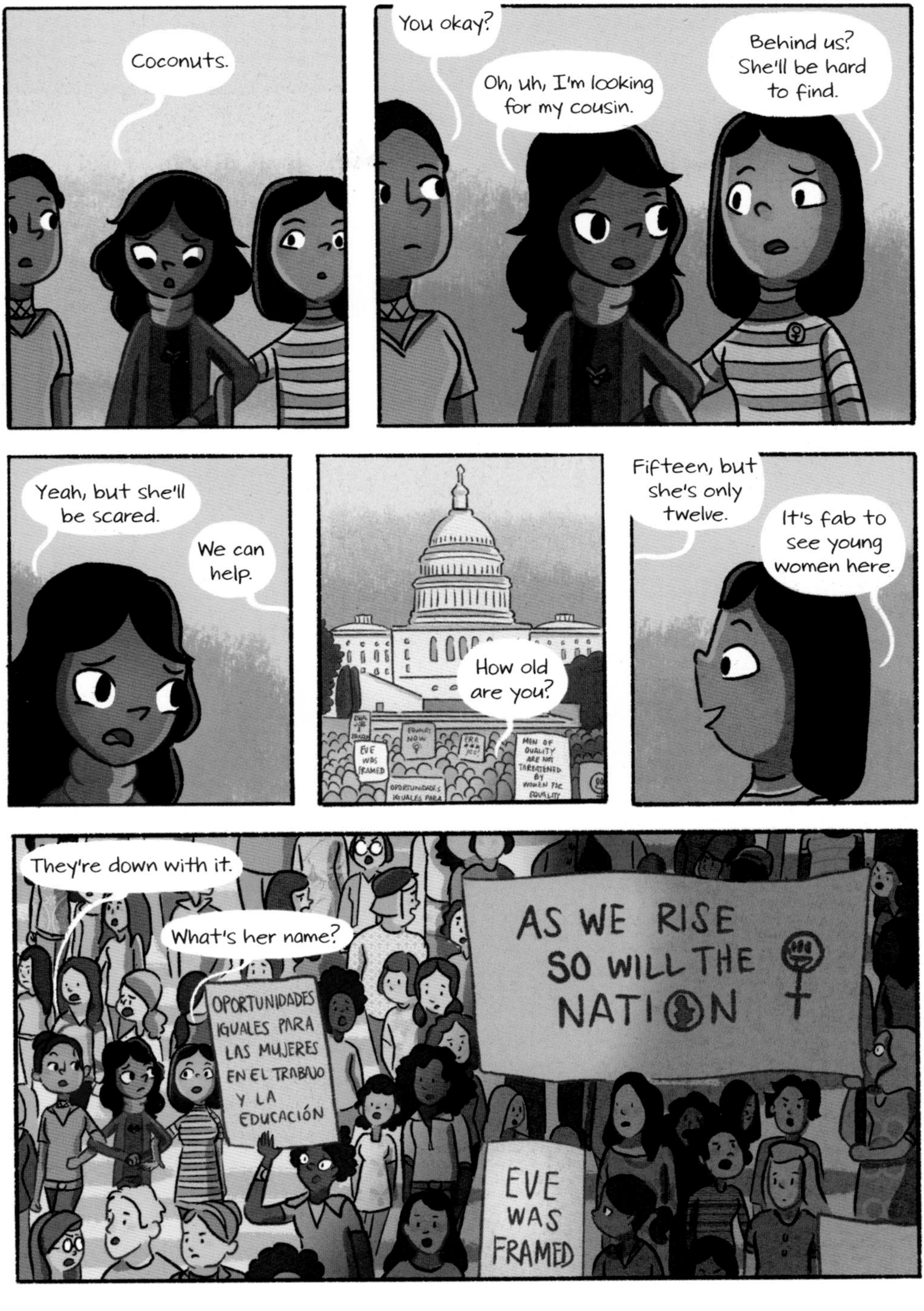

Coconuts.
You okay?
Oh, uh, I'm looking for my cousin.
Behind us? She'll be hard to find.
Yeah, but she'll be scared.
We can help.
How old are you?
Fifteen, but she's only twelve.
It's fab to see young women here.
They're down with it.
What's her name?
OPORTUNIDADES IGUALES PARA LAS MUJERES EN EL TRABAJO Y LA EDUCACIÓN
AS WE RISE SO WILL THE NATION
EVE WAS FRAMED

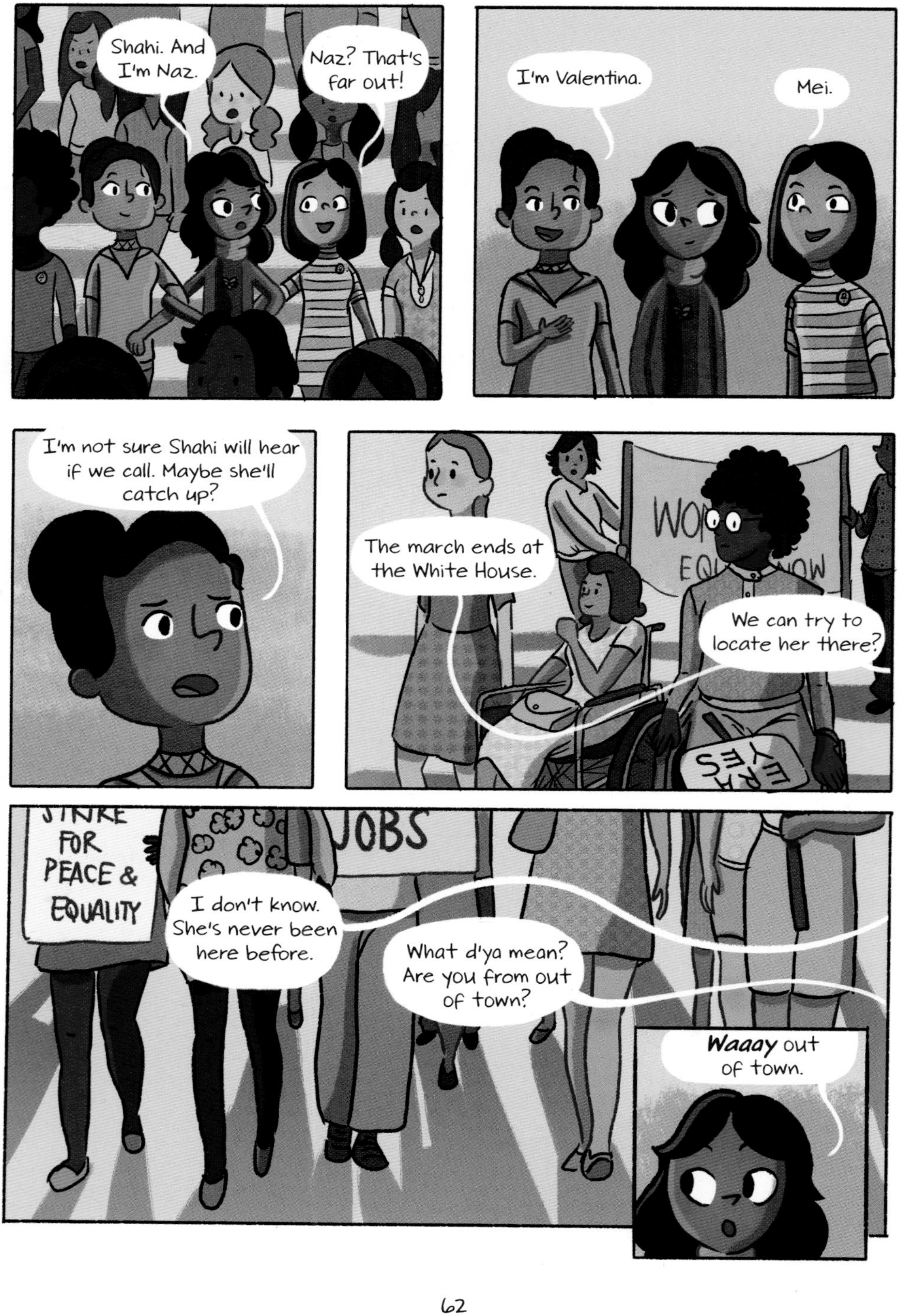
Shahi. And I'm Naz.
Naz? That's far out!
I'm Valentina.
Mei.
I'm not sure Shahi will hear if we call. Maybe she'll catch up?
WO
EQ NOW
The march ends at the White House.
We can try to locate her there?
ERA YES
FOR PEACE & EQUALITY
JOBS
I don't know. She's never been here before.
What d'ya mean? Are you from out of town?
Waaay out of town.

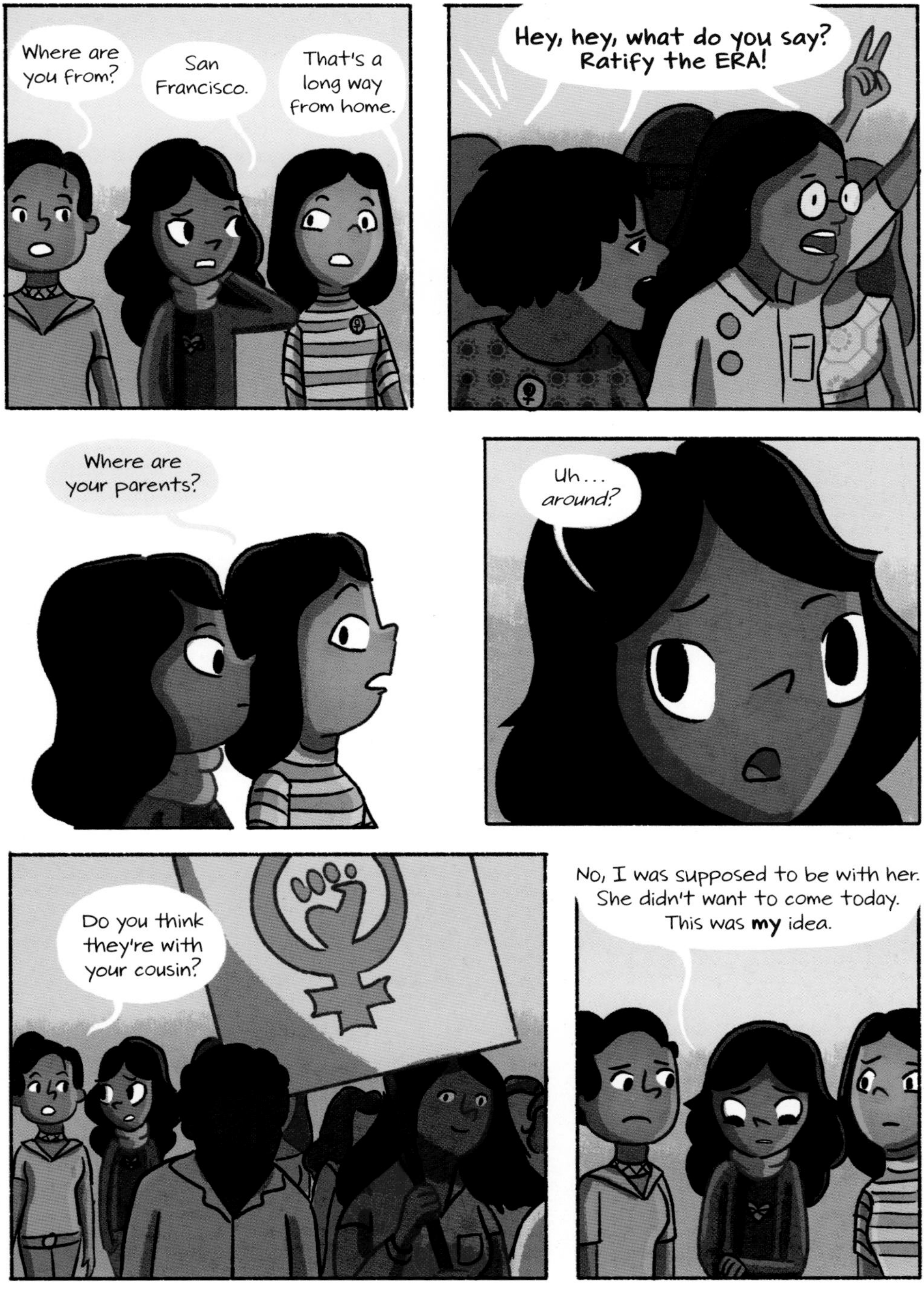
Where are you from?
San Francisco.
That's a long way from home.
Hey, hey, what do you say? Ratify the ERA!
Where are your parents?
Uh... around?
Do you think they're with your cousin?
No, I was supposed to be with her. She didn't want to come today. This was **my** idea.

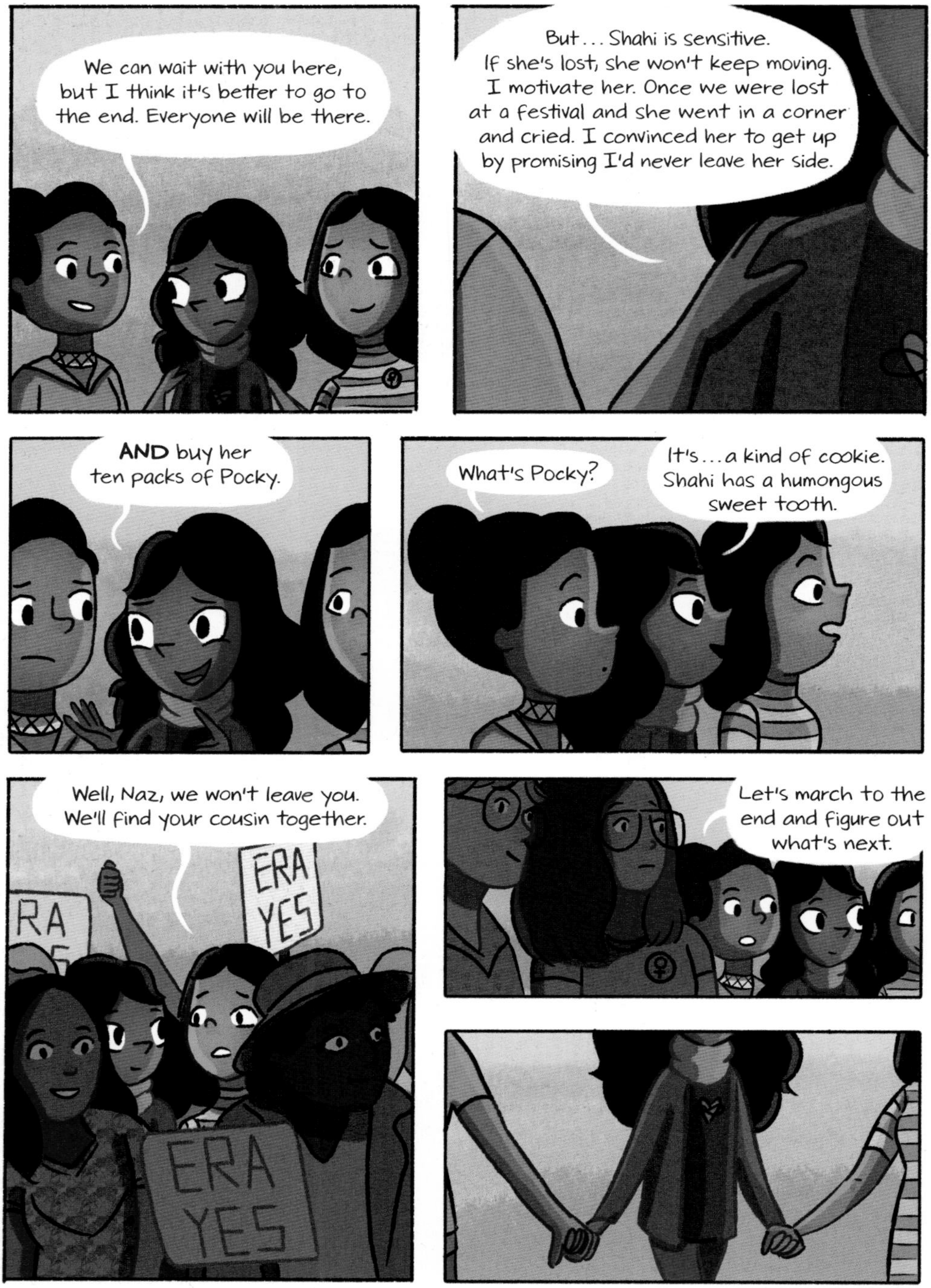
We can wait with you here, but I think it's better to go to the end. Everyone will be there.
But... Shahi is sensitive. If she's lost, she won't keep moving. I motivate her. Once we were lost at a festival and she went in a corner and cried. I convinced her to get up by promising I'd never leave her side.
AND buy her ten packs of Pocky.
What's Pocky?
It's... a kind of cookie. Shahi has a humongous sweet tooth.
Well, Naz, we won't leave you. We'll find your cousin together.
ERA YES
ERA YES
Let's march to the end and figure out what's next.

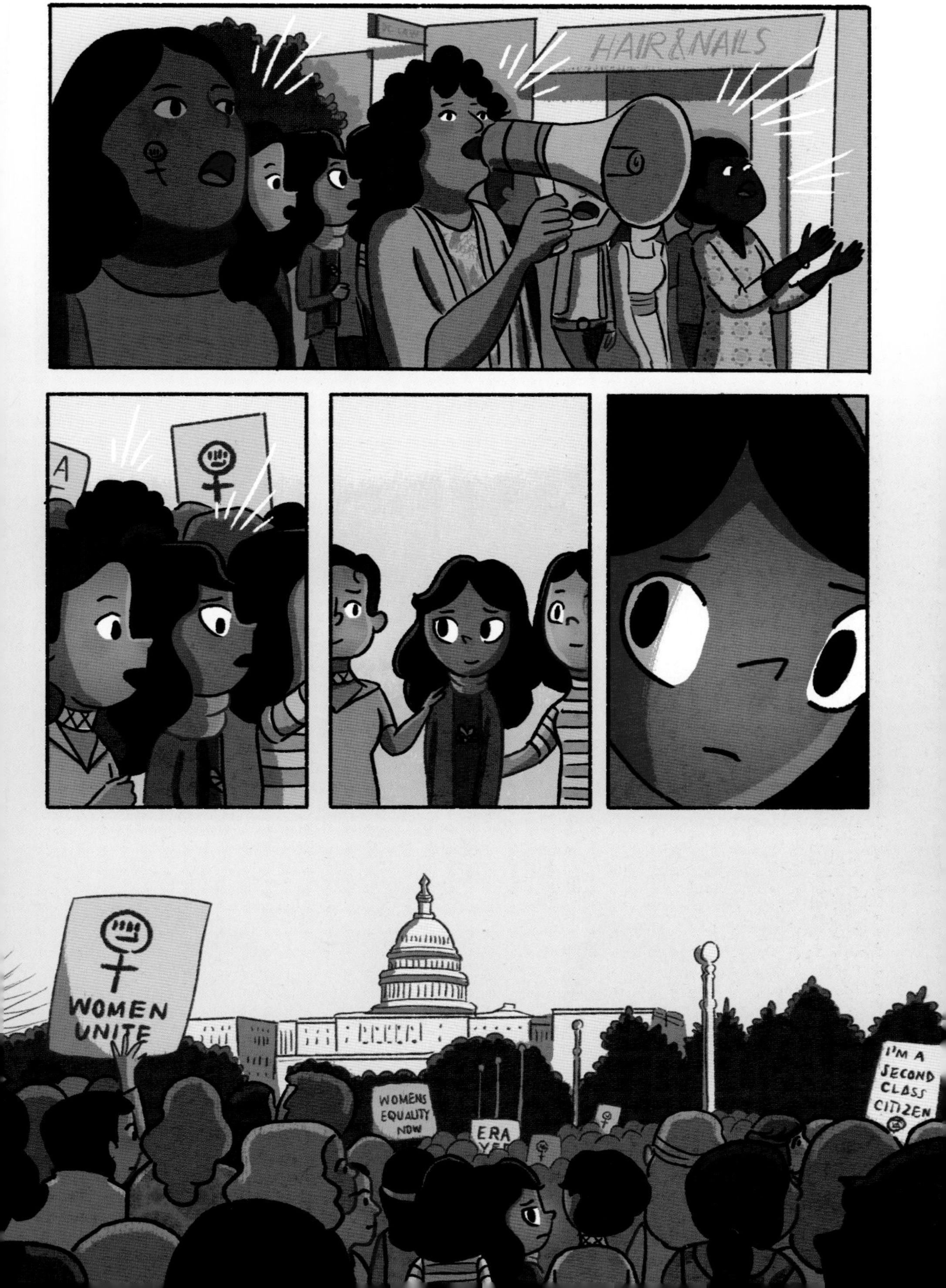

HAIR & NAILS
A
WOMEN UNITE
WOMENS EQUALITY NOW
ERA
I'M A SECOND CLASS CITIZEN

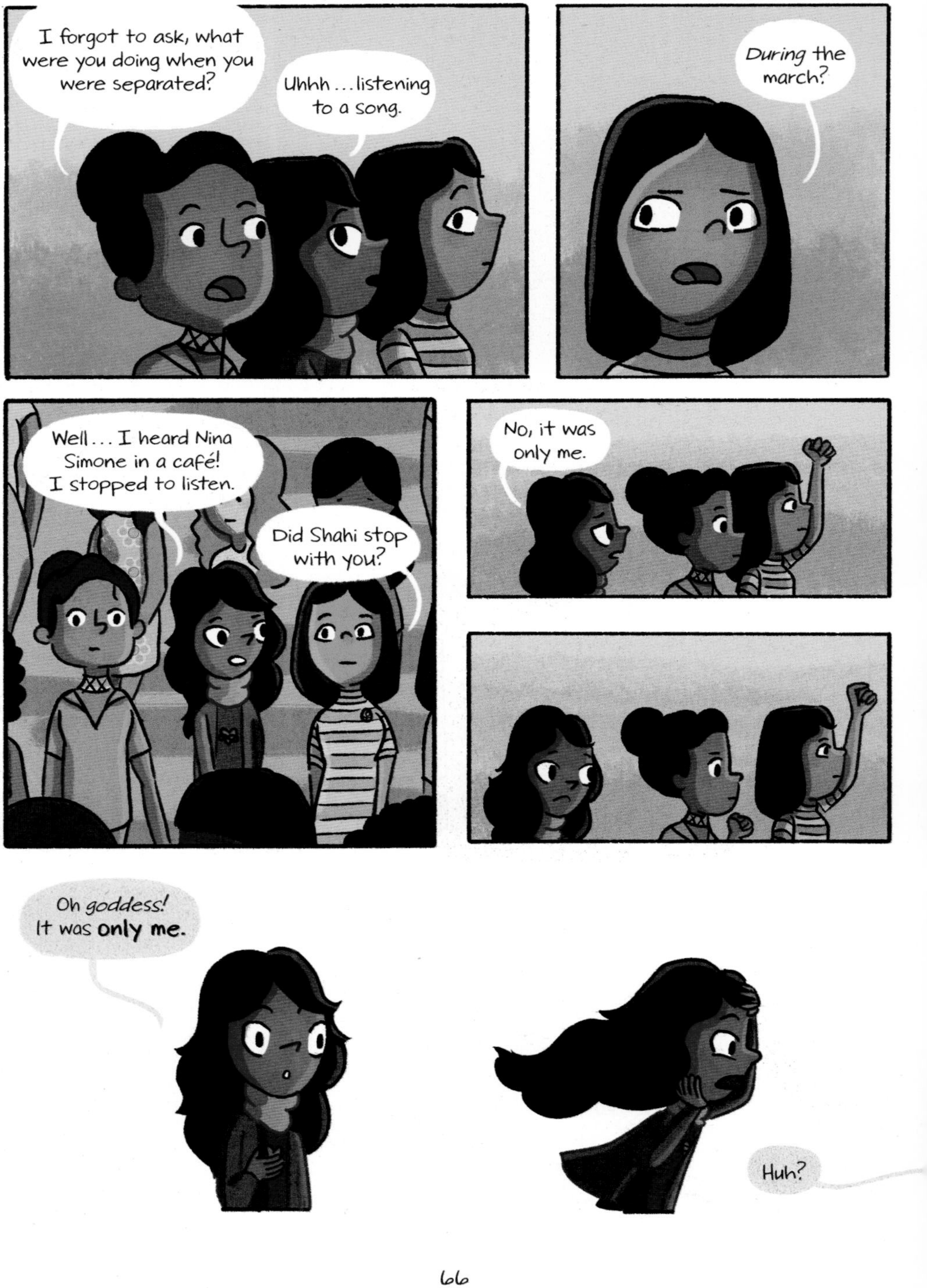
I forgot to ask, what were you doing when you were separated?
Uhhh ... listening to a song.
During the march?
Well... I heard Nina Simone in a café! I stopped to listen.
Did Shahi stop with you?
No, it was only me.
Oh goddess! It was **only me.**
Huh?

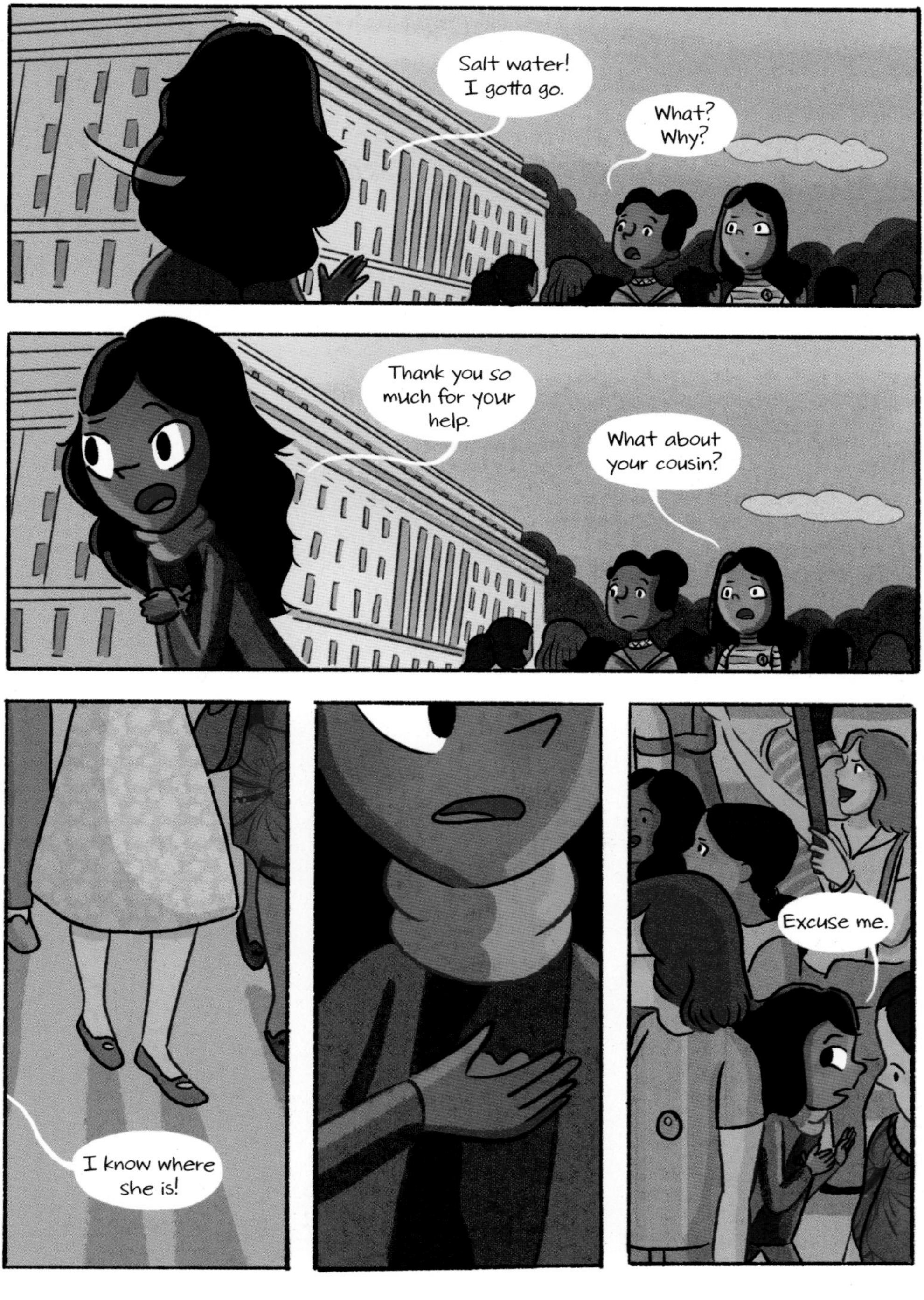
Salt water! I gotta go.
What? Why?
Thank you so much for your help.
What about your cousin?
I know where she is!
Excuse me.

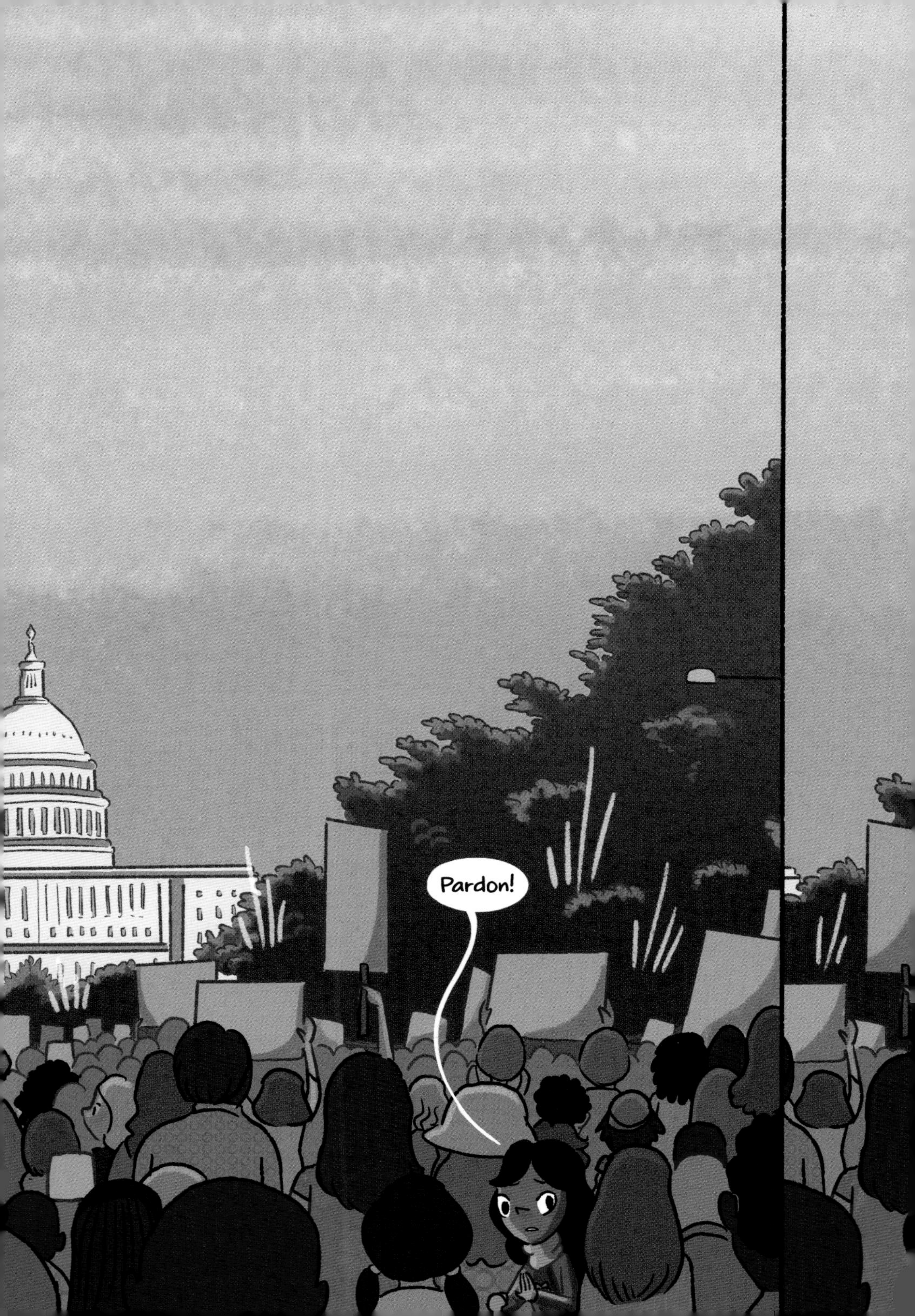
Pardon!

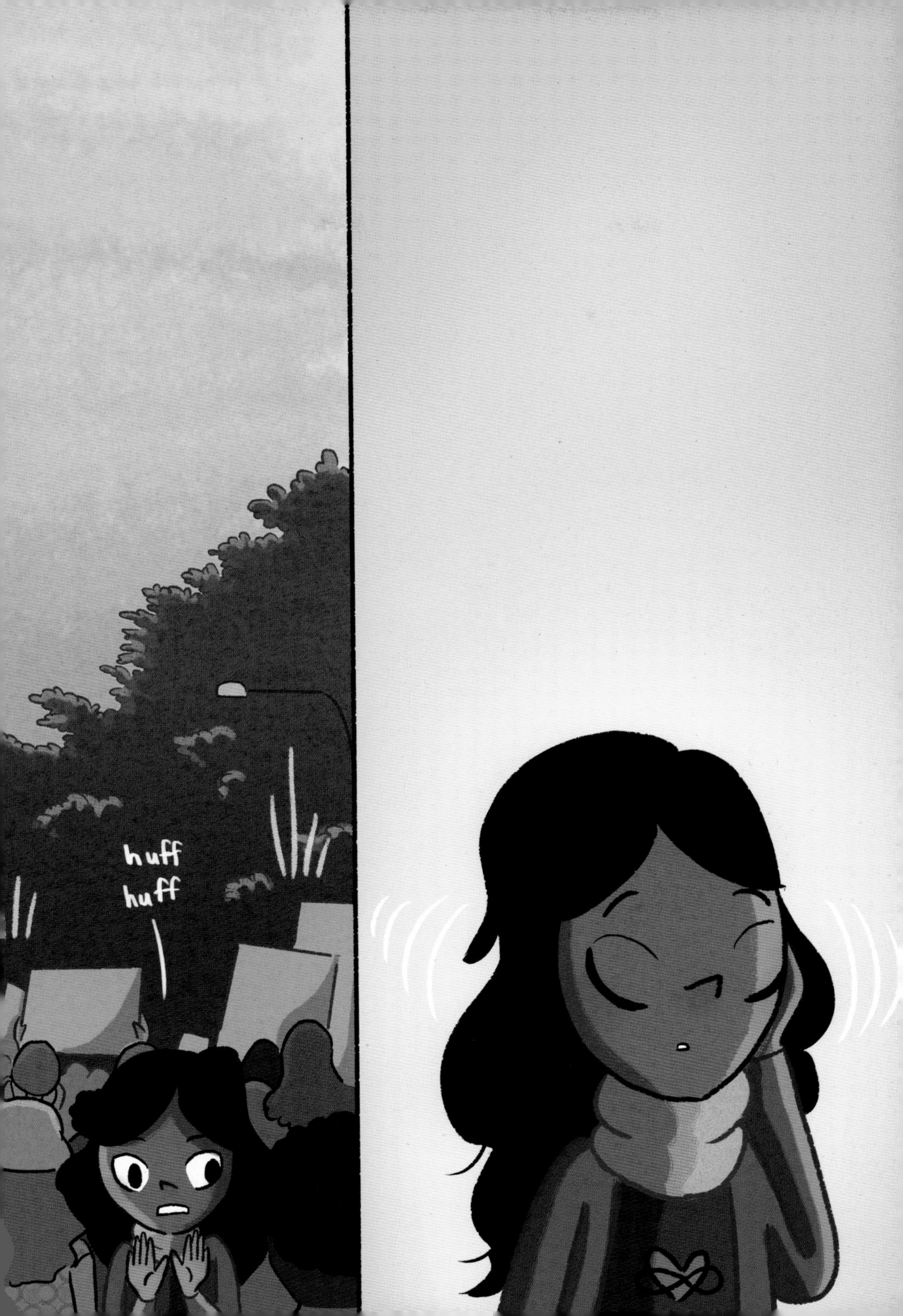
huff
huff

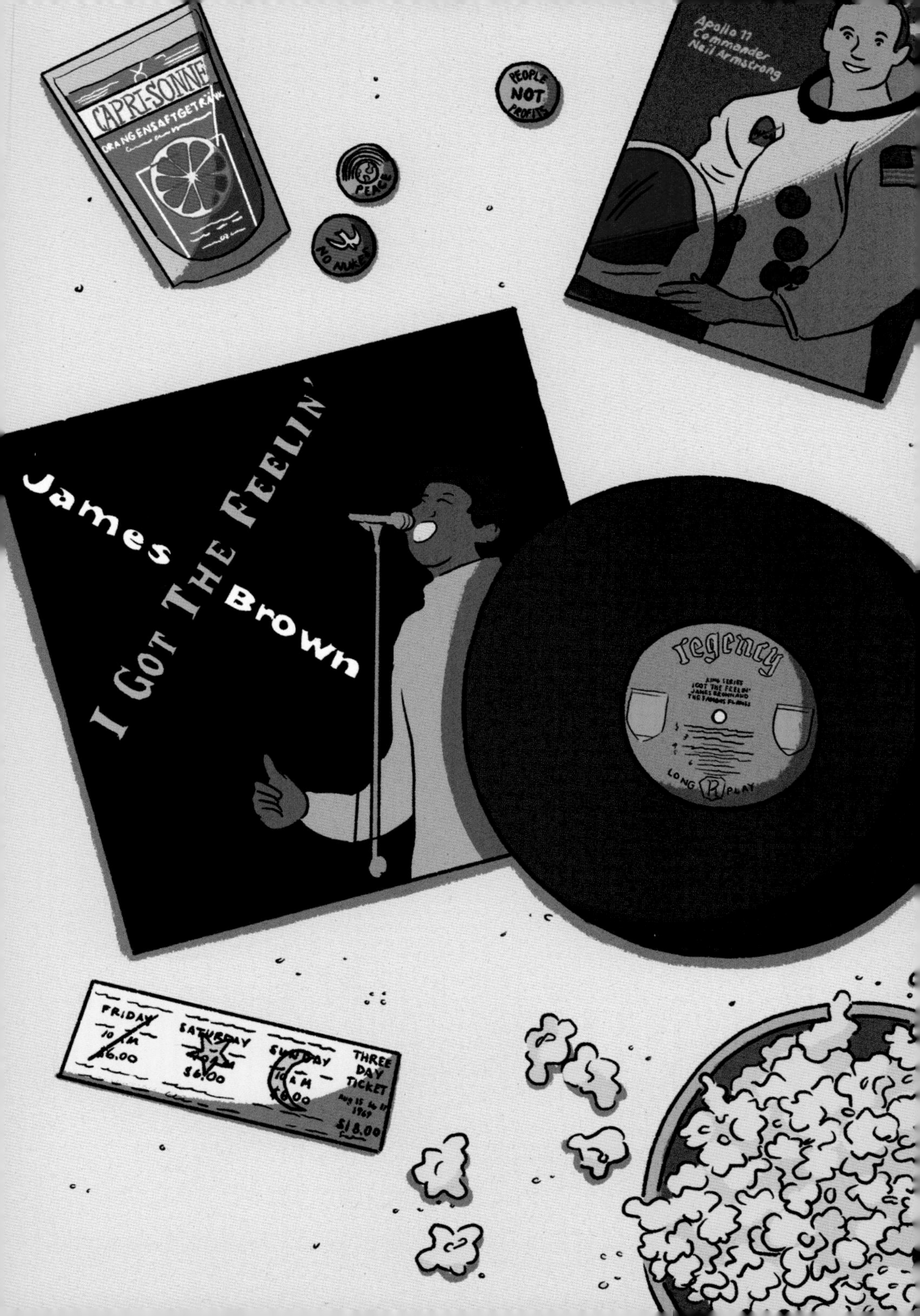

CAPRI-SONNE
ORANGENSAFTGETRÄNK
PEOPLE NOT PROFITS
PEACE
NO NUKES
Apollo 11 Commander Neil Armstrong
James Brown
I GOT THE FEELIN'
regency
LONG PLAY
FRIDAY
SATURDAY
$6.00
THREE DAY TICKET
$18.00

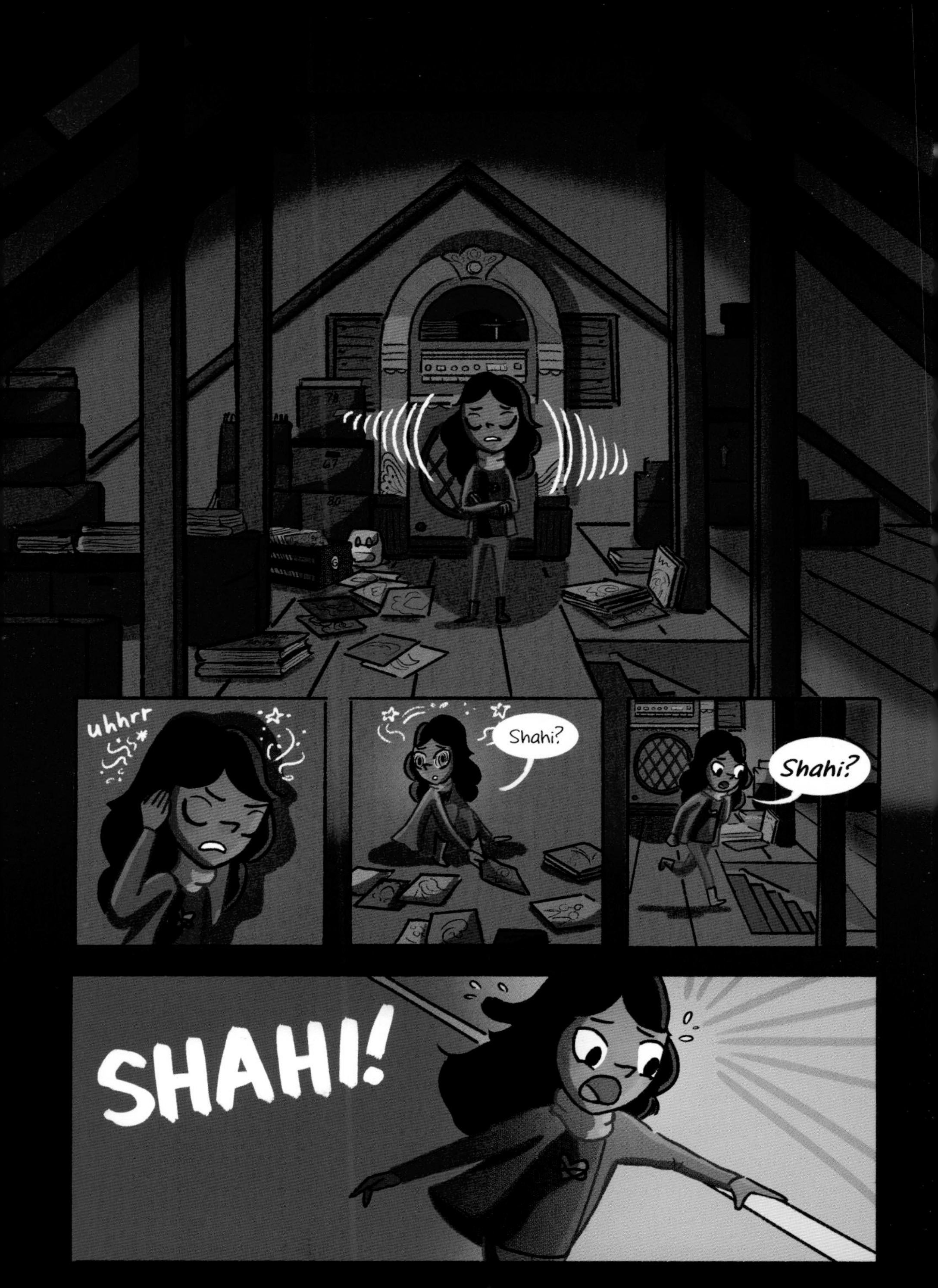
uhhrr
Shahi?
Shahi?
SHAHI!

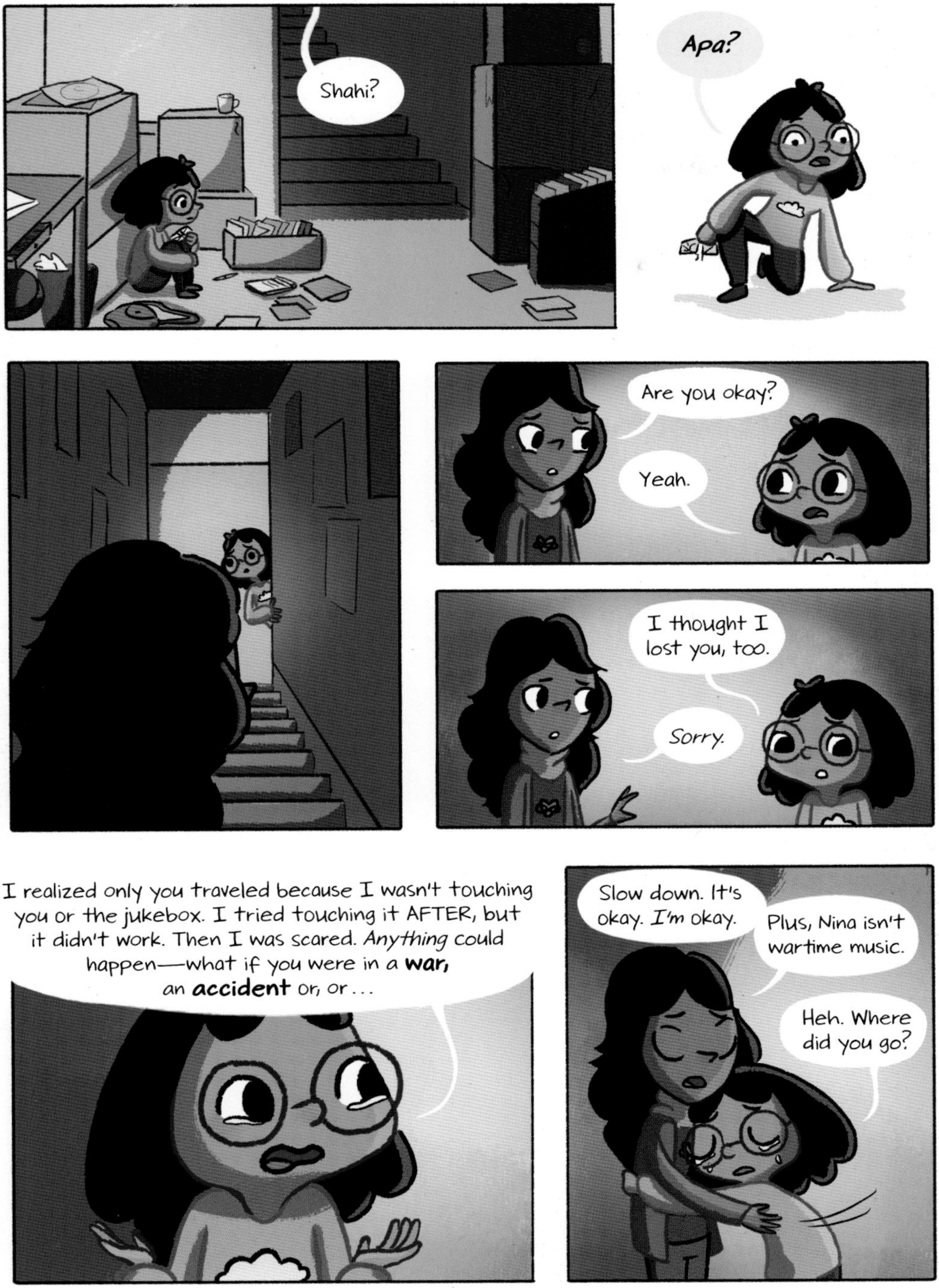
Shahi?
Apa?
Are you okay?
Yeah.
I thought I lost you, too.
Sorry.
I realized only you traveled because I wasn't touching you or the jukebox. I tried touching it AFTER, but it didn't work. Then I was scared. *Anything* could happen—what if you were in a **war,** an **accident** or, or . . .
Slow down. It's okay. *I'm* okay.
Plus, Nina isn't wartime music.
Heh. Where did you go?

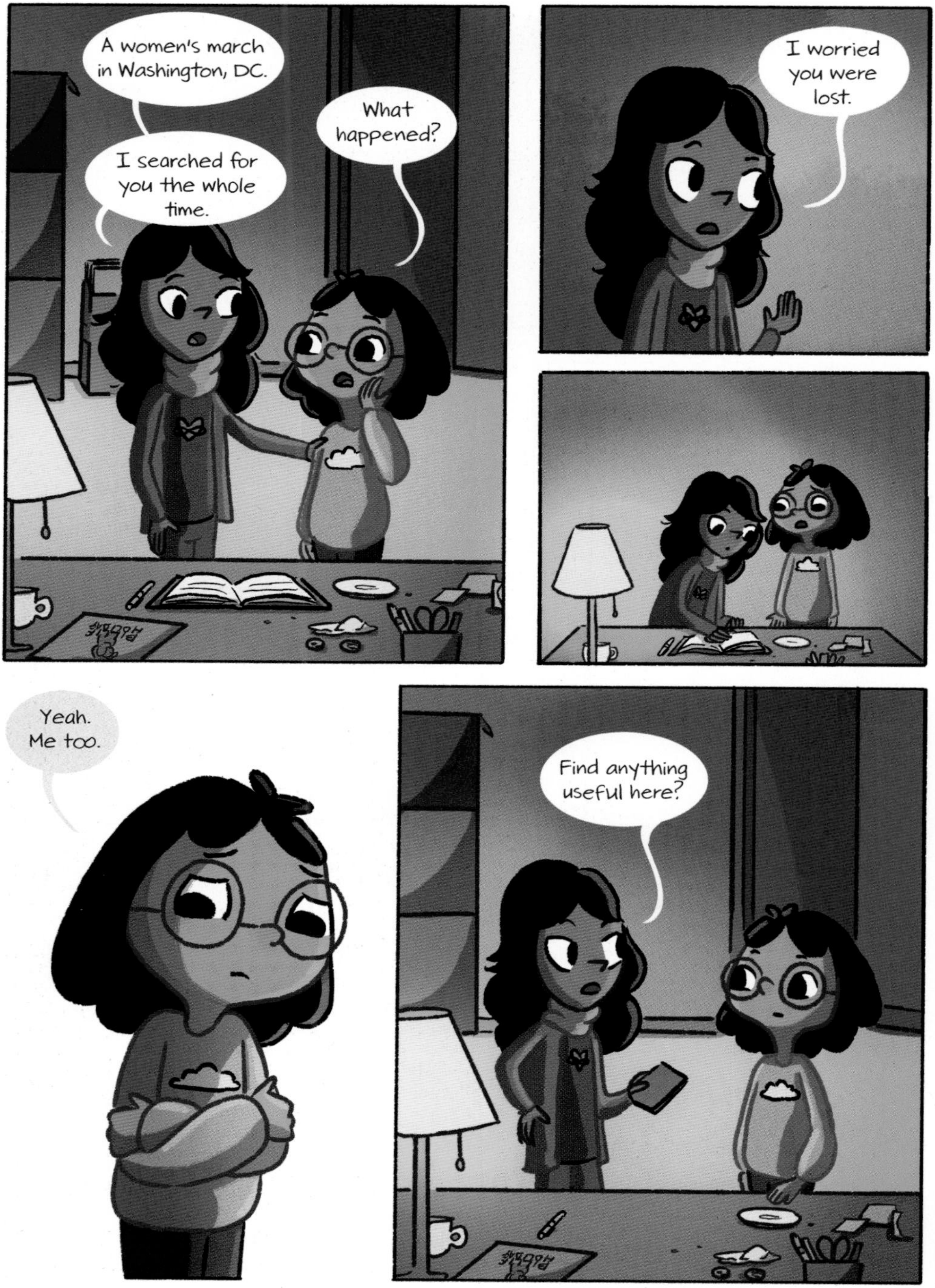
A women's march in Washington, DC.
I searched for you the whole time.
What happened?
I worried you were lost.
Yeah. Me too.
Find anything useful here?

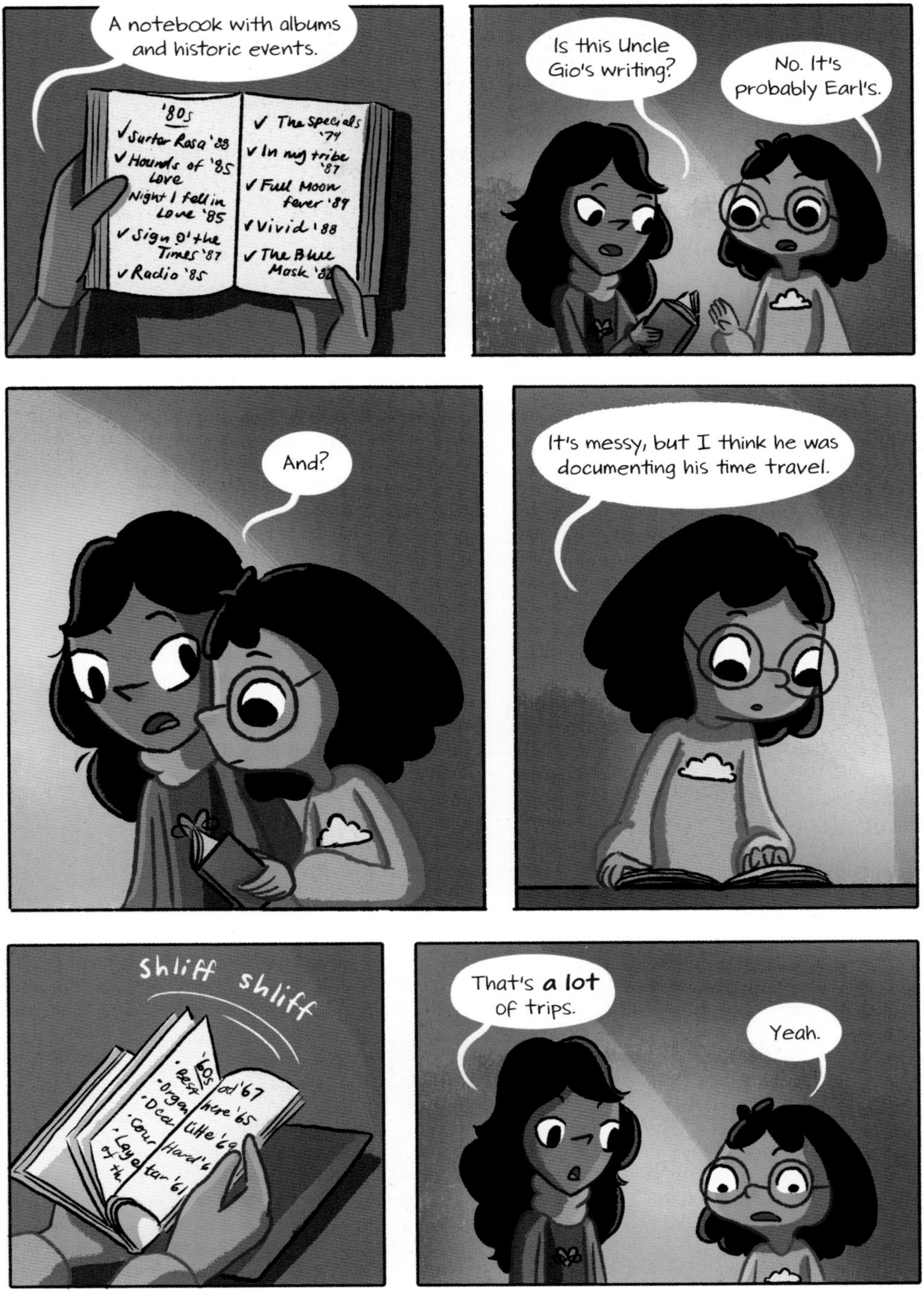
A notebook with albums and historic events.
'80s
✓Surfer Rosa '88
✓Hounds of Love '85
Night I fell in Love '85
✓Sign O' the Times '87
✓Radio '85
✓The Specials '79
✓In my tribe '87
✓Full Moon fever '89
✓Vivid '88
✓The Blue Mask '82
Is this Uncle Gio's writing?
No. It's probably Earl's.
And?
It's messy, but I think he was documenting his time travel.
shliff shliff
That's **a lot** of trips.
Yeah.

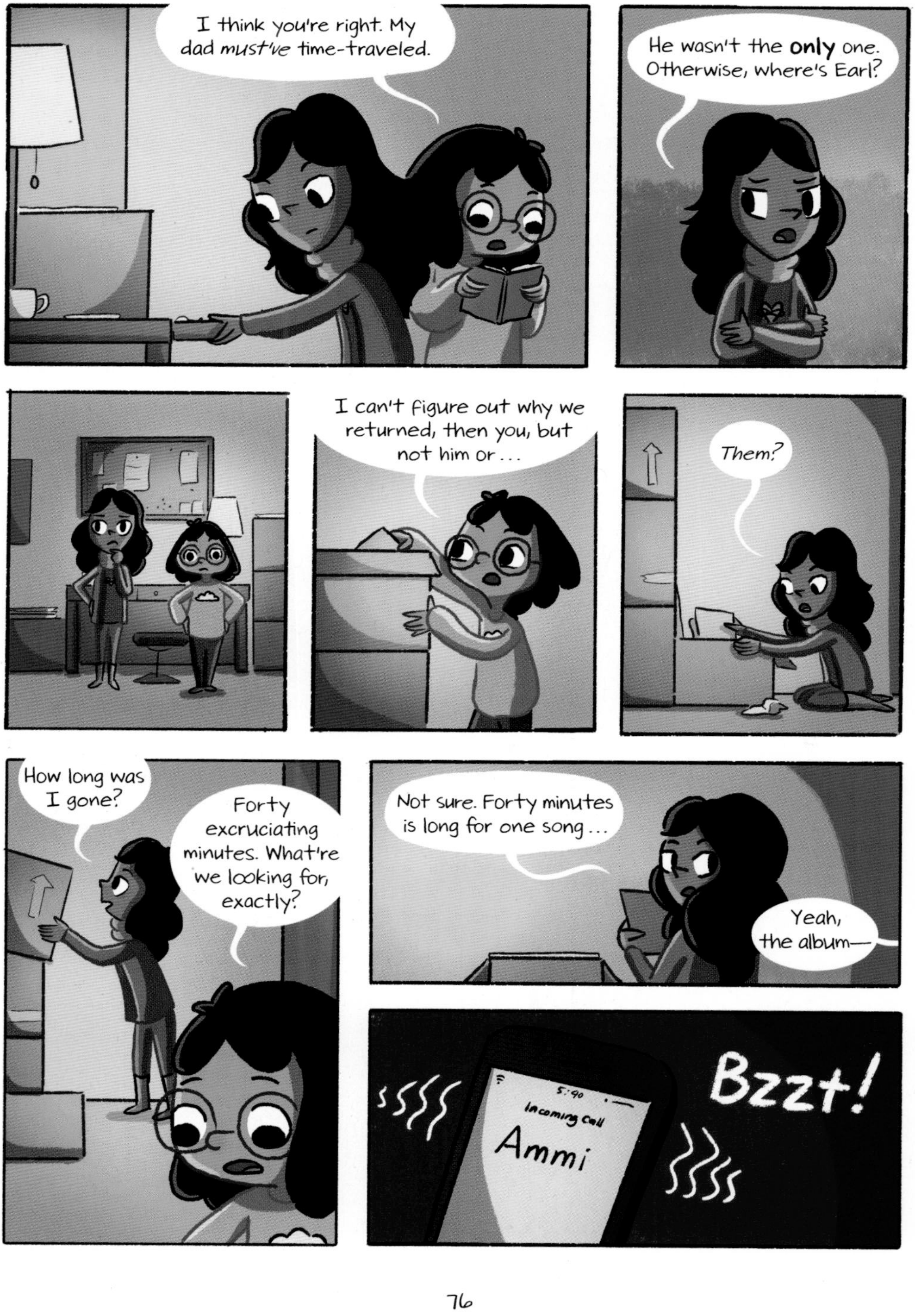
I think you're right. My dad *must've* time-traveled.
He wasn't the **only** one. Otherwise, where's Earl?
I can't figure out why we returned, then you, but not him or...
Them?
How long was I gone?
Forty excruciating minutes. What're we looking for, exactly?
Not sure. Forty minutes is long for one song...
Yeah, the album—
5:40
Incoming call
Ammi
Bzzt!

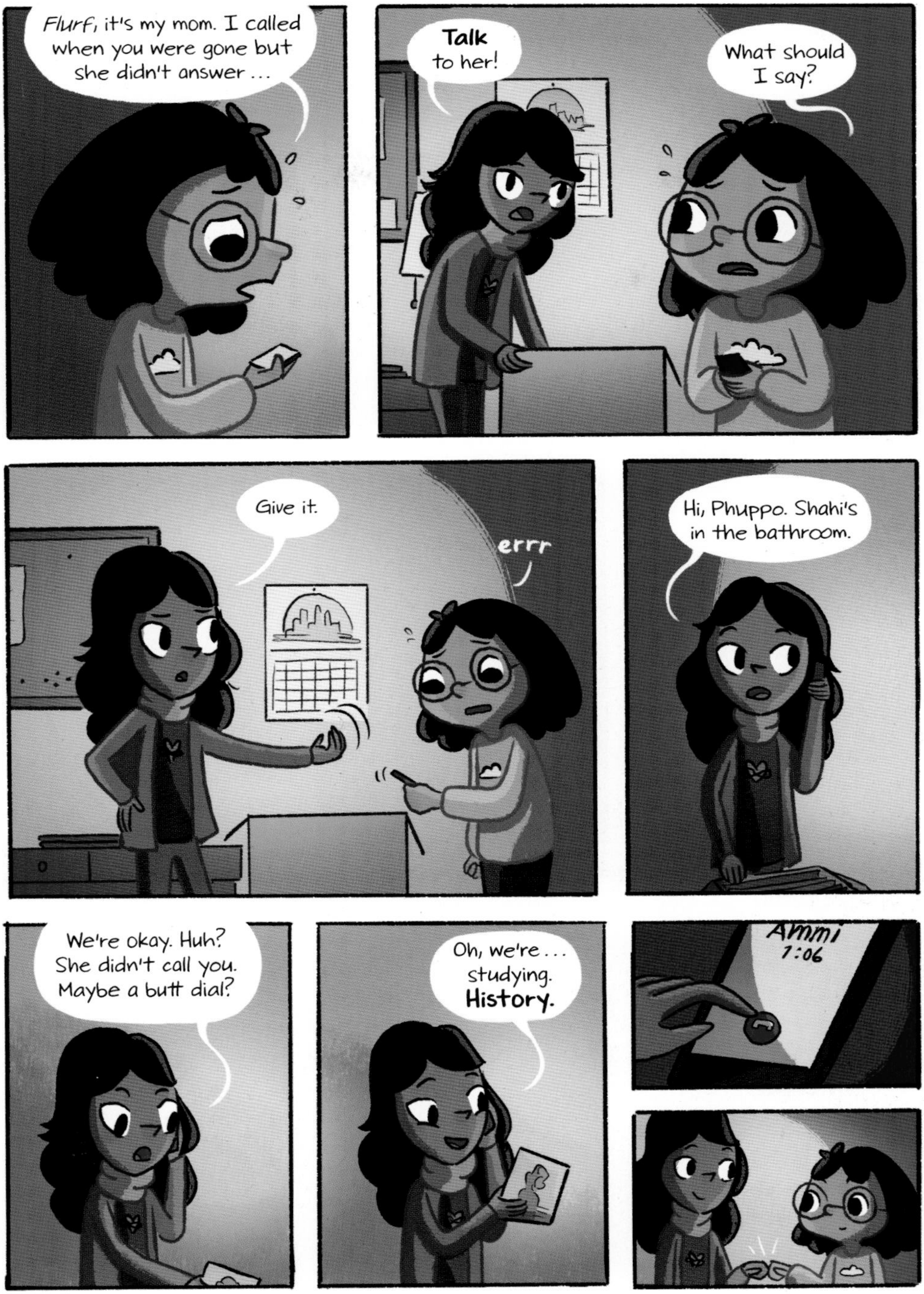
Flurf, it's my mom. I called when you were gone but she didn't answer . . .
Talk to her!
What should I say?
Give it.
errr
Hi, Phuppo. Shahi's in the bathroom.
We're okay. Huh? She didn't call you. Maybe a butt dial?
Oh, we're . . . studying. History.
Ammi
1:06

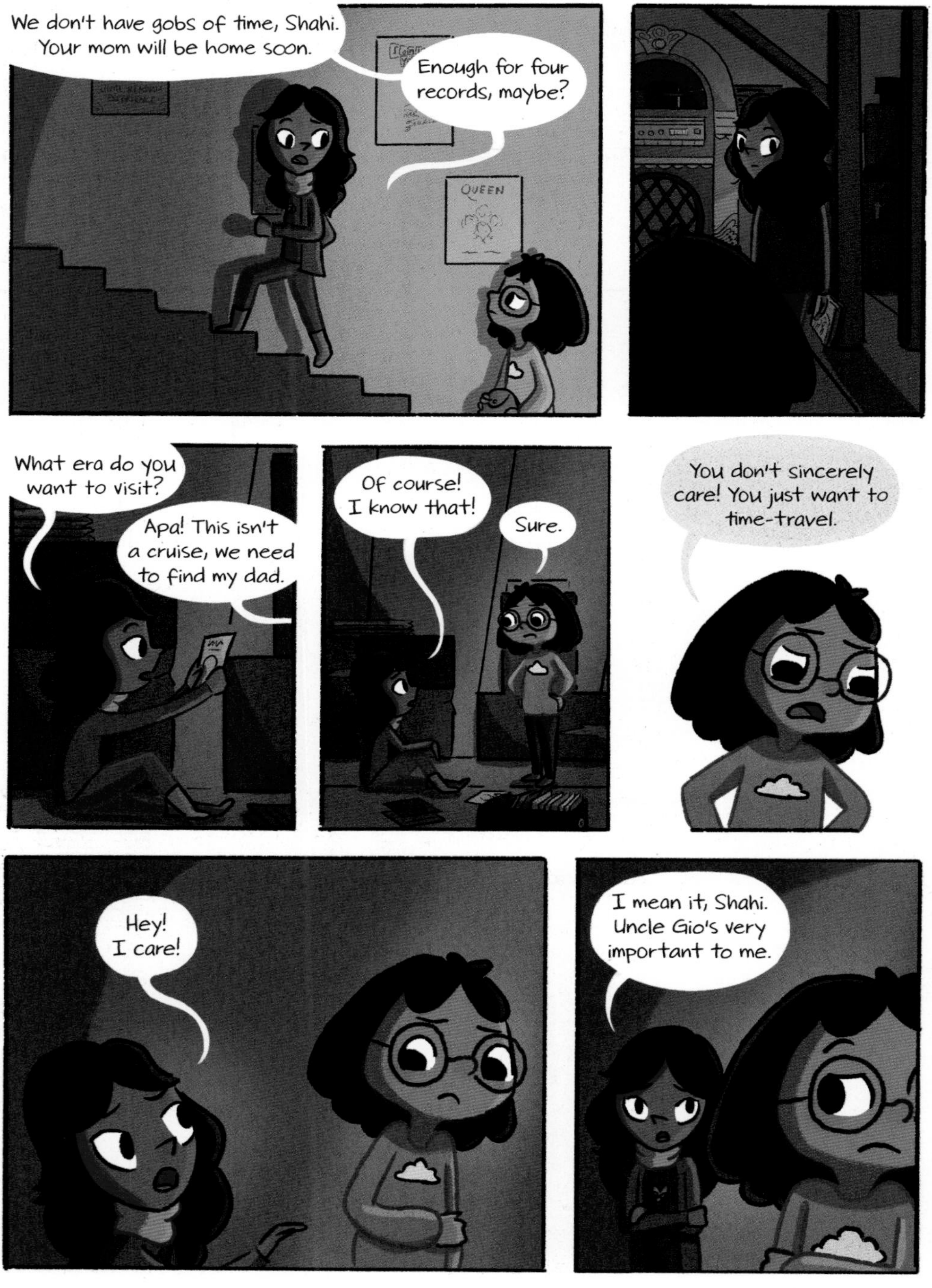
We don't have gobs of time, Shahi. Your mom will be home soon.
Enough for four records, maybe?
QUEEN
What era do you want to visit?
Apa! This isn't a cruise, we need to find my dad.
Of course! I know that!
Sure.
You don't sincerely care! You just want to time-travel.
Hey! I care!
I mean it, Shahi. Uncle Gio's very important to me.

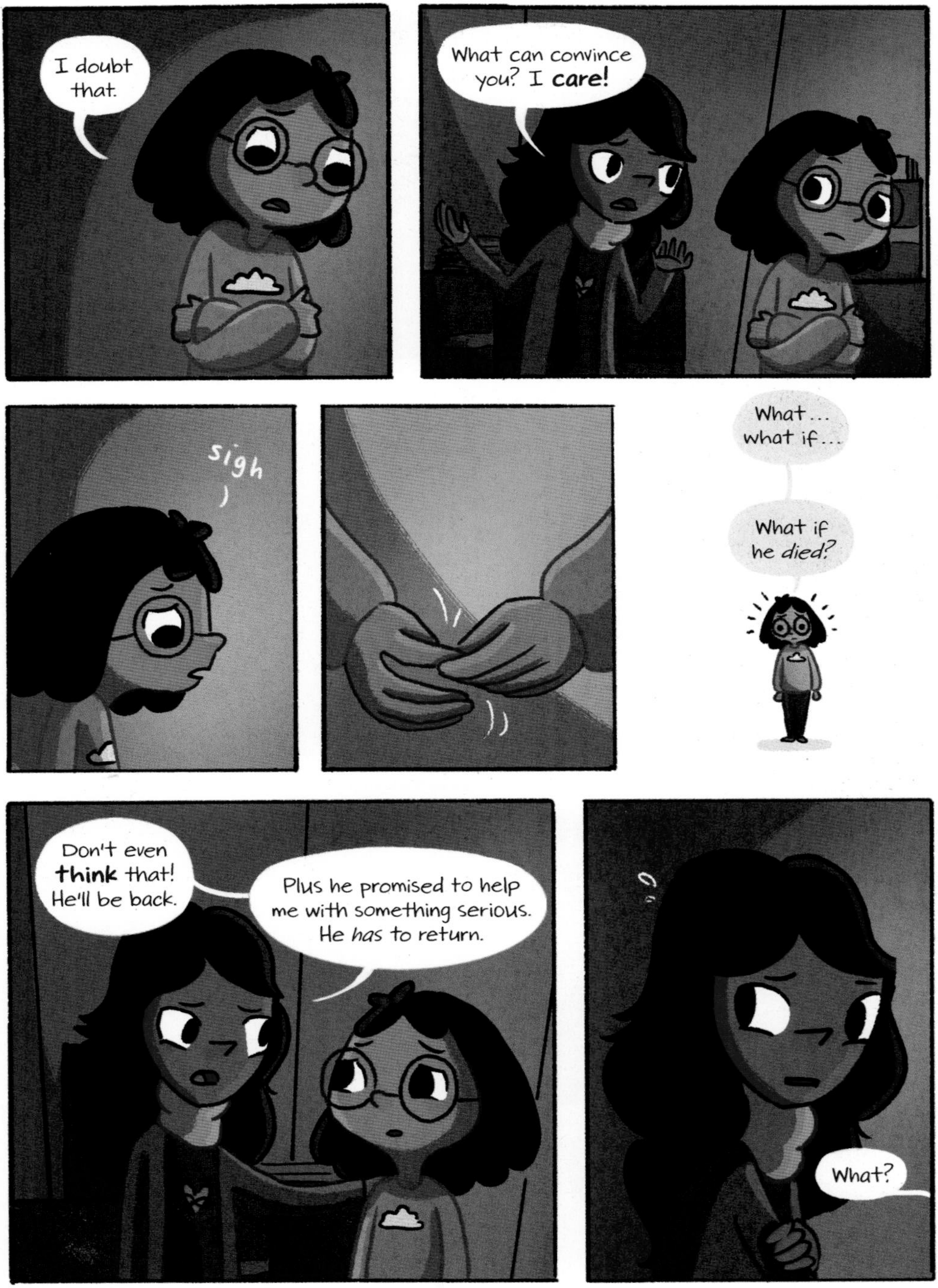
I doubt that.
What can convince you? I **care!**
sigh
What... what if...
What if he *died?*
Don't even **think** that! He'll be back.
Plus he promised to help me with something serious. He *has* to return.
What?

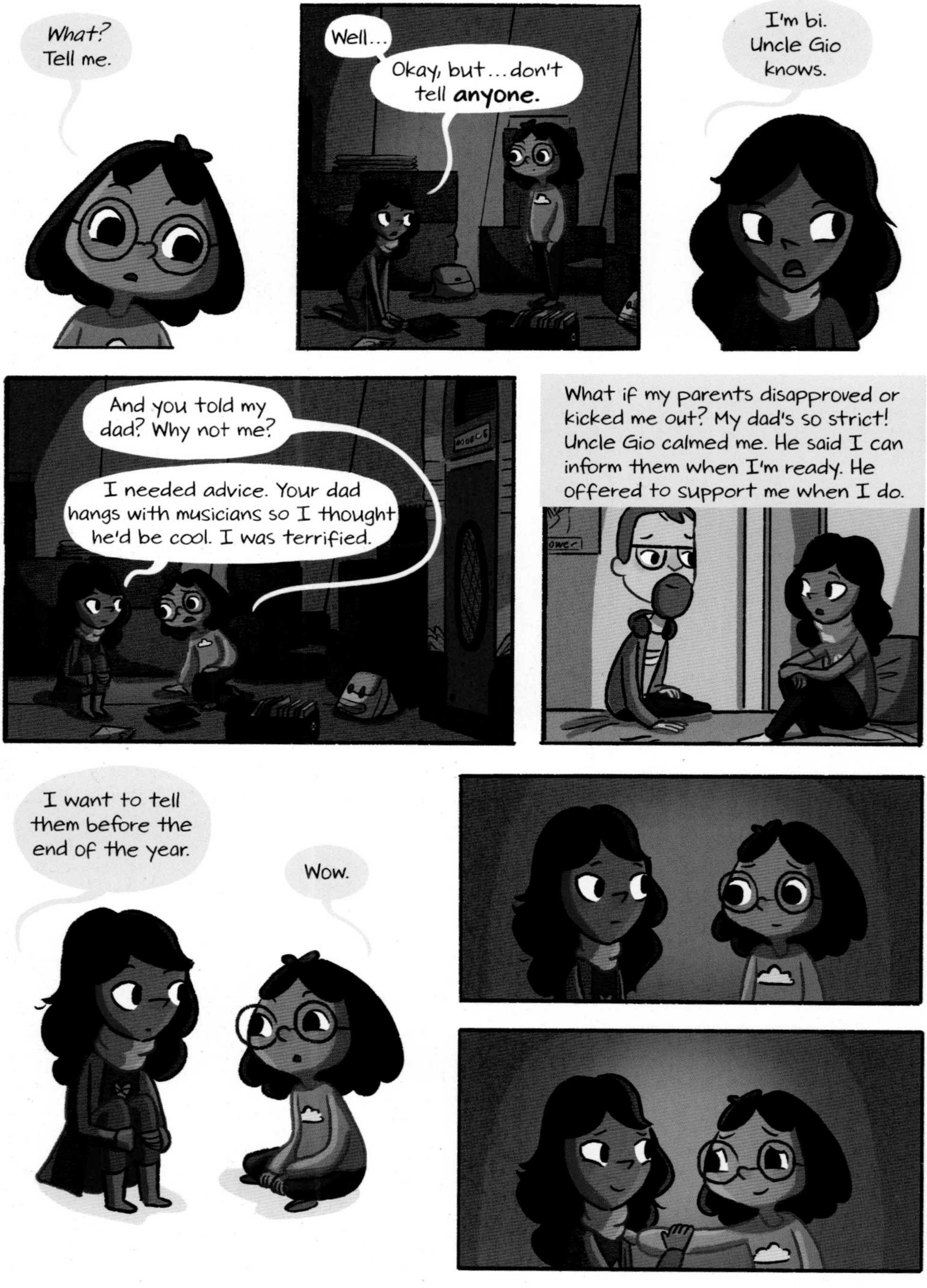

What? Tell me.
Well...
Okay, but...don't tell **anyone.**
I'm bi. Uncle Gio knows.
And you told my dad? Why not me?
I needed advice. Your dad hangs with musicians so I thought he'd be cool. I was terrified.
What if my parents disapproved or kicked me out? My dad's so strict! Uncle Gio calmed me. He said I can inform them when I'm ready. He offered to support me when I do.
I want to tell them before the end of the year.
Wow.

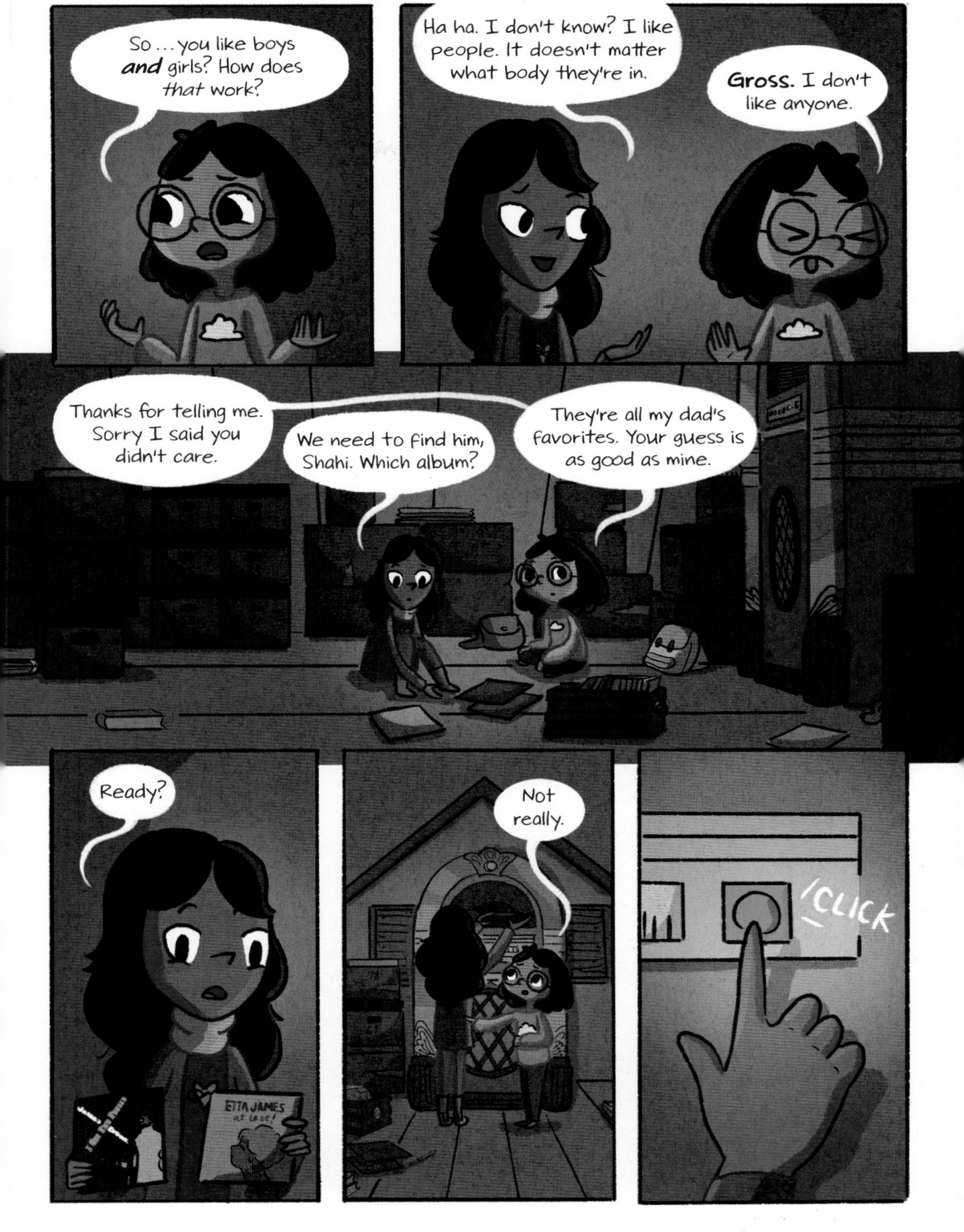

So... you like boys *and* girls? How does *that* work?
Ha ha. I don't know? I like people. It doesn't matter what body they're in.
Gross. I don't like anyone.
Thanks for telling me. Sorry I said you didn't care.
We need to find him, Shahi. Which album?
They're all my dad's favorites. Your guess is as good as mine.
Ready?
ETTA JAMES at last!
Not really.
CLICK

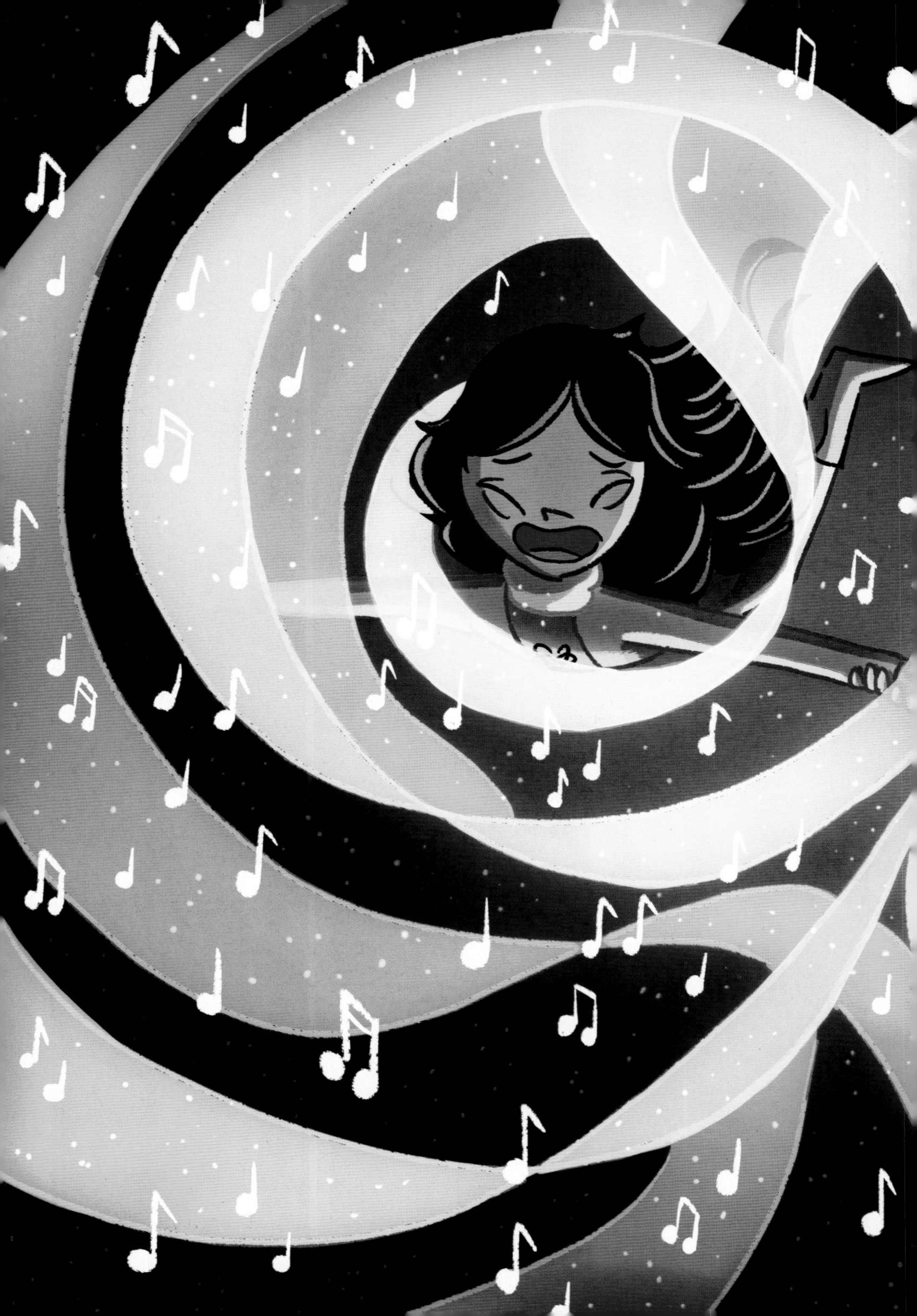

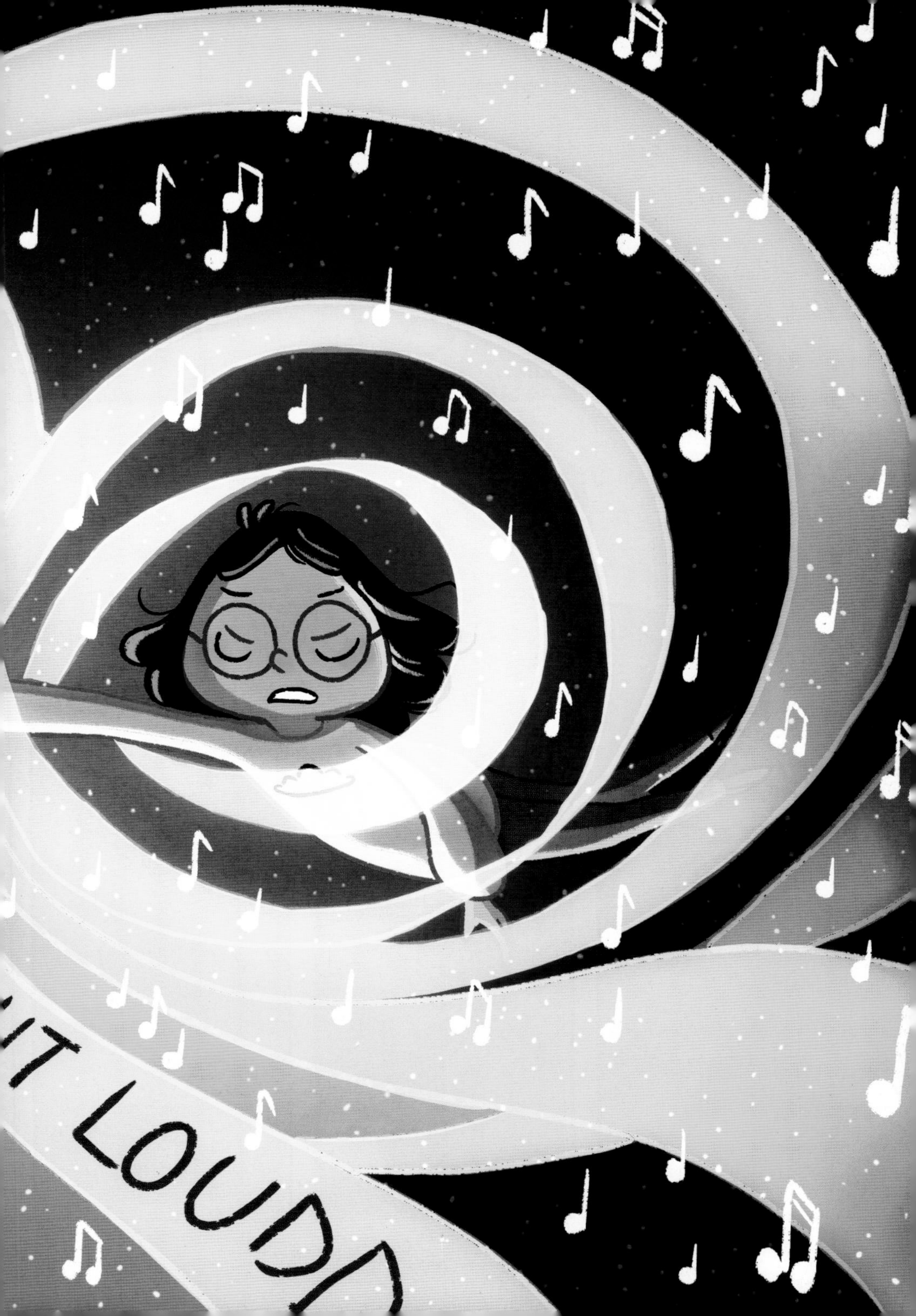
IT LOUD

We have a special announcement, ladies and gentlemen. We've received a report that the city is very quiet and calm, and that everyone is home watching the TV program. The fact that we have television cameras here is a big success. Let's have a big round of applause for the staff of the city!

Now it's showtime. Mr. Please, Please, Please himself.

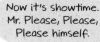

JAMES... BROWN!

You got the *feeling?*

You got the *feeling?*

BABY, BABY, BABY!

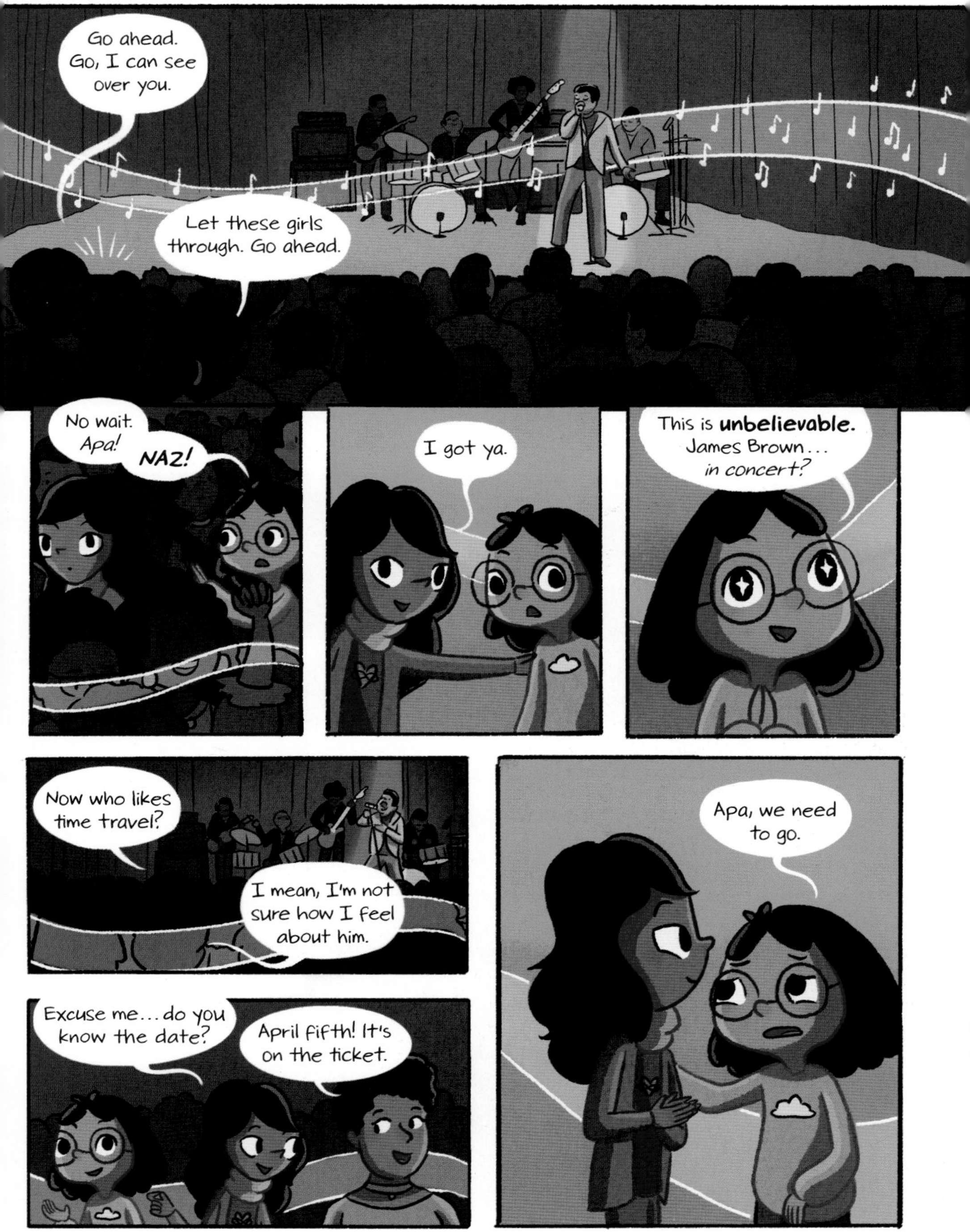
Go ahead. Go, I can see over you.
Let these girls through. Go ahead.
No wait. Apa!
NAZ!
I got ya.
This is **unbelievable.** James Brown... *in concert?*
Now who likes time travel?
I mean, I'm not sure how I feel about him.
Excuse me... do you know the date?
April fifth! It's on the ticket.
Apa, we need to go.

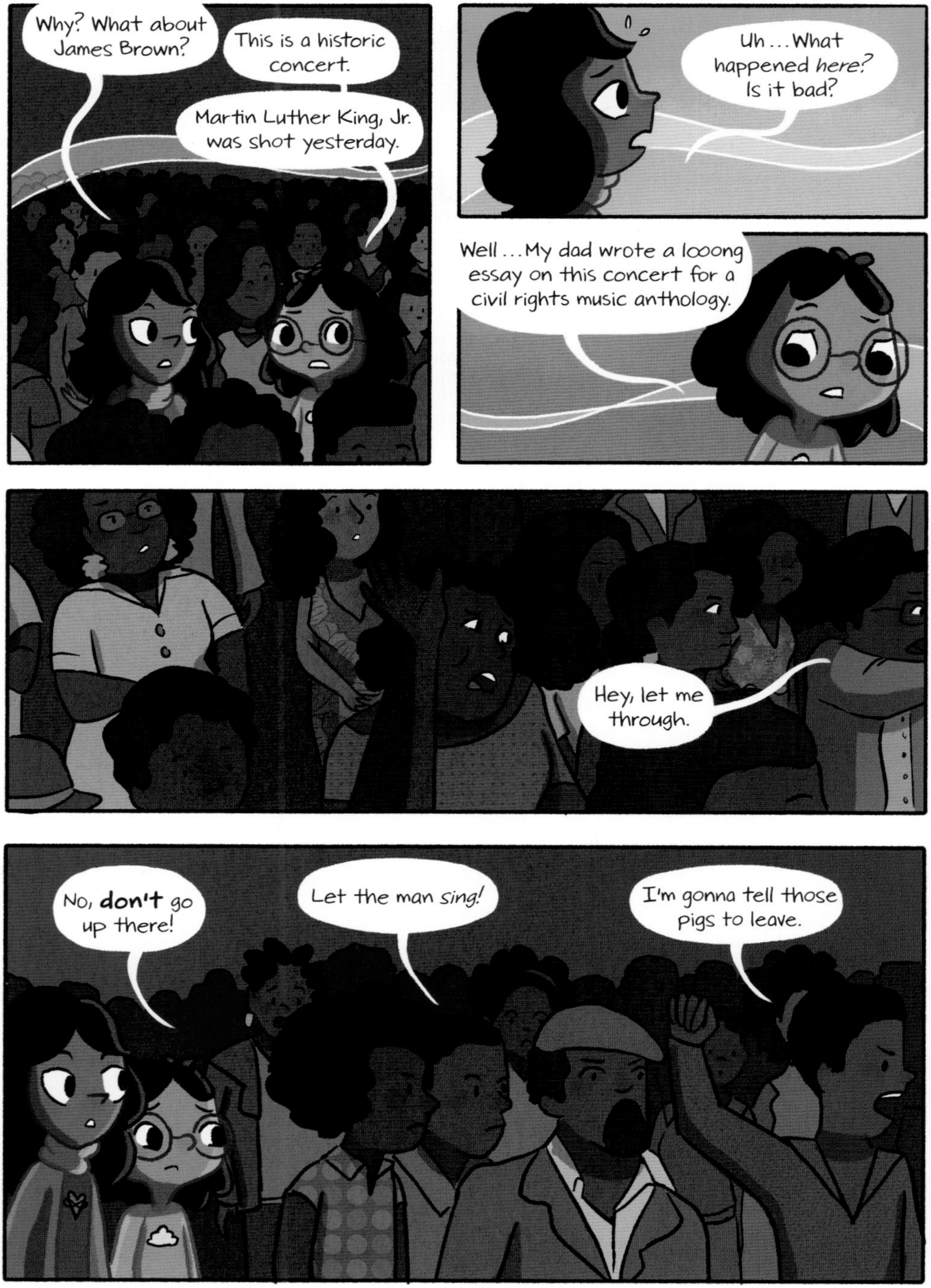
Why? What about James Brown?
This is a historic concert.
Martin Luther King, Jr. was shot yesterday.
Uh... What happened *here?* Is it bad?
Well... My dad wrote a looong essay on this concert for a civil rights music anthology.
Hey, let me through.
No, **don't** go up there!
Let the man *sing!*
I'm gonna tell those pigs to leave.

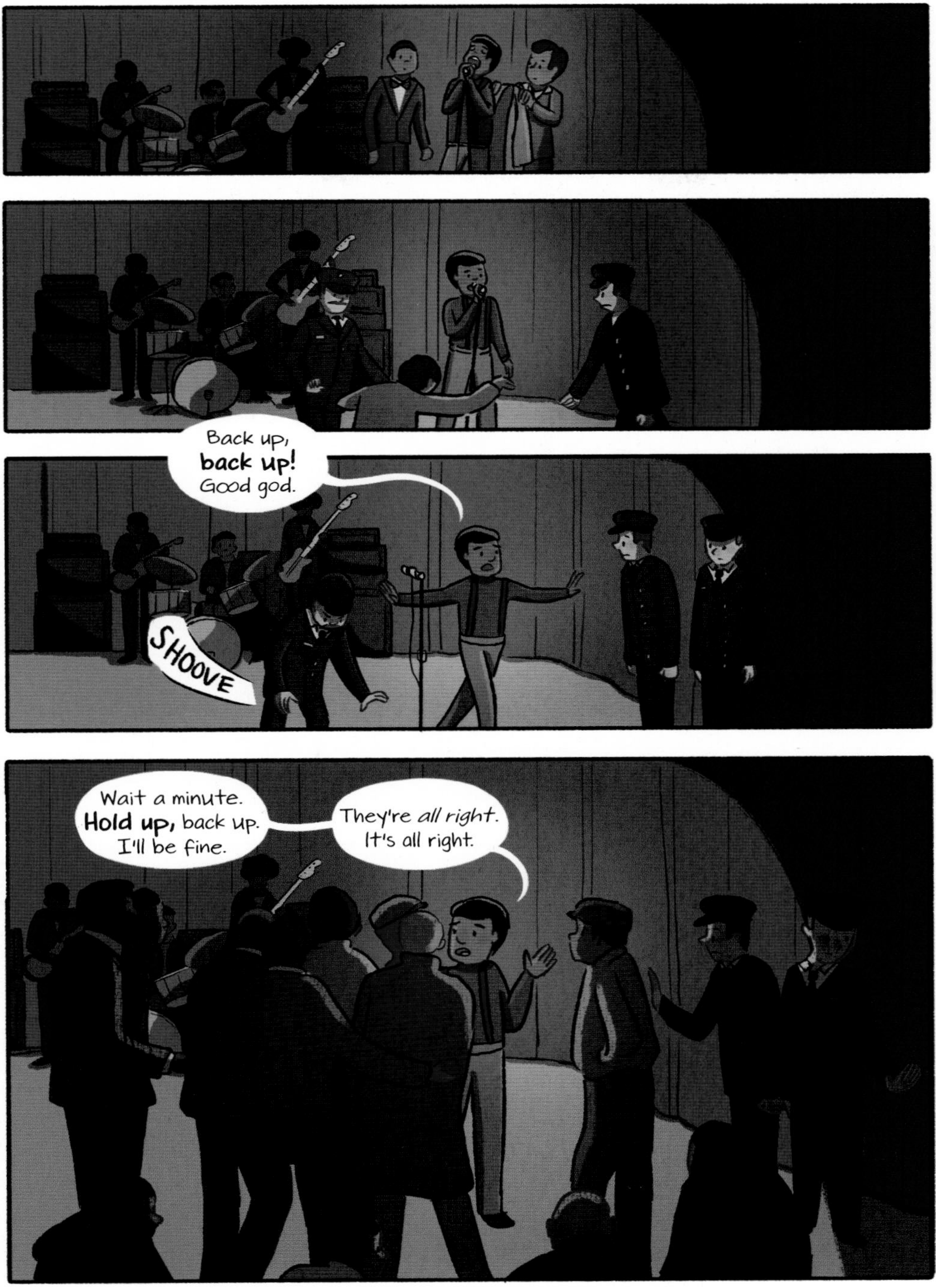
Back up, **back up!** Good god.
SHOOVE
Wait a minute. **Hold up,** back up. I'll be fine.
They're *all right.* It's all right.

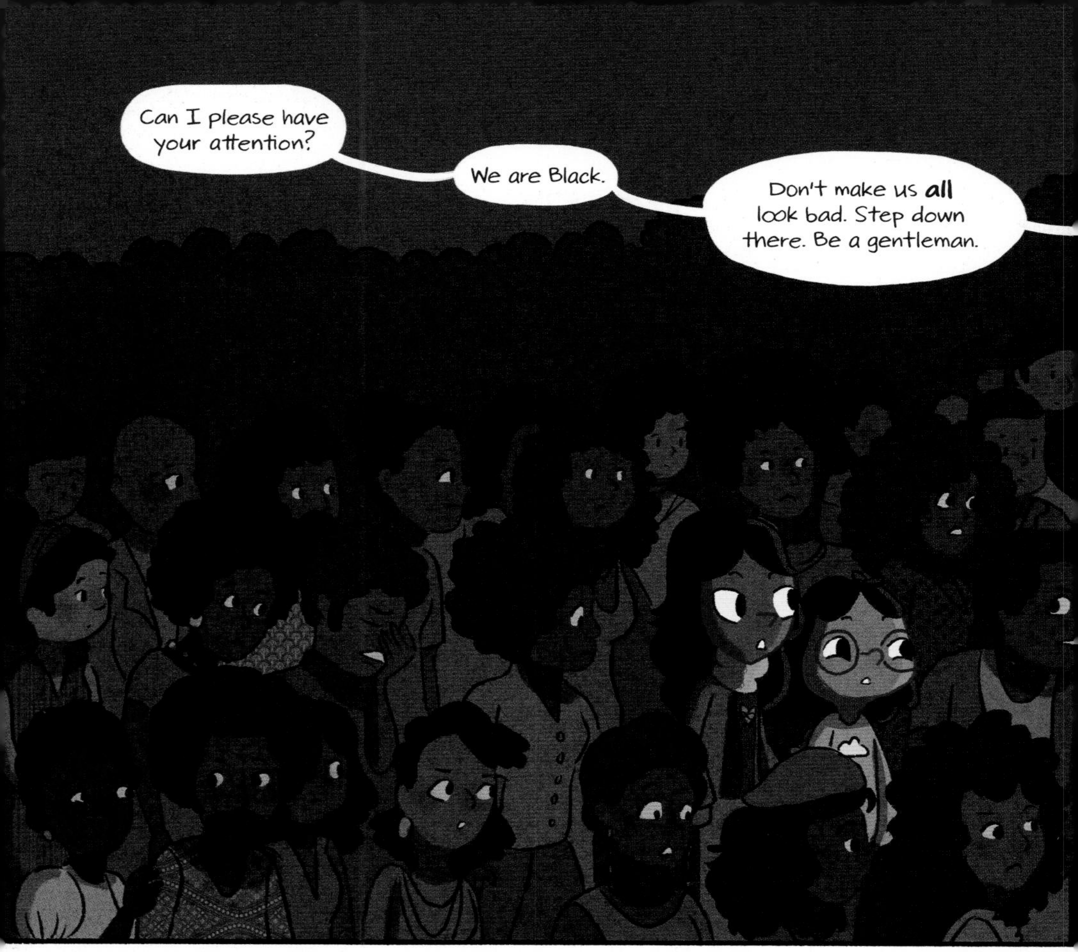
Can I please have your attention?
We are Black.
Don't make us **all** look bad. Step down there. Be a gentleman.

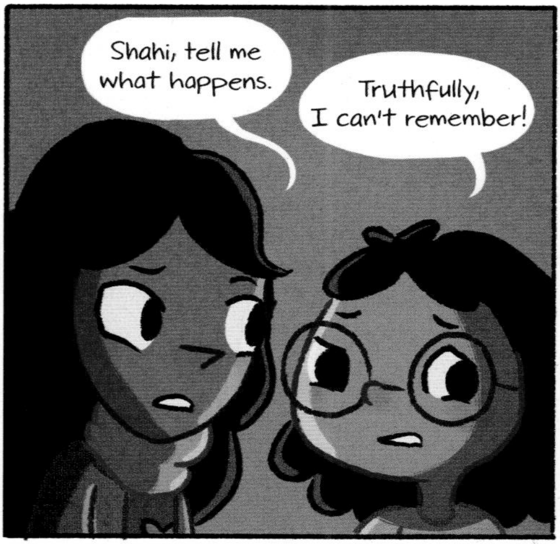
Shahi, tell me what happens.
Truthfully, I can't remember!

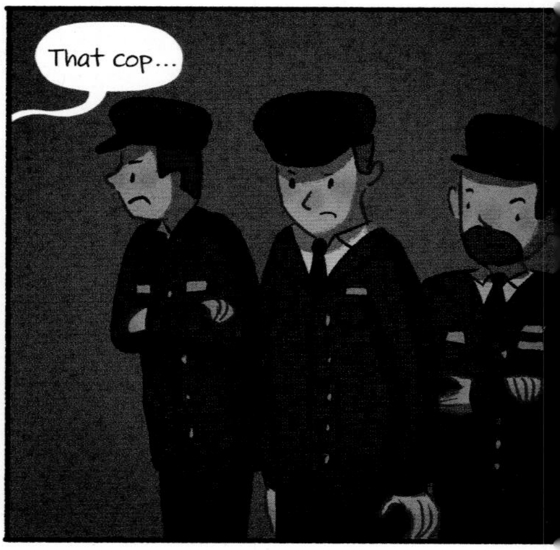
That cop...

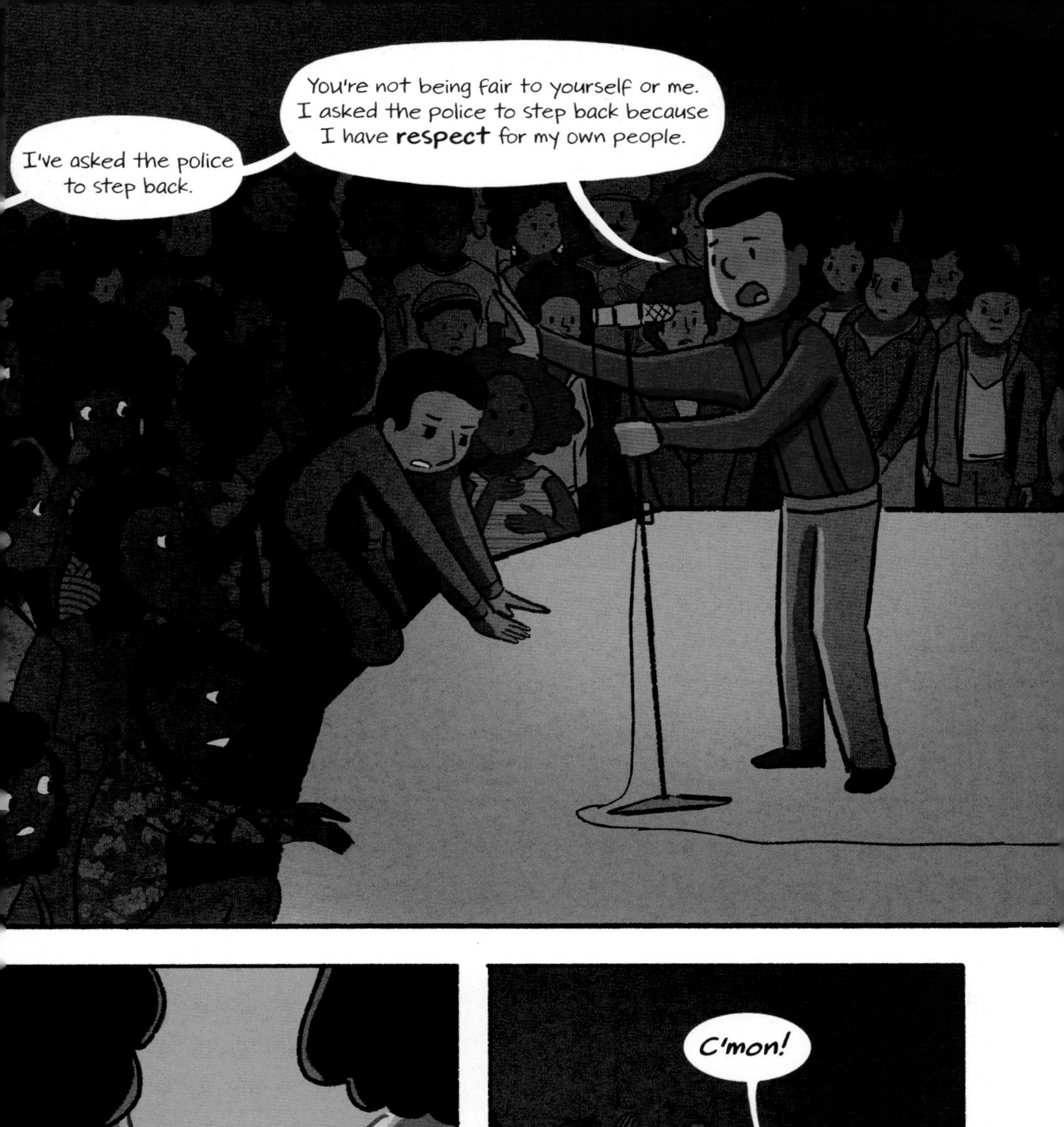
I've asked the police to step back.
You're not being fair to yourself or me. I asked the police to step back because I have **respect** for my own people.

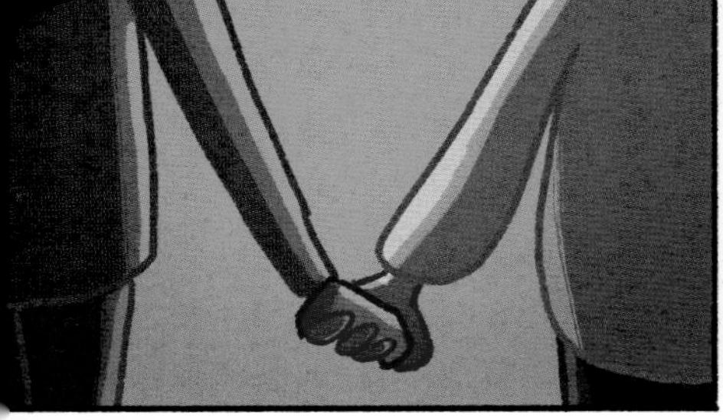

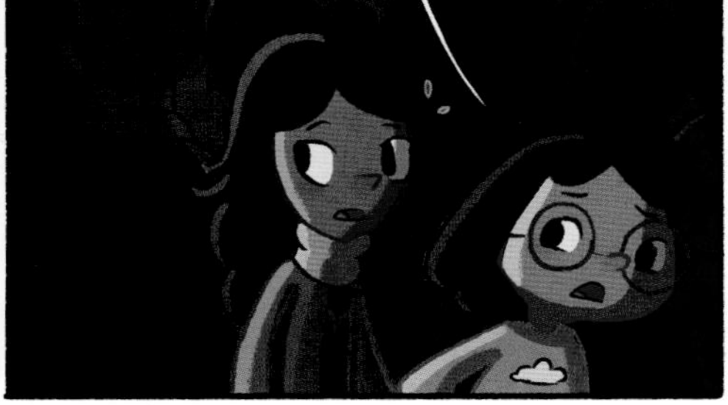
C'mon!

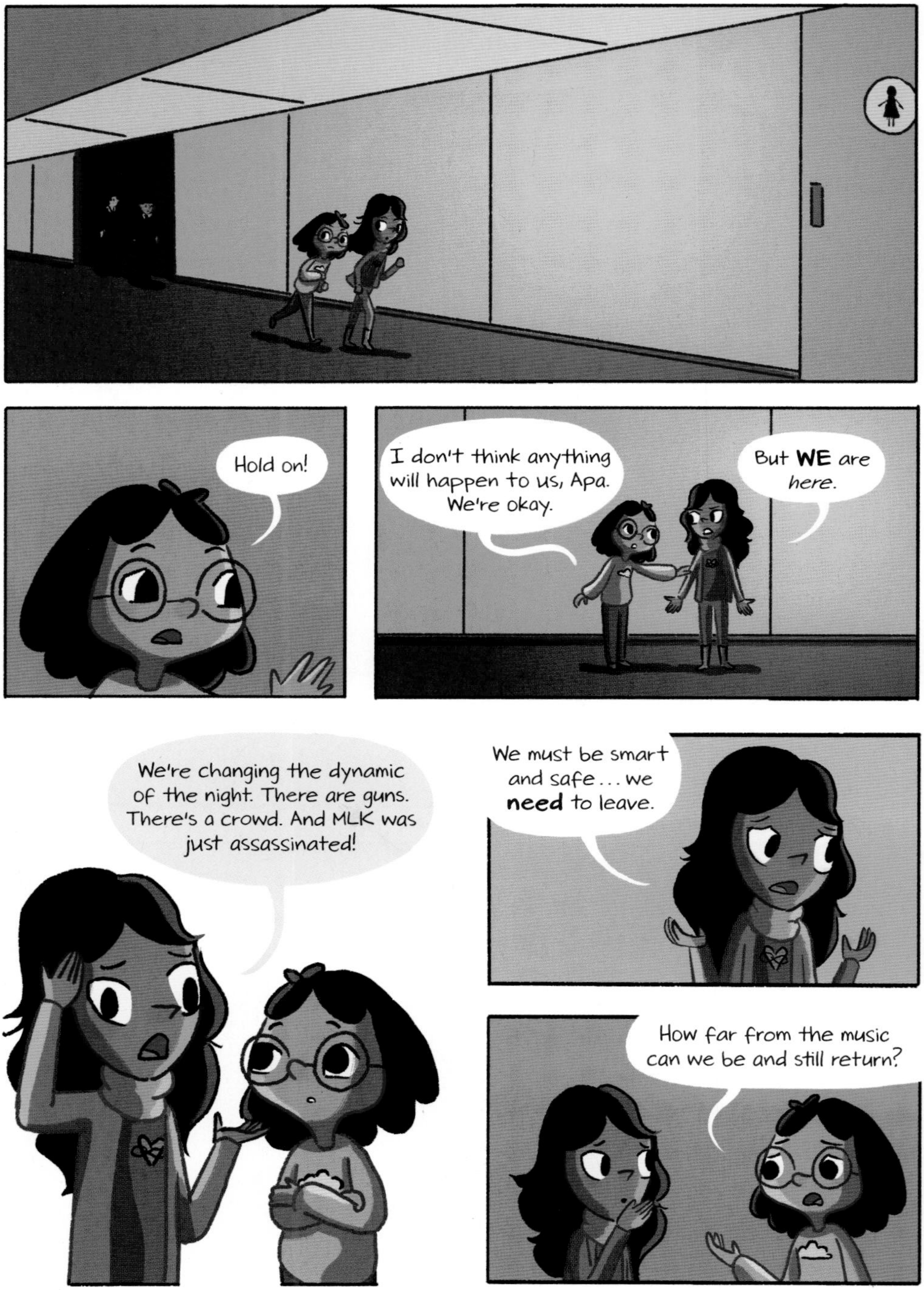
Hold on!
I don't think anything will happen to us, Apa. We're okay.
But WE are here.
We're changing the dynamic of the night. There are guns. There's a crowd. And MLK was just assassinated!
We must be smart and safe... we need to leave.
How far from the music can we be and still return?

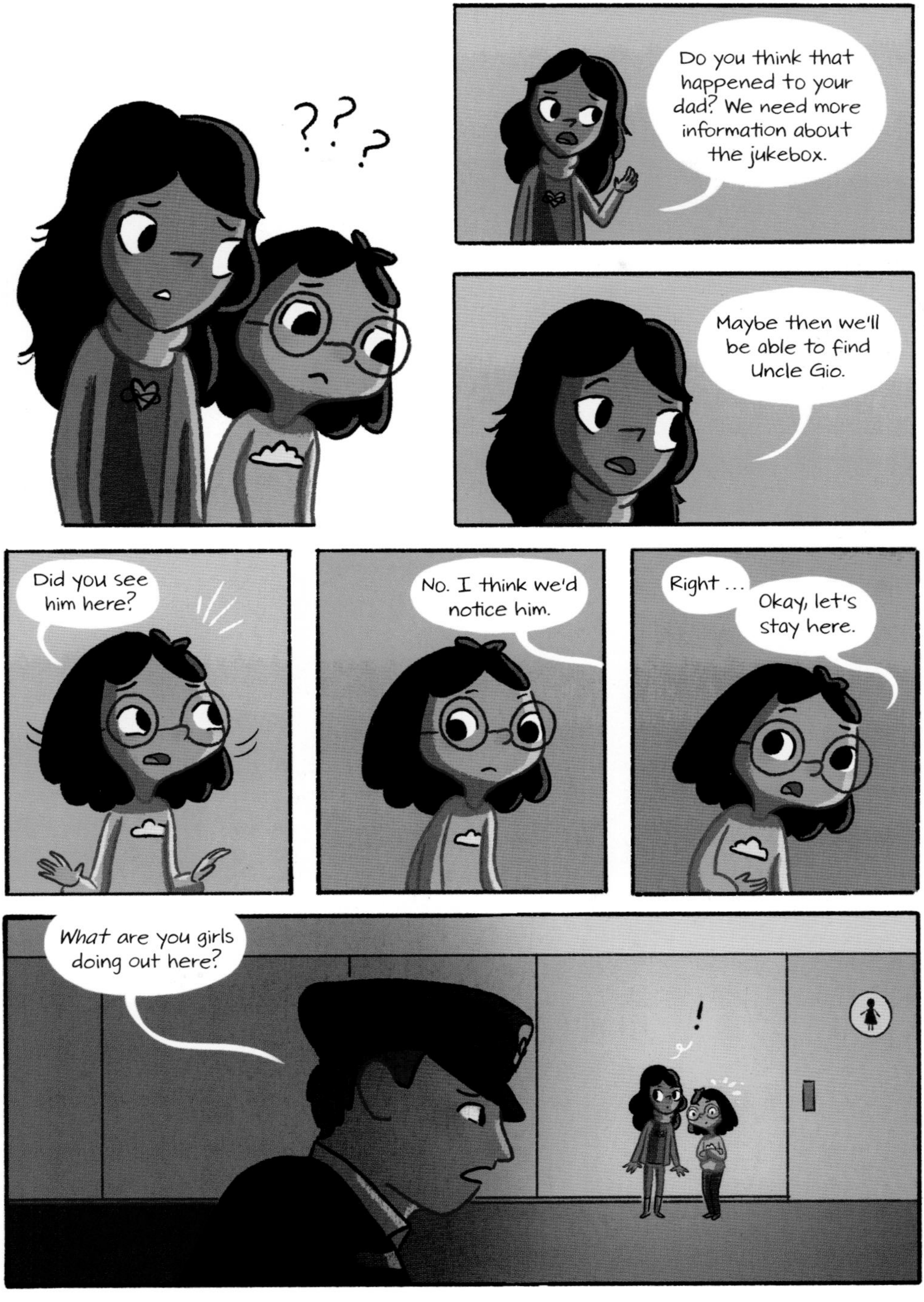

Do you think that happened to your dad? We need more information about the jukebox.
Maybe then we'll be able to find Uncle Gio.
Did you see him here?
No. I think we'd notice him.
Right ...
Okay, let's stay here.
What are you girls doing out here?

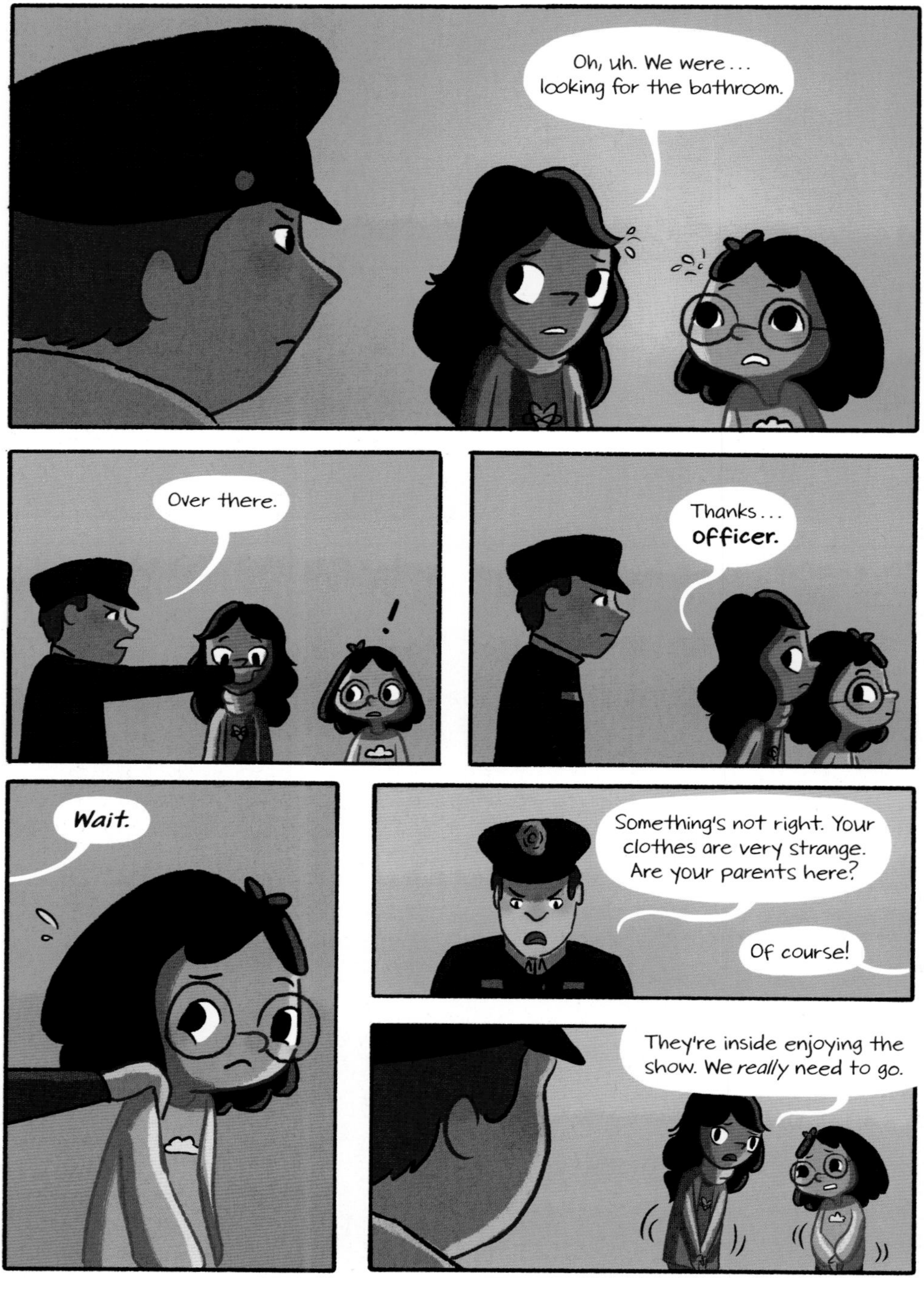

Oh, uh. We were... looking for the bathroom.
Over there.
!
Thanks... **officer.**
Wait.
Something's not right. Your clothes are very strange. Are your parents here?
Of course!
They're inside enjoying the show. We *really* need to go.

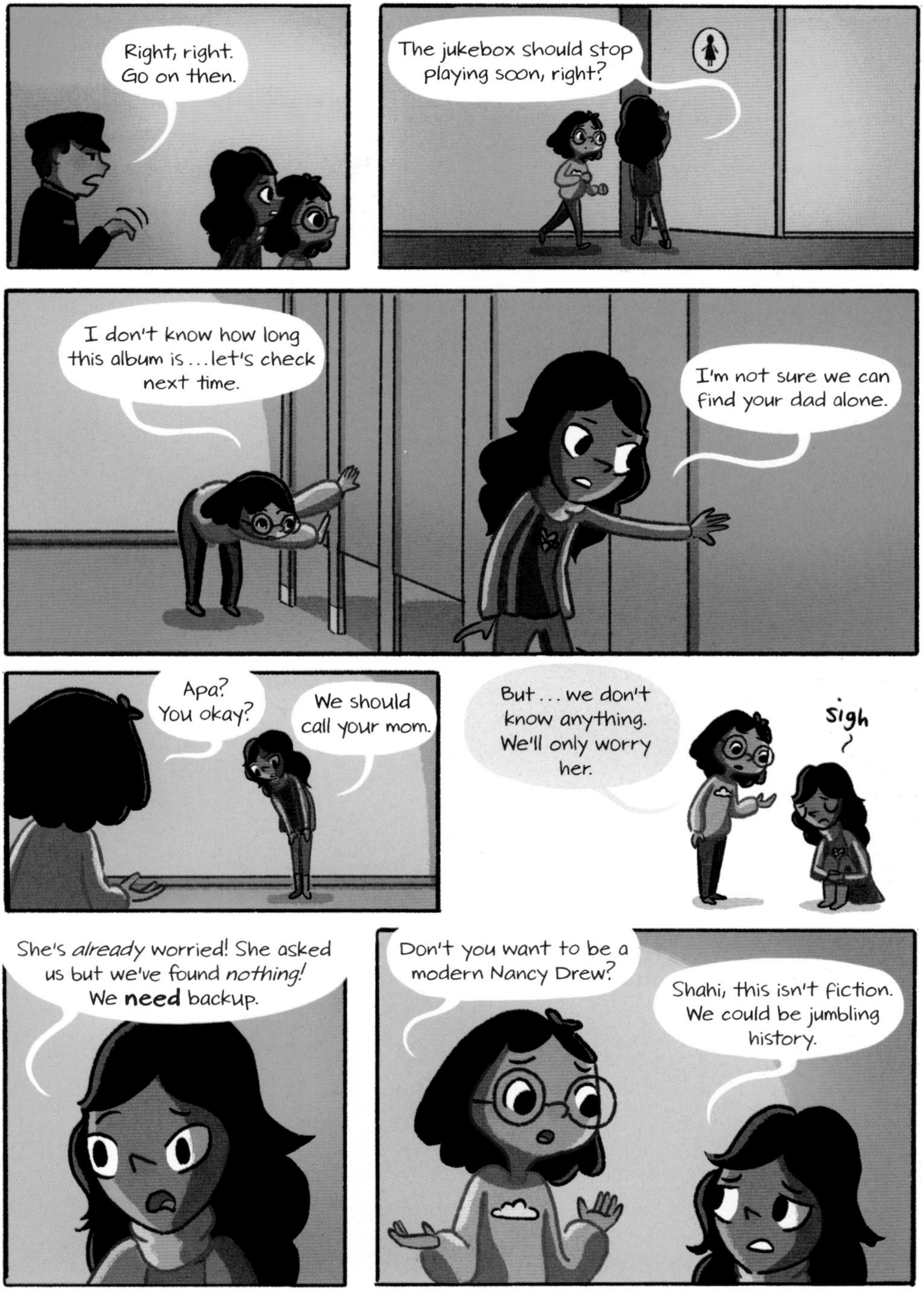

Right, right.
Go on then.
The jukebox should stop playing soon, right?
I don't know how long this album is...let's check next time.
I'm not sure we can find your dad alone.
Apa?
You okay?
We should call your mom.
But... we don't know anything. We'll only worry her.
Sigh
She's *already* worried! She asked us but we've found *nothing!* We **need** backup.
Don't you want to be a modern Nancy Drew?
Shahi, this isn't fiction. We could be jumbling history.

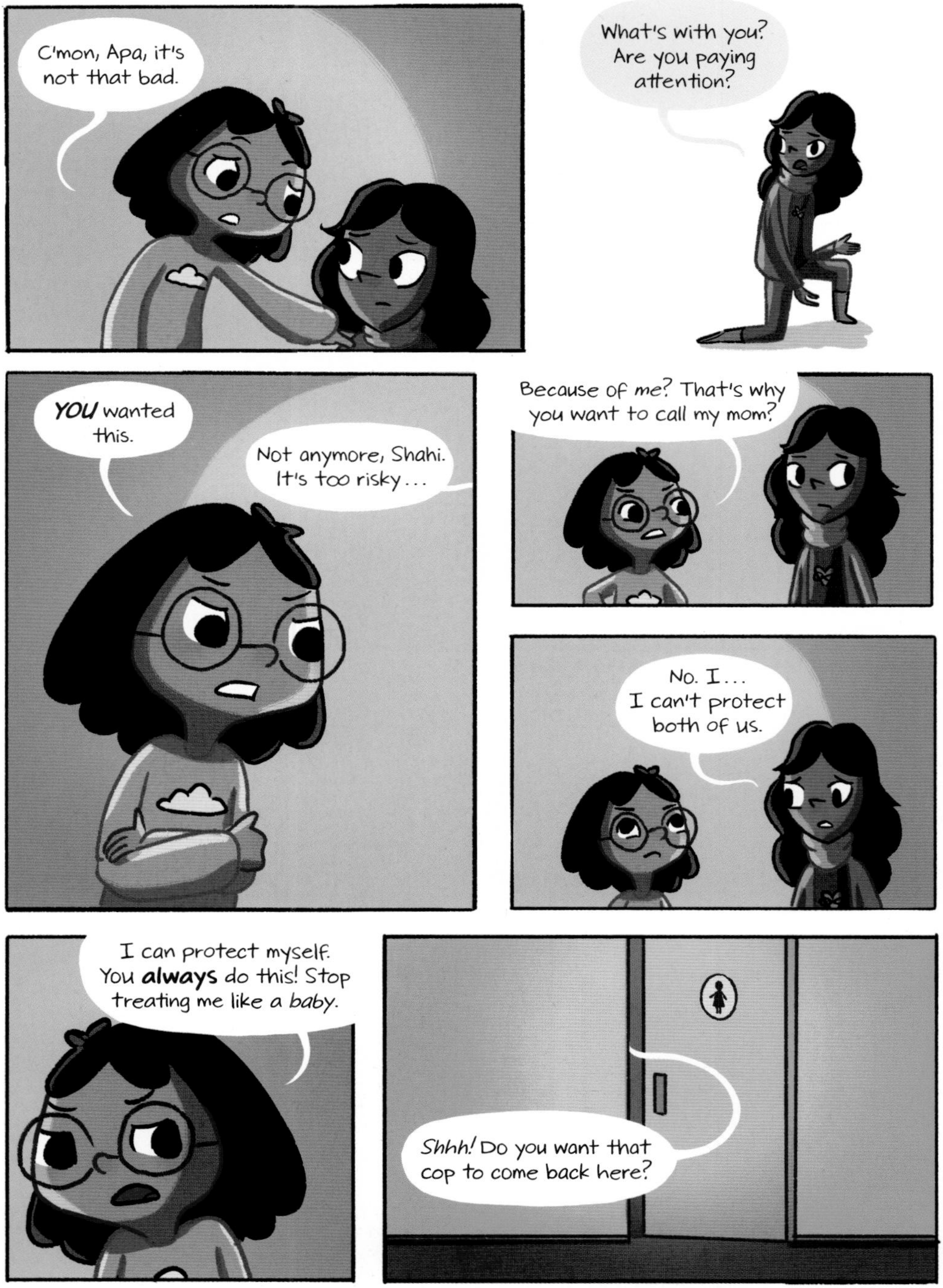
C'mon, Apa, it's not that bad.
What's with you? Are you paying attention?
YOU wanted this.
Not anymore, Shahi. It's too risky...
Because of *me*? That's why you want to call my mom?
No. I... I can't protect both of us.
I can protect myself. You **always** do this! Stop treating me like a *baby*.
Shhh! Do you want that cop to come back here?

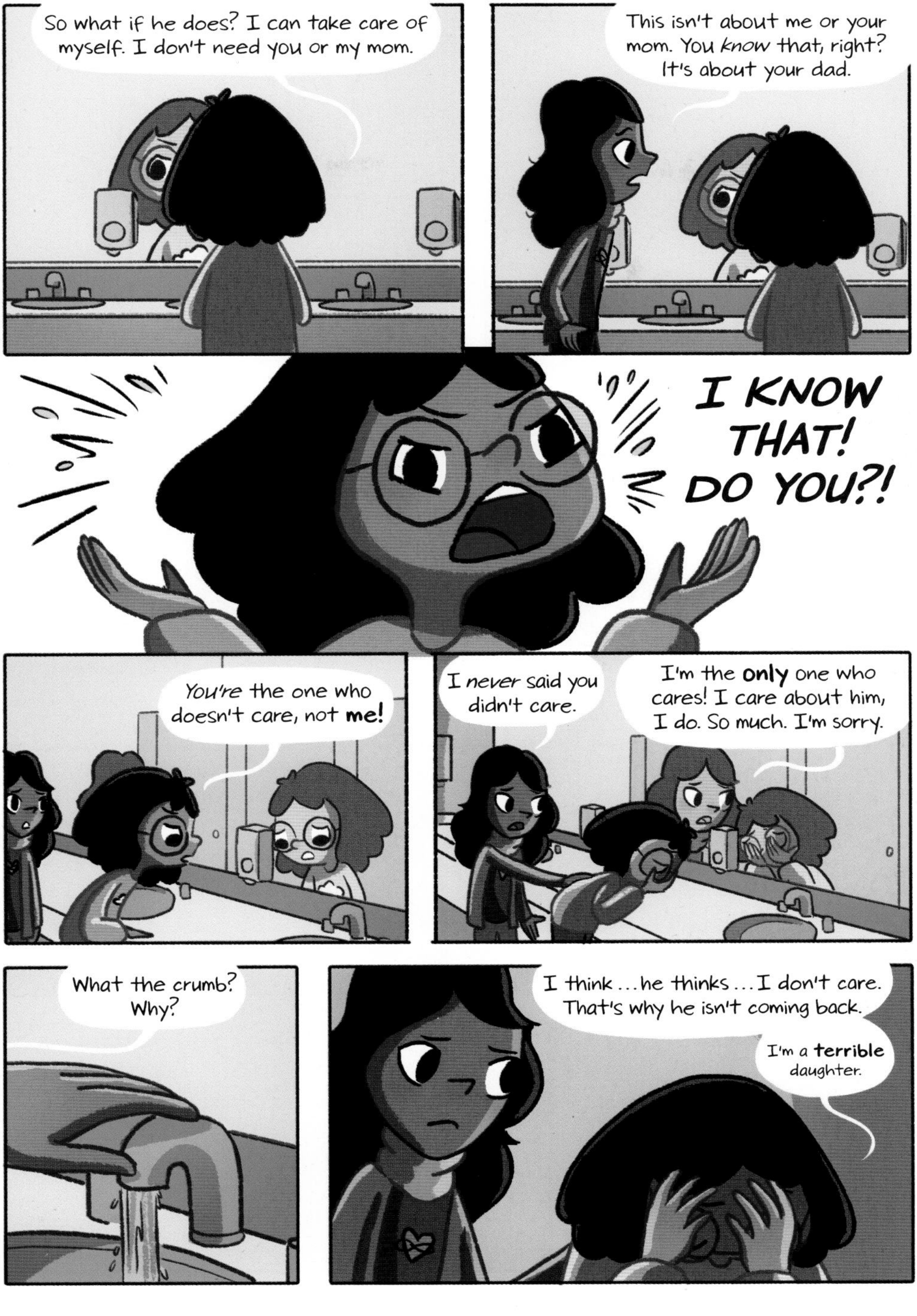

So what if he does? I can take care of myself. I don't need you or my mom.
This isn't about me or your mom. You *know* that, right? It's about your dad.
I KNOW THAT! DO YOU?!
You're the one who doesn't care, not **me**!
I *never* said you didn't care.
I'm the **only** one who cares! I care about him, I do. So much. I'm sorry.
What the crumb? Why?
I think ... he thinks ... I don't care. That's why he isn't coming back.
I'm a **terrible** daughter.

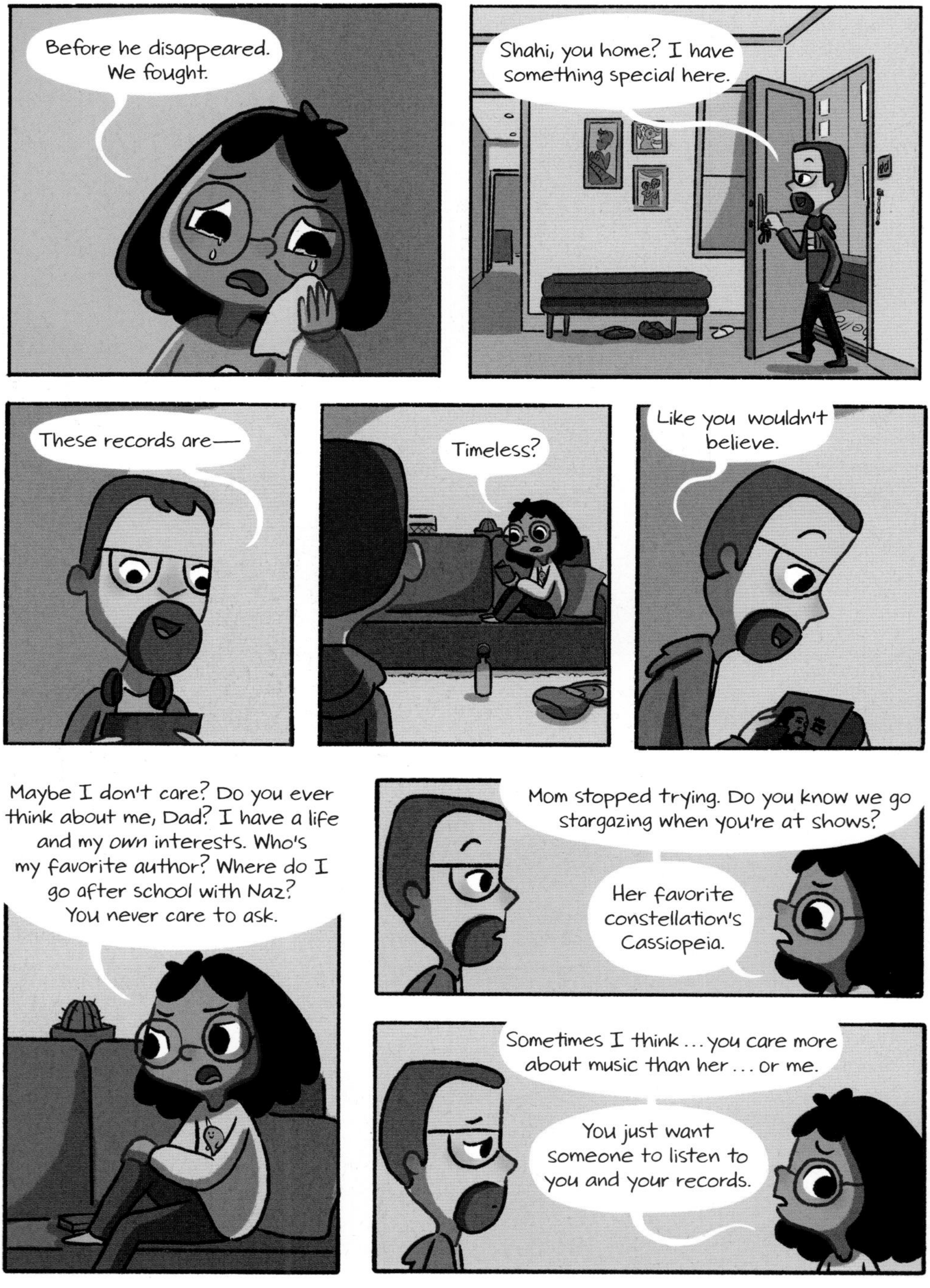
Before he disappeared. We fought.
Shahi, you home? I have something special here.
These records are—
Timeless?
Like you wouldn't believe.
Maybe I don't care? Do you ever think about me, Dad? I have a life and my own interests. Who's my favorite author? Where do I go after school with Naz? You never care to ask.
Mom stopped trying. Do you know we go stargazing when you're at shows?
Her favorite constellation's Cassiopeia.
Sometimes I think . . . you care more about music than her . . . or me.
You just want someone to listen to you and your records.

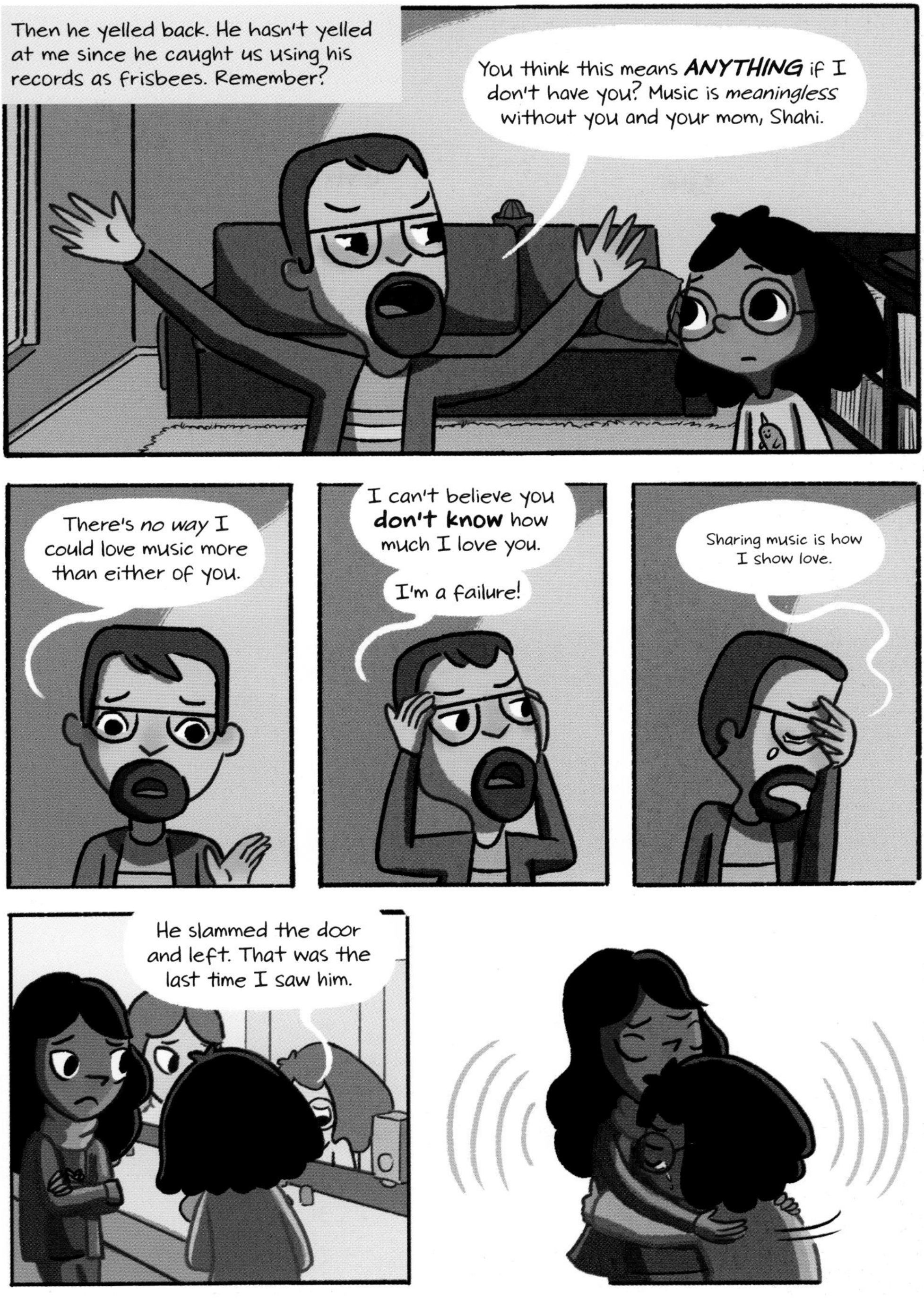
Then he yelled back. He hasn't yelled at me since he caught us using his records as frisbees. Remember?
You think this means ANYTHING if I don't have you? Music is meaningless without you and your mom, Shahi.
There's no way I could love music more than either of you.
I can't believe you don't know how much I love you.
I'm a failure!
Sharing music is how I show love.
He slammed the door and left. That was the last time I saw him.

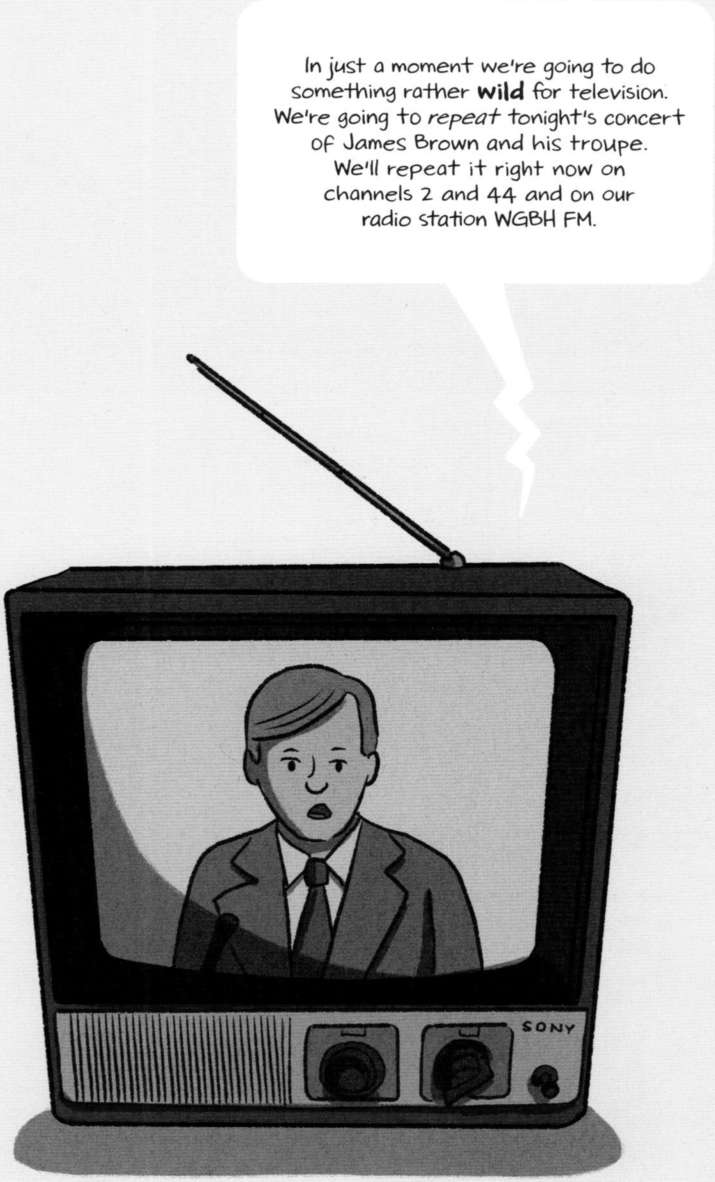
In just a moment we're going to do something rather **wild** for television. We're going to *repeat* tonight's concert of James Brown and his troupe. We'll repeat it right now on channels 2 and 44 and on our radio station WGBH FM.
SONY

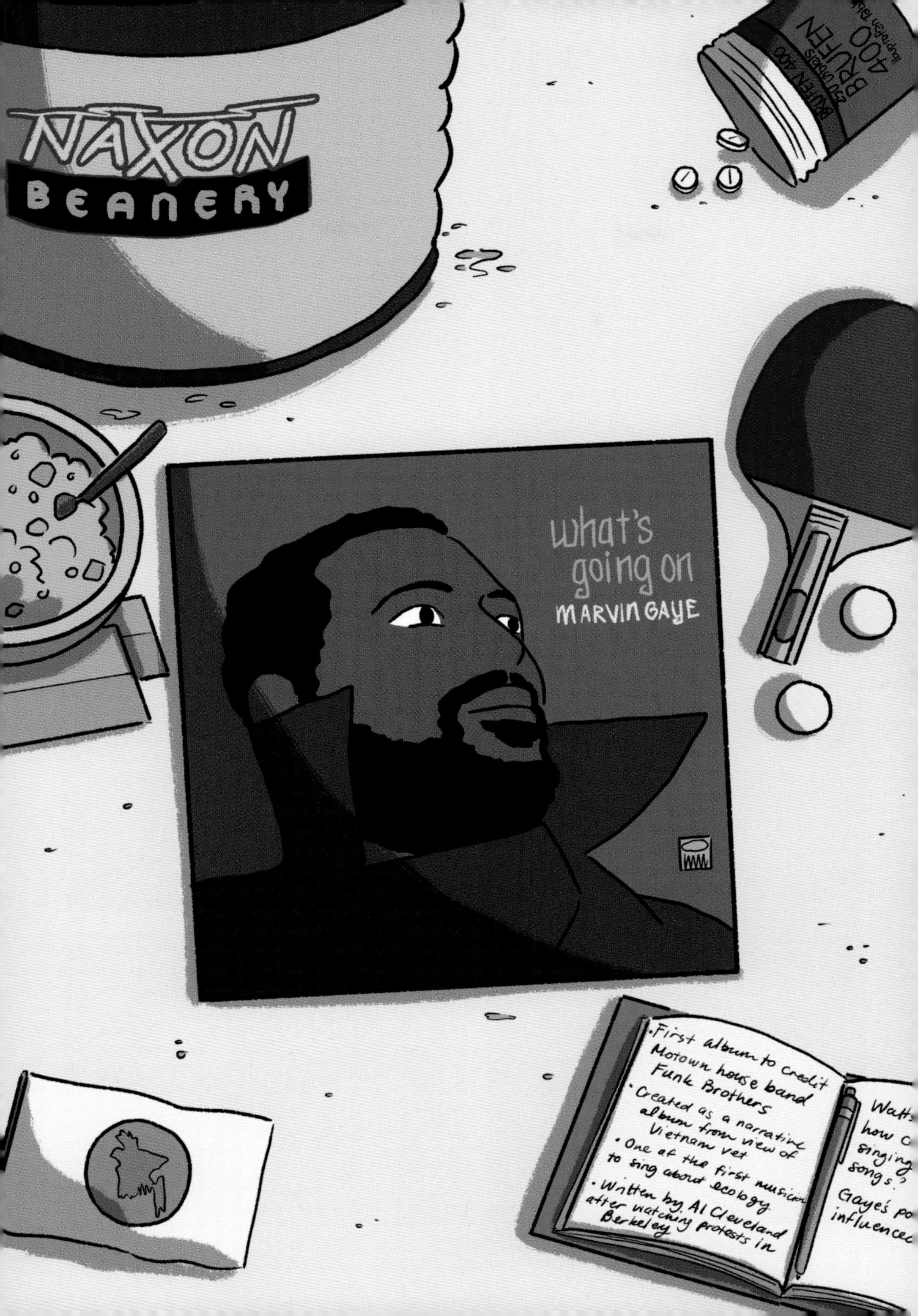
NAXON
BEANERY
BRUFEN 400
400
BRUFEN
what's going on
MARVIN GAYE
• First album to credit Motown house band Funk Brothers
• Created as a narrative album from view of Vietnam vet
• One of the first musician to sing about ecology
• Written by Al Cleveland after watching protests in Berkeley
how
singing
songs."
Gaye's

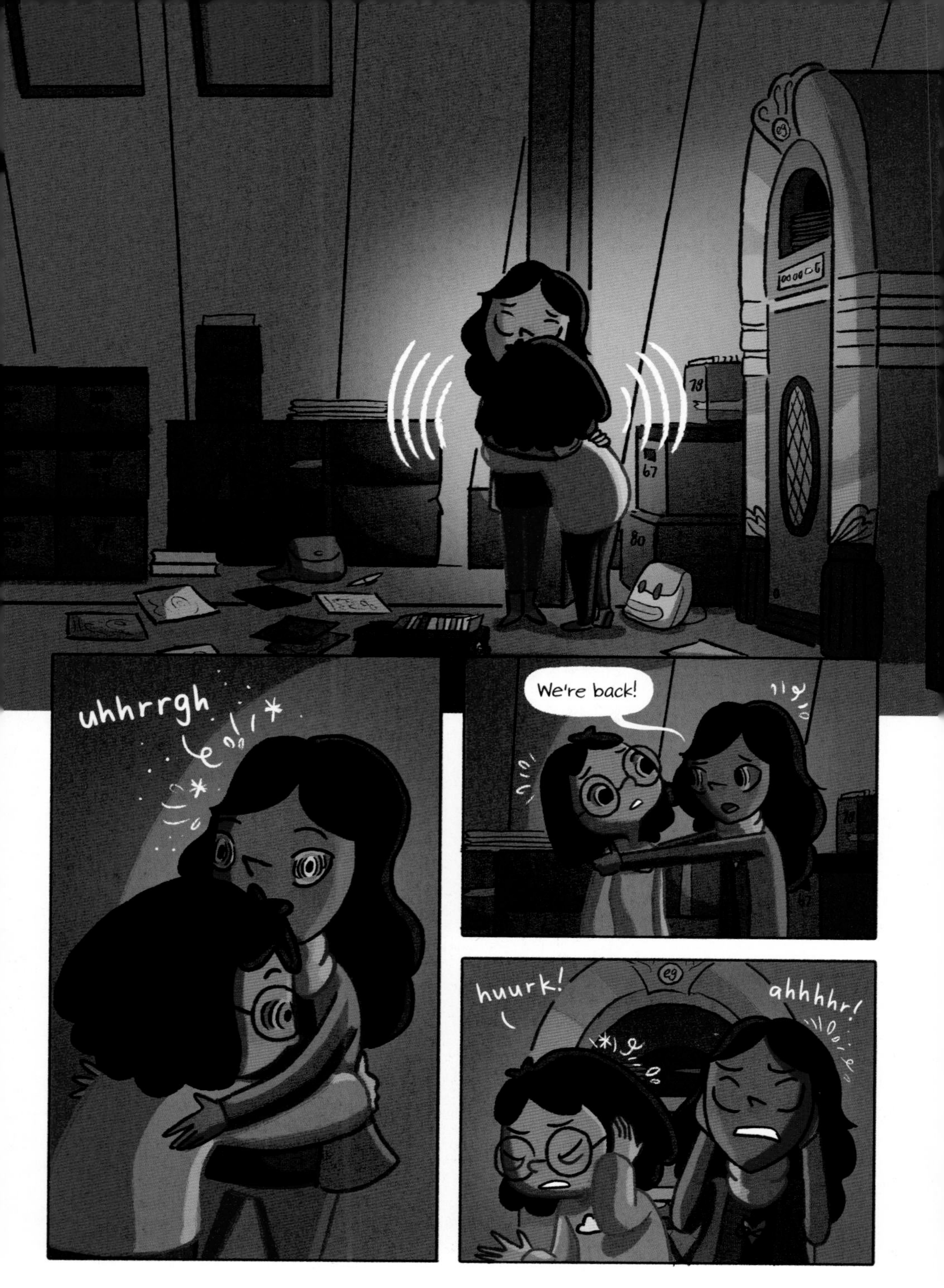
uhhrrgh
We're back!
huurk!
ahhhhr!

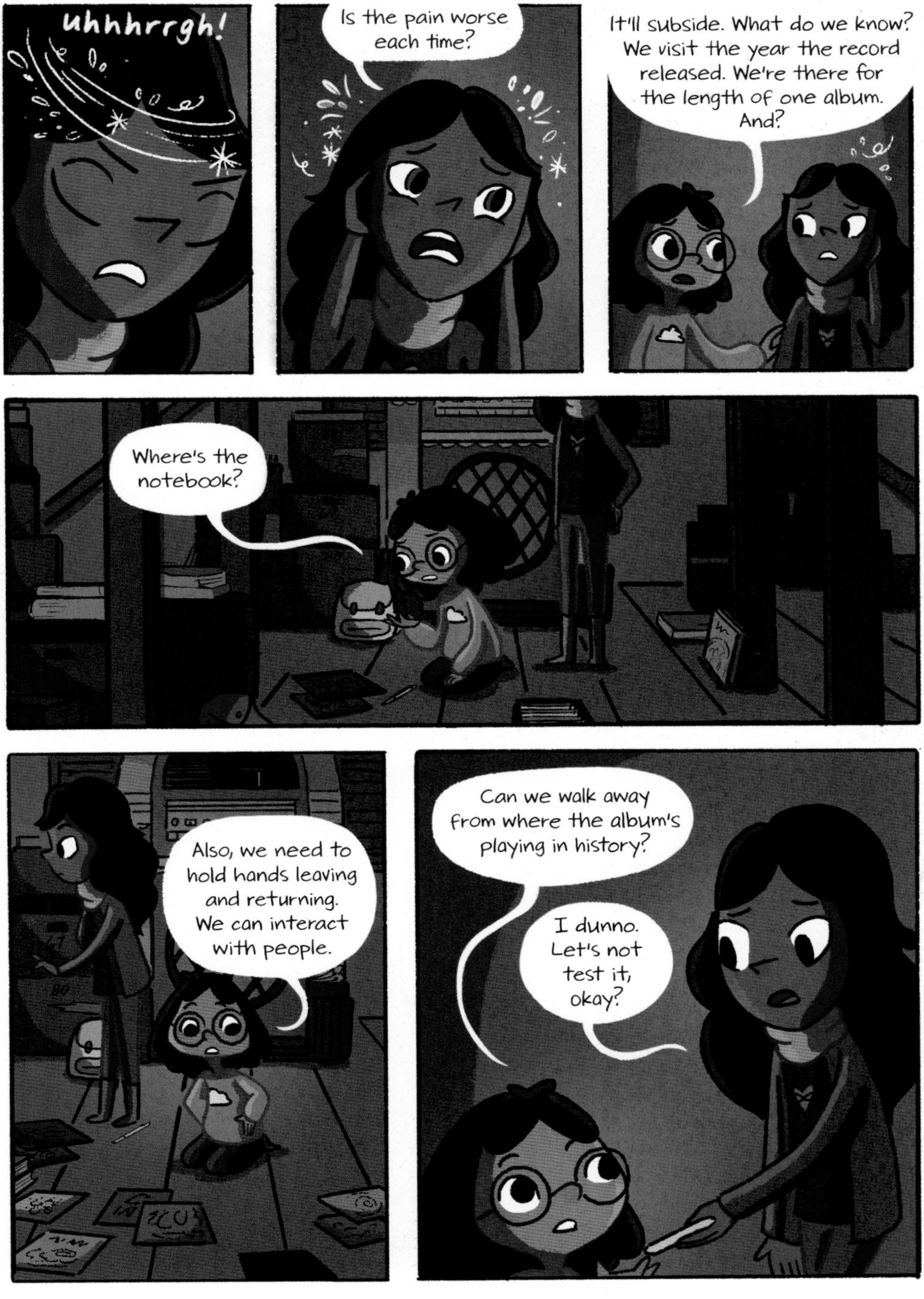
uhhhrrgh!
Is the pain worse each time?
It'll subside. What do we know? We visit the year the record released. We're there for the length of one album. And?
Where's the notebook?
Also, we need to hold hands leaving and returning. We can interact with people.
Can we walk away from where the album's playing in history?
I dunno. Let's not test it, okay?

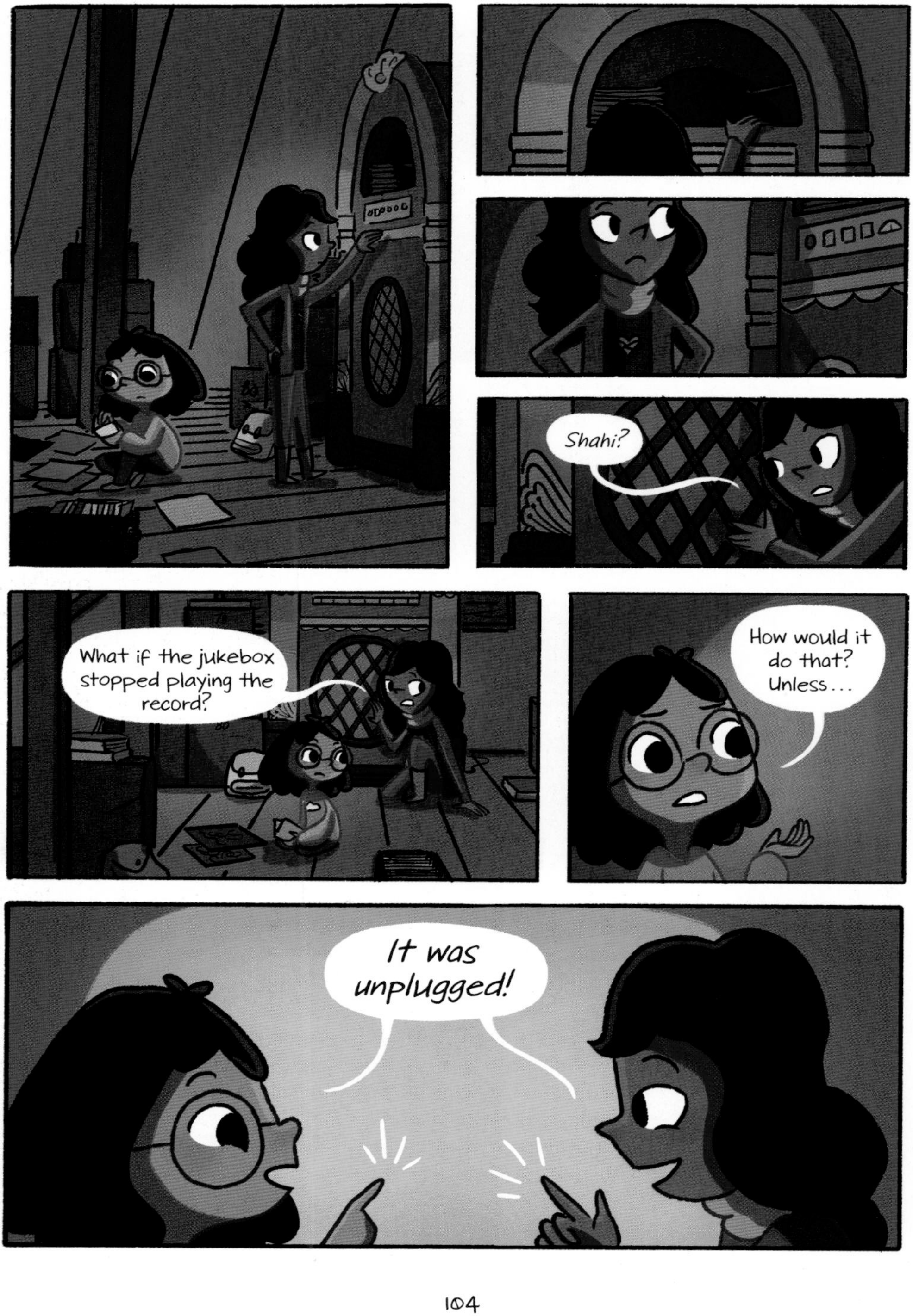
Shahi?
What if the jukebox stopped playing the record?
How would it do that? Unless...
It was unplugged!

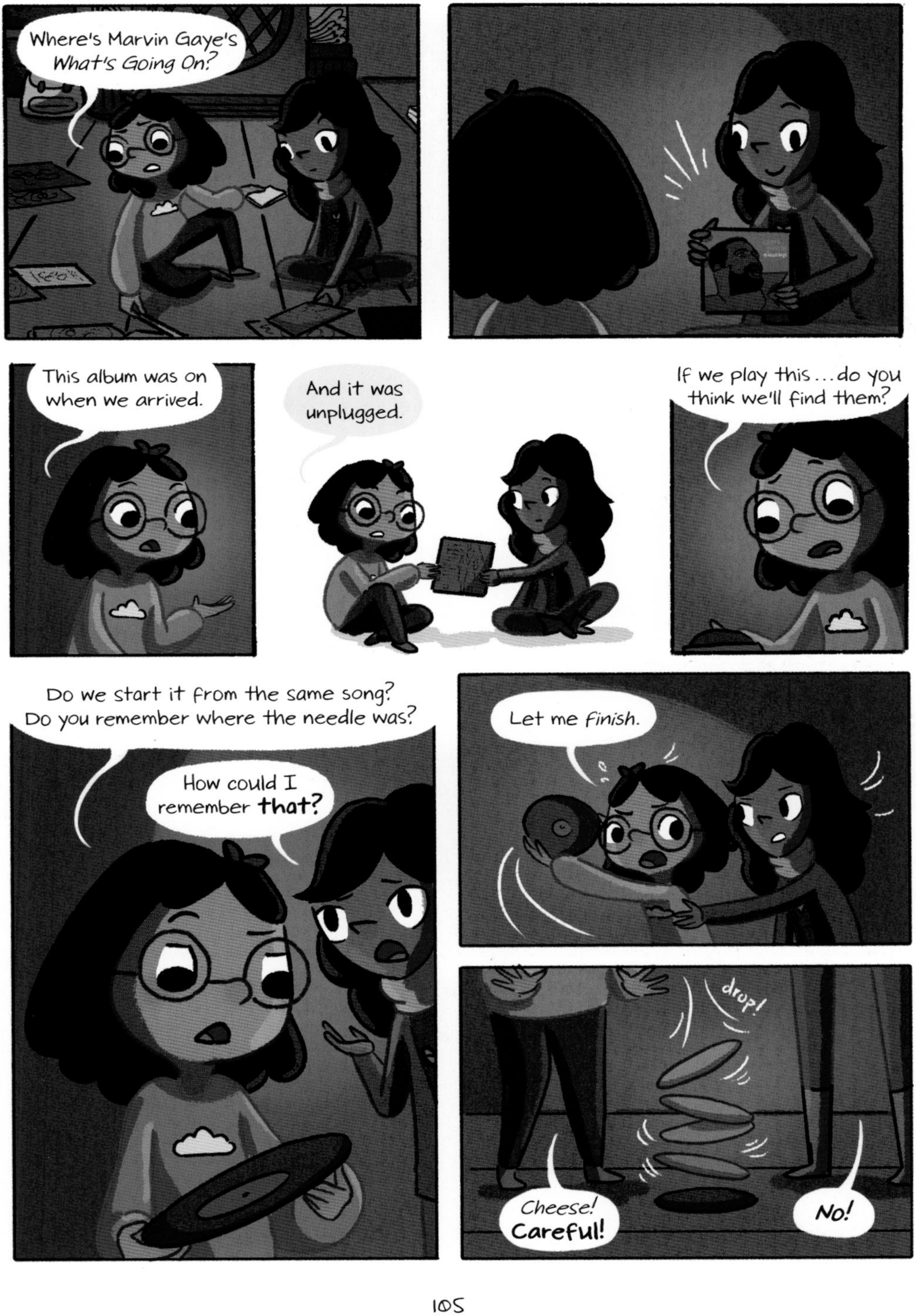

Where's Marvin Gaye's *What's Going On?*
This album was on when we arrived.
And it was unplugged.
If we play this...do you think we'll find them?
Do we start it from the same song? Do you remember where the needle was?
How could I remember **that?**
Let me *finish.*
drop!
Cheese! **Careful!**
No!

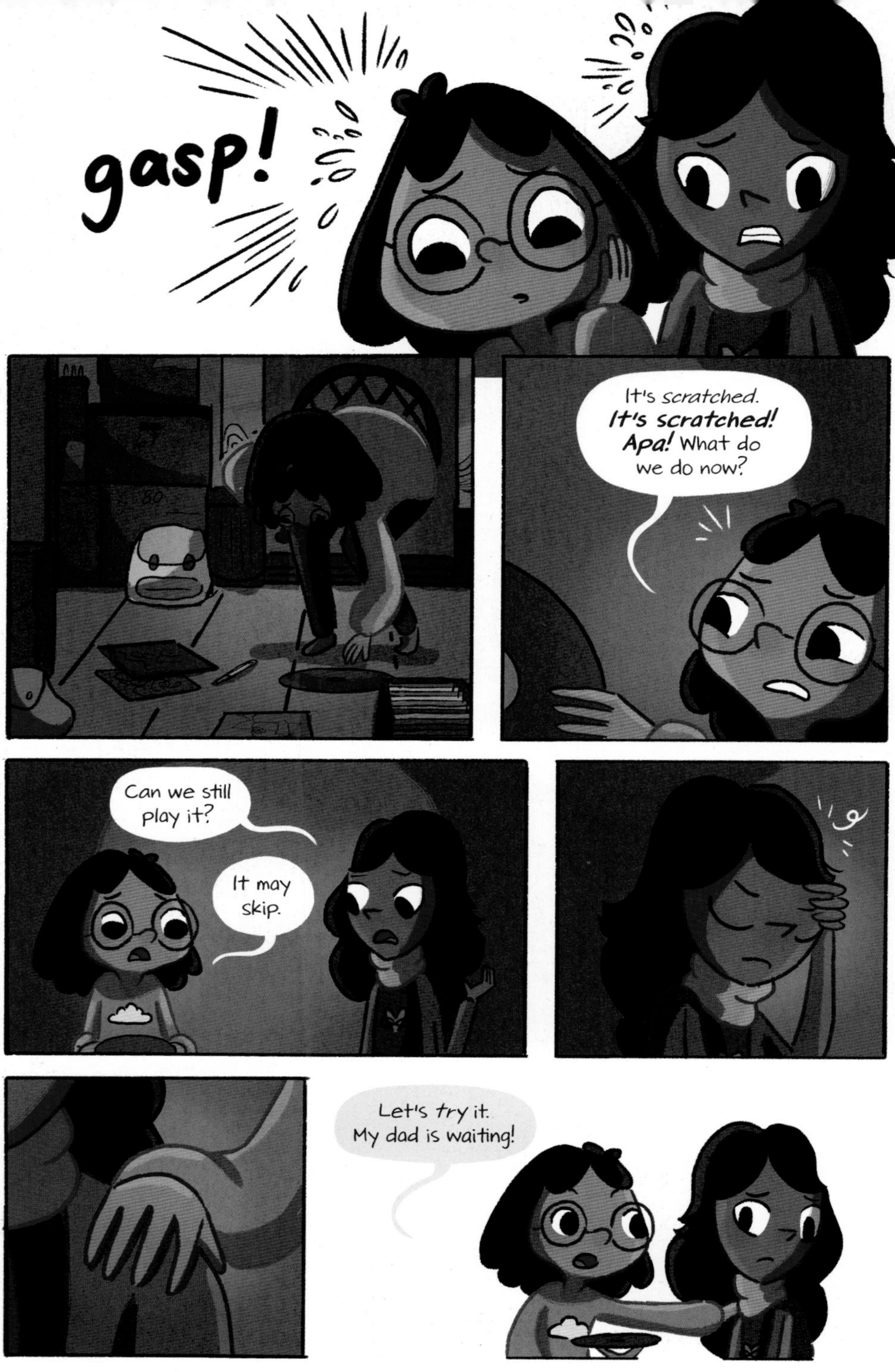
gasp!
It's *scratched*. **It's scratched! Apa!** What do we do now?
Can we still play it?
It may skip.
Let's *try* it. My dad is waiting!

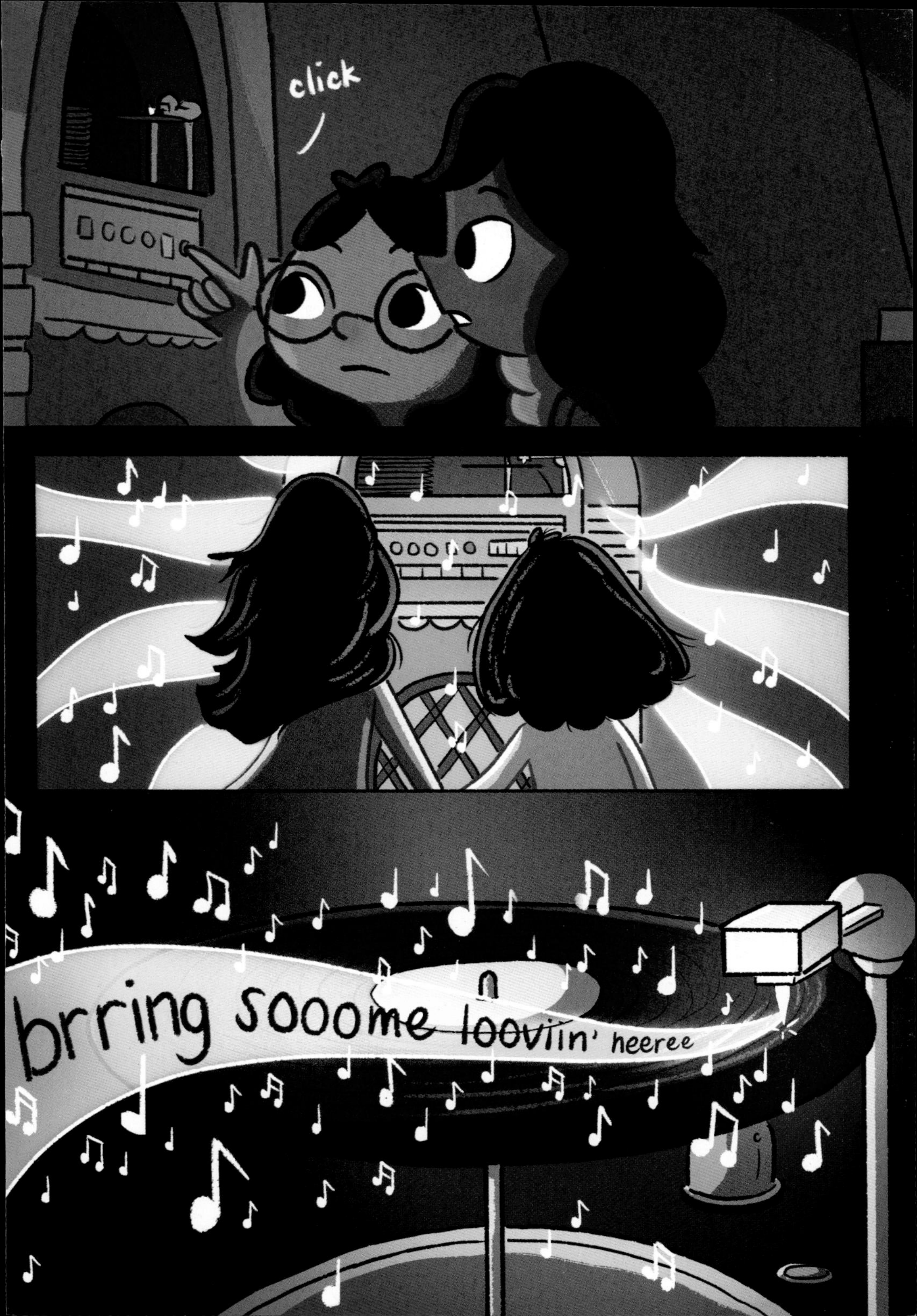
click
brring sooome loovin' heeree

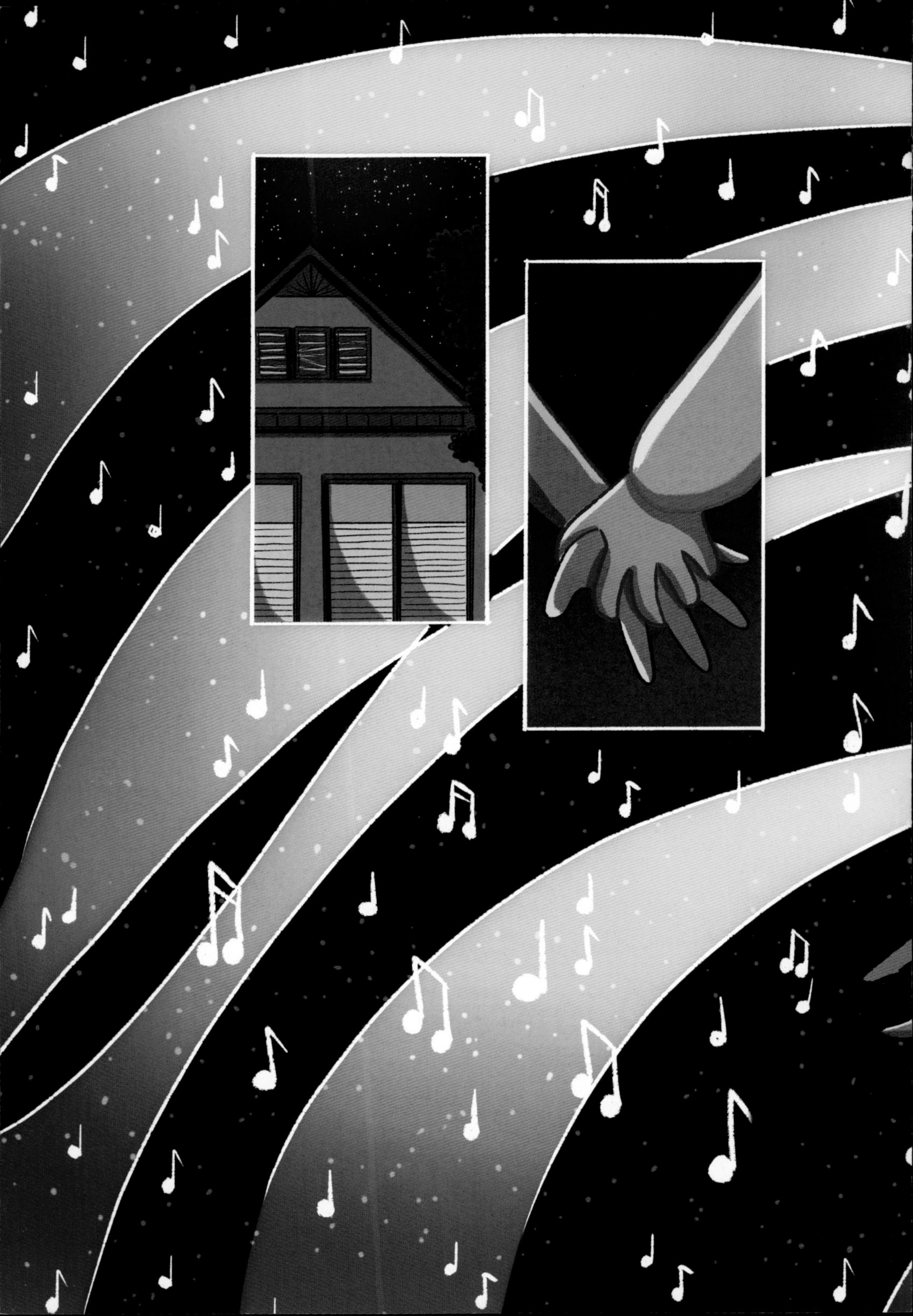

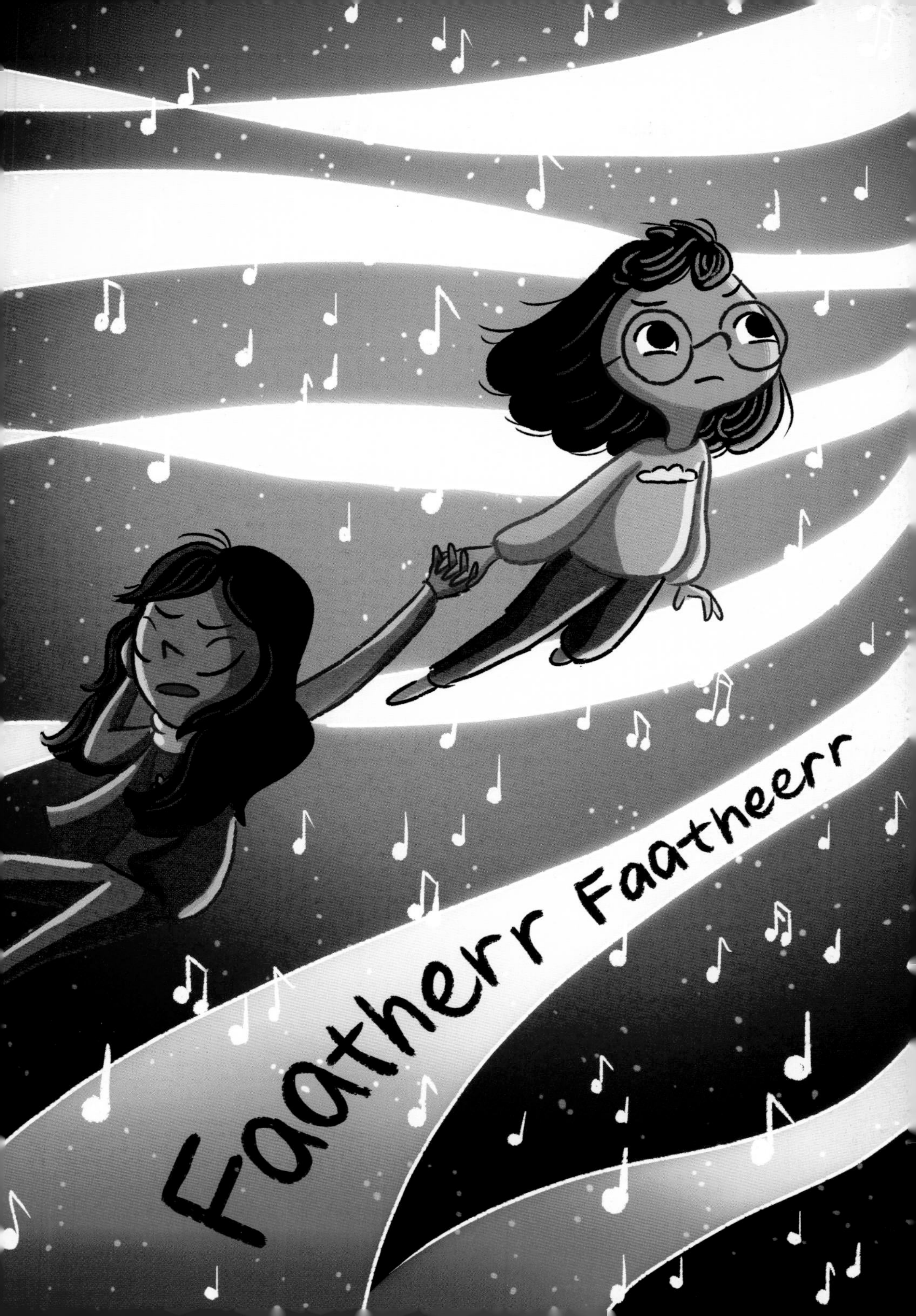
Faatherr Faatheerr

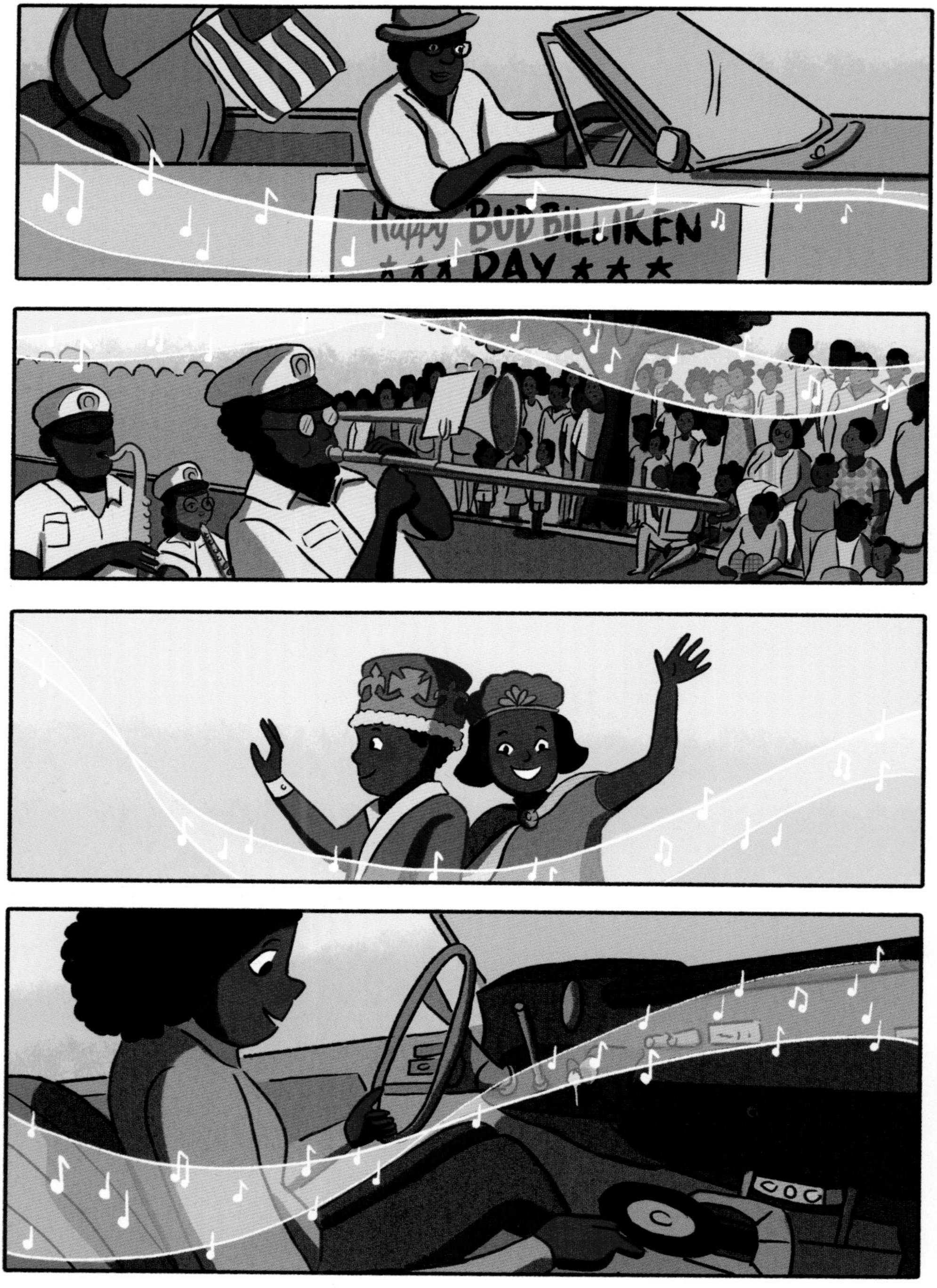
Happy BUD BILLIKEN
DAY ★★★

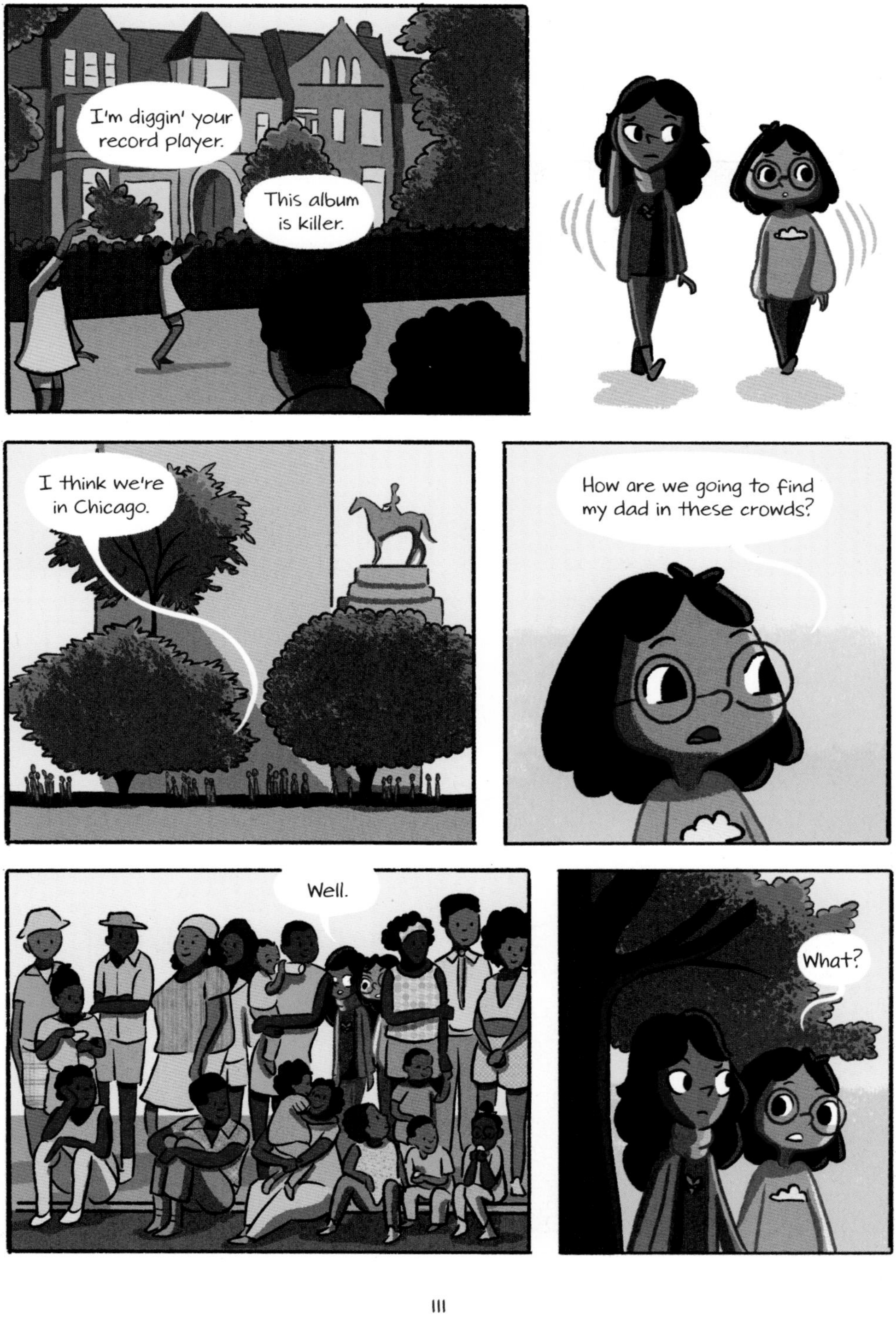
I'm diggin' your record player.
This album is killer.
I think we're in Chicago.
How are we going to find my dad in these crowds?
Well.
What?

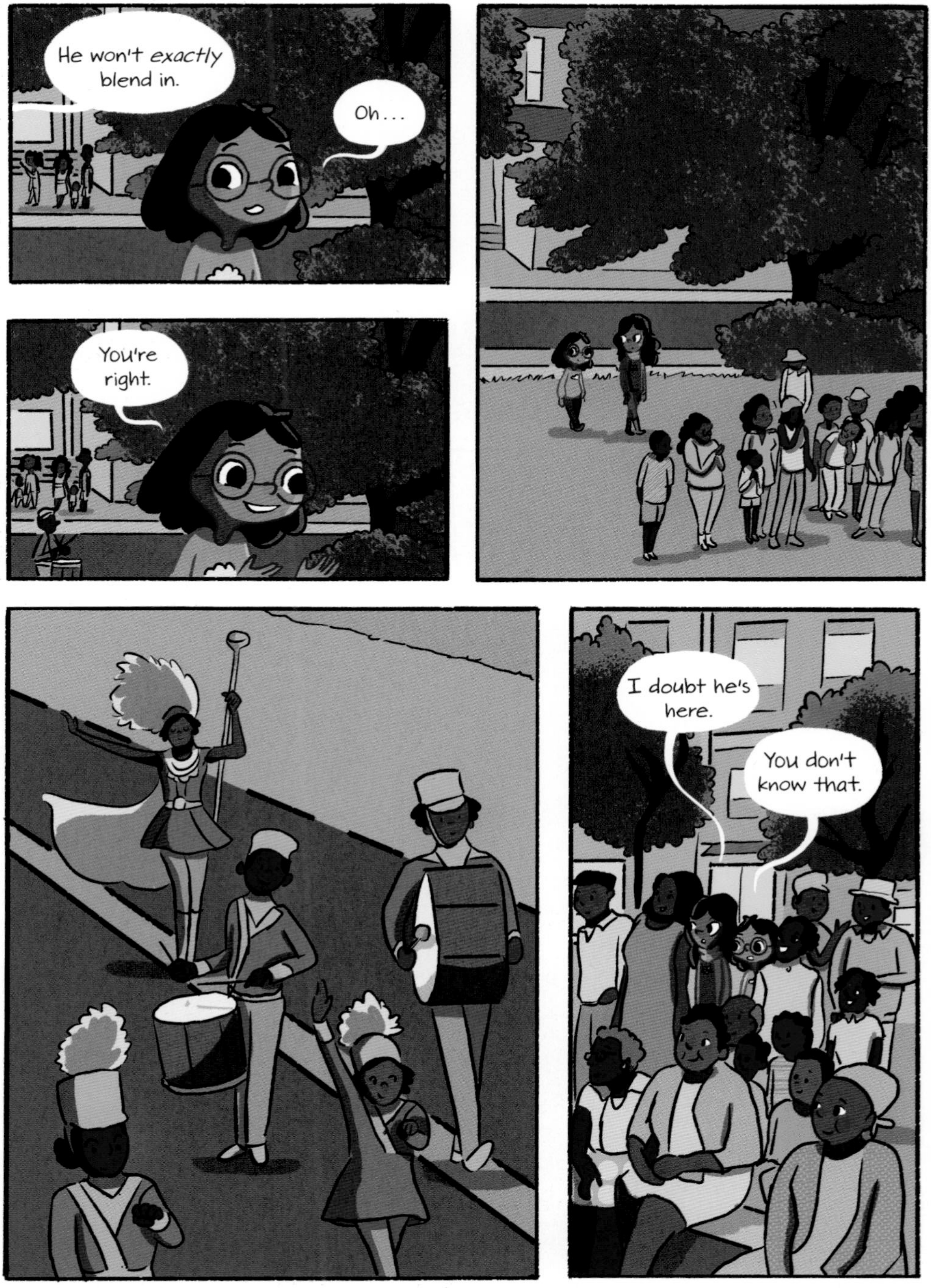
He won't *exactly* blend in.
Oh...
You're right.
I doubt he's here.
You don't know that.

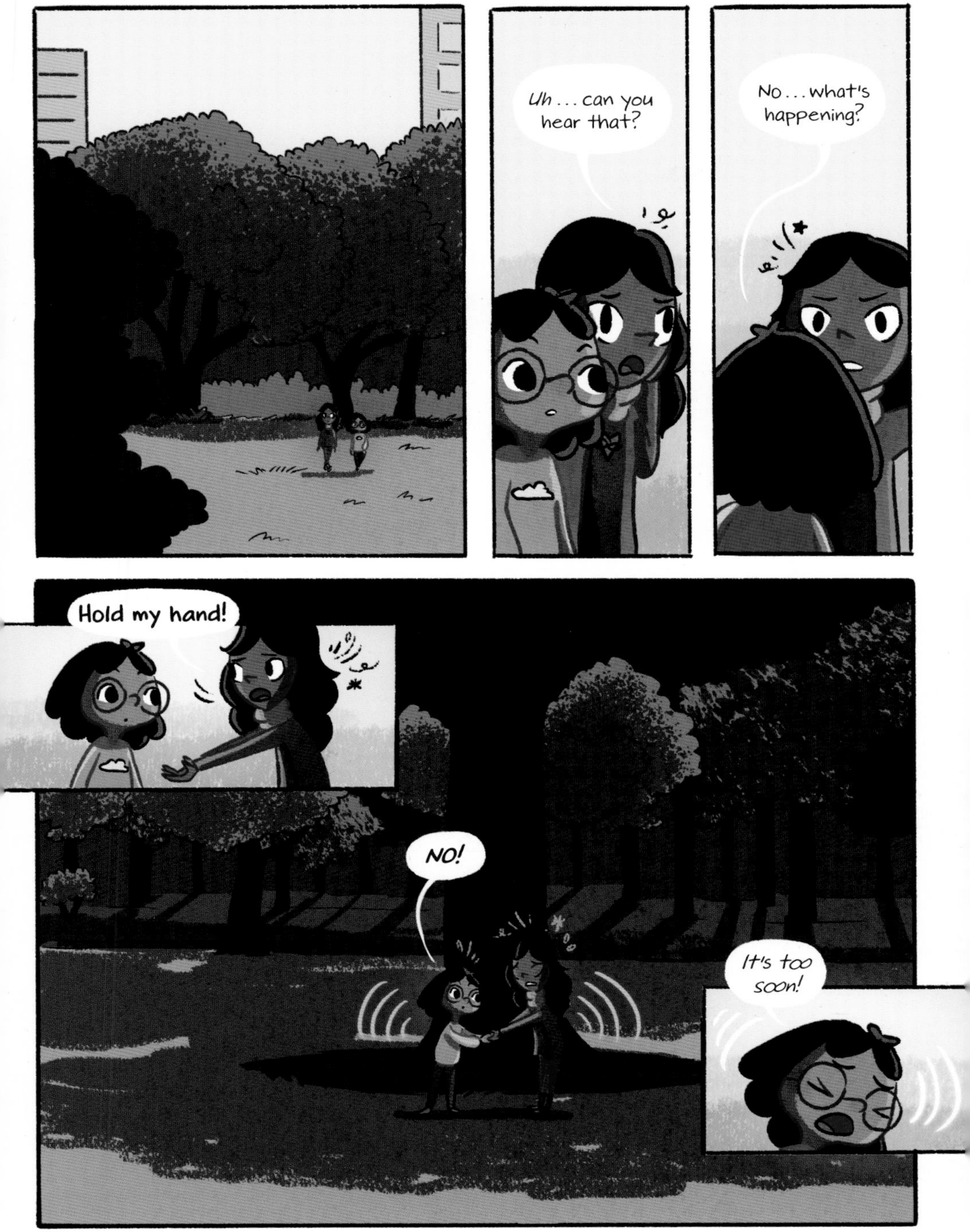

Uh... can you hear that?
No... what's happening?
Hold my hand!
NO!
It's too soon!

Considered the most
important hip hop
album

"edge" not threat but a
statement about the
effect of poverty on
mental health

launched hip hop into
the realm of social
commentary

sampled on
one of the frequently
sampled songs
during hip-hop's rise
to prominence

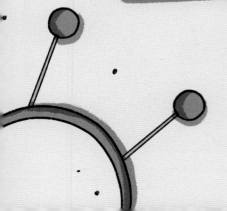

Graceland
Guest Pass
0017

GRANDMASTER FLASH
& THE FURIOUS FIVE

THE MESSAGE

Sugar Hill

JELL·O·
Pudding
Pops

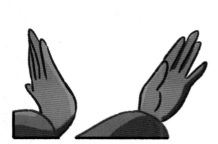

POP!

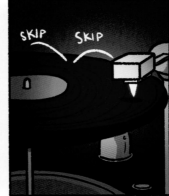

SKIP   SKIP

It's *skipping!* That's why we returned so quickly.

He wasn't there.

We didn't look *everywhere*. It's *not that* scratched—let's play it again.

Shahi, we would've noticed the *one* white guy there, trust me.

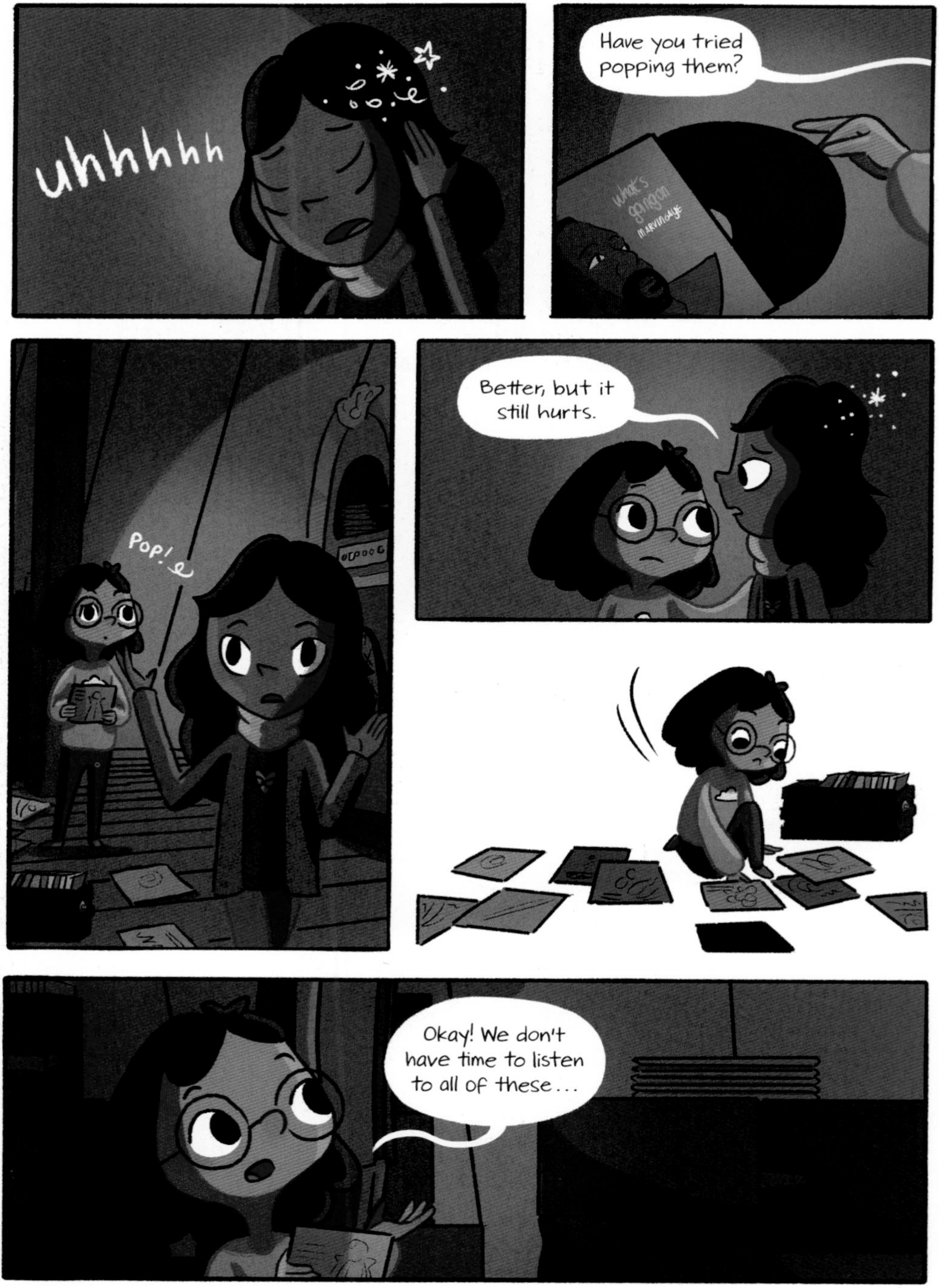

uhhhhh
Have you tried popping them?
what's going on
MARVIN GAYE
POP!
Better, but it still hurts.
Okay! We don't have time to listen to all of these...

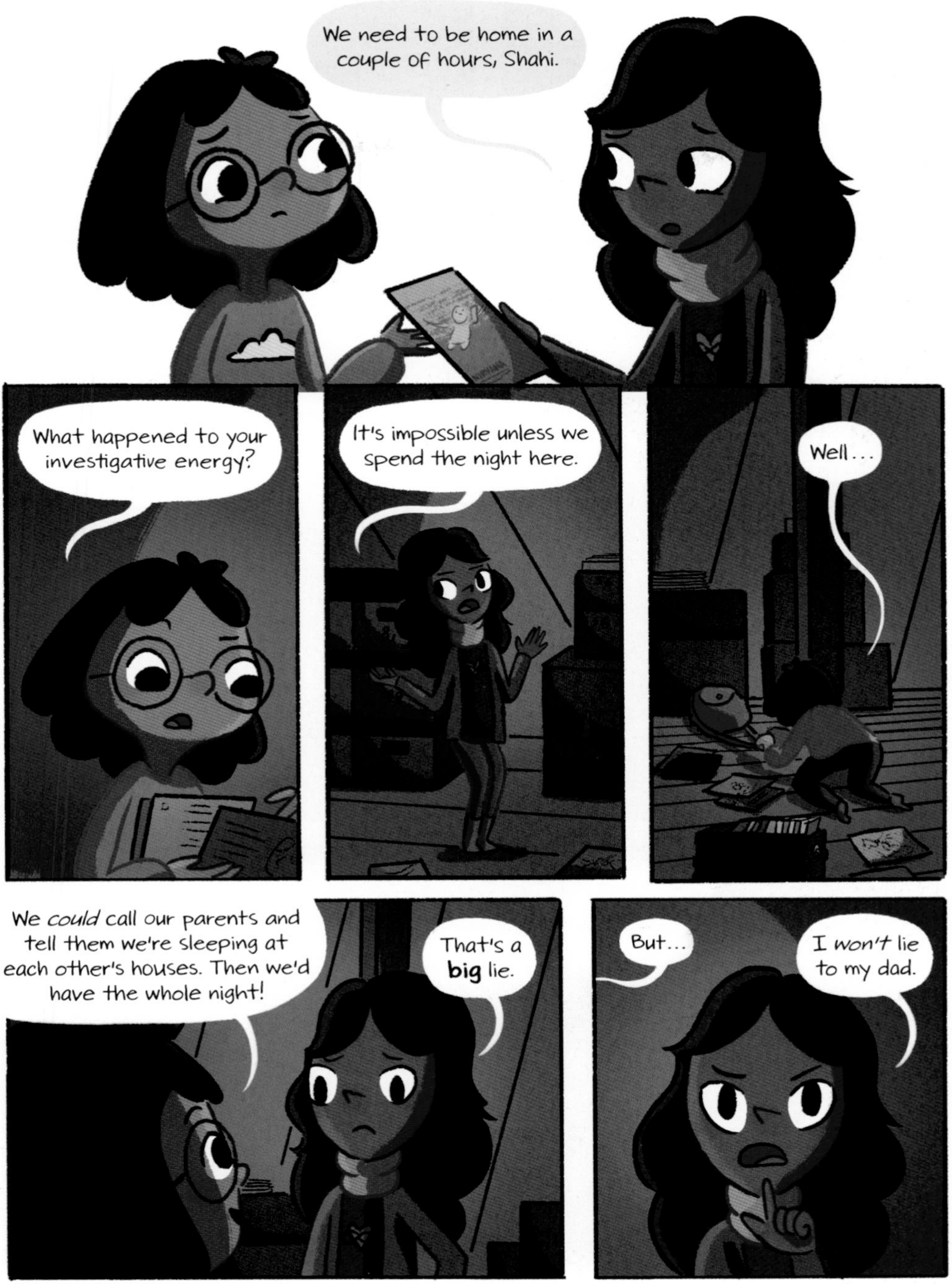
We need to be home in a couple of hours, Shahi.
What happened to your investigative energy?
It's impossible unless we spend the night here.
Well...
We *could* call our parents and tell them we're sleeping at each other's houses. Then we'd have the whole night!
That's a **big** lie.
But...
I *won't* lie to my dad.

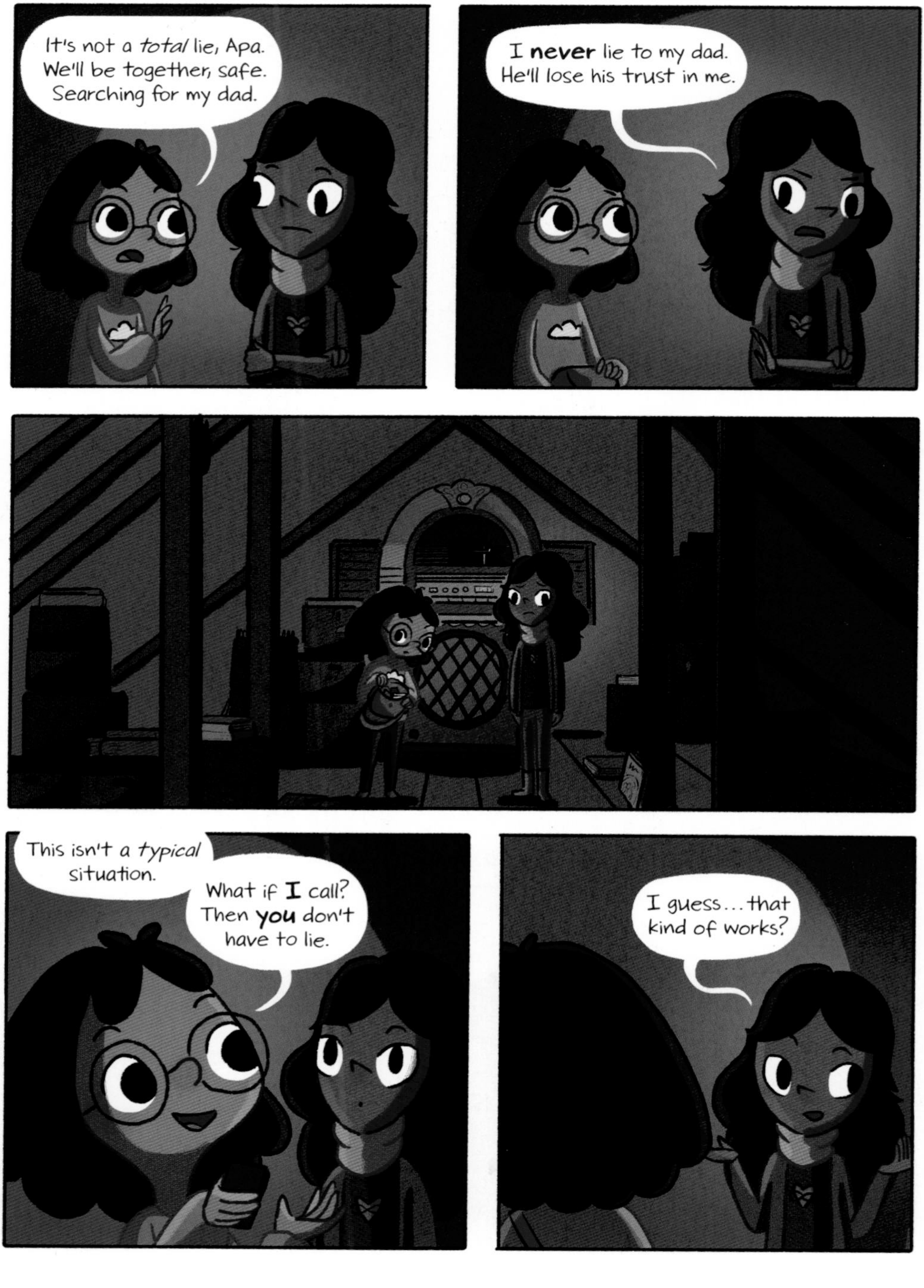
It's not a *total* lie, Apa. We'll be together, safe. Searching for my dad.
I **never** lie to my dad. He'll lose his trust in me.
This isn't a *typical* situation.
What if **I** call? Then **you** don't have to lie.
I guess... that kind of works?

Hi, Mom. I'm going to sleep over at Naz's house.

Yeah, Mamu and Mami are fine with it. Okay, I will.

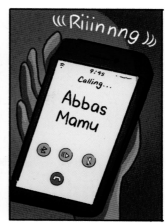

《《 Riiinnng 》》

9:45
Calling...

Abbas
Mamu

Hi, Mamu! How are you? Yeah. Is it okay if Naz sleeps over?

Oh, sure. She's right here.

mmgrrr

Hi, Abbu. Yeah, I just... want to spend more time with Shaheen.

Yes, I'll tell Phuppo Faiza. Okay. Good night.

Sorry.

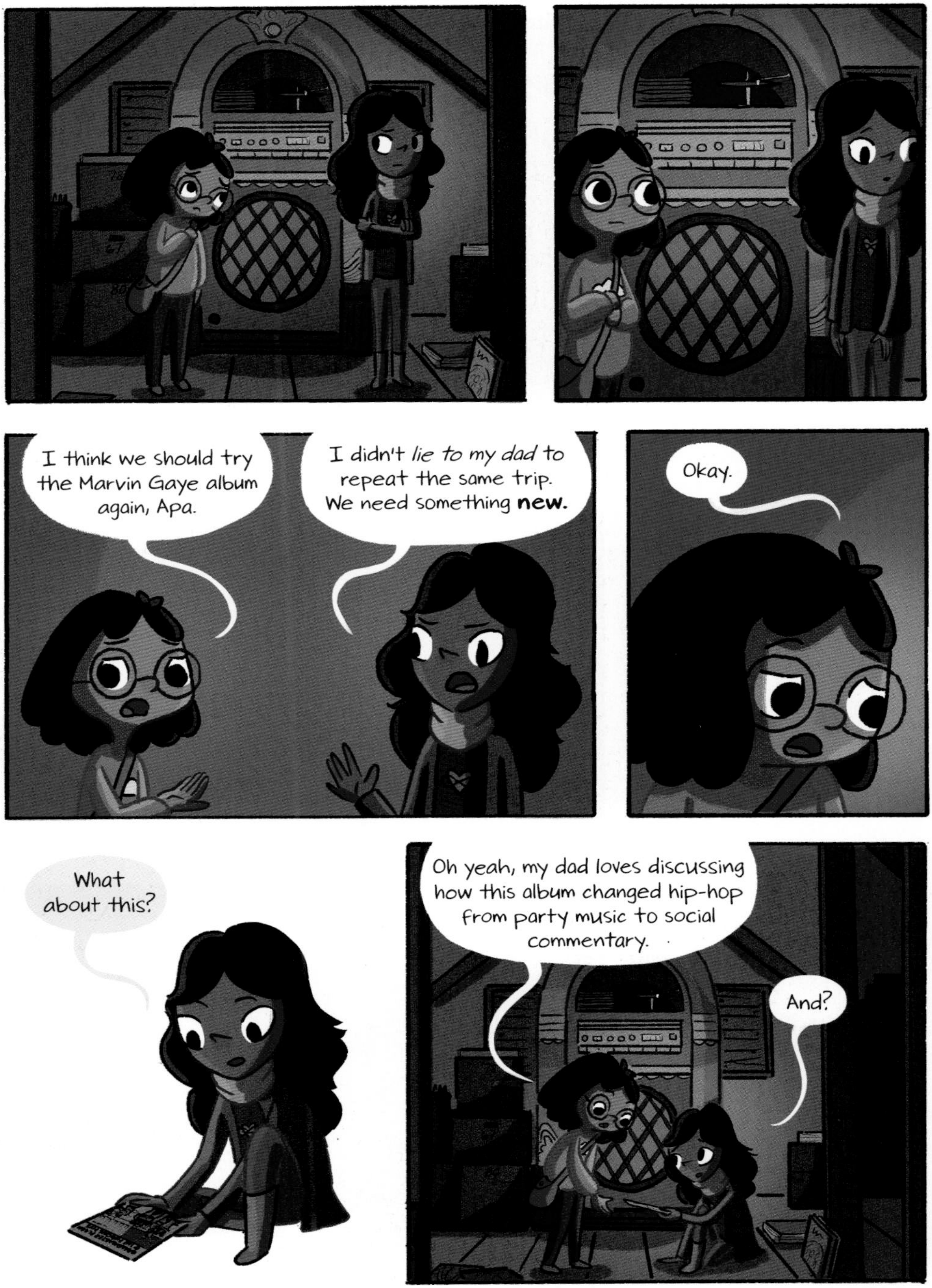

I think we should try the Marvin Gaye album again, Apa.
I didn't *lie to my dad* to repeat the same trip. We need something **new.**
Okay.
What about this?
Oh yeah, my dad loves discussing how this album changed hip-hop from party music to social commentary.
And?

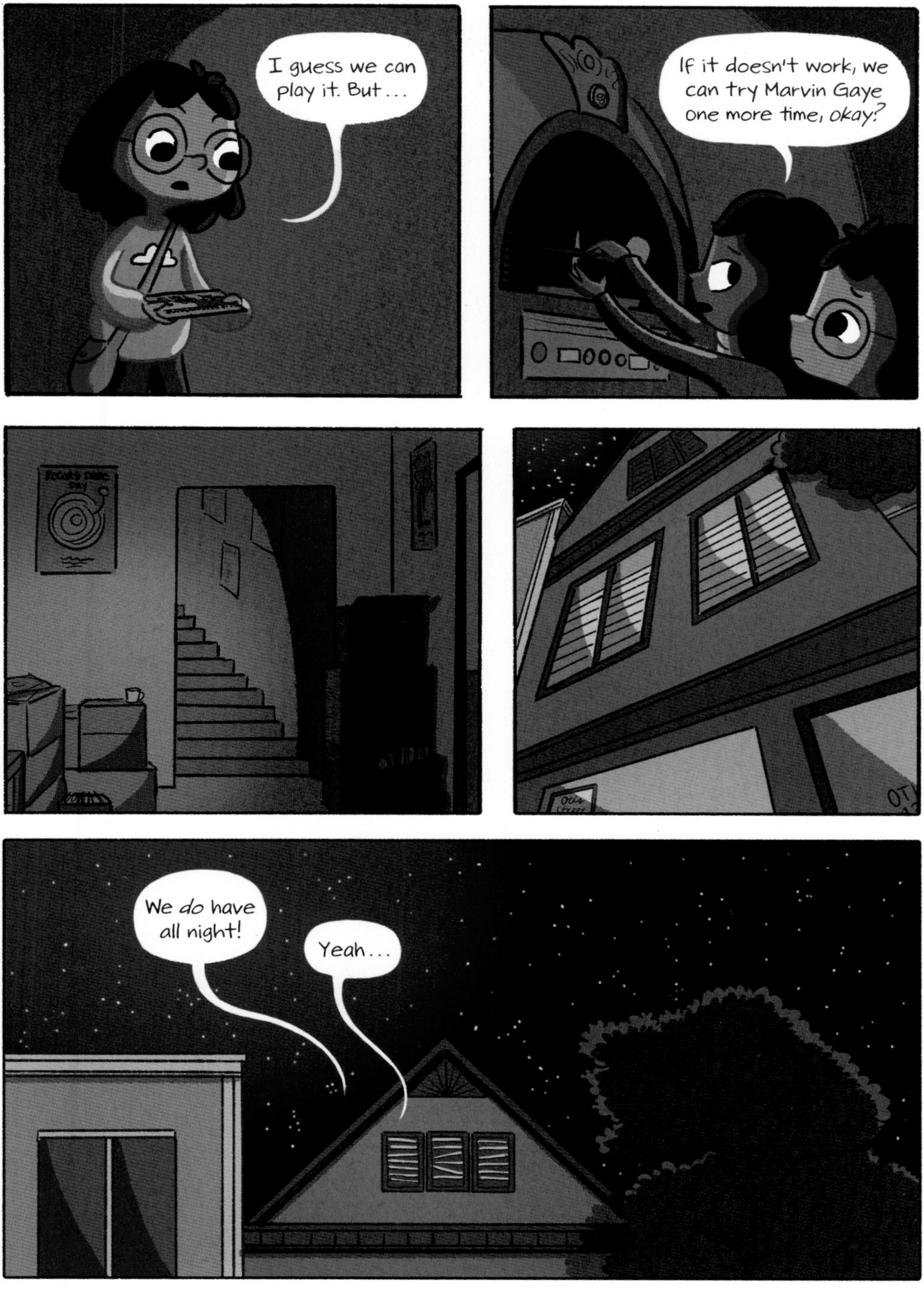
I guess we can play it. But . . .
If it doesn't work, we can try Marvin Gaye one more time, *okay?*
We *do* have all night!
Yeah . . .

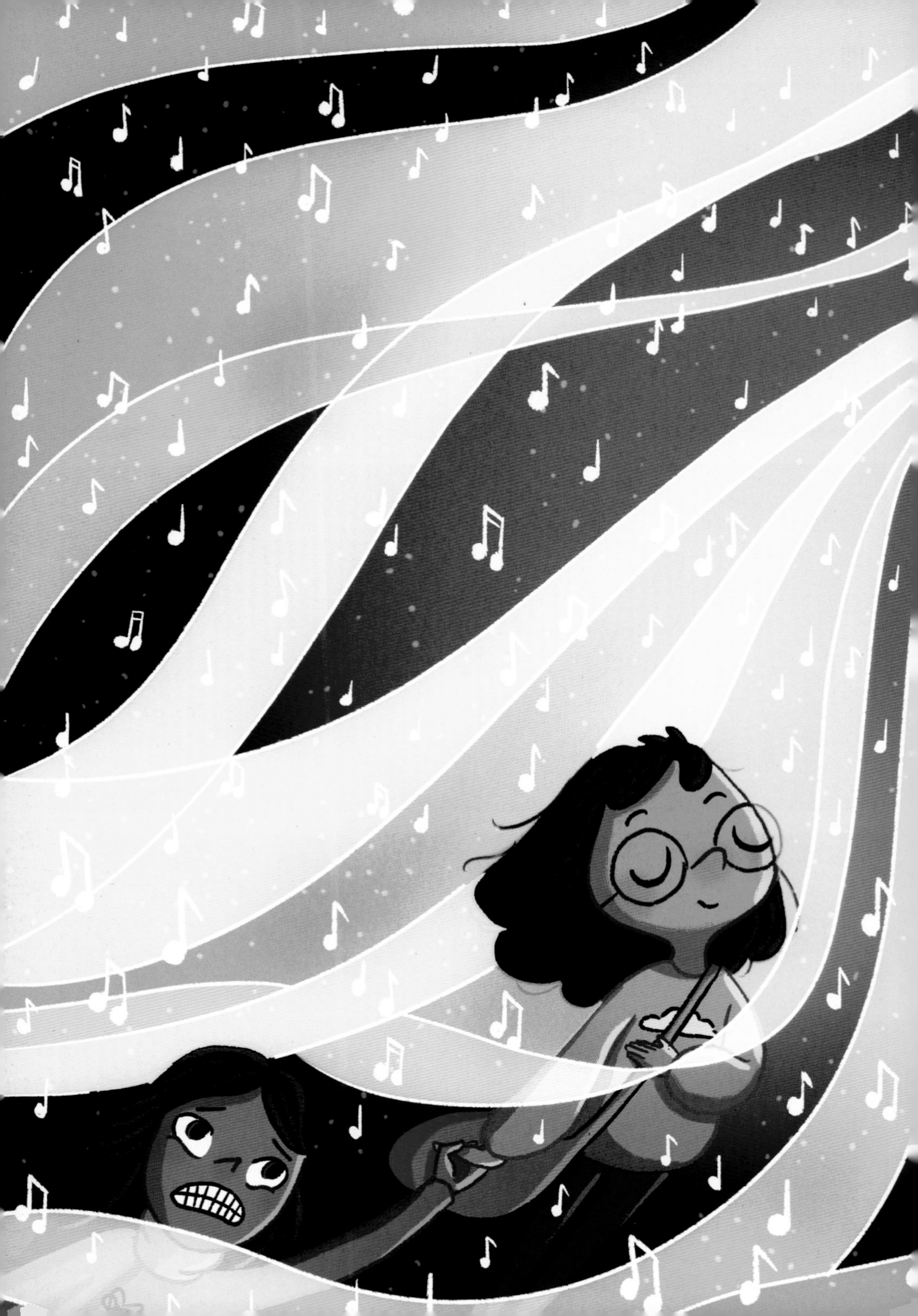

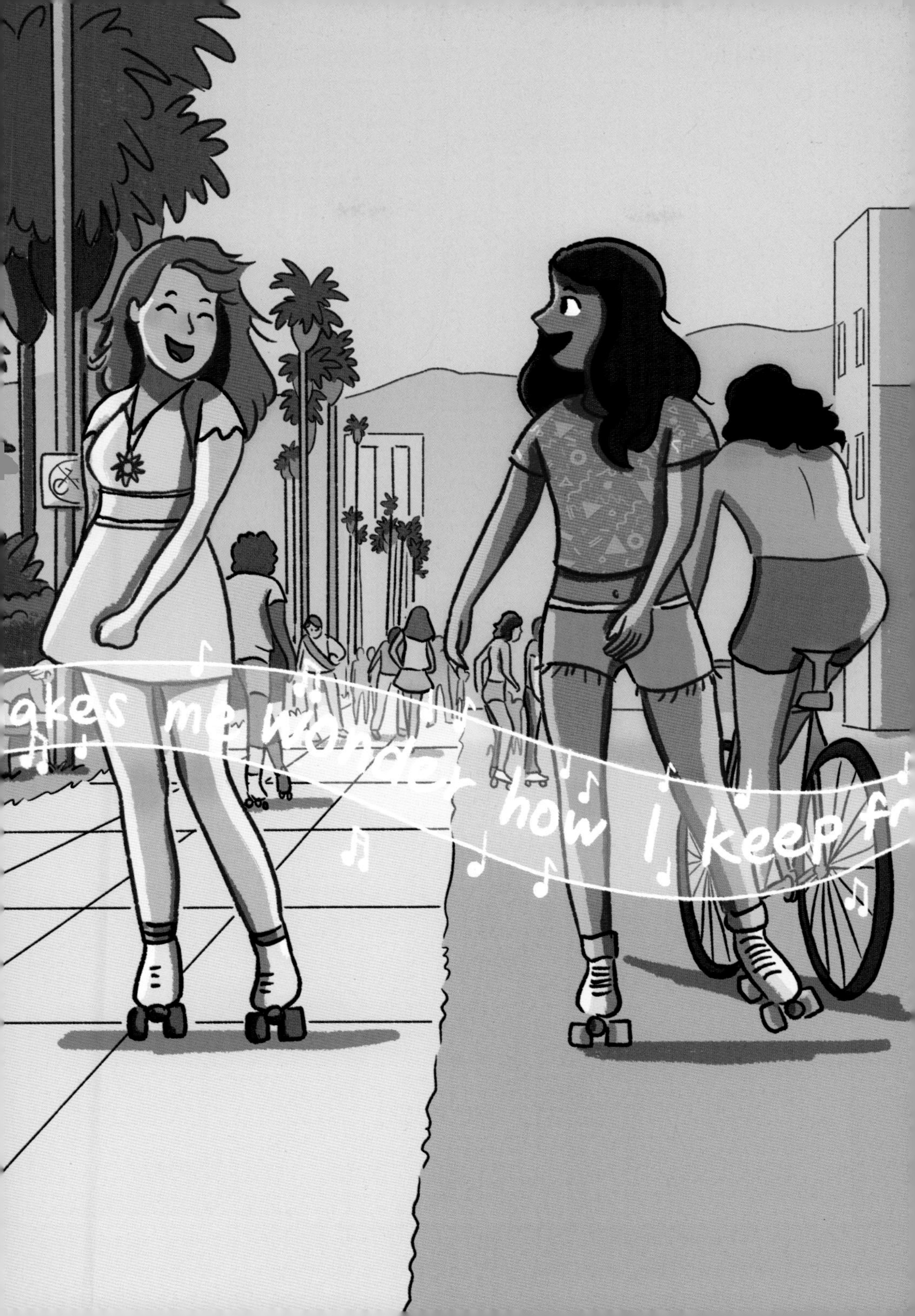
akes me wonder how I keep fr

Don't push me cause I'm close to the
Whoa.

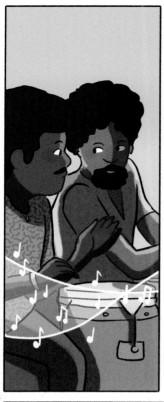

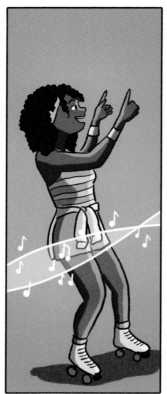

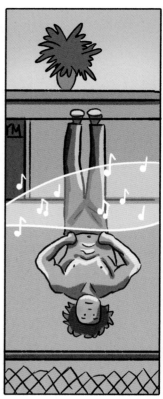

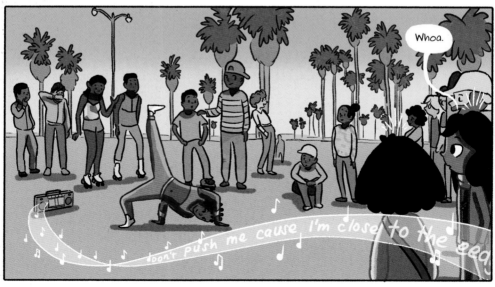

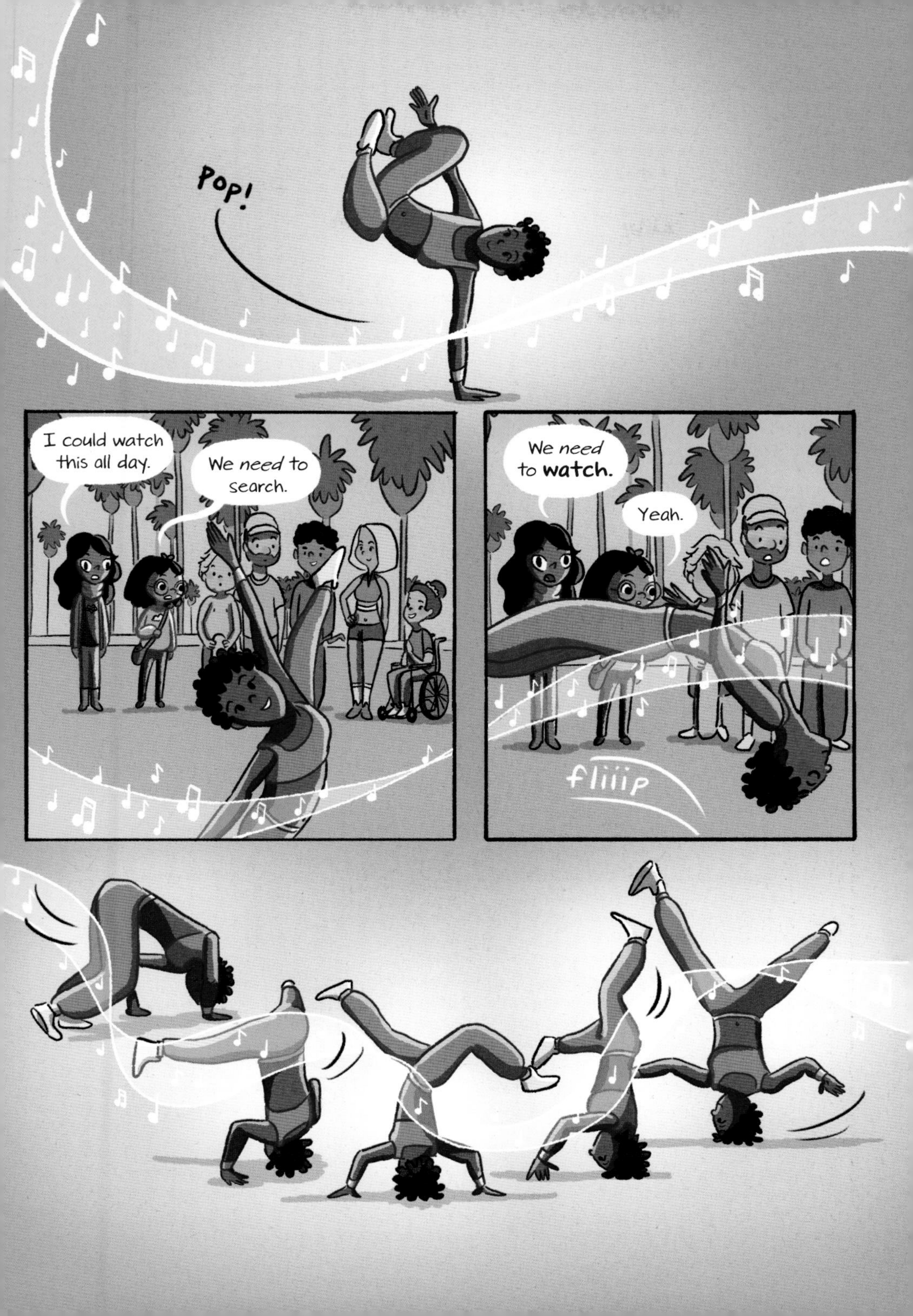
POP!
I could watch this all day.
We need to search.
We need to watch.
Yeah.
fliiip

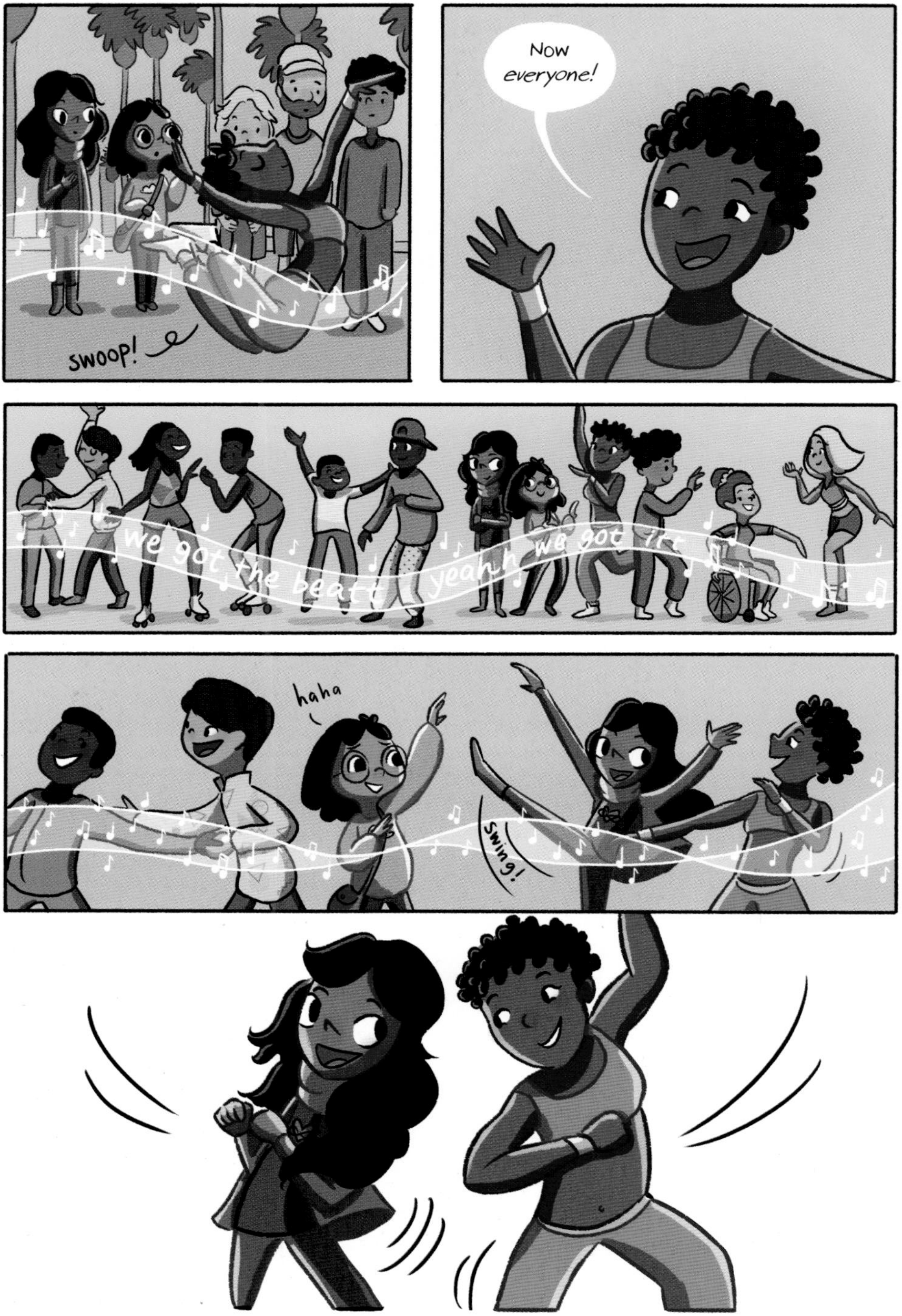
SWOOP!
Now everyone!
we got the beatt yeahh we got itt
haha
Swing!

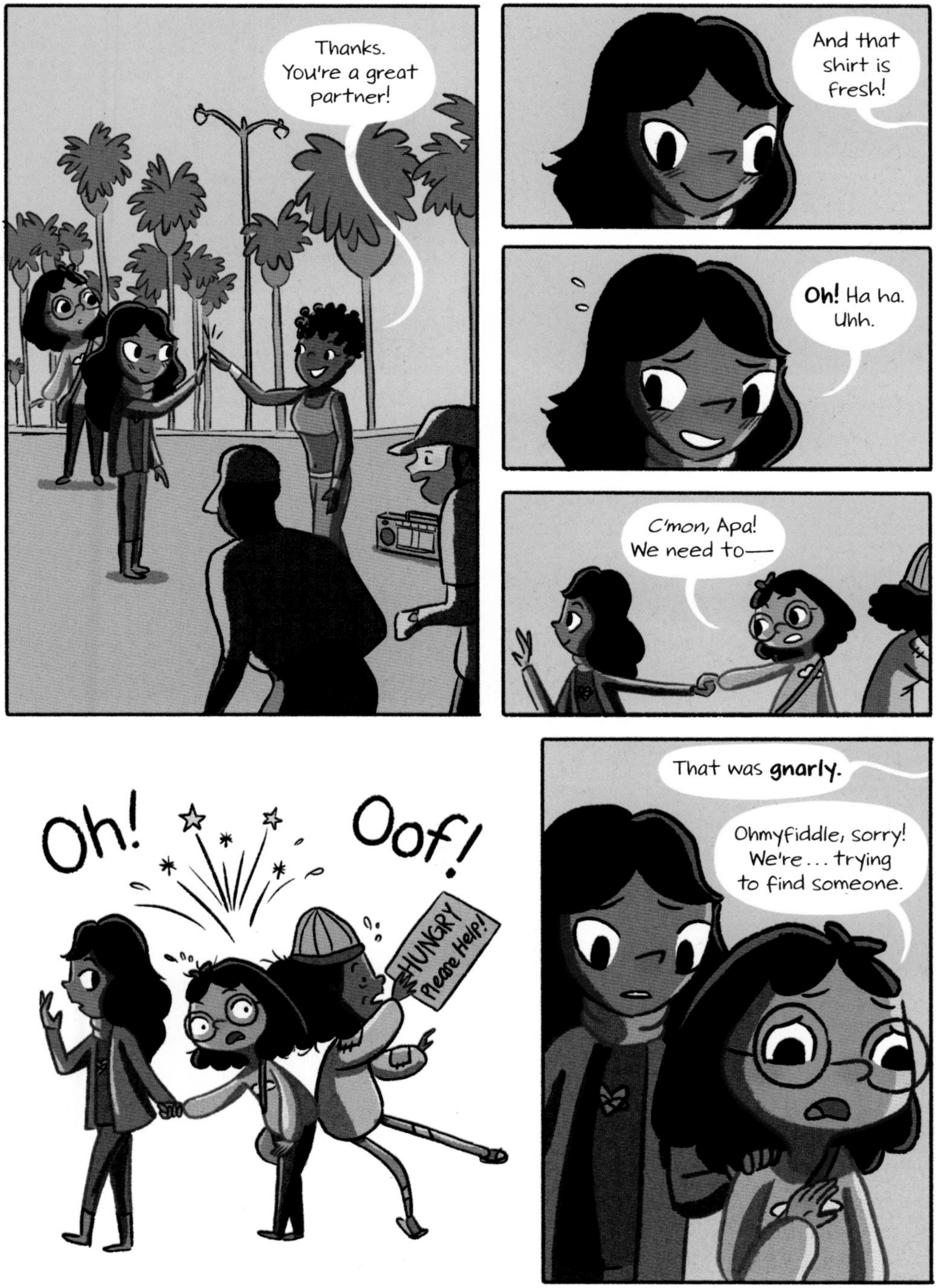
Thanks. You're a great partner!
And that shirt is fresh!
Oh! Ha ha. Uhh.
C'mon, Apa! We need to—
Oh!
Oof!
HUNGRY Please Help!
That was **gnarly.**
Ohmyfiddle, sorry! We're . . . trying to find someone.

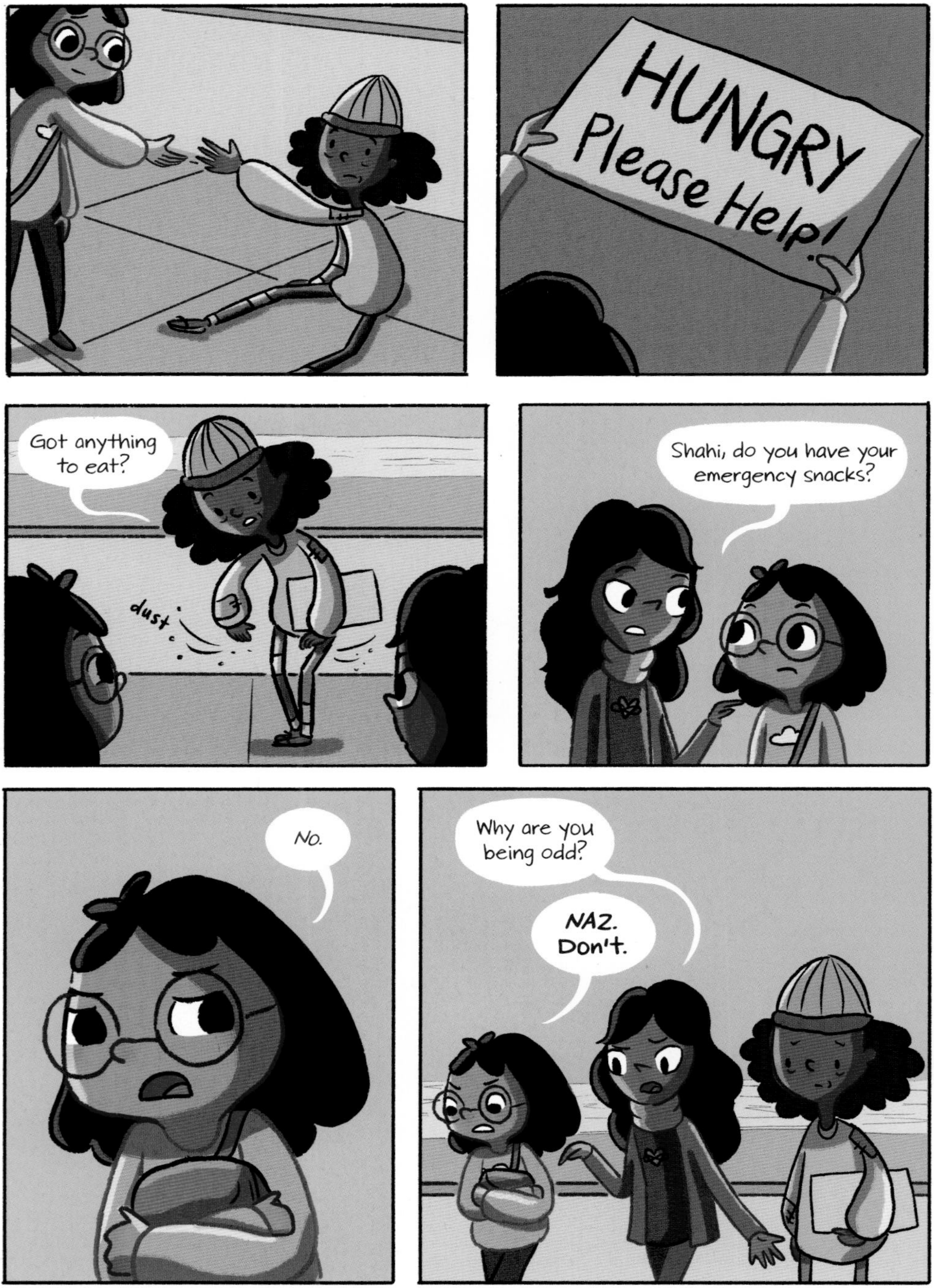
HUNGRY
Please Help!
Got anything to eat?
dust
Shahi, do you have your emergency snacks?
No.
Why are you being odd?
NAZ. Don't.

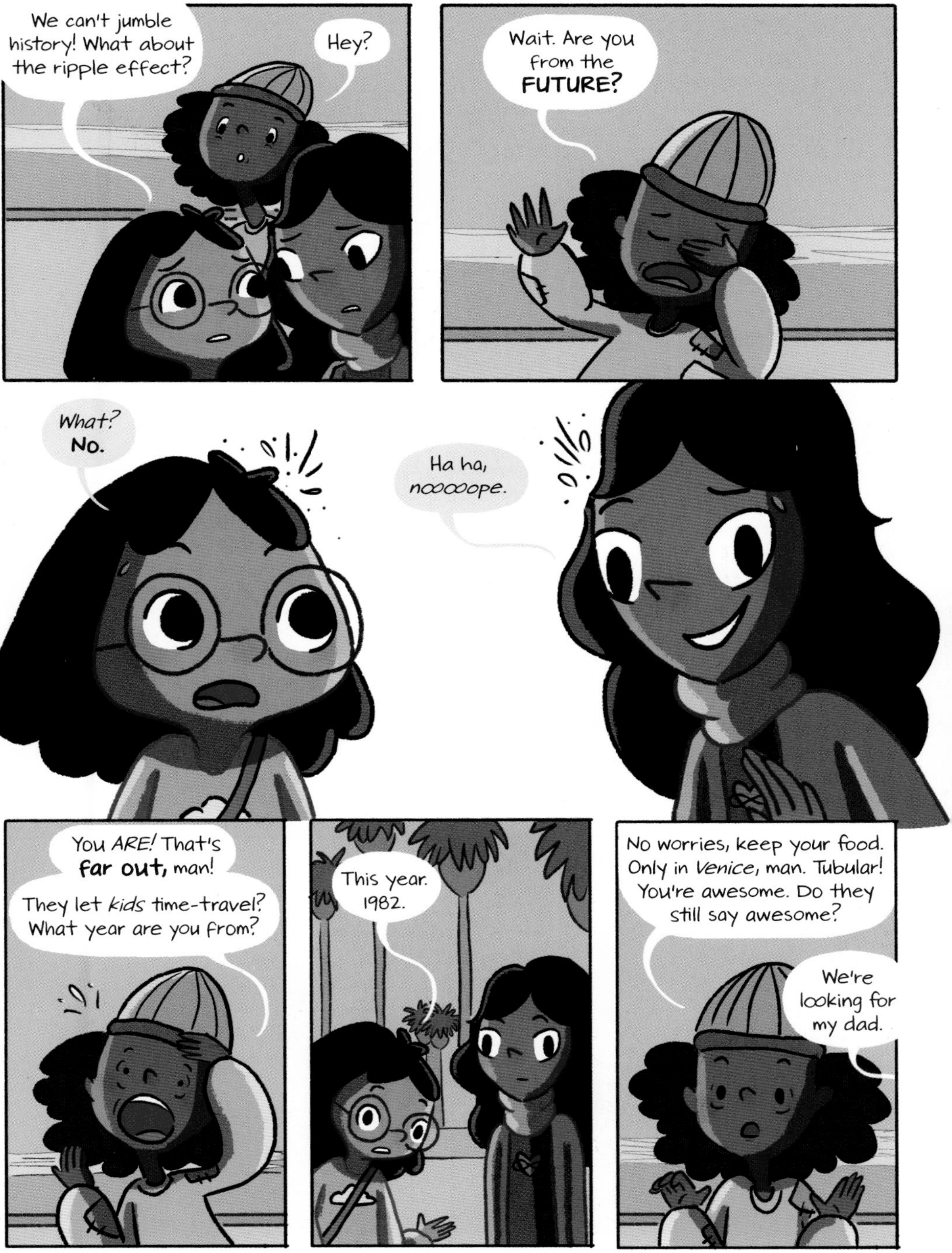
We can't jumble history! What about the ripple effect?
Hey?
Wait. Are you from the **FUTURE?**
What? **No.**
Ha ha, *nooooope.*
You *ARE!* That's **far out,** man!
They let *kids* time-travel? What year are you from?
This year. 1982.
No worries, keep your food. Only in *Venice*, man. Tubular! You're awesome. Do they still say awesome?
We're looking for my dad.

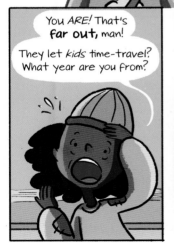

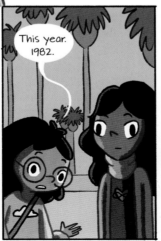

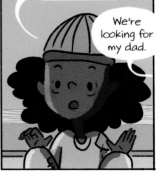

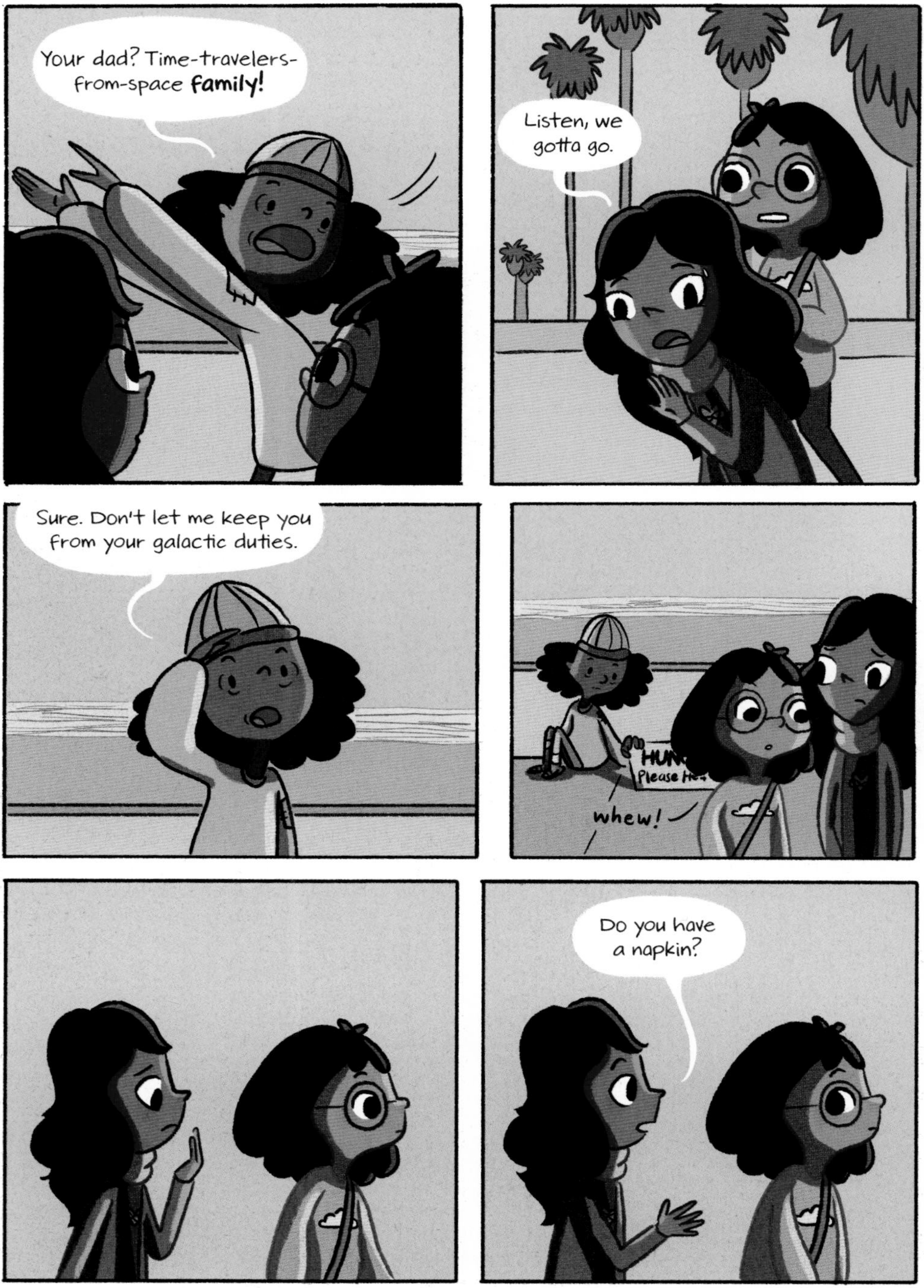
Your dad? Time-travelers-from-space **family!**
Listen, we gotta go.
Sure. Don't let me keep you from your galactic duties.
whew!
Do you have a napkin?

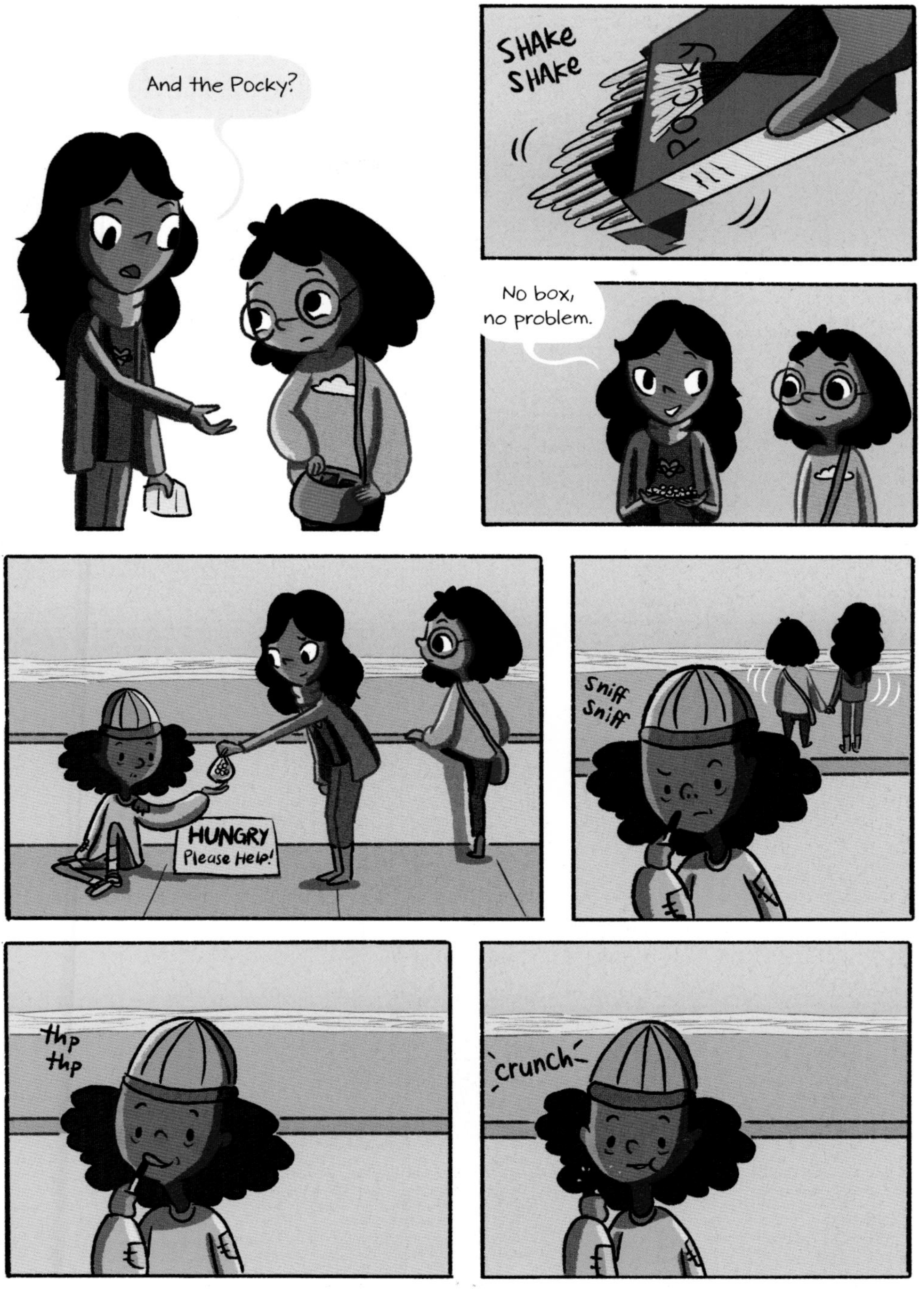
And the Pocky?
SHAKE SHAKE
POCKY
No box, no problem.
HUNGRY Please Help!
Sniff Sniff
thp thp
crunch

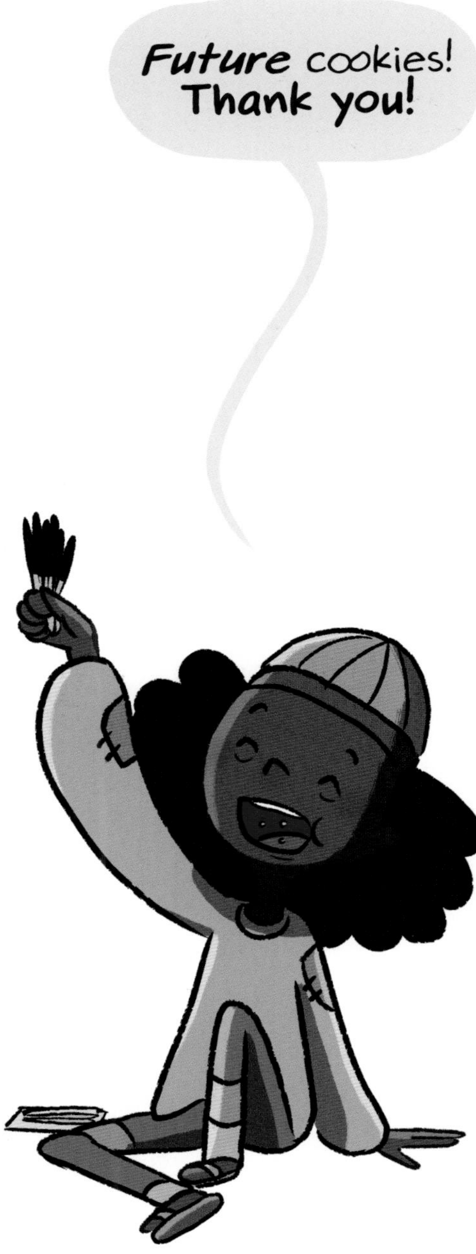
Future cookies! Thank you!

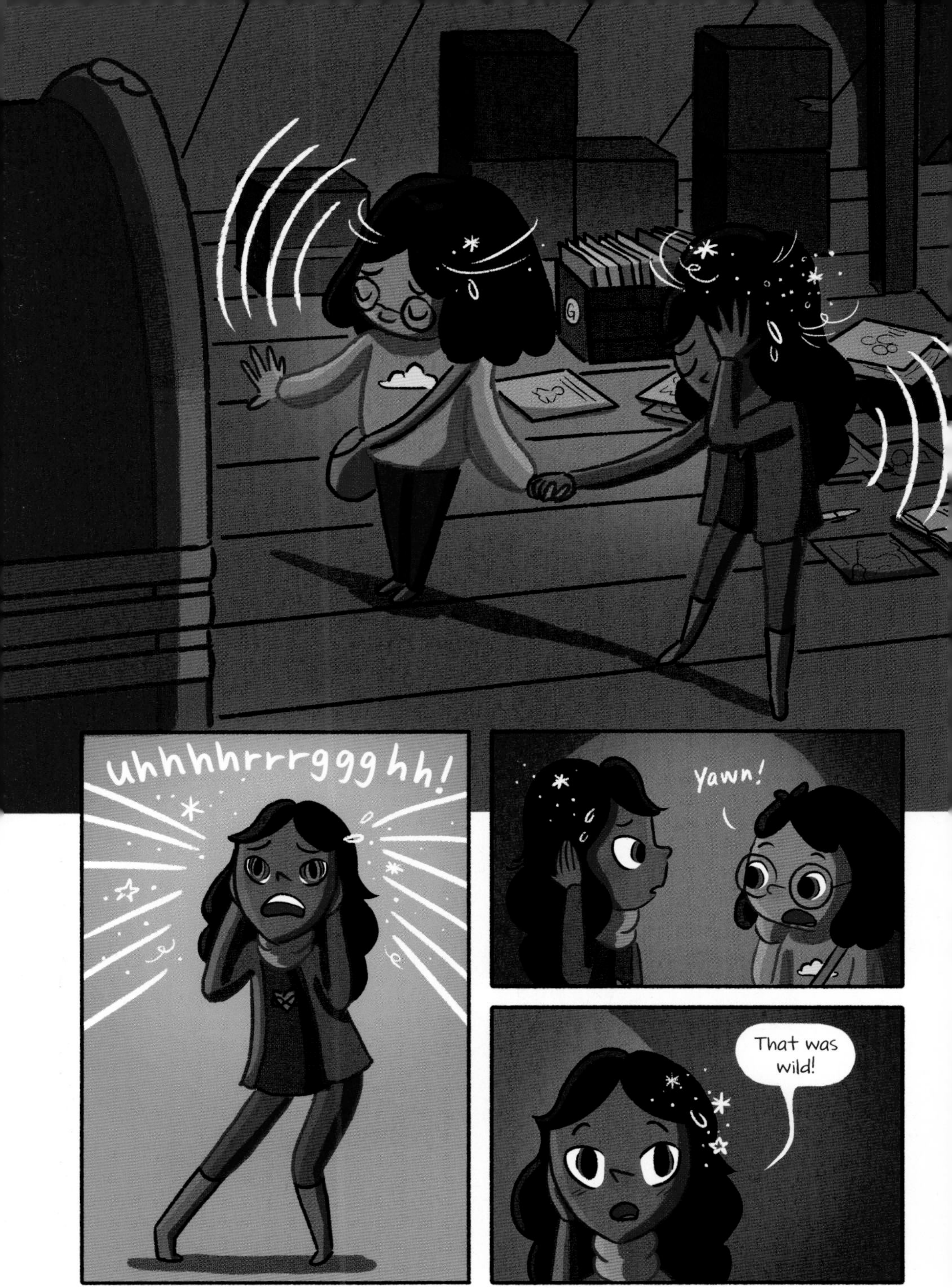
uhhhhrrrggghh!
Yawn!
That was wild!

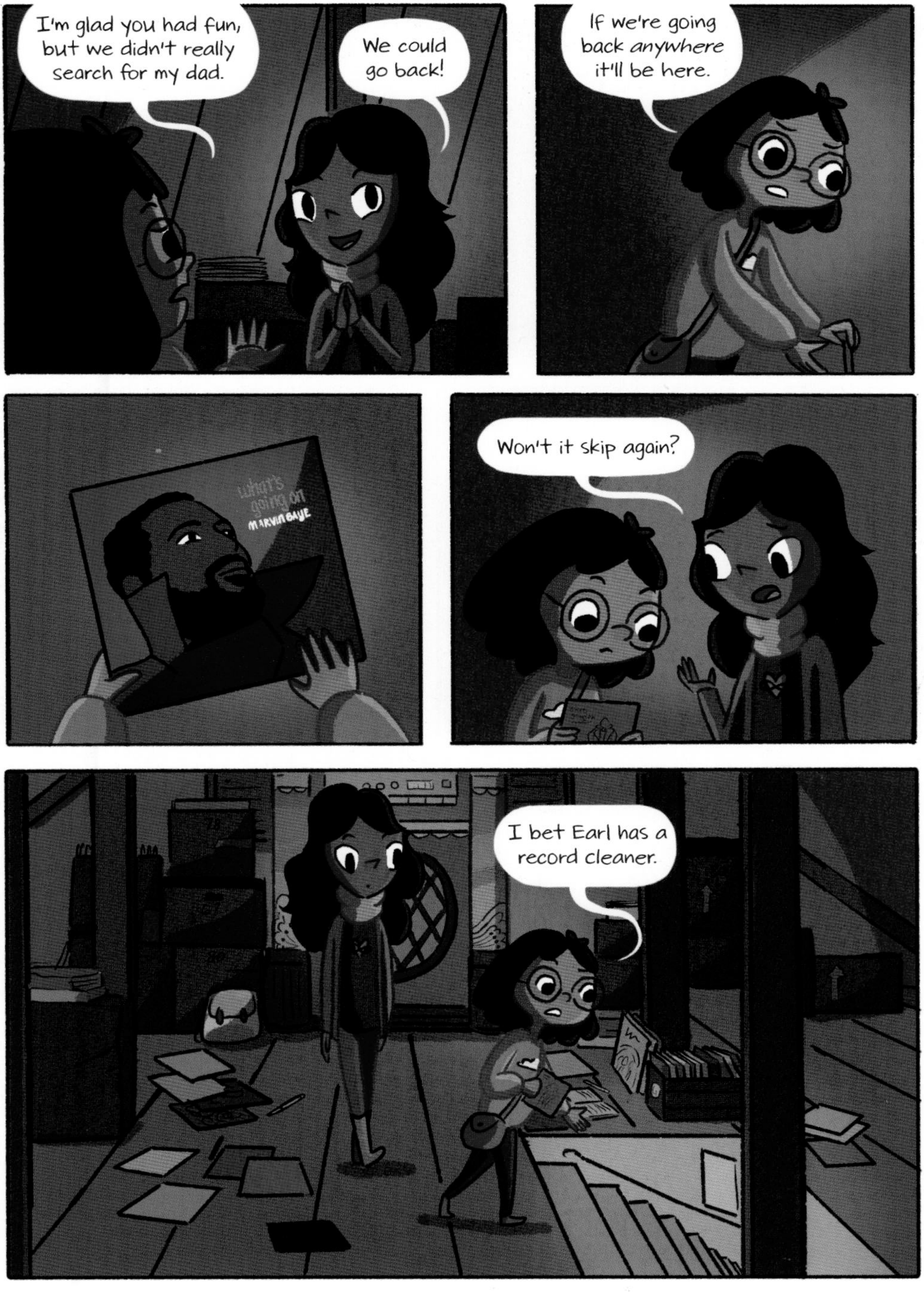

I'm glad you had fun, but we didn't really search for my dad.
We could go back!
If we're going back anywhere it'll be here.
what's going on
MARVIN GAYE
Won't it skip again?
I bet Earl has a record cleaner.

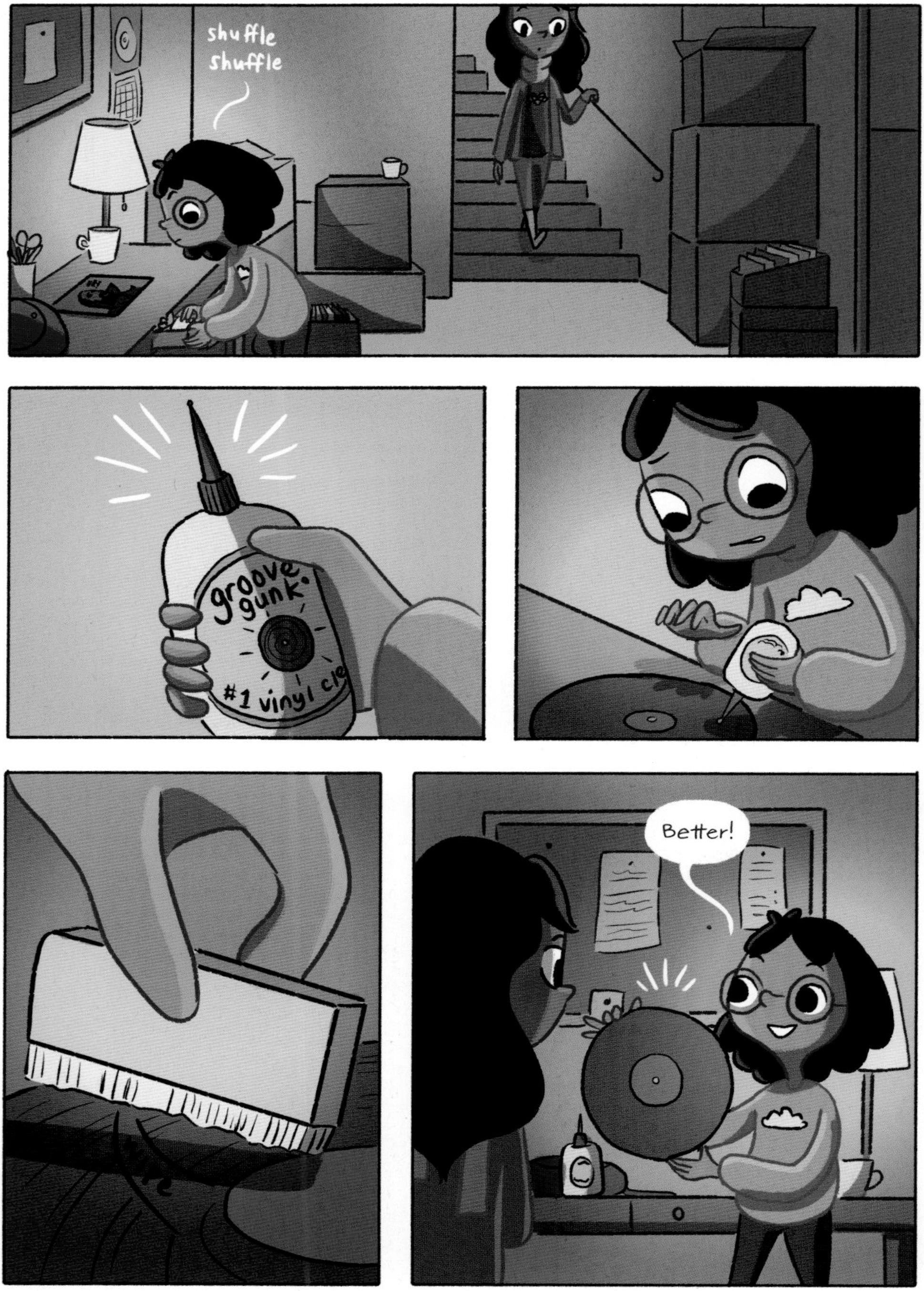
shuffle
shuffle
groove gunk.
#1 vinyl cle
Better!

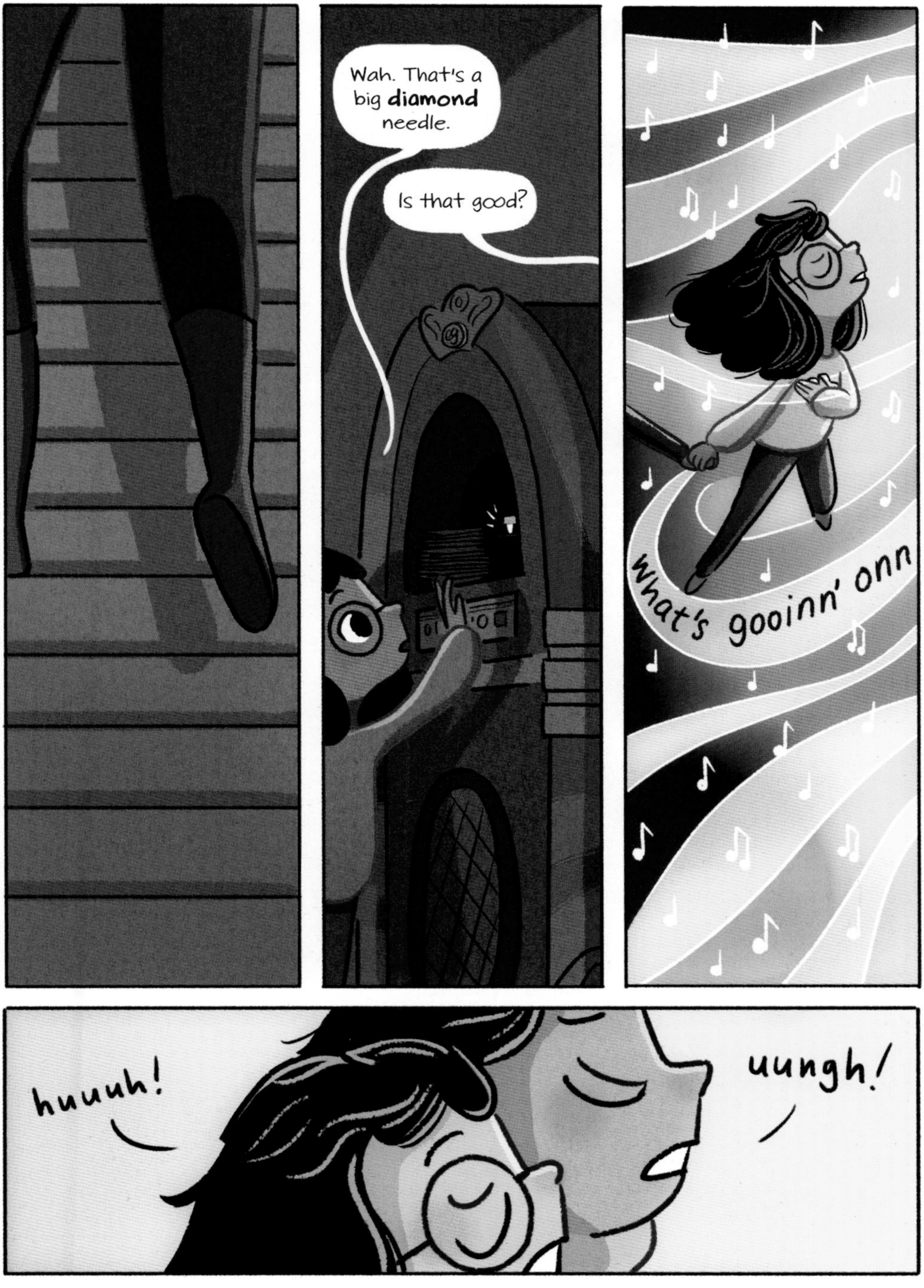
Wah. That's a big diamond needle.
Is that good?
What's gooinn' onn
huuuh!
uungh!

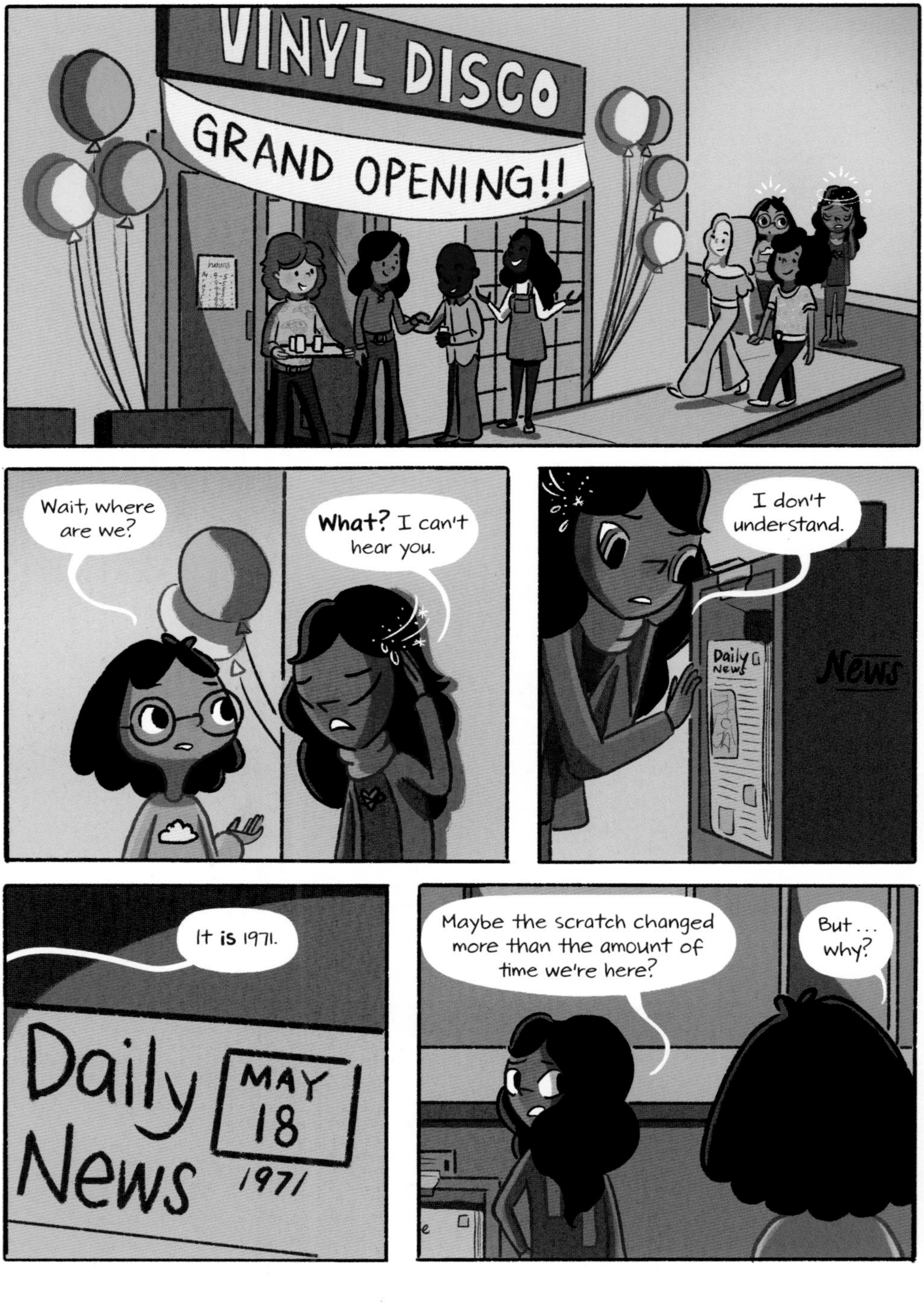
VINYL DISCO
GRAND OPENING!!
hours
Wait, where are we?
What? I can't hear you.
I don't understand.
Daily News
News
It is 1971.
Daily News
MAY 18
1971
Maybe the scratch changed more than the amount of time we're here?
But... why?

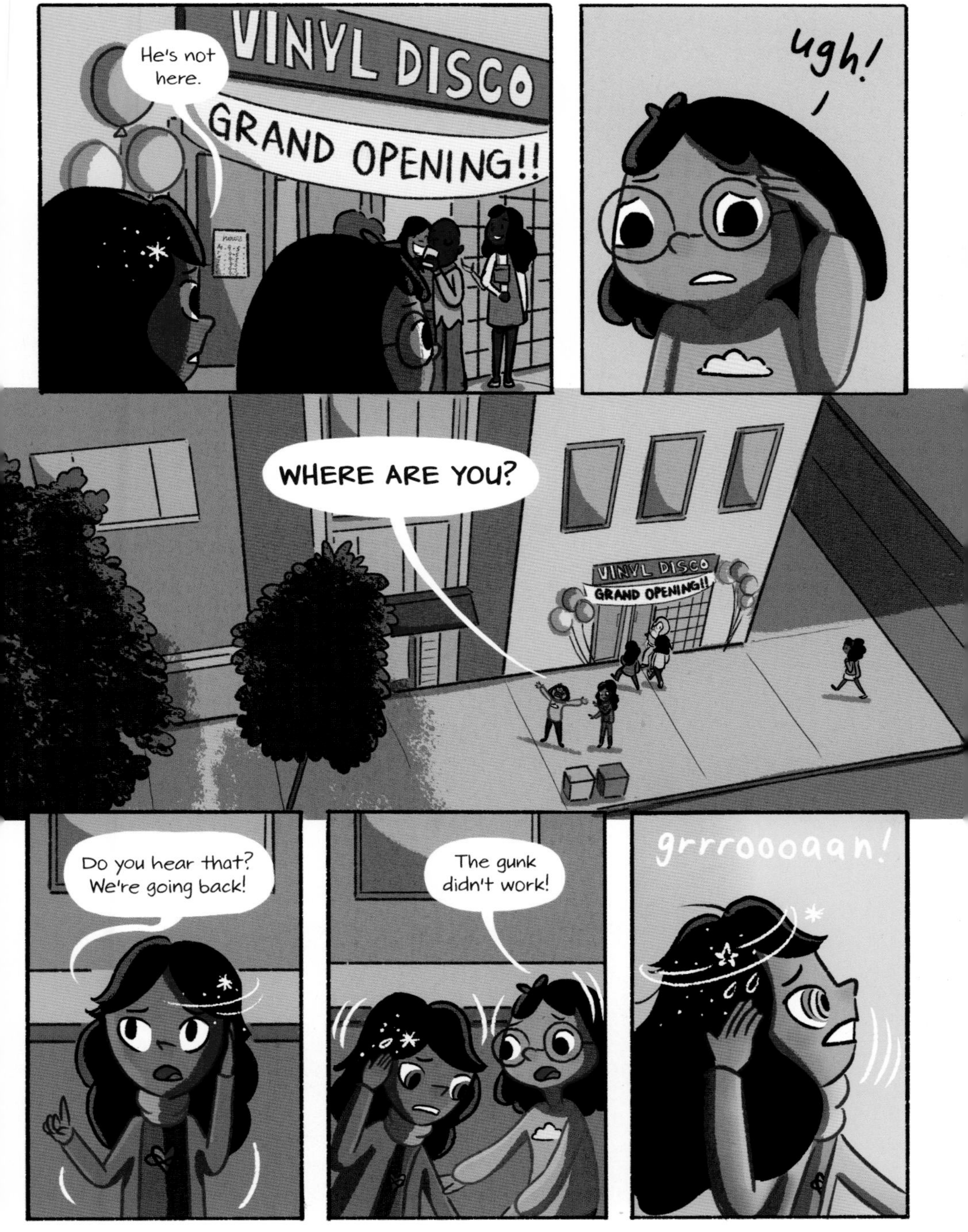
VINYL DISCO
GRAND OPENING!!
He's not here.
ugh!
WHERE ARE YOU?
VINYL DISCO
GRAND OPENING!!
Do you hear that? We're going back!
The gunk didn't work!
grrroooaan!

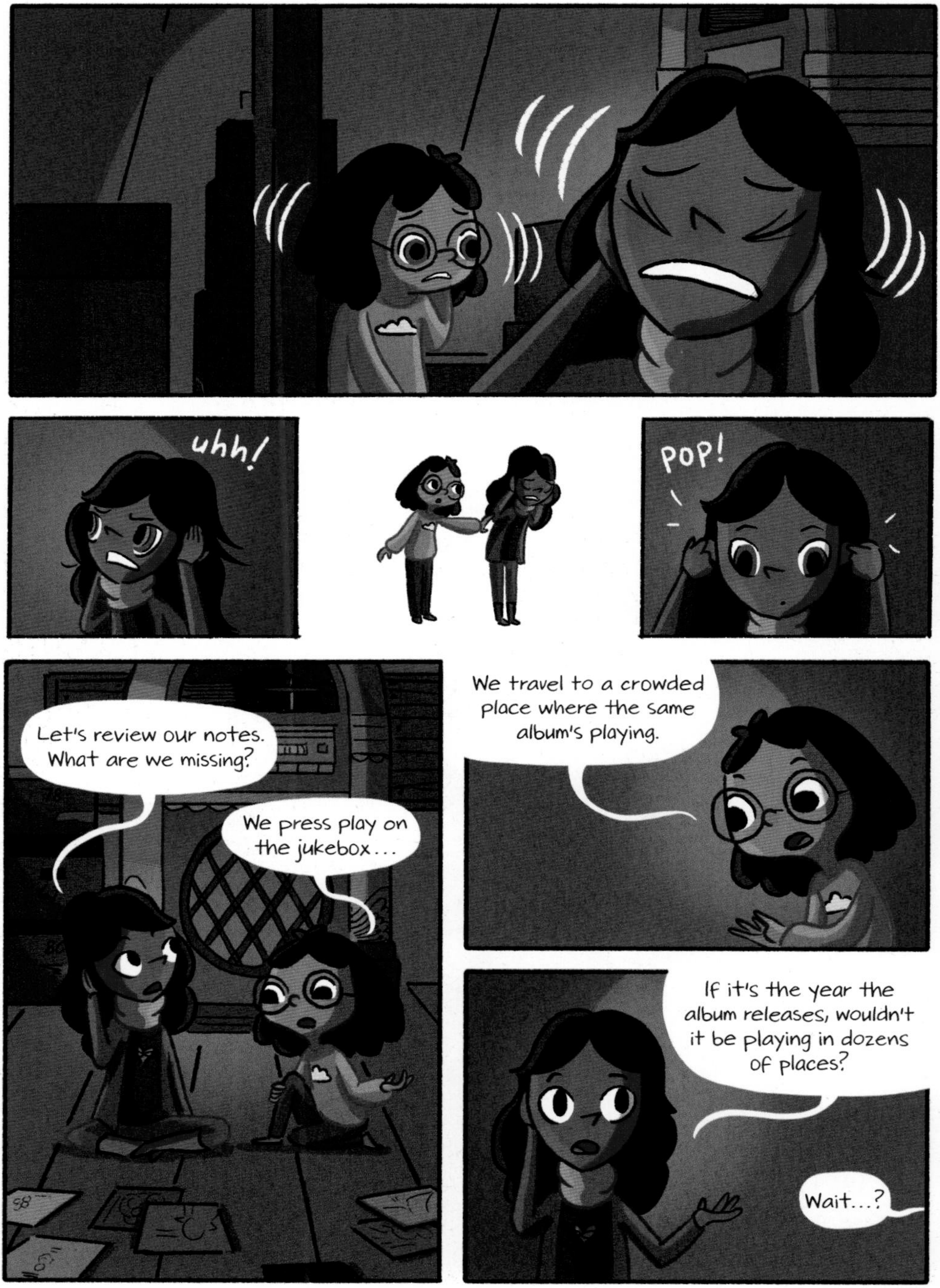
uhh!
POP!
Let's review our notes. What are we missing?
We press play on the jukebox...
We travel to a crowded place where the same album's playing.
If it's the year the album releases, wouldn't it be playing in dozens of places?
Wait...?

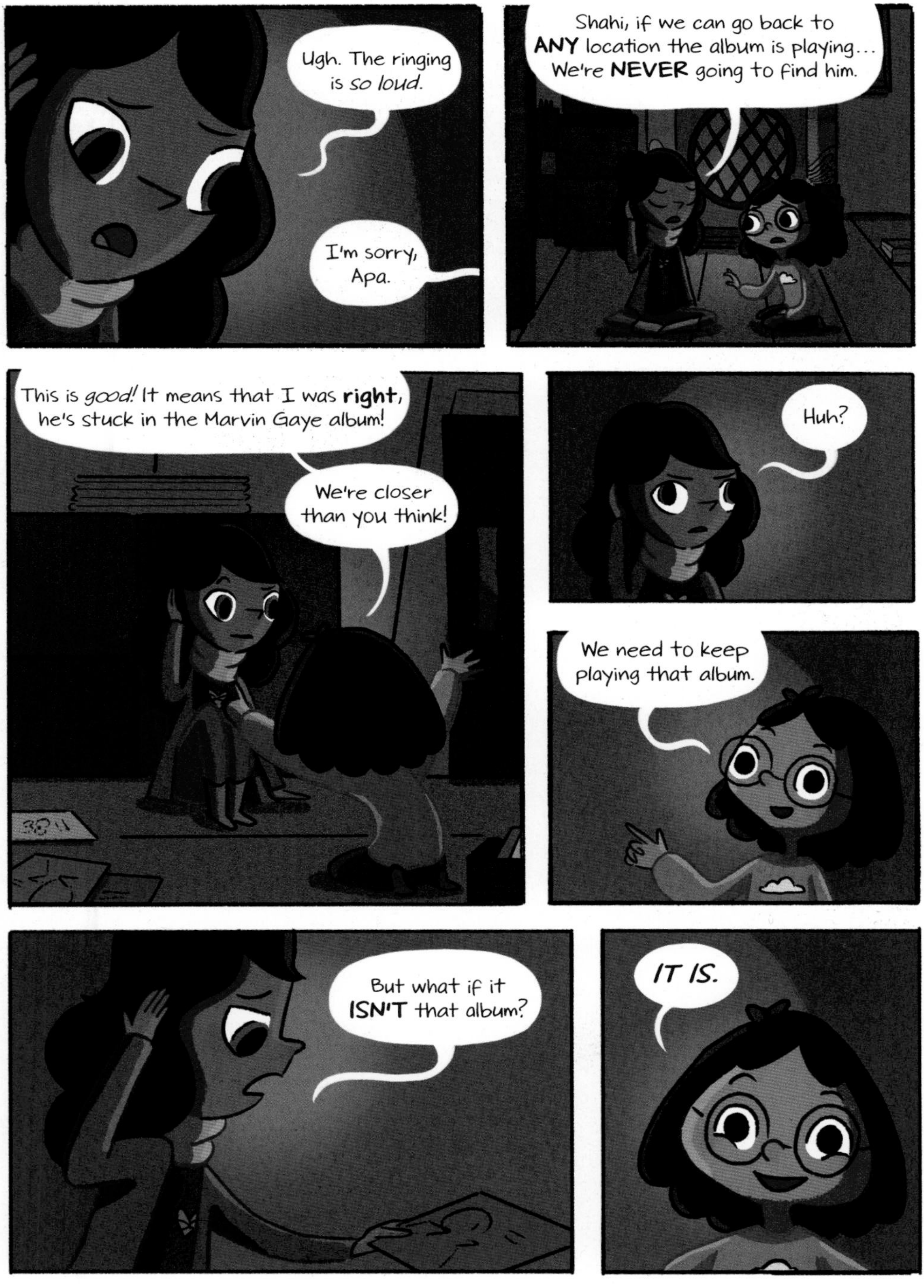
Ugh. The ringing is *so loud*.
I'm sorry, Apa.
Shahi, if we can go back to **ANY** location the album is playing... We're **NEVER** going to find him.
This is *good!* It means that I was **right**, he's stuck in the Marvin Gaye album!
We're closer than you think!
Huh?
We need to keep playing that album.
But what if it **ISN'T** that album?
IT IS.

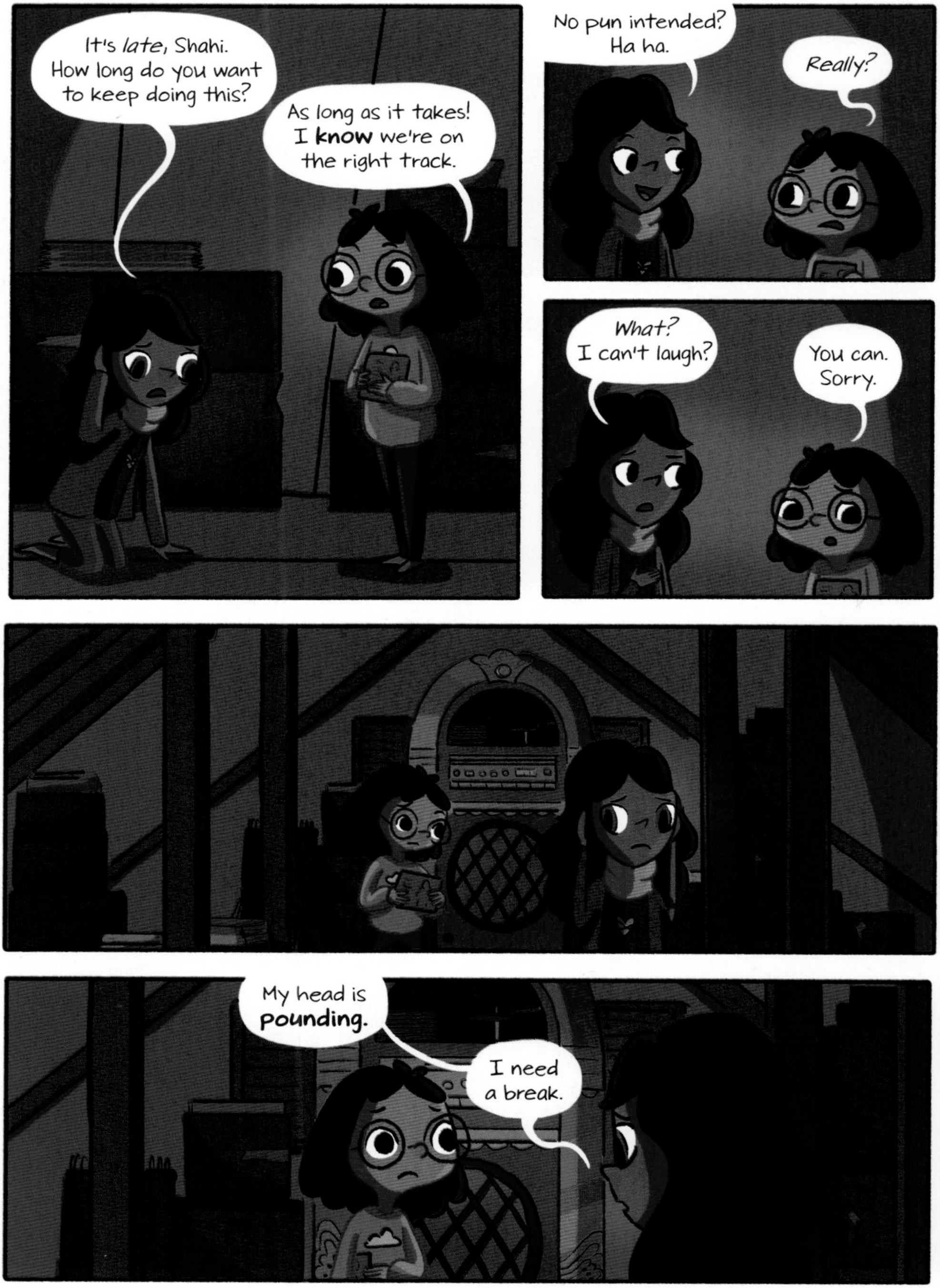
It's *late*, Shahi. How long do you want to keep doing this?
As long as it takes! I **know** we're on the right track.
No pun intended? Ha ha.
Really?
What? I can't laugh?
You can. Sorry.
My head is **pounding.**
I need a break.

It's not affecting me the same way.

I can...go alone.

I **can't** let you do that!

My ears will recover.

And...if they don't?

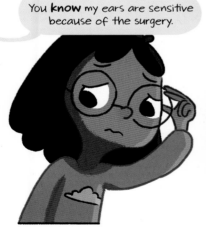

You **know** my ears are sensitive because of the surgery.

But...I can't lose you both.

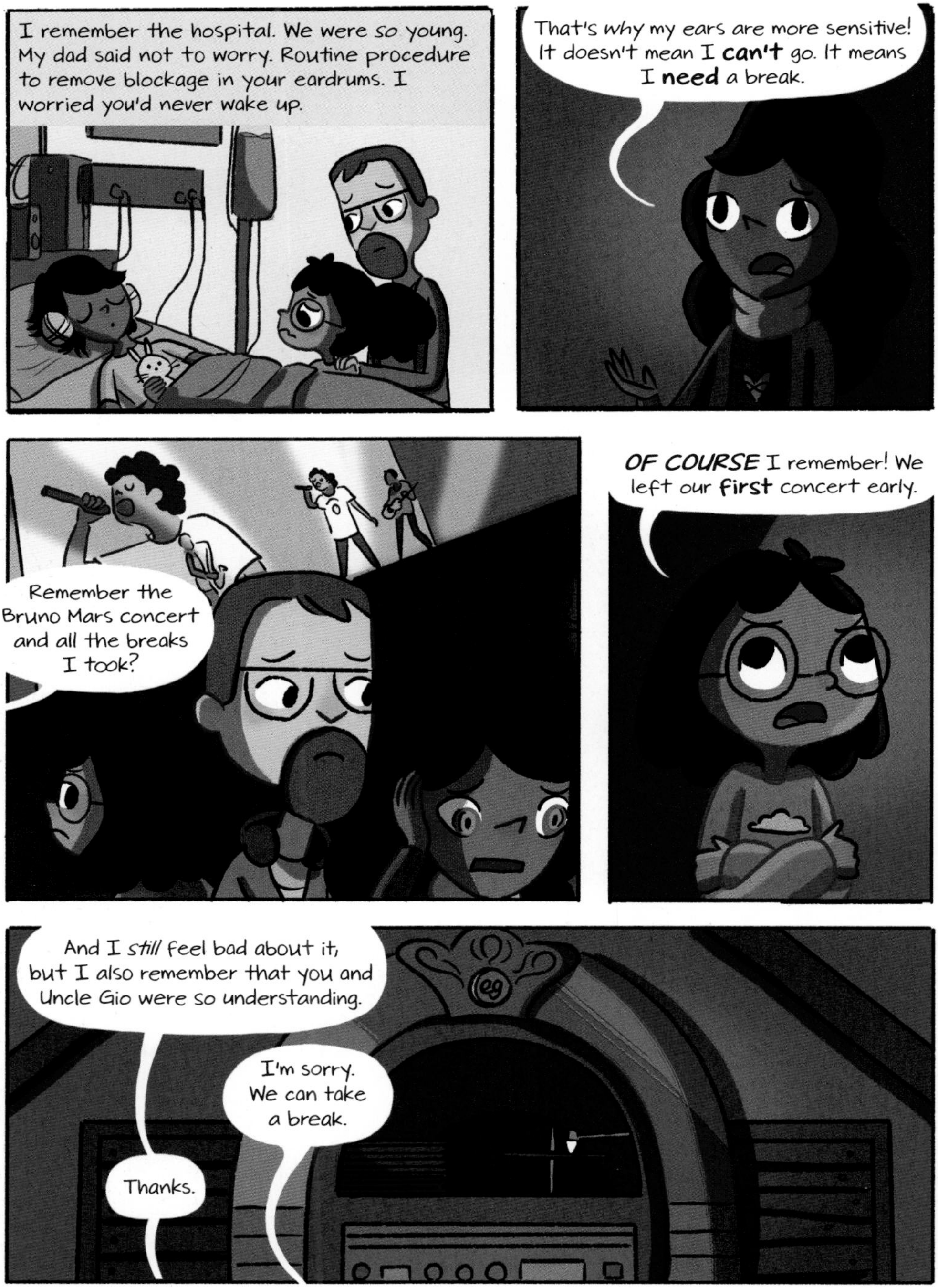

I remember the hospital. We were so young. My dad said not to worry. Routine procedure to remove blockage in your eardrums. I worried you'd never wake up.
That's *why* my ears are more sensitive! It doesn't mean I **can't** go. It means I **need** a break.
Remember the Bruno Mars concert and all the breaks I took?
OF COURSE I remember! We left our **first** concert early.
And I *still* feel bad about it, but I also remember that you and Uncle Gio were so understanding.
I'm sorry. We can take a break.
Thanks.

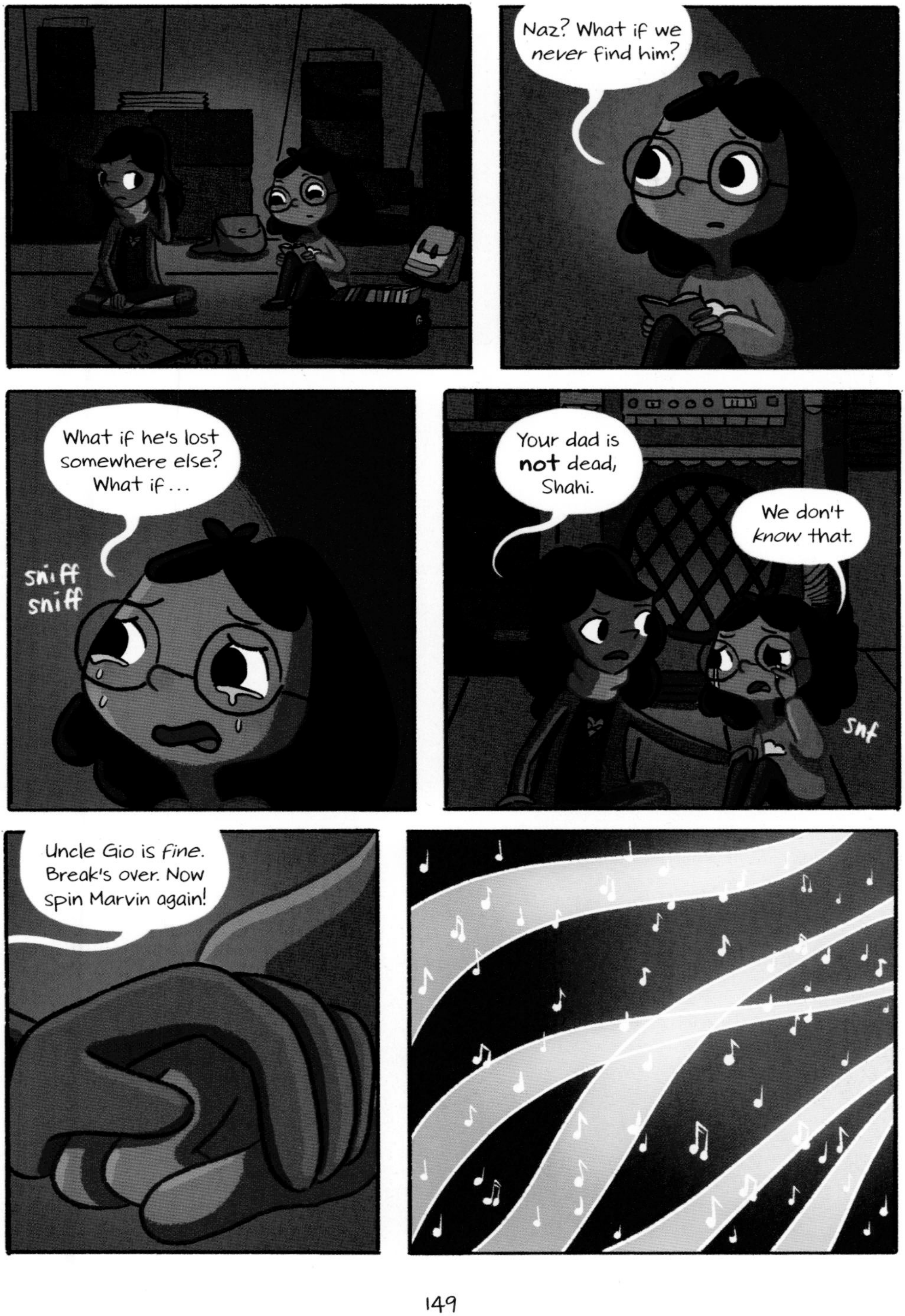
Naz? What if we never find him?
What if he's lost somewhere else? What if...
sniff sniff
Your dad is **not** dead, Shahi.
We don't know that.
snf
Uncle Gio is *fine*. Break's over. Now spin Marvin again!

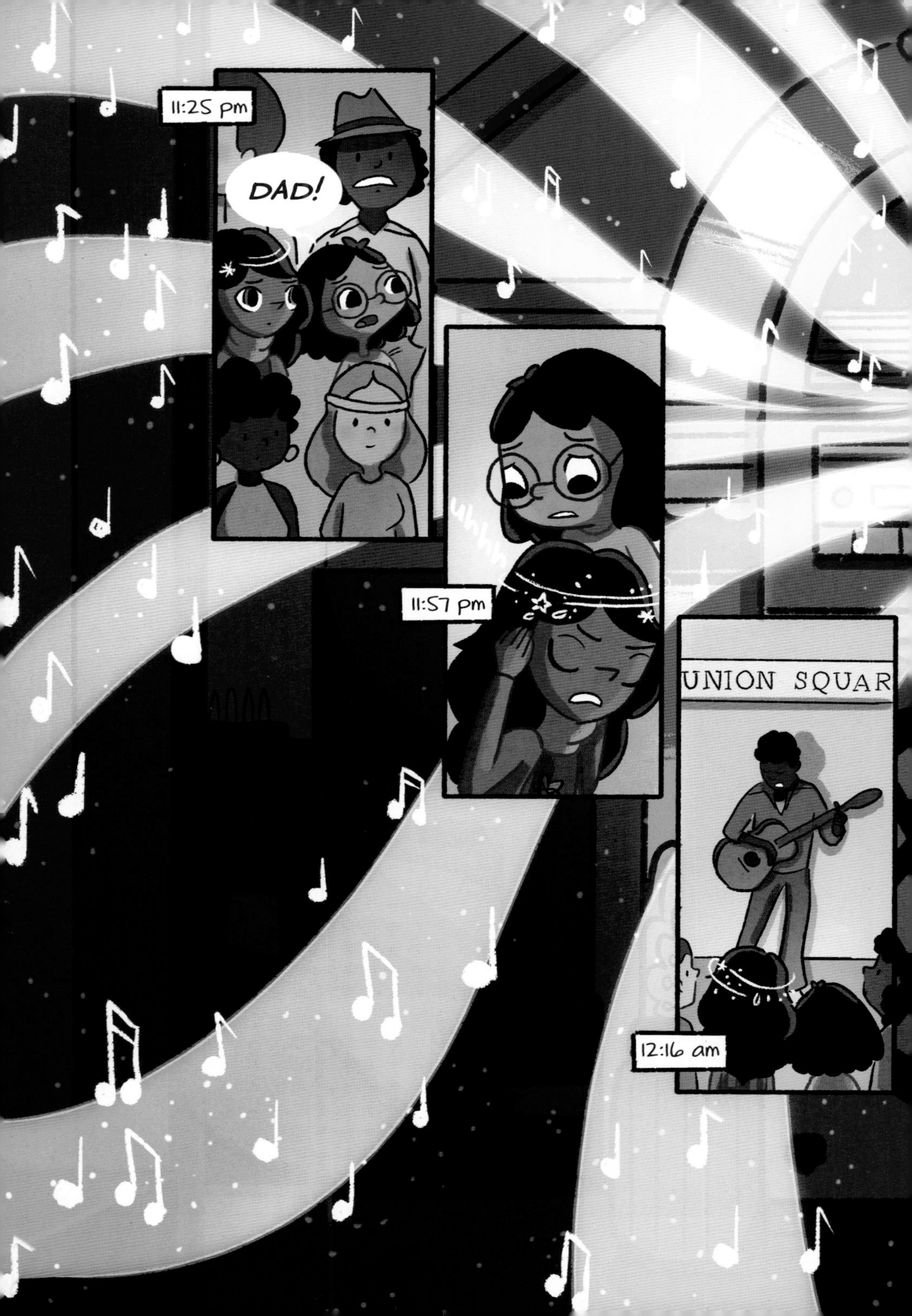
11:25 pm
DAD!
11:57 pm
UNION SQUAR
12:16 am

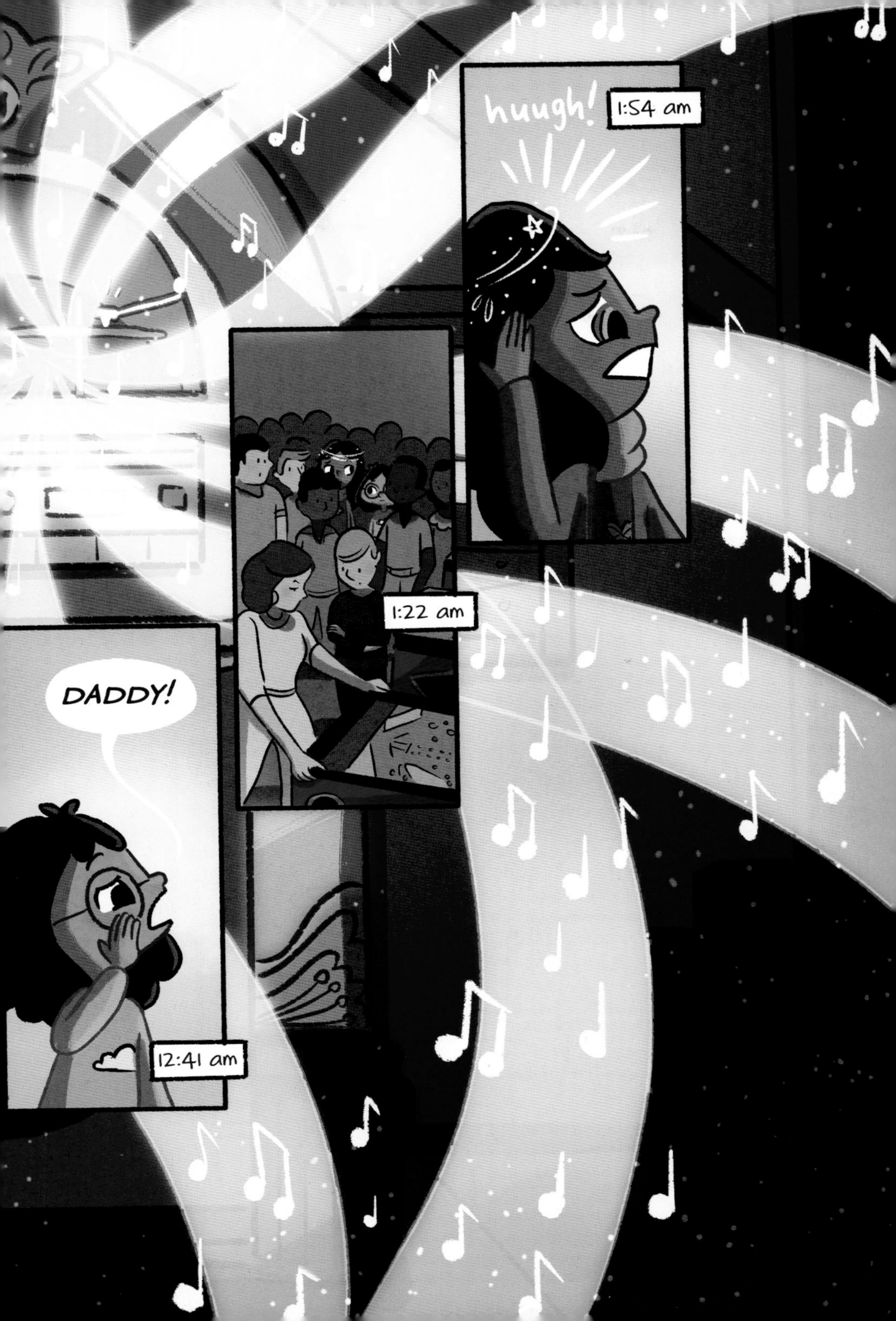
DADDY!
12:41 am
1:22 am
huugh!
1:54 am

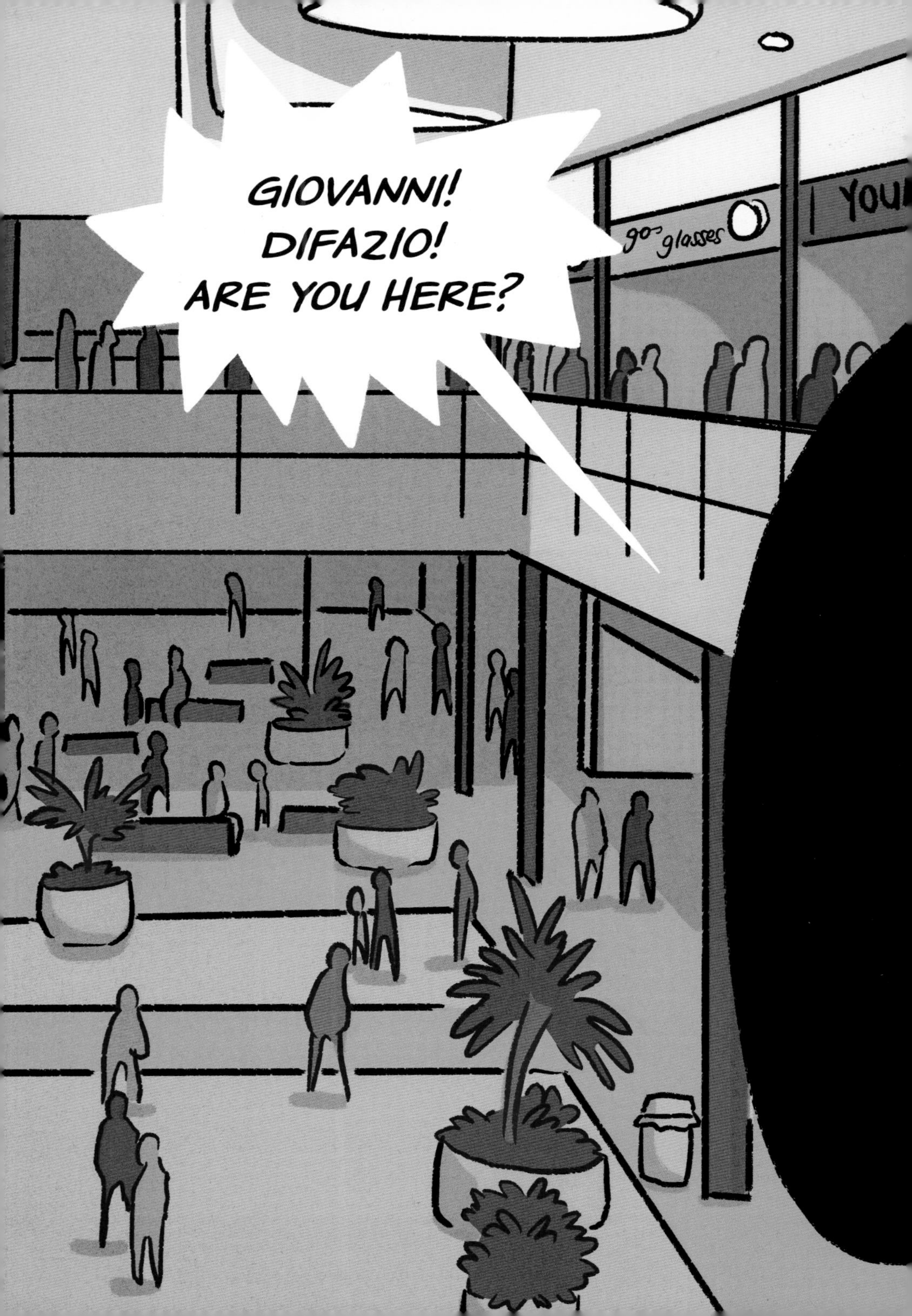
GIOVANNI! DIFAZIO! ARE YOU HERE?
go glasses
YOU

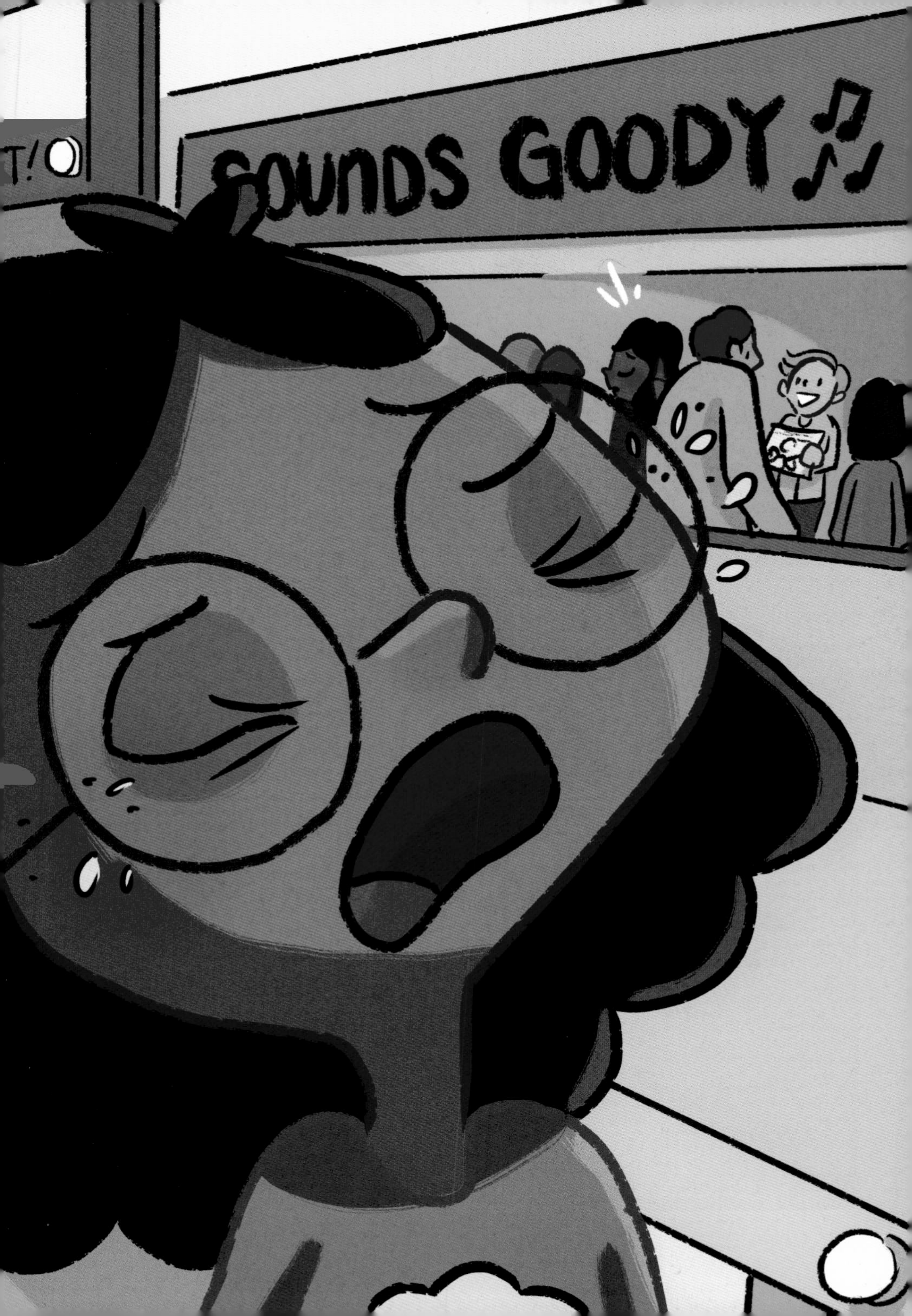
SOUNDS GOODY

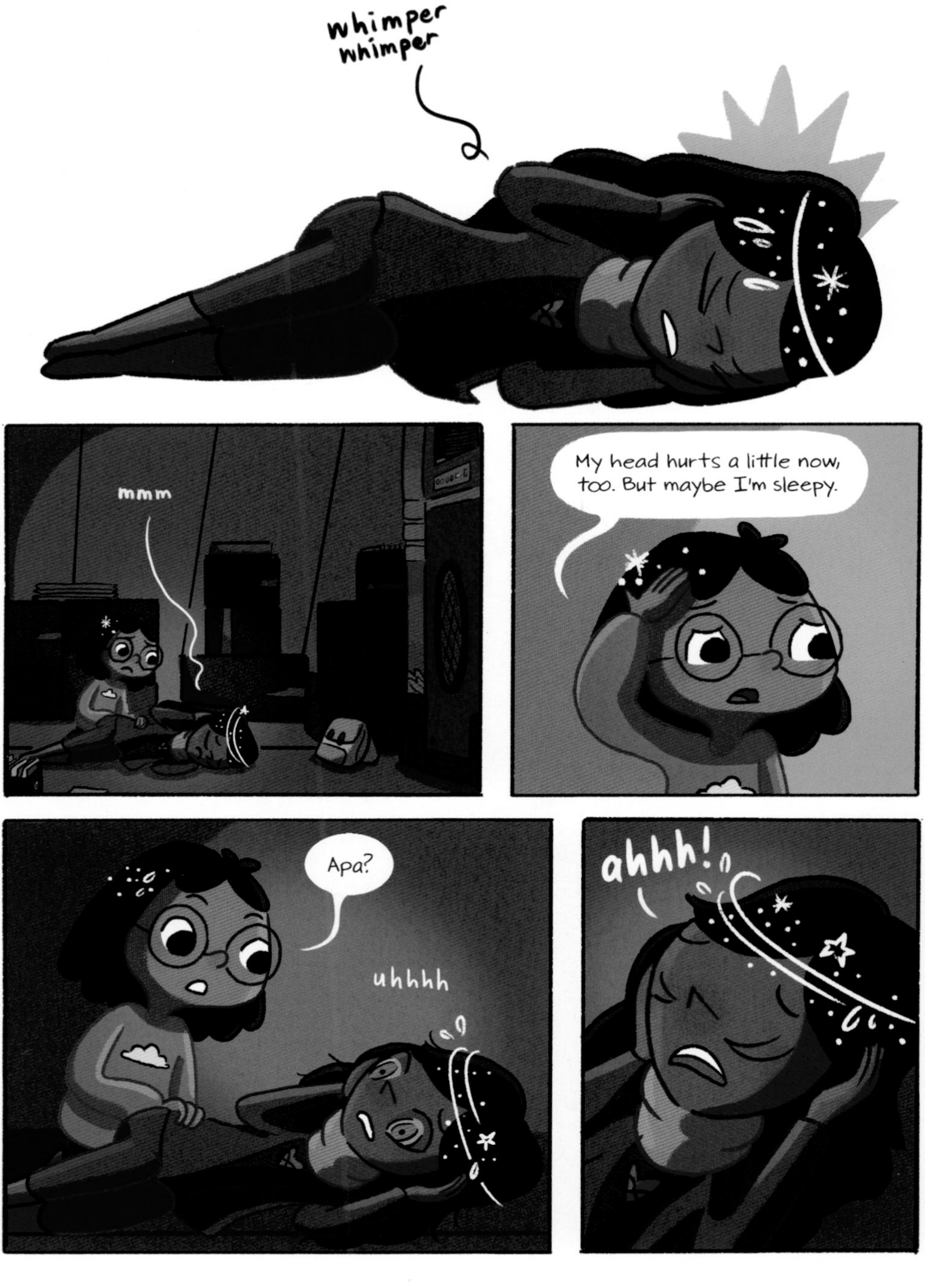
whimper
whimper
mmm
My head hurts a little now, too. But maybe I'm sleepy.
Apa?
uhhhh
ahhh!

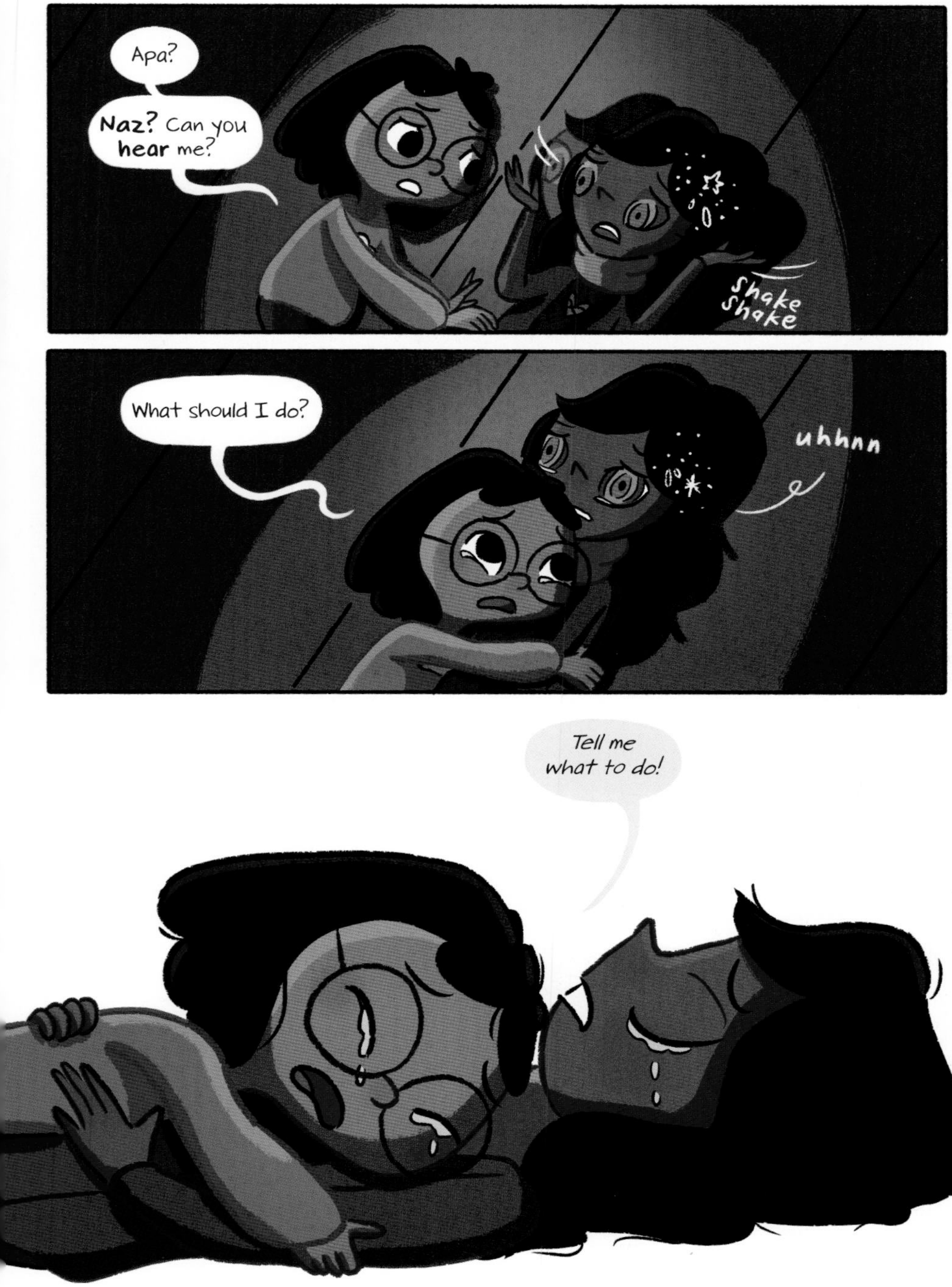

Apa?
Naz? Can you **hear** me?
Shake Shake
What should I do?
uhhnn
Tell me what to do!

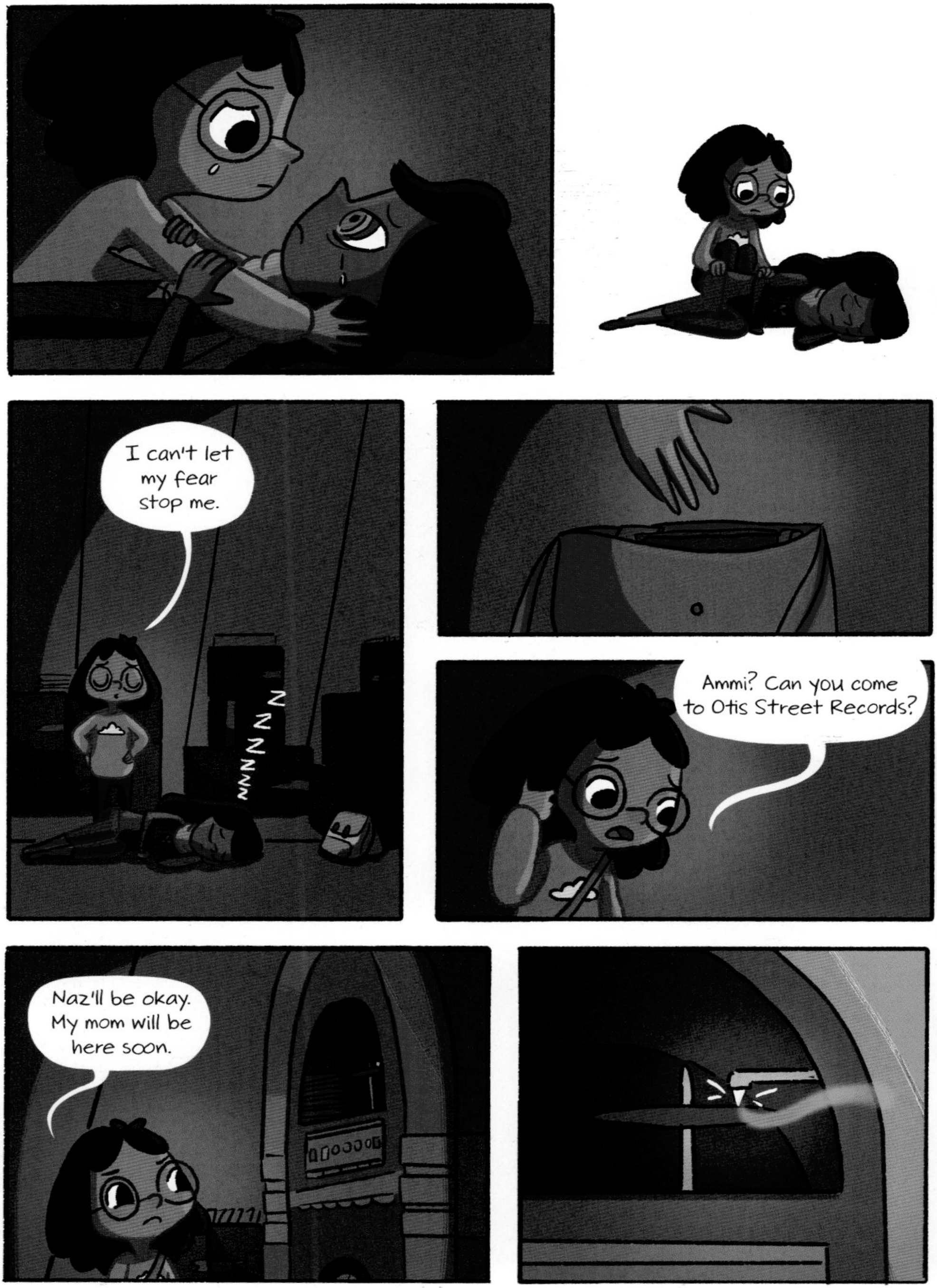
I can't let my fear stop me.
Ammi? Can you come to Otis Street Records?
Naz'll be okay. My mom will be here soon.

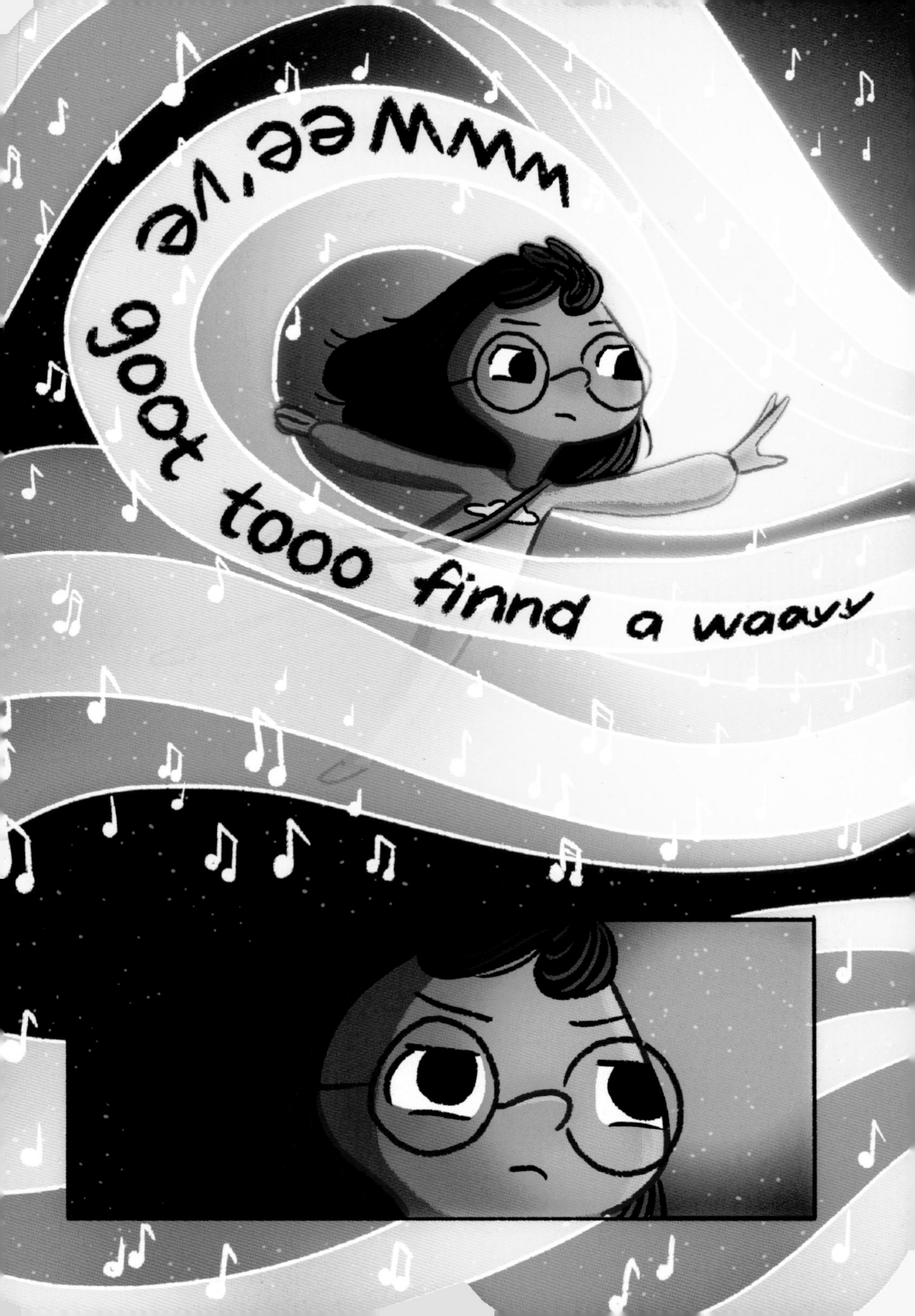
wwwee've goot tooo finnd a waayy

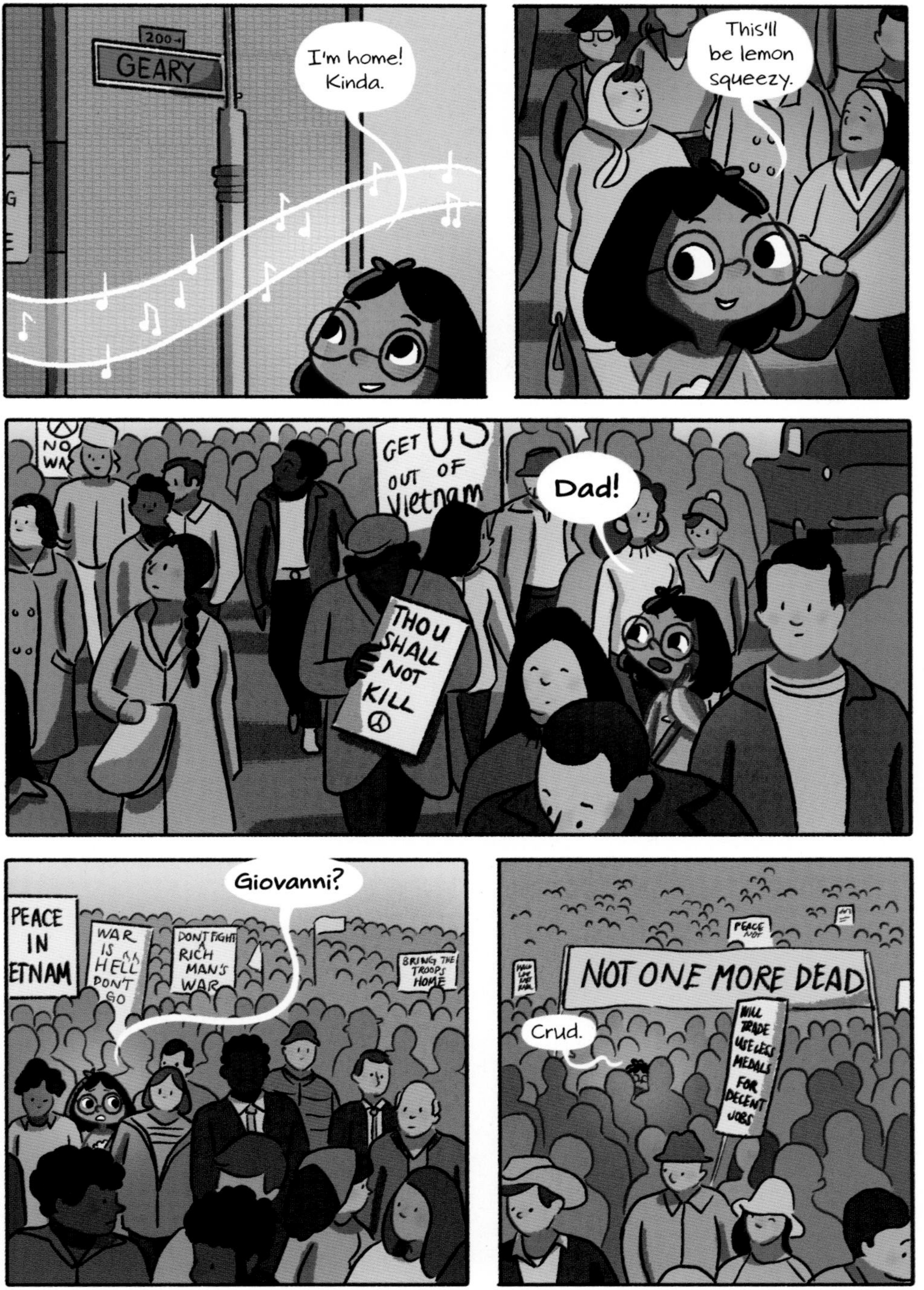
200
GEARY
I'm home! Kinda.
This'll be lemon squeezy.
GET US OUT OF Vietnam
Dad!
THOU SHALL NOT KILL
Giovanni?
WAR IS HELL DON'T GO
DONT FIGHT A RICH MAN'S WAR
BRING THE TROOPS HOME
NOT ONE MORE DEAD
Crud.
WILL TRADE USELESS MEDALS FOR DECENT JOBS

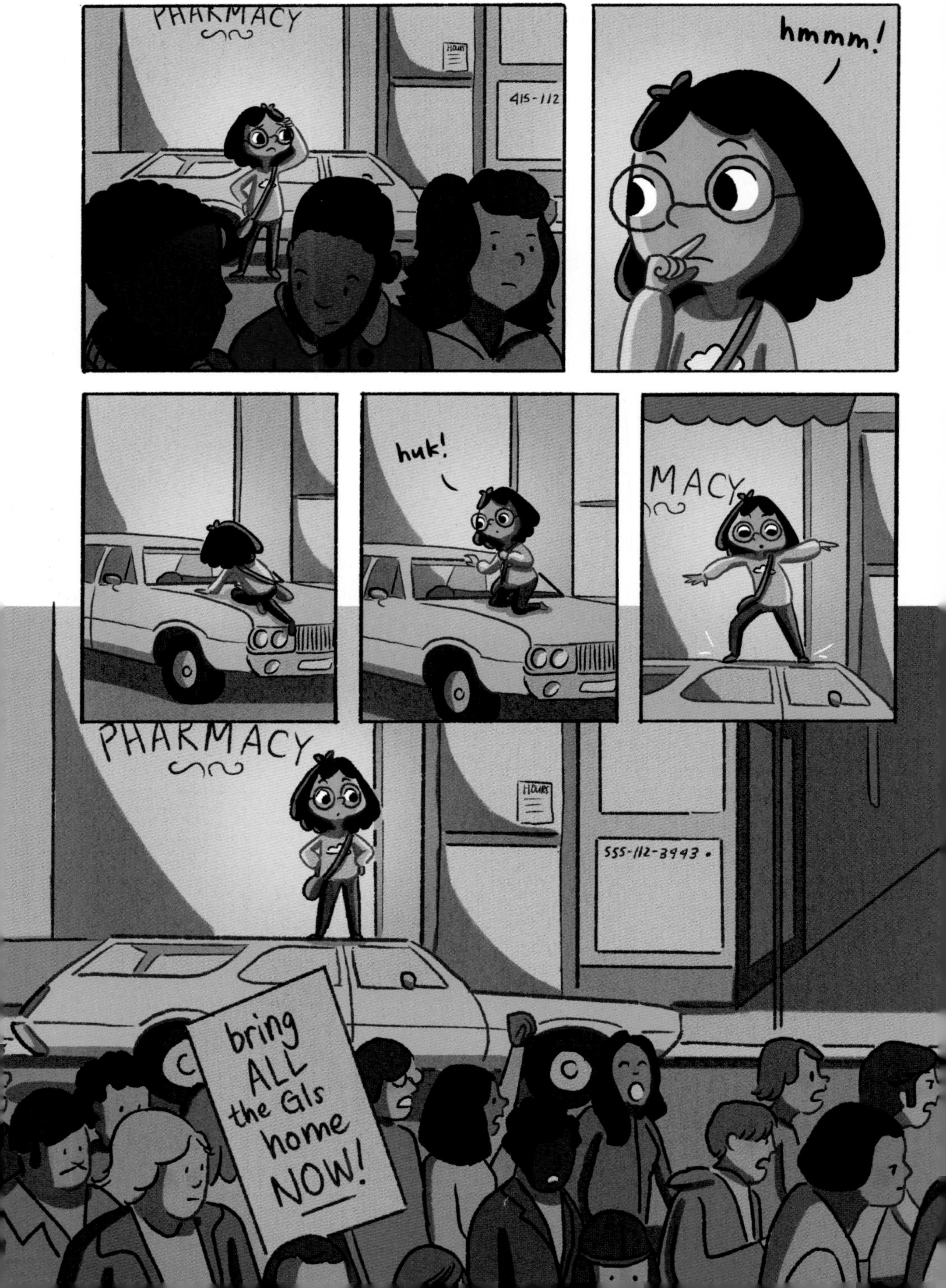

PHARMACY
HOURS
415-112
hmmm!
huk!
MACY
PHARMACY
HOURS
555-112-3943
bring ALL the GIs home NOW!

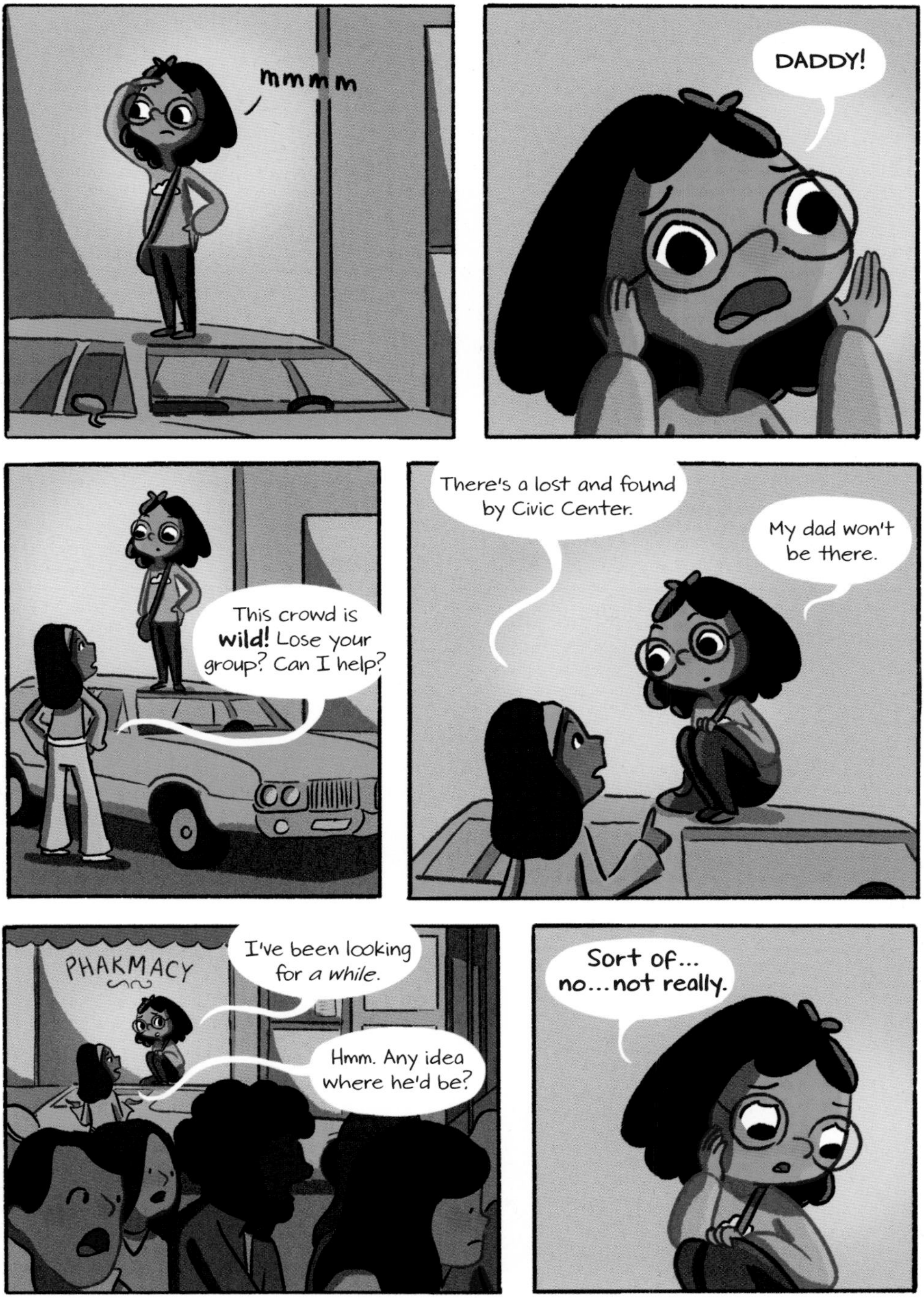
mmmm
DADDY!
This crowd is **wild!** Lose your group? Can I help?
There's a lost and found by Civic Center.
My dad won't be there.
PHARMACY
I've been looking for a *while*.
Hmm. Any idea where he'd be?
Sort of... no...not really.

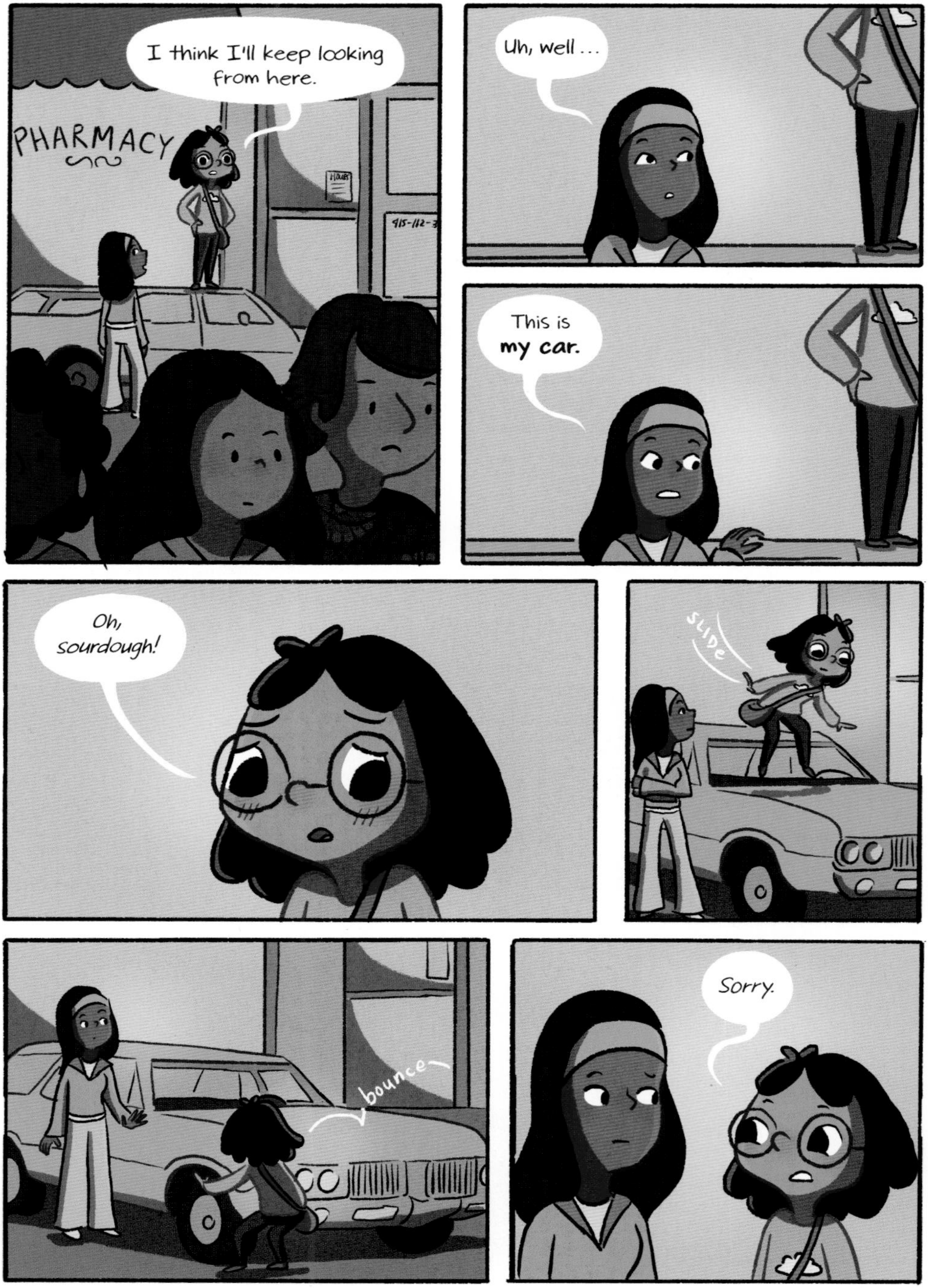
I think I'll keep looking from here.
PHARMACY
Uh, well...
This is my car.
Oh, sourdough!
SLIDE
bounce
Sorry.

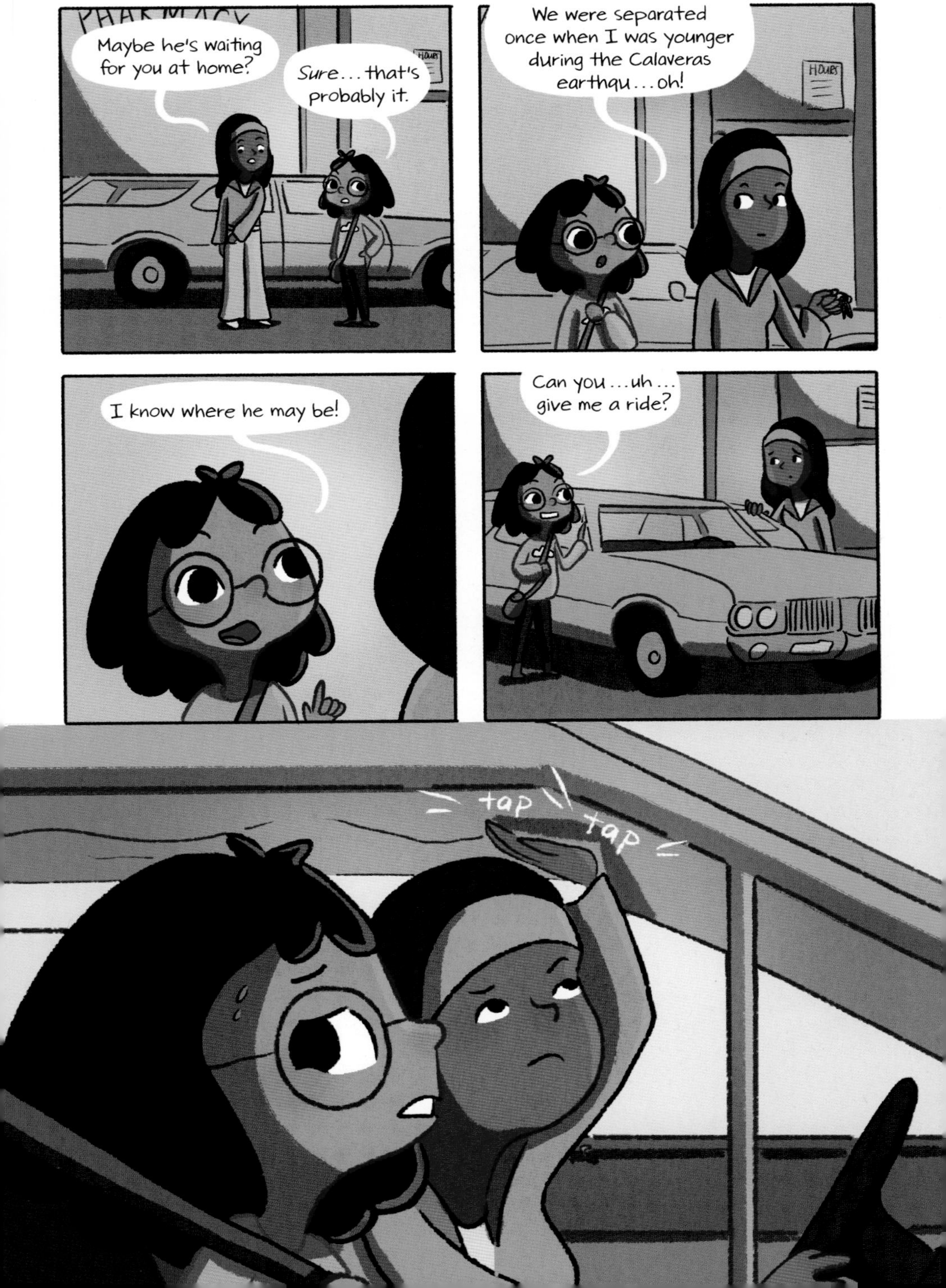
PHARMACY
Maybe he's waiting for you at home?
Sure... that's probably it.
HOURS
We were separated once when I was younger during the Calaveras earthqu...oh!
HOURS
I know where he may be!
Can you...uh... give me a ride?
tap
tap

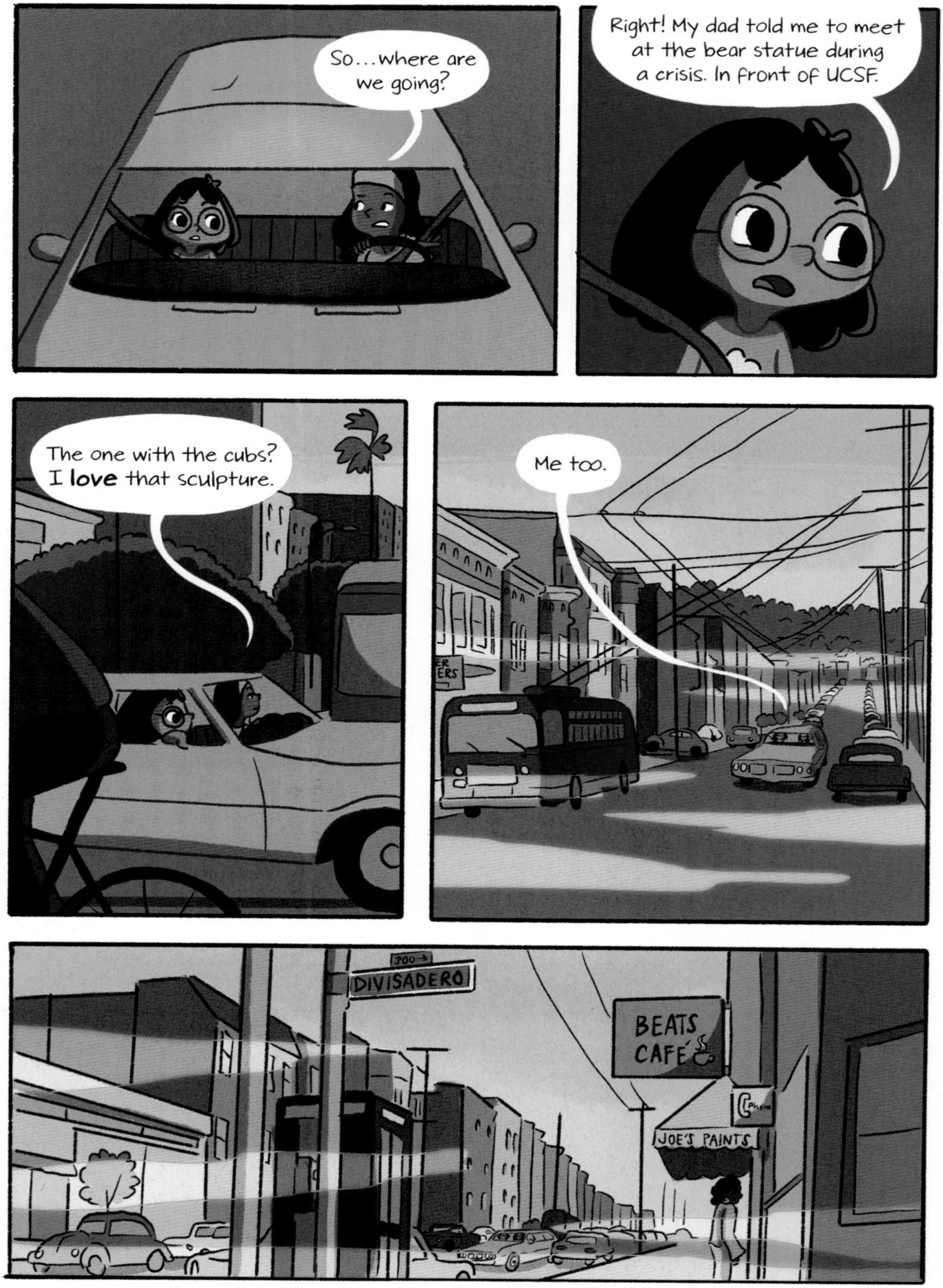
So...where are we going?
Right! My dad told me to meet at the bear statue during a crisis. In front of UCSF.
The one with the cubs? I **love** that sculpture.
Me too.
300
DIVISADERO
BEATS CAFÉ
Phone
JOE'S PAINTS

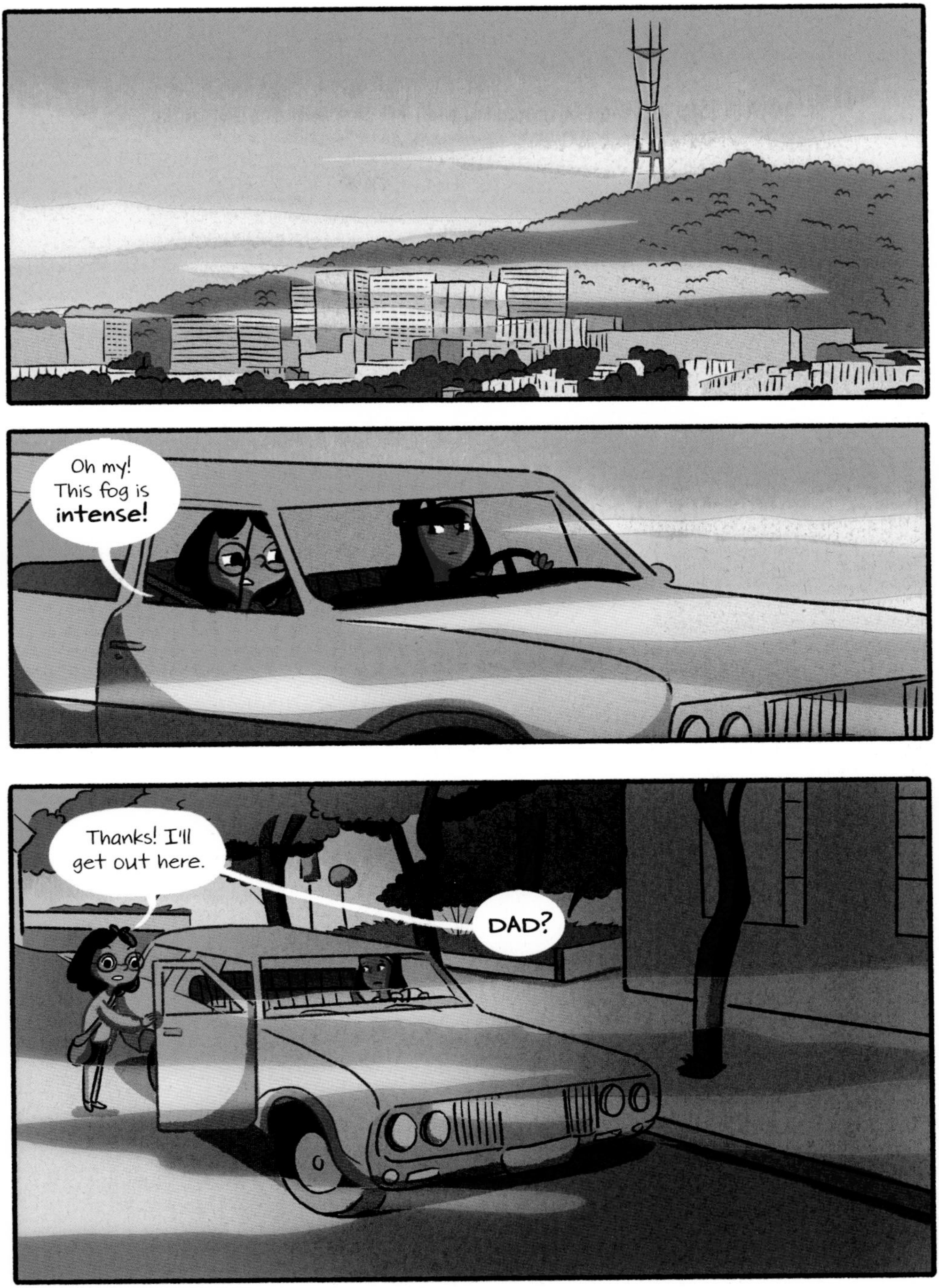
Oh my! This fog is **intense!**
Thanks! I'll get out here.
DAD?

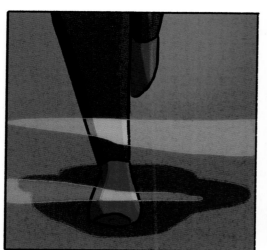

DADDY?

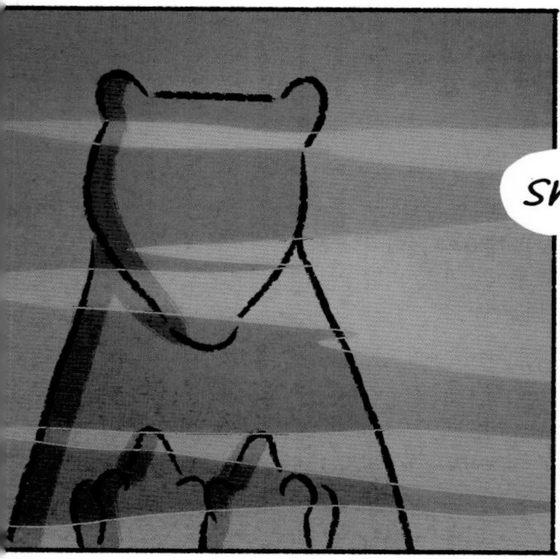

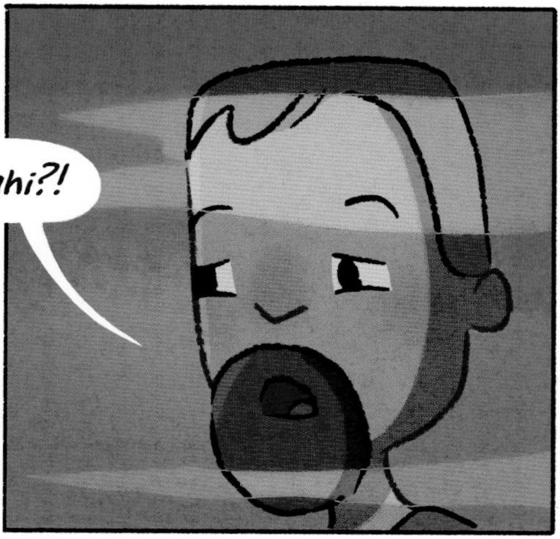
Shahi?!

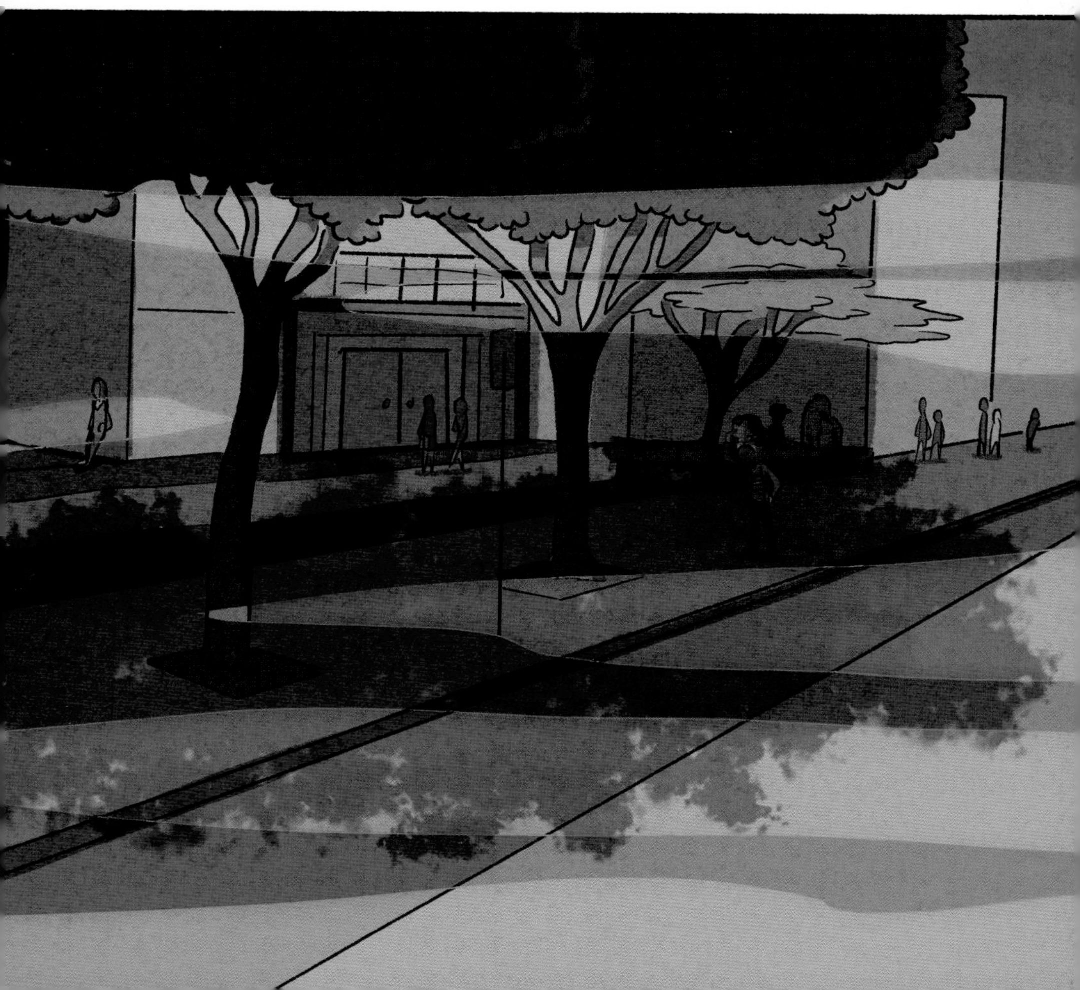

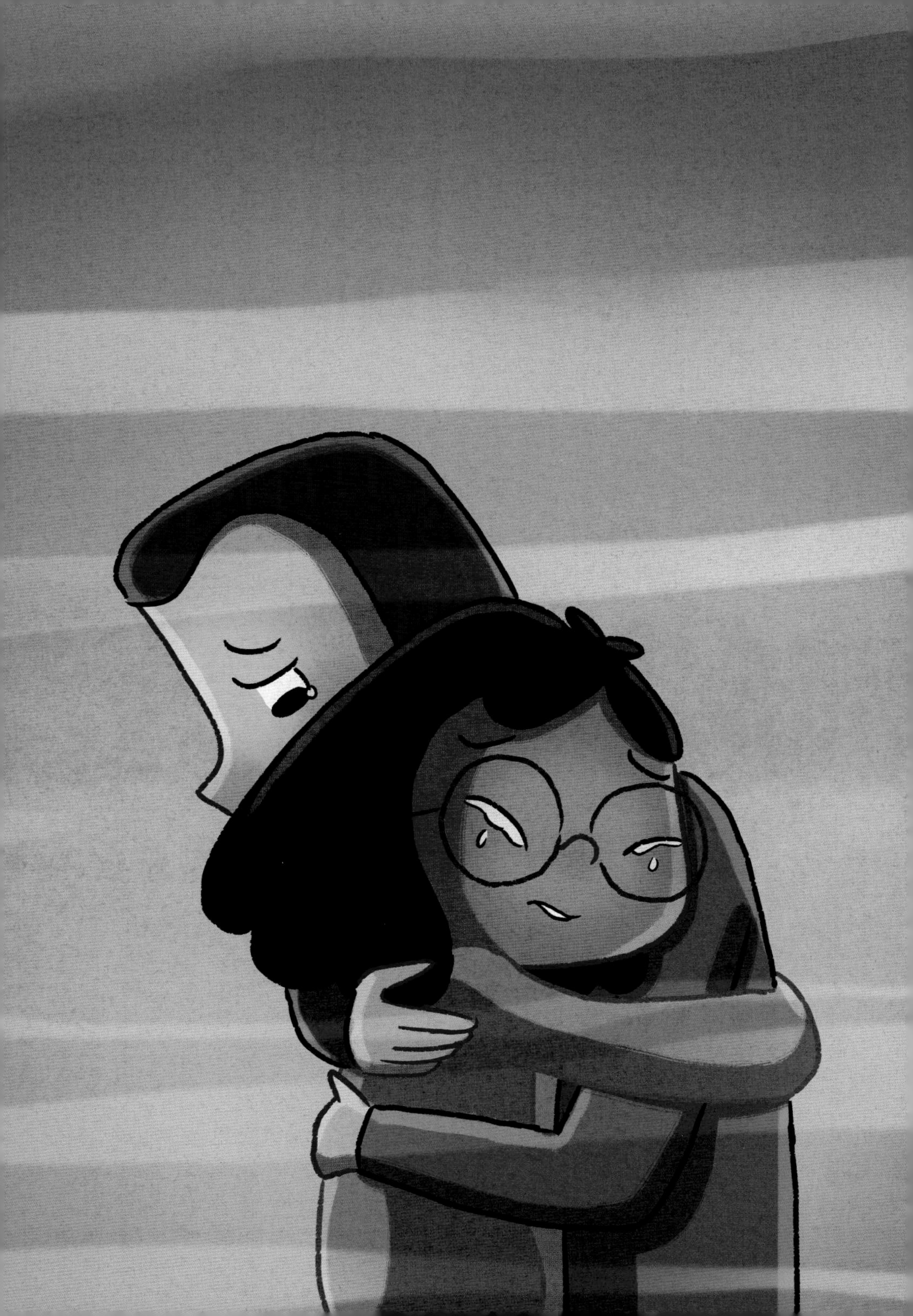

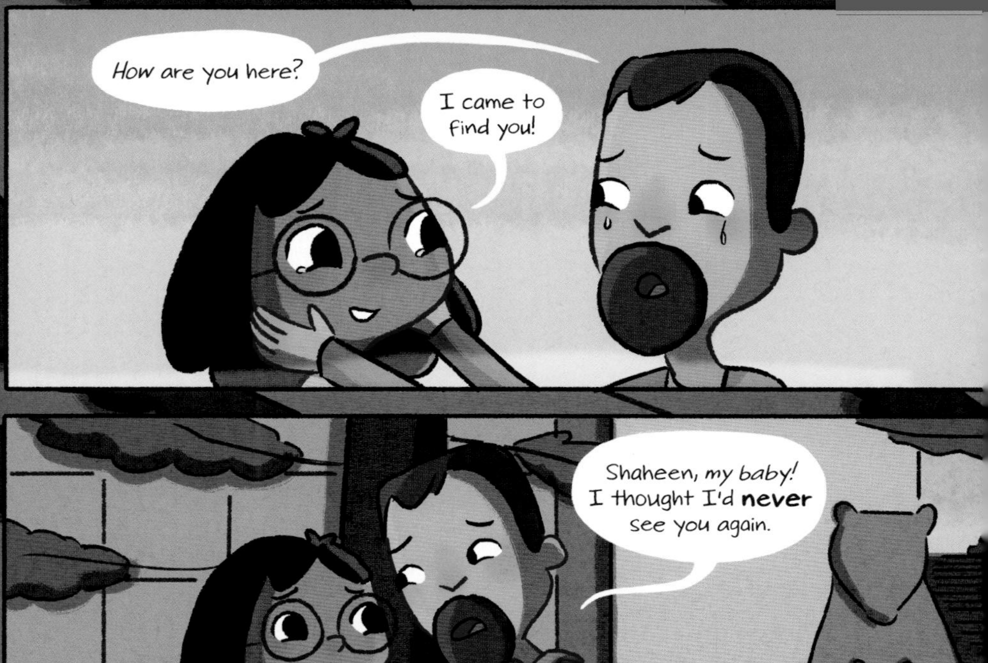
How are you here?
I came to find you!
Shaheen, *my baby!* I thought I'd **never** see you again.
Here, they're a li'l cracked.
slide
Yeah, I kinda lost myself when I found the jukebox.
I'm just so happy to see you.

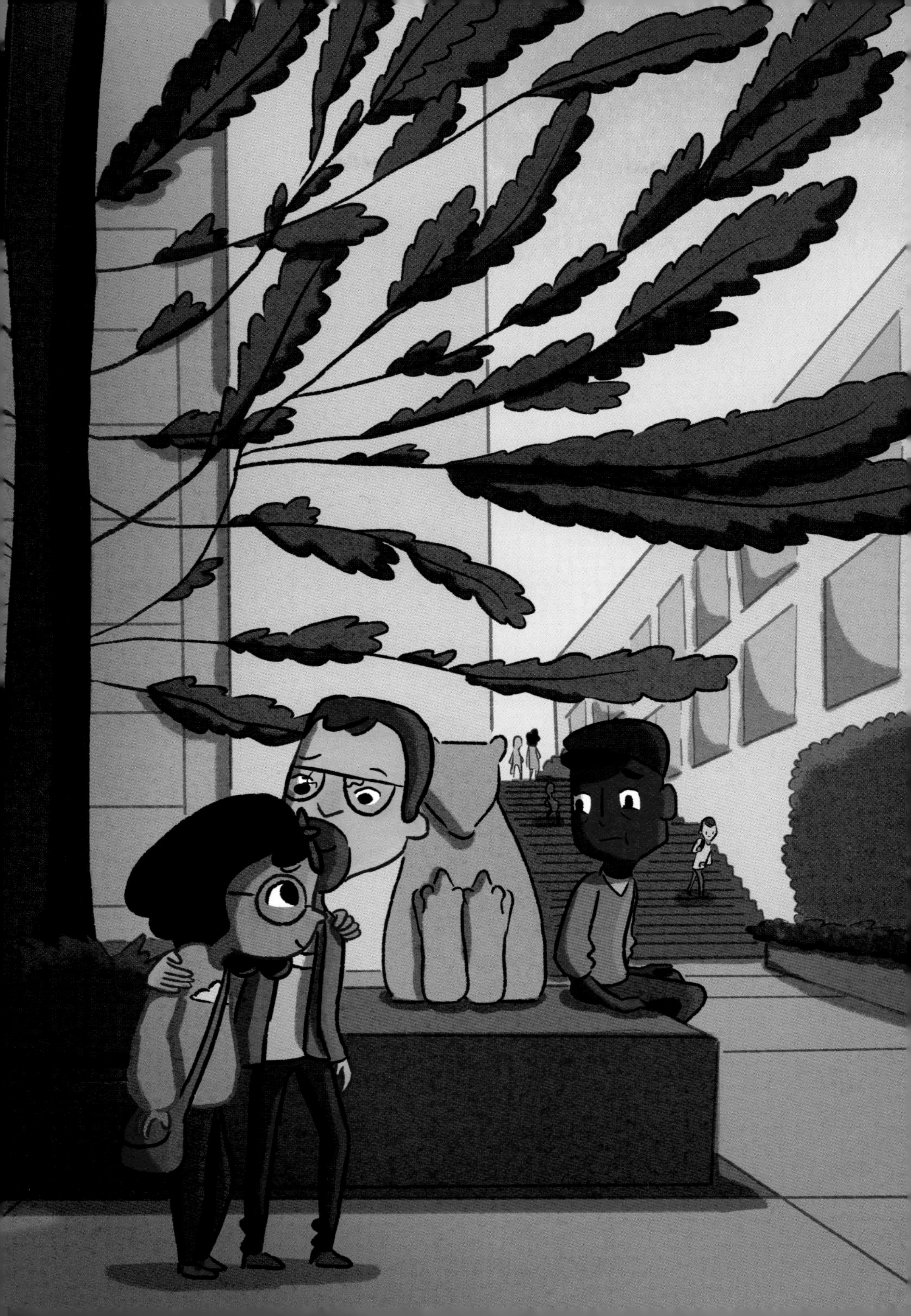

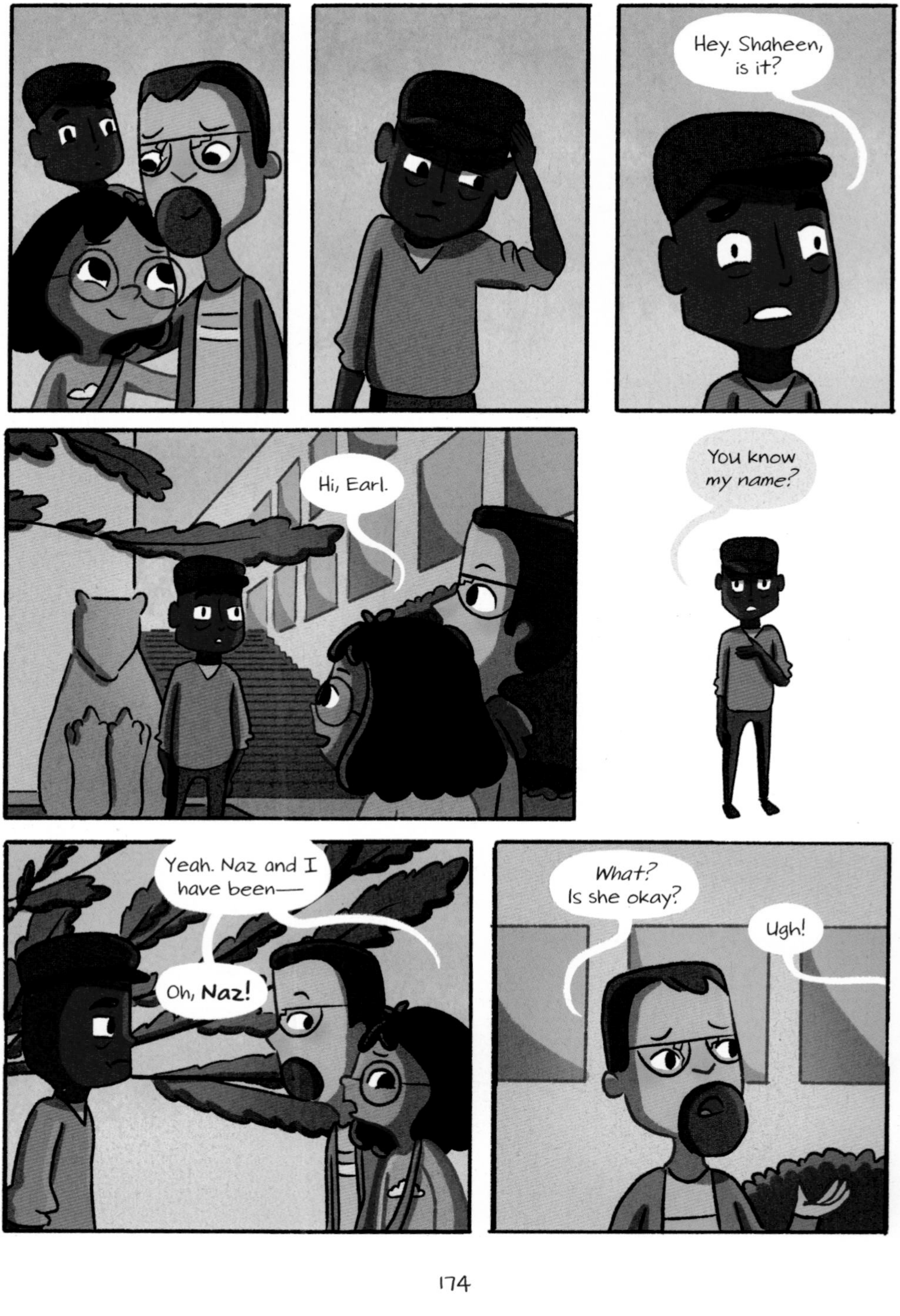
Hey. Shaheen,
is it?
Hi, Earl.
You know
my name?
Yeah. Naz and I
have been—
Oh, Naz!
What?
Is she okay?
Ugh!

Naz lost her hearing because of **YOUR** jukebox.

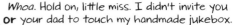

Whoa. Hold on, little miss. I didn't invite you **or** your dad to touch my handmade jukebox.

Wait... *you made it?*

Hmph! You can't buy a jukebox like that.

Is Naz *here?*

No, she was... tired. We searched all night.

I should've **known** you'd never stop.

You can stop now. And keep your hands off **my property.**

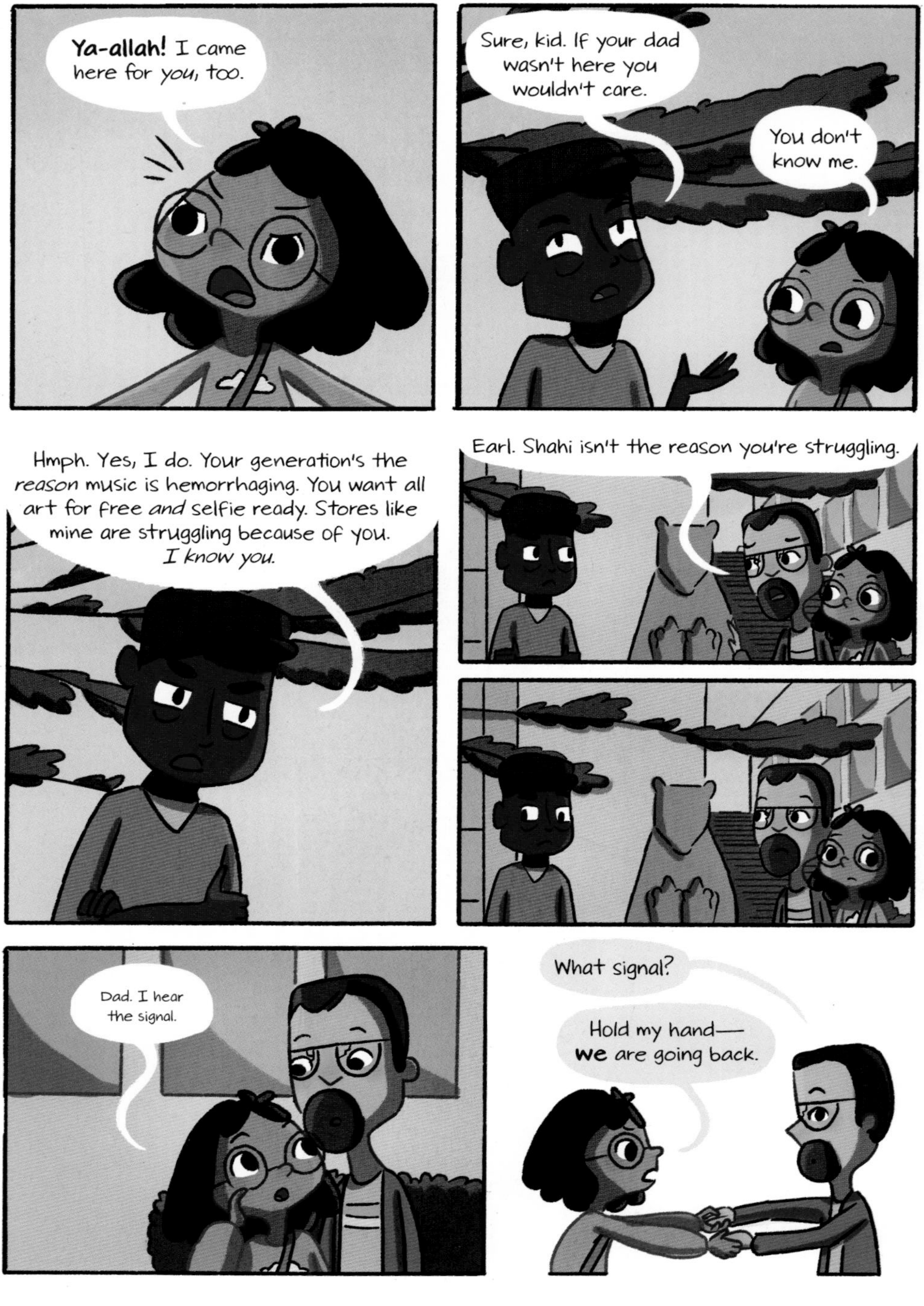

Ya-allah! I came here for *you*, too.
Sure, kid. If your dad wasn't here you wouldn't care.
You don't know me.
Hmph. Yes, I do. Your generation's the *reason* music is hemorrhaging. You want all art for free *and* selfie ready. Stores like mine are struggling because of you. *I know you.*
Earl. Shahi isn't the reason you're struggling.
Dad. I hear the signal.
What signal?
Hold my hand— **we** are going back.

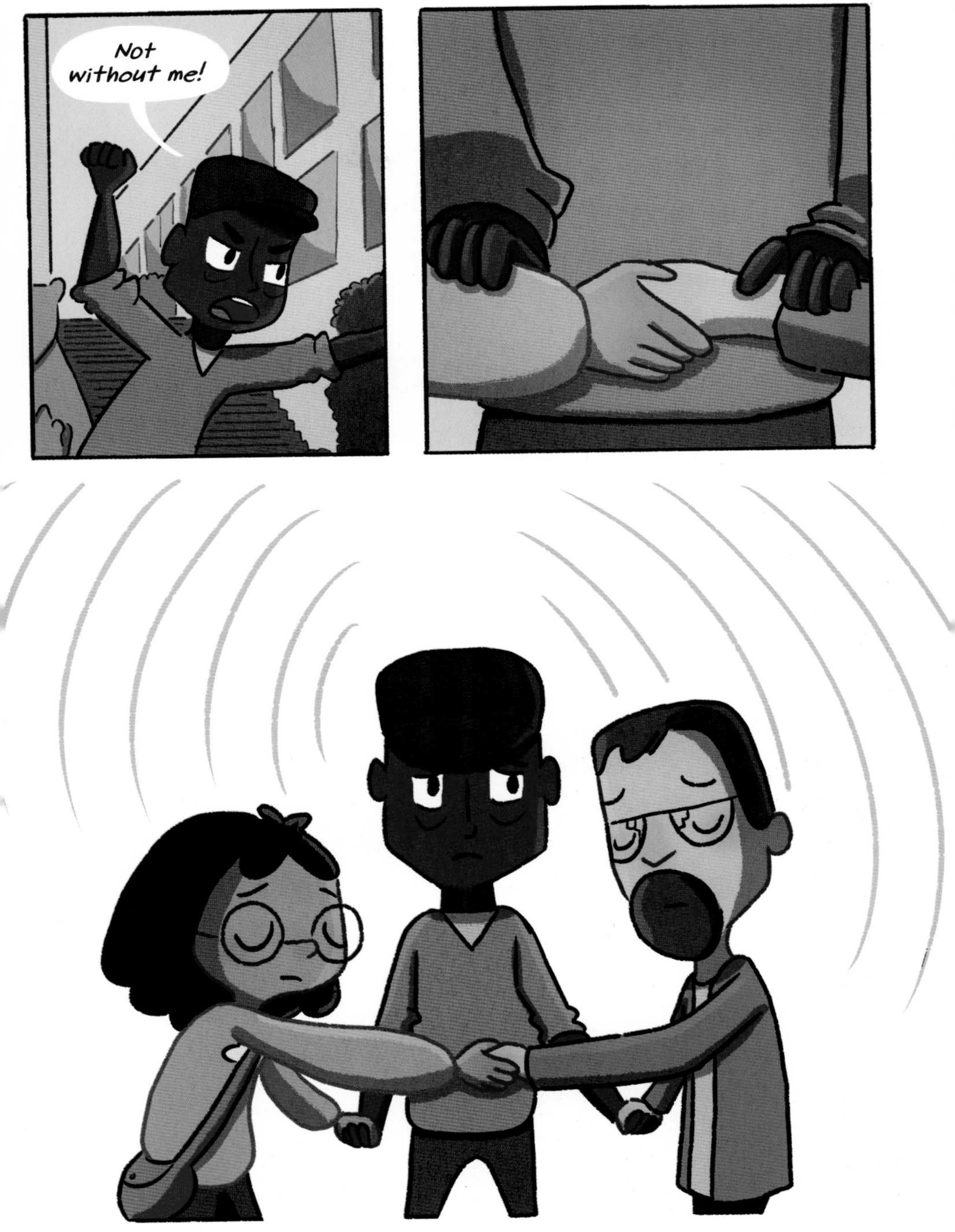
Not without me!

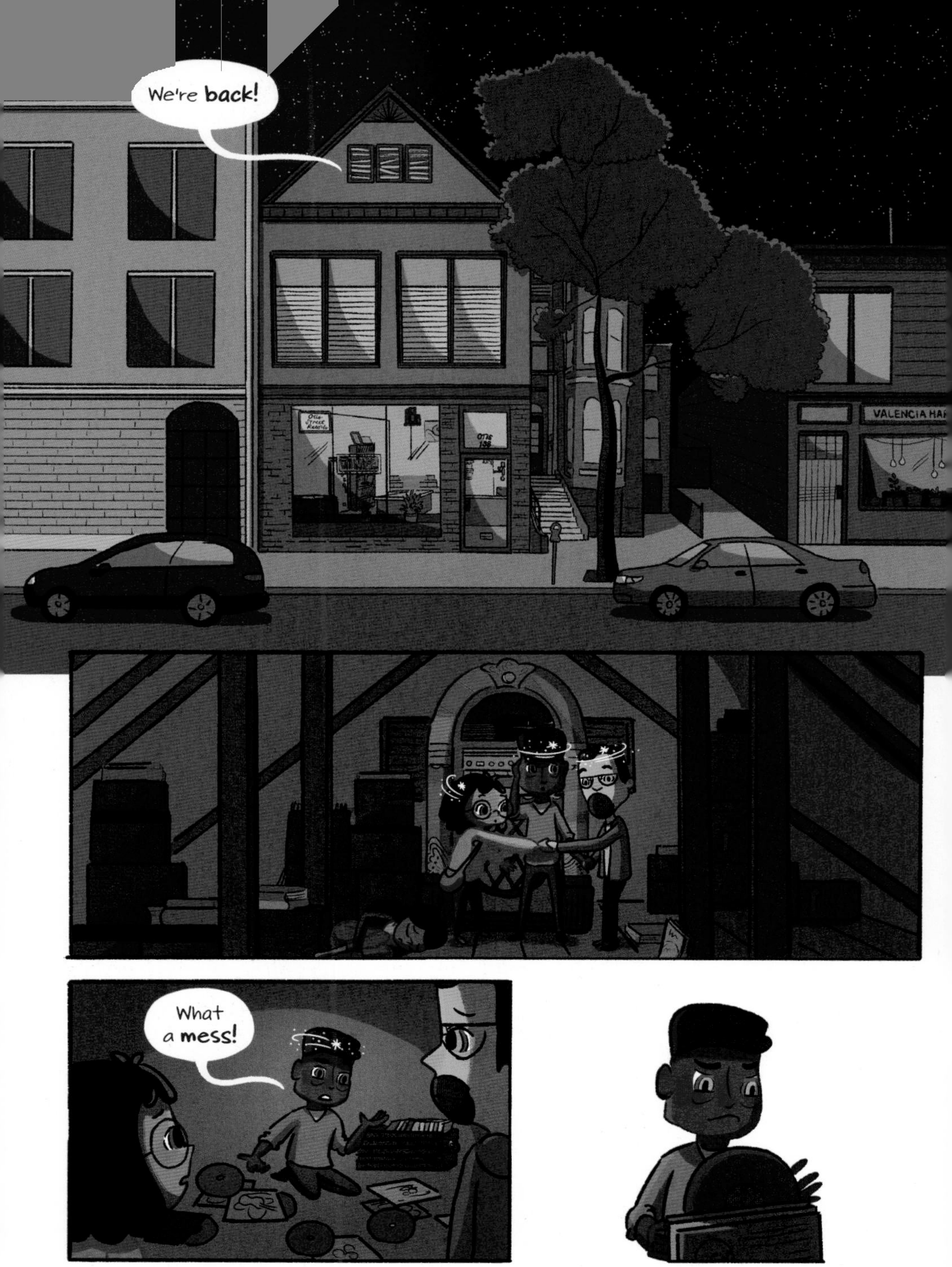
We're **back**!
What a **mess**!

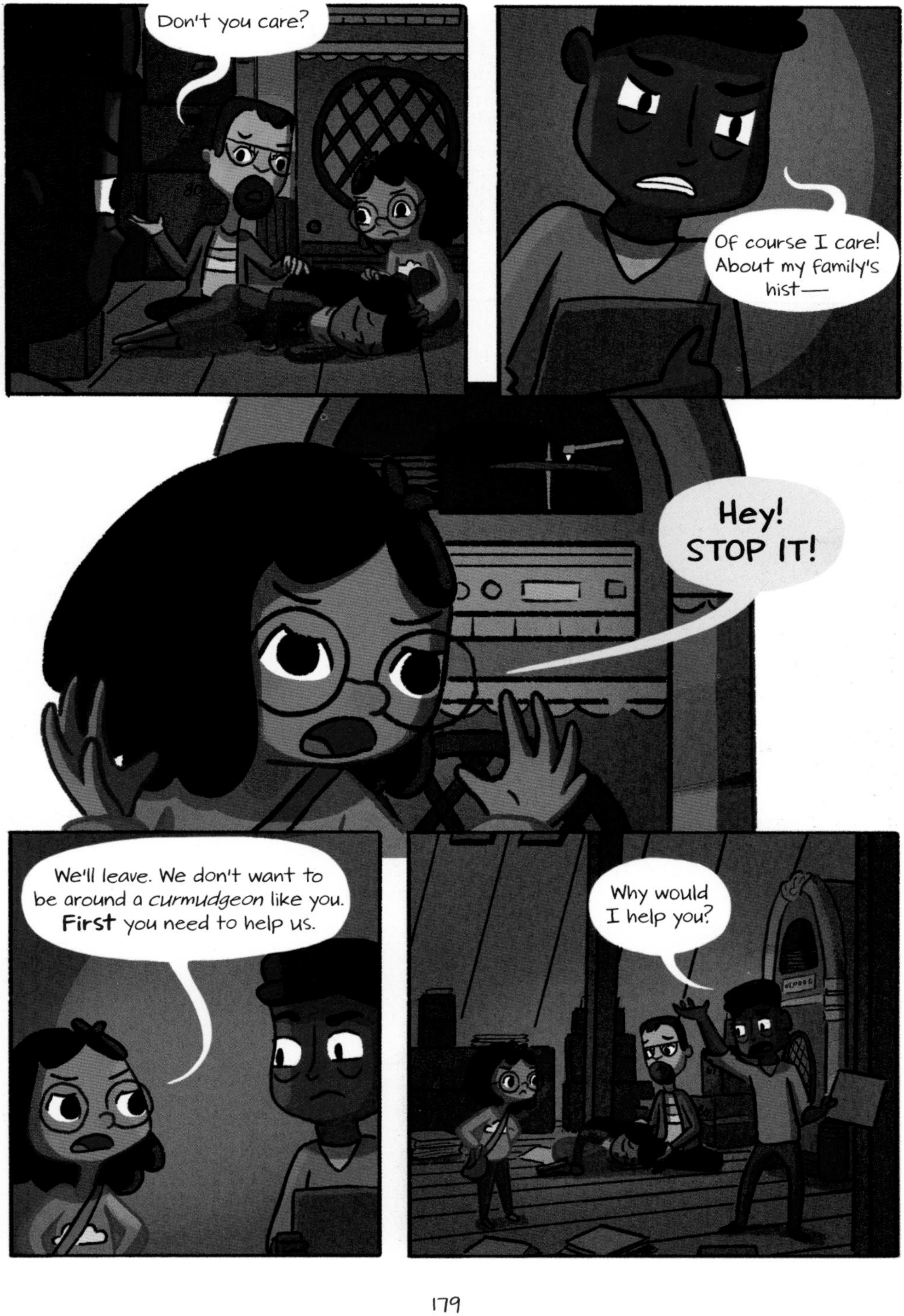
Don't you care?
Of course I care! About my family's hist—
Hey! STOP IT!
We'll leave. We don't want to be around a *curmudgeon* like you. **First** you need to help us.
Why would I help you?

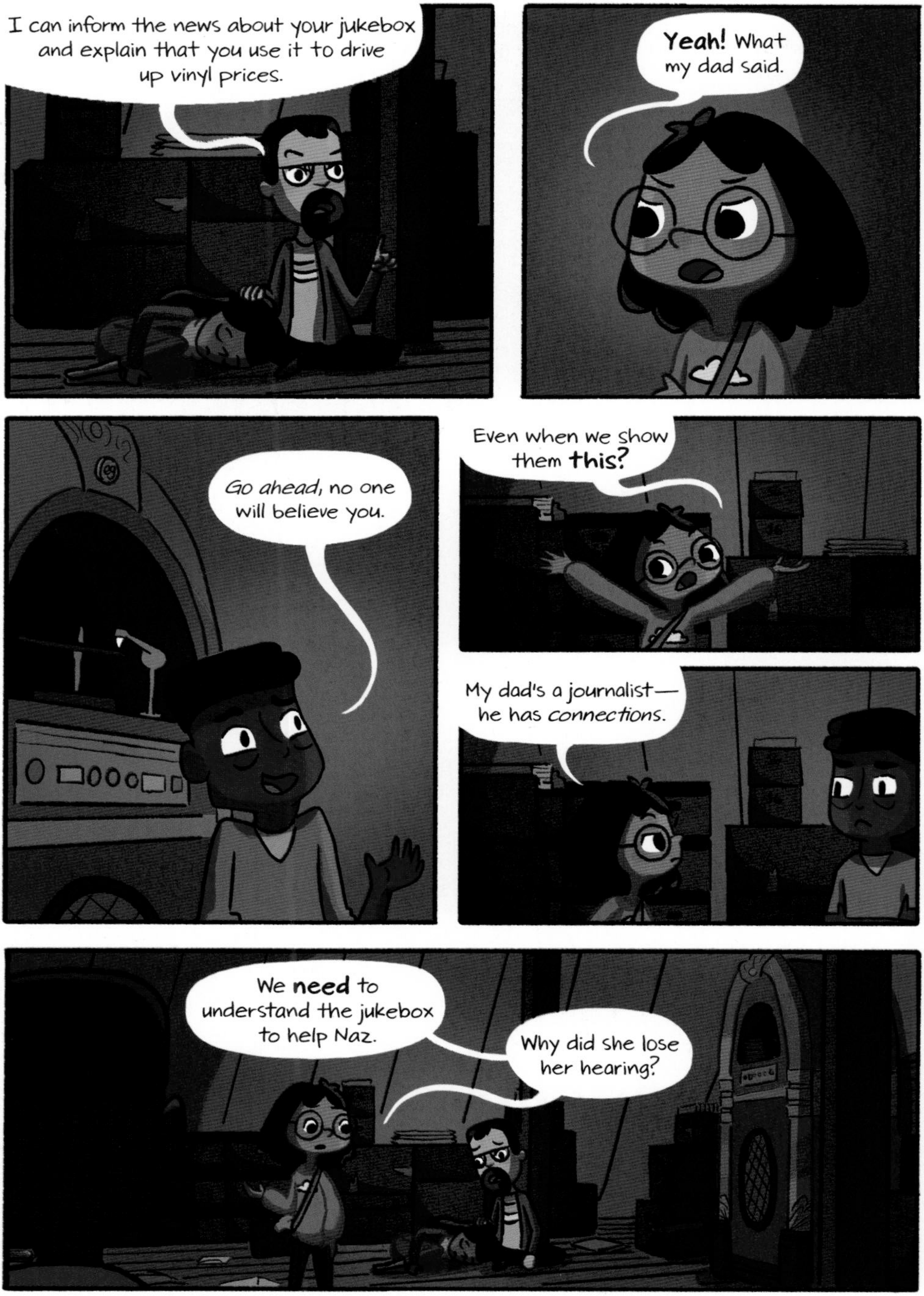
I can inform the news about your jukebox and explain that you use it to drive up vinyl prices.
Yeah! What my dad said.
Go ahead, no one will believe you.
Even when we show them this?
My dad's a journalist— he has connections.
We need to understand the jukebox to help Naz.
Why did she lose her hearing?

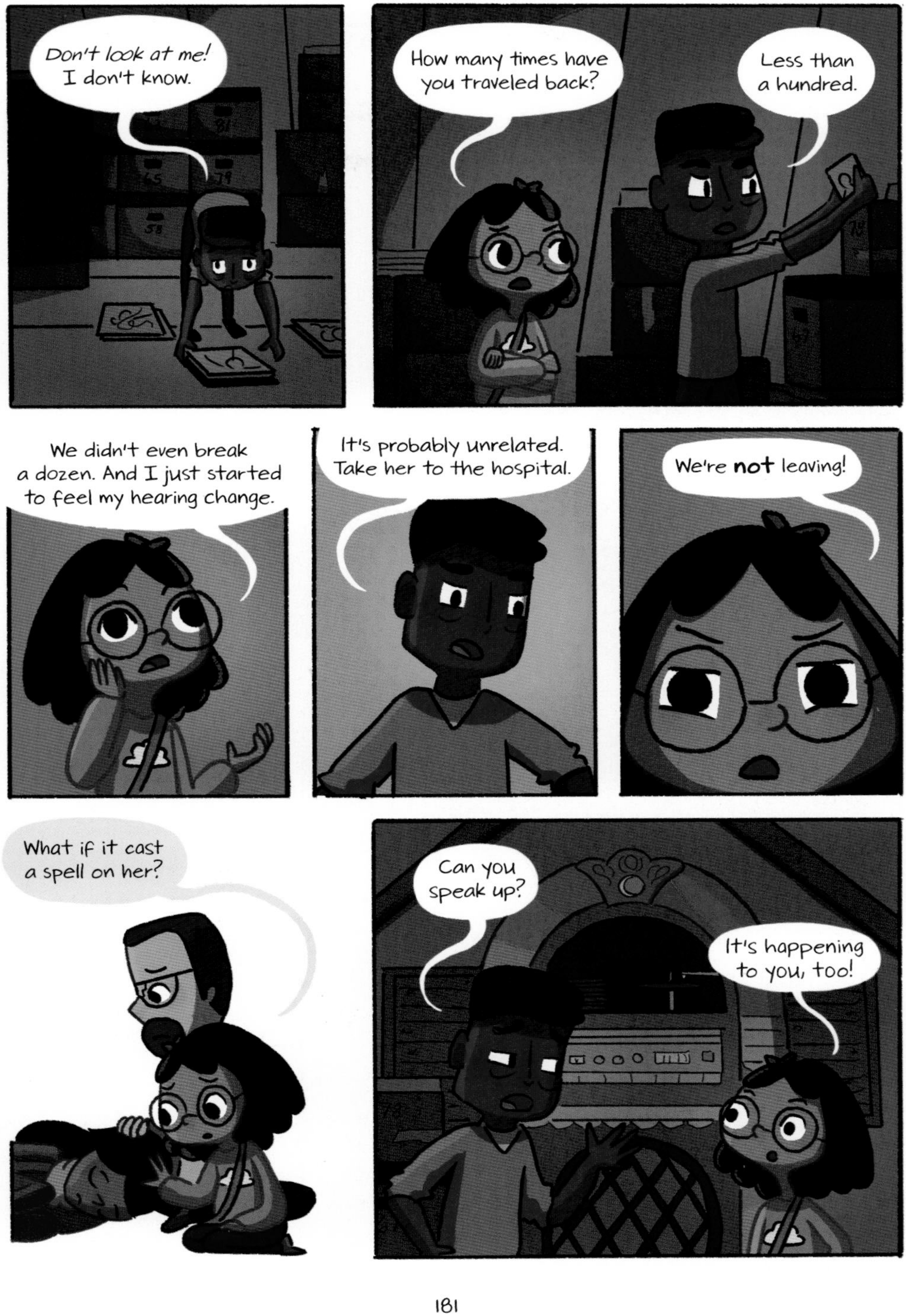
Don't look at me! I don't know.
How many times have you traveled back?
Less than a hundred.
We didn't even break a dozen. And I just started to feel my hearing change.
It's probably unrelated. Take her to the hospital.
We're **not** leaving!
What if it cast a spell on her?
Can you speak up?
It's happening to you, too!

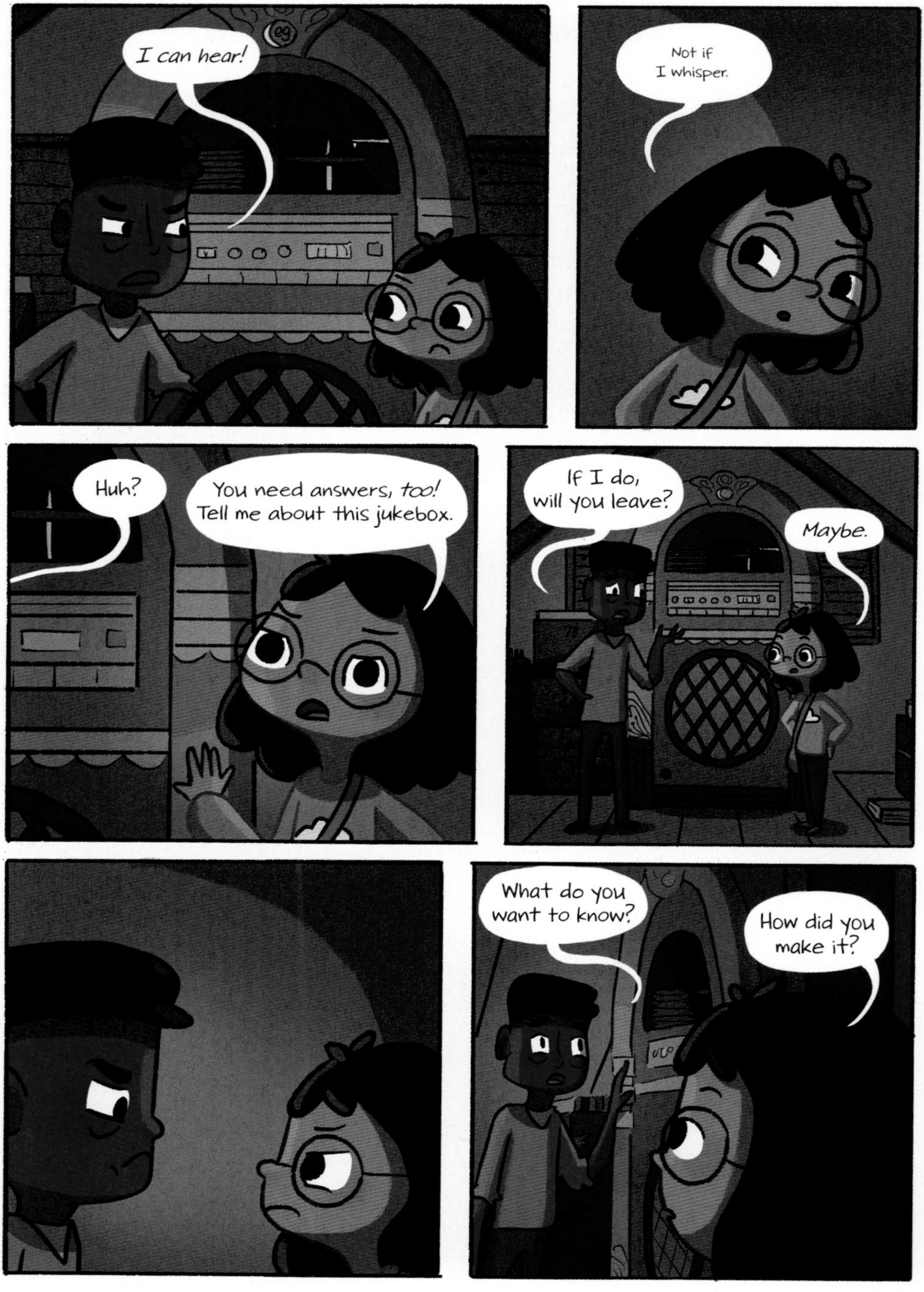
I can hear!
Not if I whisper.
Huh?
You need answers, *too!* Tell me about this jukebox.
If I do, will you leave?
Maybe.
What do you want to know?
How did you make it?

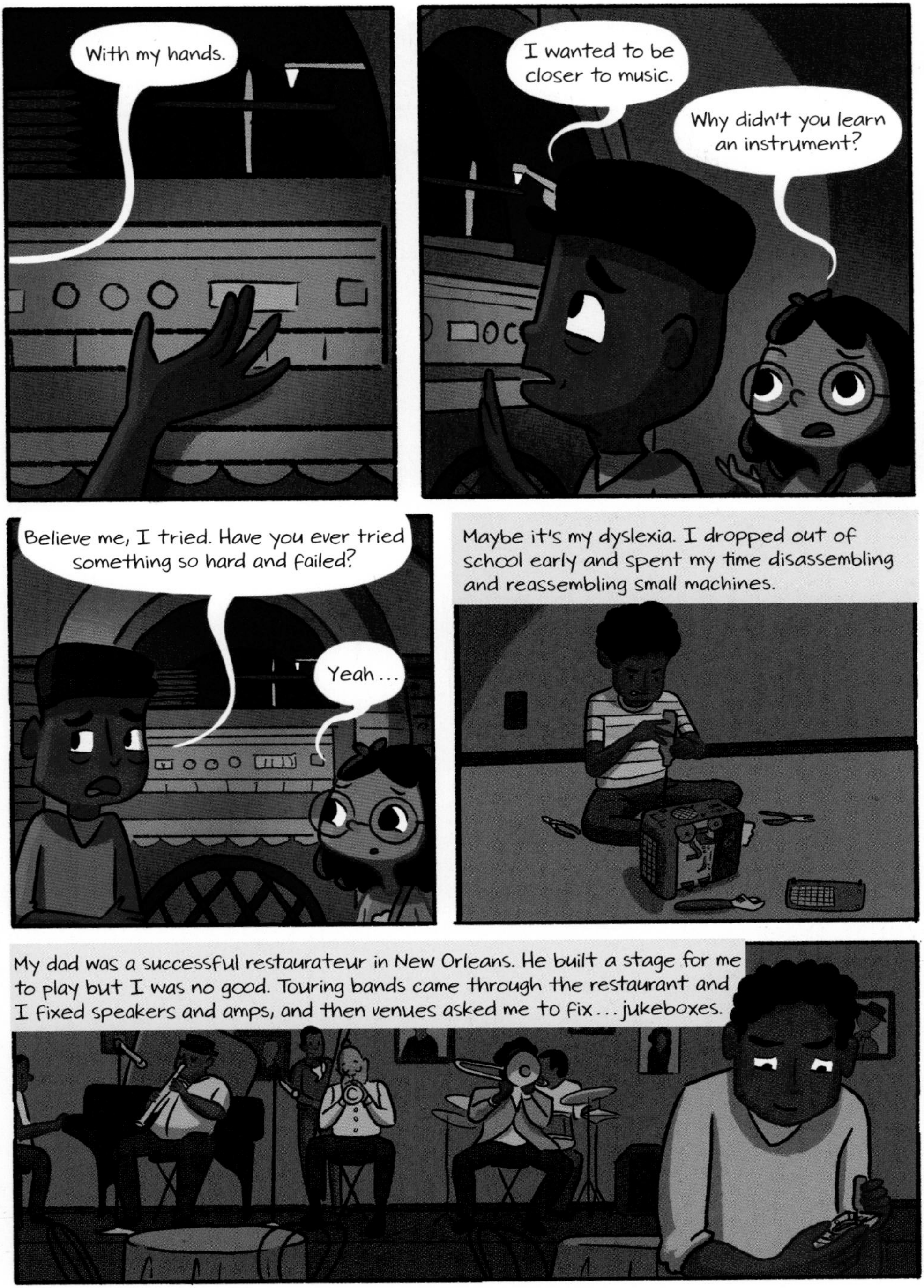
With my hands.
I wanted to be closer to music.
Why didn't you learn an instrument?
Believe me, I tried. Have you ever tried something so hard and failed?
Yeah...
Maybe it's my dyslexia. I dropped out of school early and spent my time disassembling and reassembling small machines.
My dad was a successful restaurateur in New Orleans. He built a stage for me to play but I was no good. Touring bands came through the restaurant and I fixed speakers and amps, and then venues asked me to fix... jukeboxes.

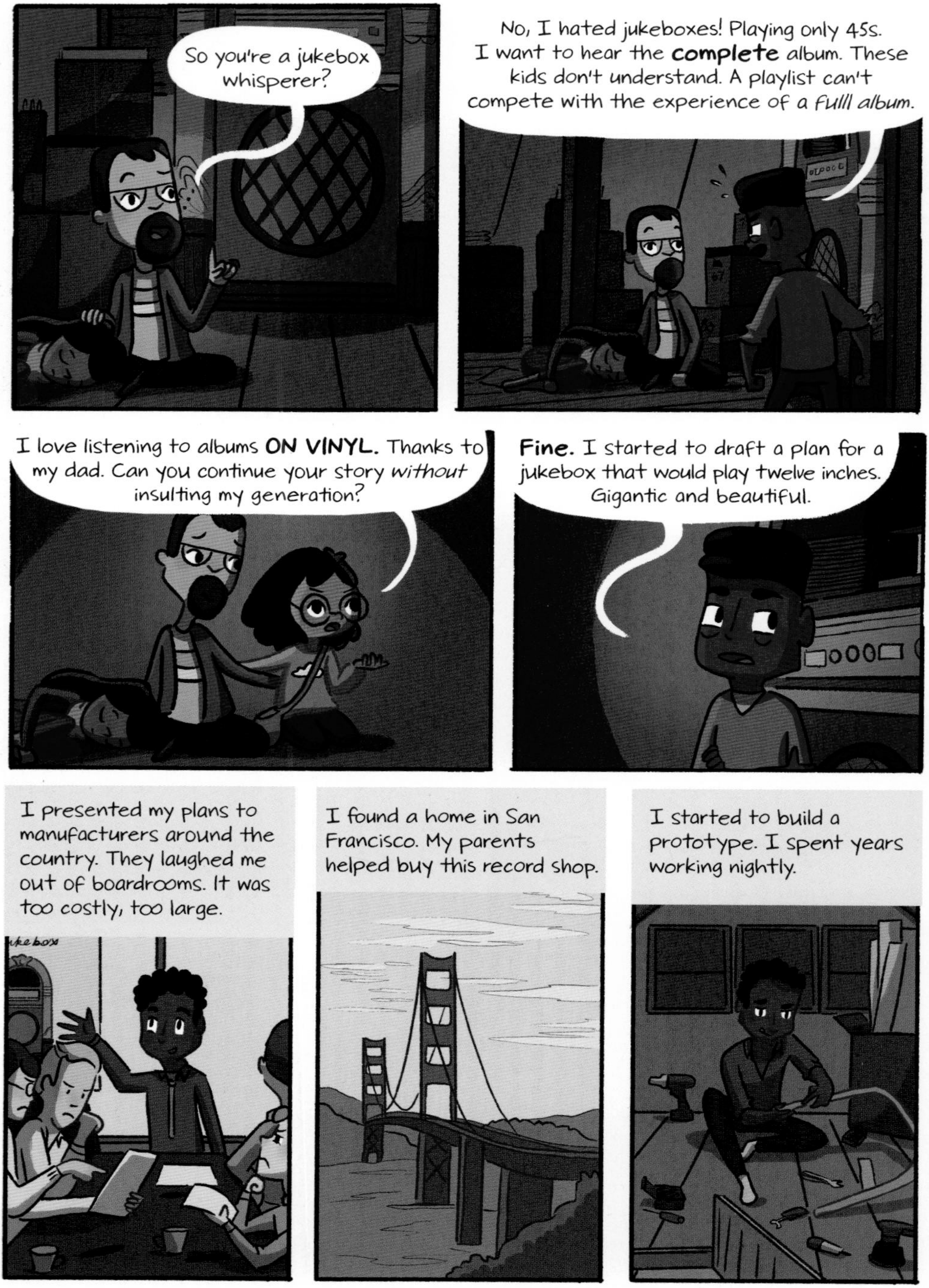
So you're a jukebox whisperer?
No, I hated jukeboxes! Playing only 45s. I want to hear the **complete** album. These kids don't understand. A playlist can't compete with the experience of a *fulll album.*
I love listening to albums **ON VINYL.** Thanks to my dad. Can you continue your story *without* insulting my generation?
Fine. I started to draft a plan for a jukebox that would play twelve inches. Gigantic and beautiful.
I presented my plans to manufacturers around the country. They laughed me out of boardrooms. It was too costly, too large.
I found a home in San Francisco. My parents helped buy this record shop.
I started to build a prototype. I spent years working nightly.

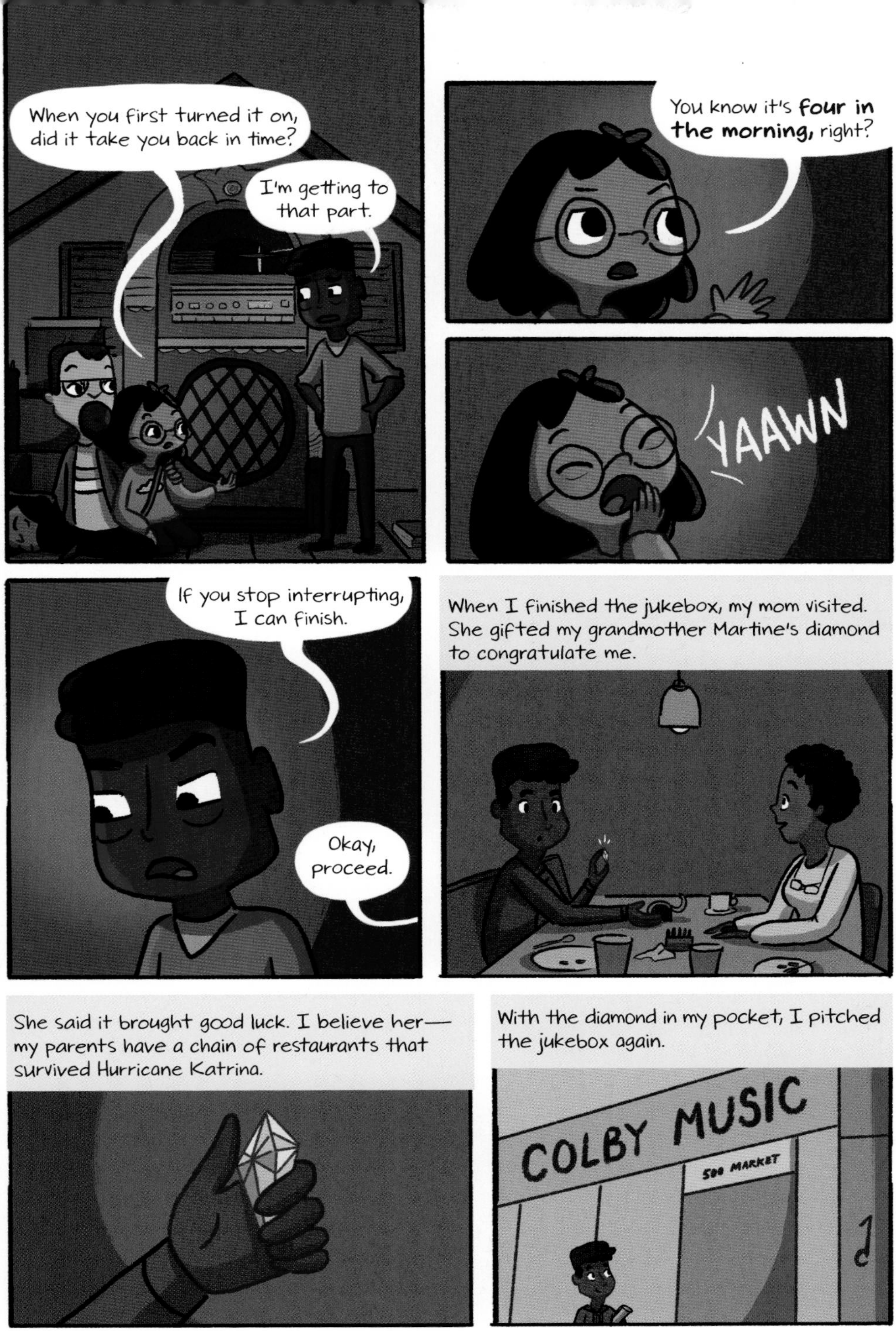
When you first turned it on, did it take you back in time?
I'm getting to that part.
You know it's **four in the morning,** right?
YAAWN
If you stop interrupting, I can finish.
Okay, proceed.
When I finished the jukebox, my mom visited. She gifted my grandmother Martine's diamond to congratulate me.
She said it brought good luck. I believe her—my parents have a chain of restaurants that survived Hurricane Katrina.
With the diamond in my pocket, I pitched the jukebox again.
COLBY MUSIC
500 MARKET

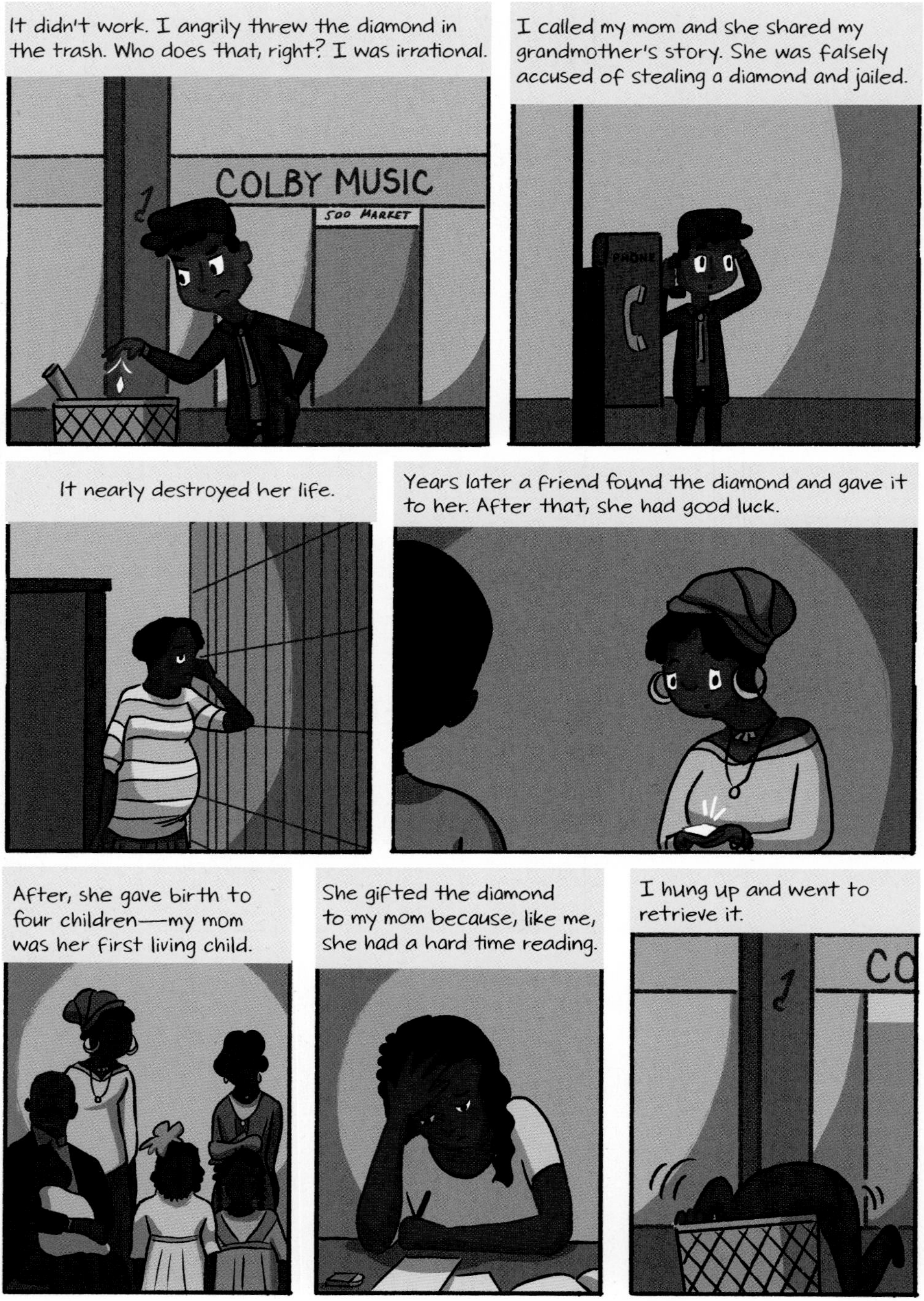
It didn't work. I angrily threw the diamond in the trash. Who does that, right? I was irrational.
COLBY MUSIC
500 MARKET
I called my mom and she shared my grandmother's story. She was falsely accused of stealing a diamond and jailed.
PHONE
It nearly destroyed her life.
Years later a friend found the diamond and gave it to her. After that, she had good luck.
After, she gave birth to four children—my mom was her first living child.
She gifted the diamond to my mom because, like me, she had a hard time reading.
I hung up and went to retrieve it.
CO

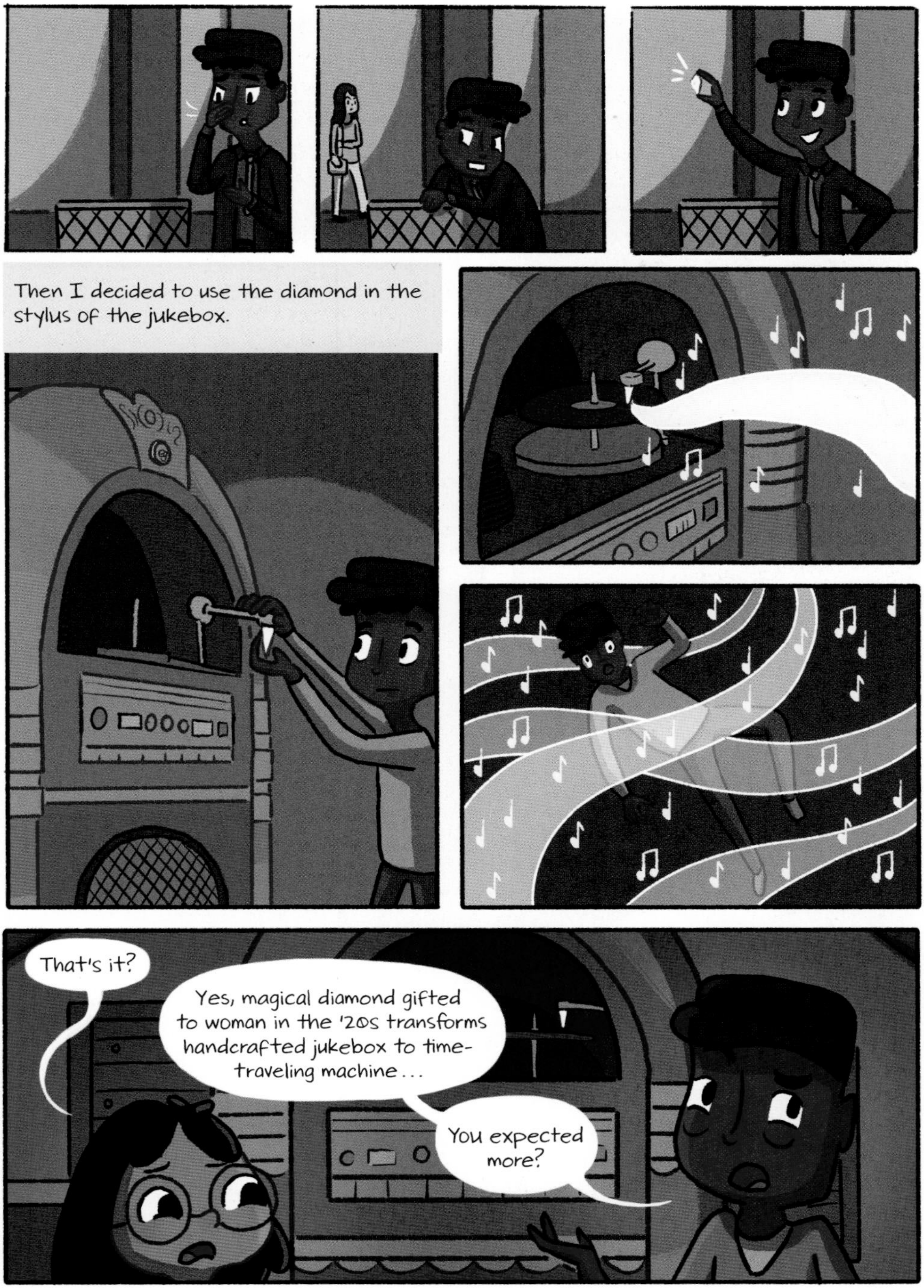
Then I decided to use the diamond in the stylus of the jukebox.
That's it?
Yes, magical diamond gifted to woman in the '20s transforms handcrafted jukebox to time-traveling machine...
You expected more?

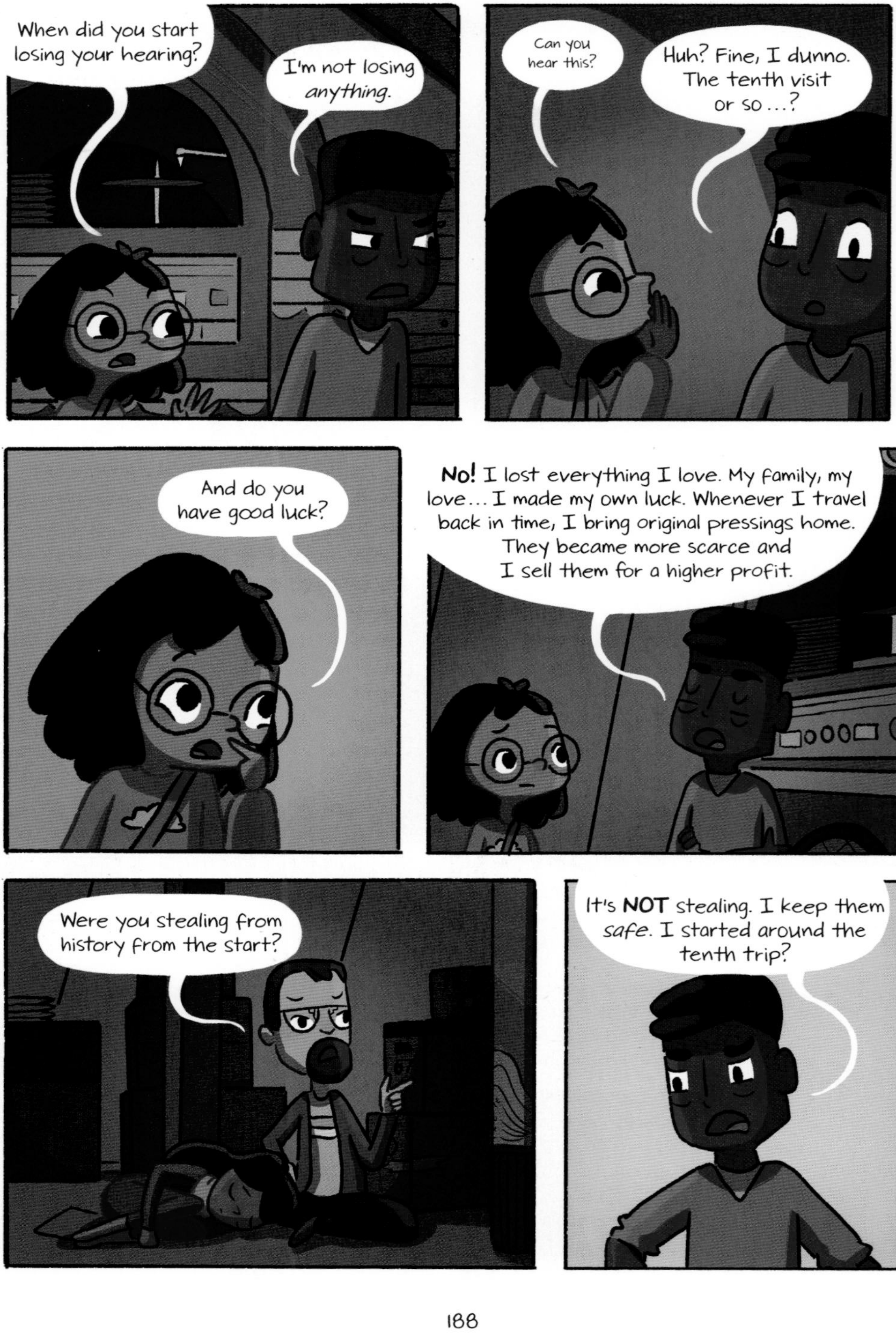
When did you start losing your hearing?
I'm not losing *anything.*
Can you hear this?
Huh? Fine, I dunno. The tenth visit or so...?
And do you have good luck?
No! I lost everything I love. My family, my love... I made my own luck. Whenever I travel back in time, I bring original pressings home. They became more scarce and I sell them for a higher profit.
Were you stealing from history from the start?
It's **NOT** stealing. I keep them *safe.* I started around the tenth trip?

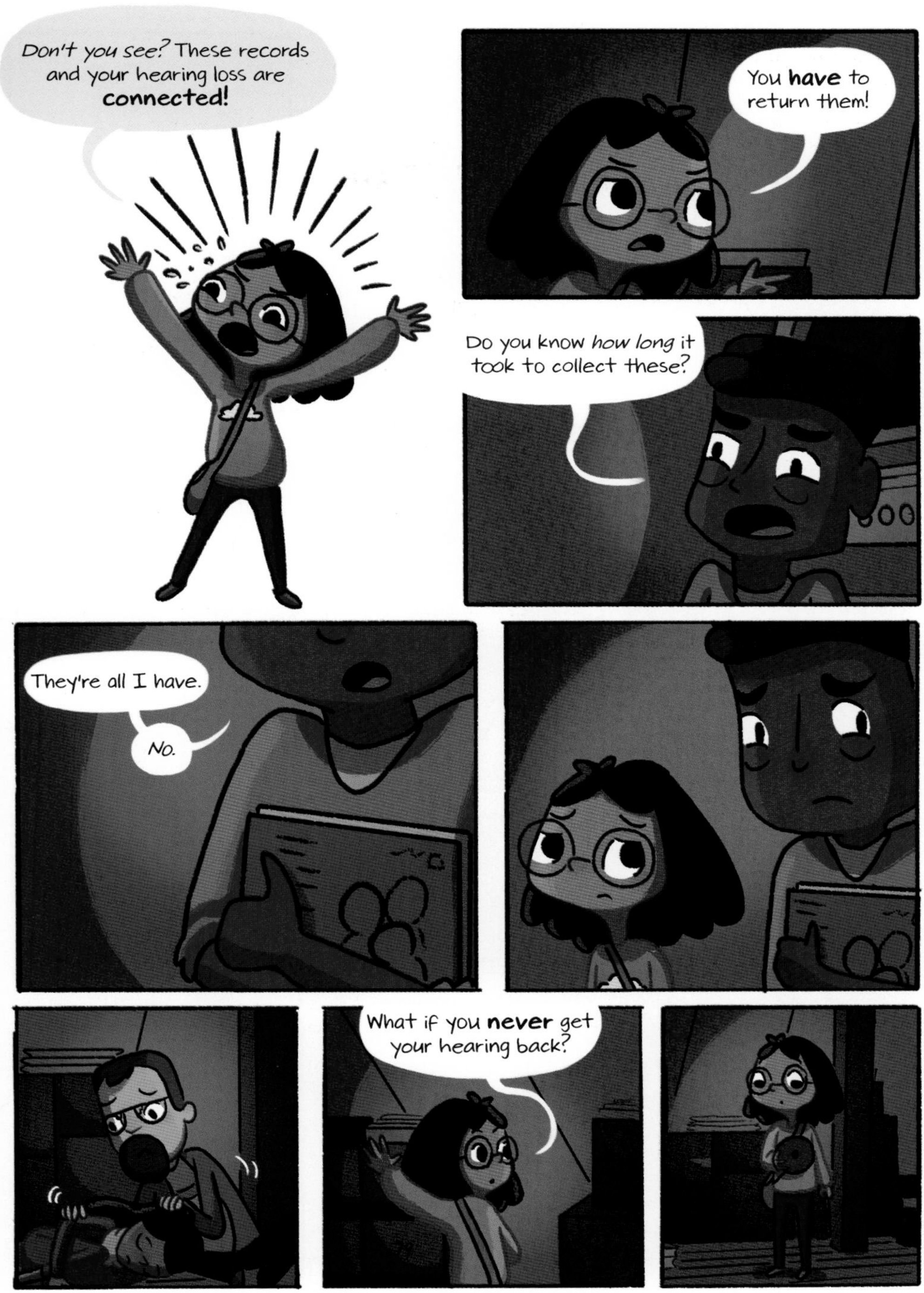

Don't you see? These records and your hearing loss are **connected!**
You **have** to return them!
Do you know *how long* it took to collect these?
They're all I have.
No.
What if you **never** get your hearing back?

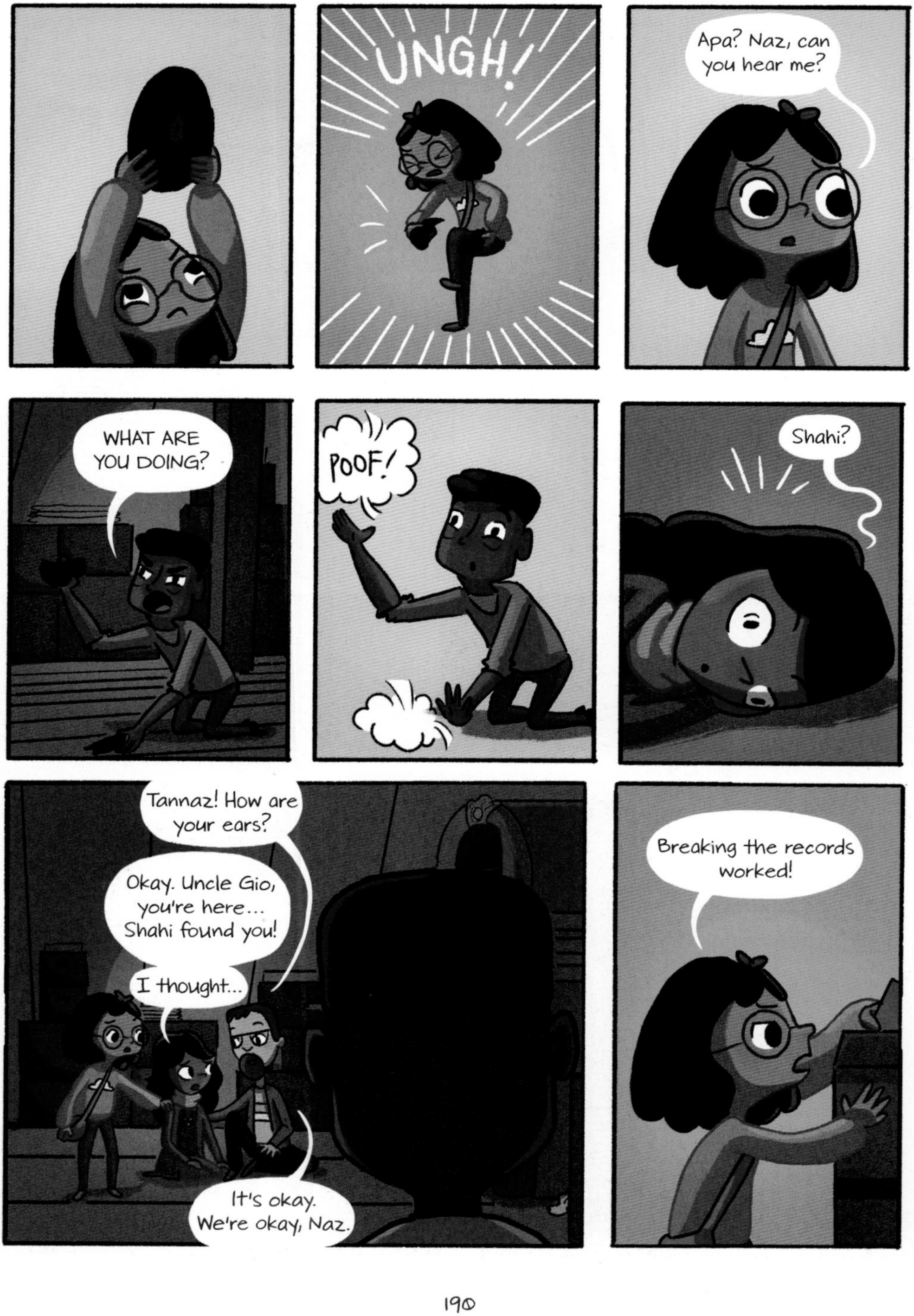
UNGH!
Apa? Naz, can you hear me?
WHAT ARE YOU DOING?
POOF!
Shahi?
Tannaz! How are your ears?
Okay. Uncle Gio, you're here... Shahi found you!
I thought...
It's okay. We're okay, Naz.
Breaking the records worked!

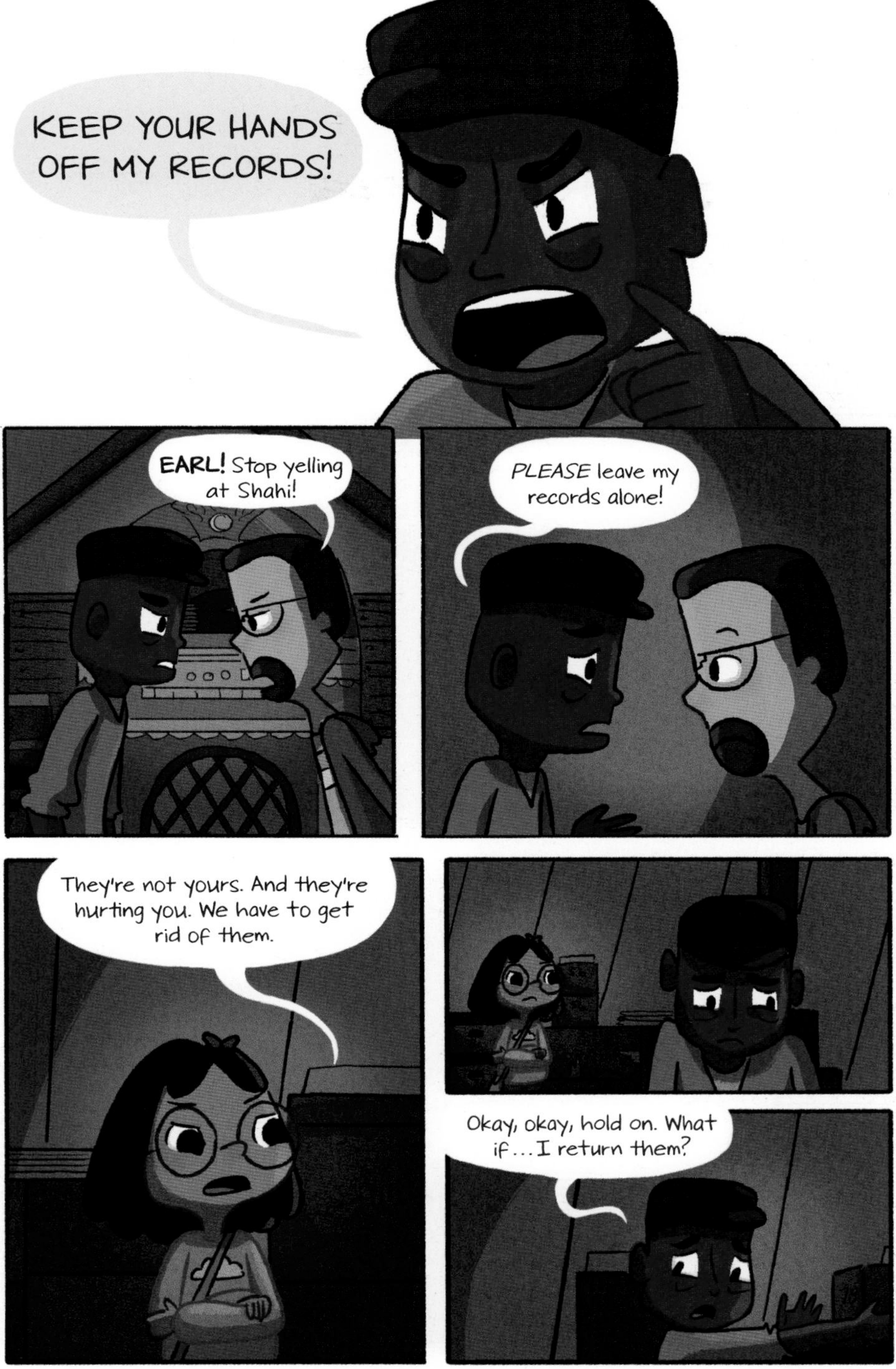
KEEP YOUR HANDS OFF MY RECORDS!
EARL! Stop yelling at Shahi!
PLEASE leave my records alone!
They're not yours. And they're hurting you. We have to get rid of them.
Okay, okay, hold on. What if... I return them?

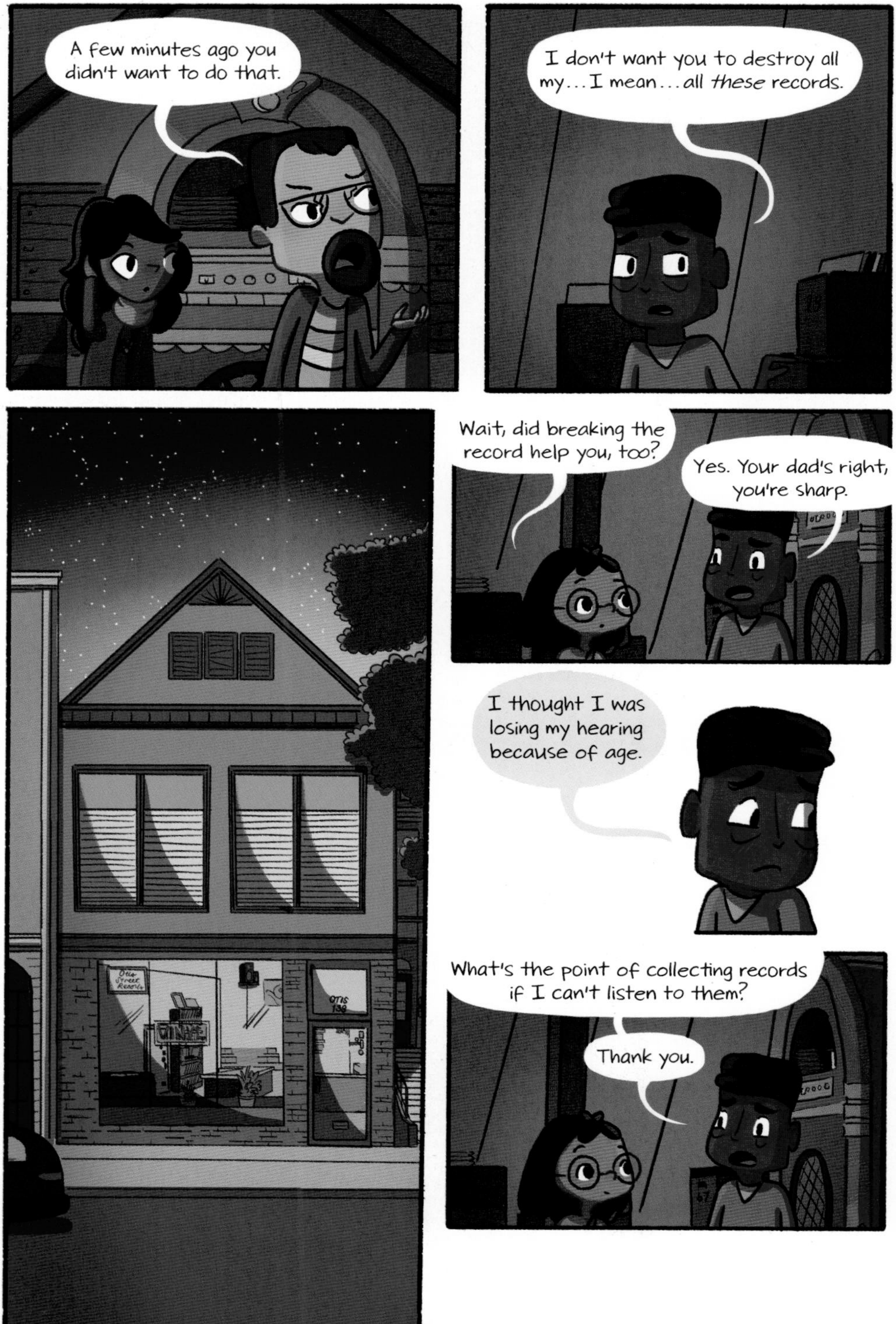
A few minutes ago you didn't want to do that.
I don't want you to destroy all my... I mean... all *these* records.
Wait, did breaking the record help you, too?
Yes. Your dad's right, you're sharp.
I thought I was losing my hearing because of age.
What's the point of collecting records if I can't listen to them?
Thank you.

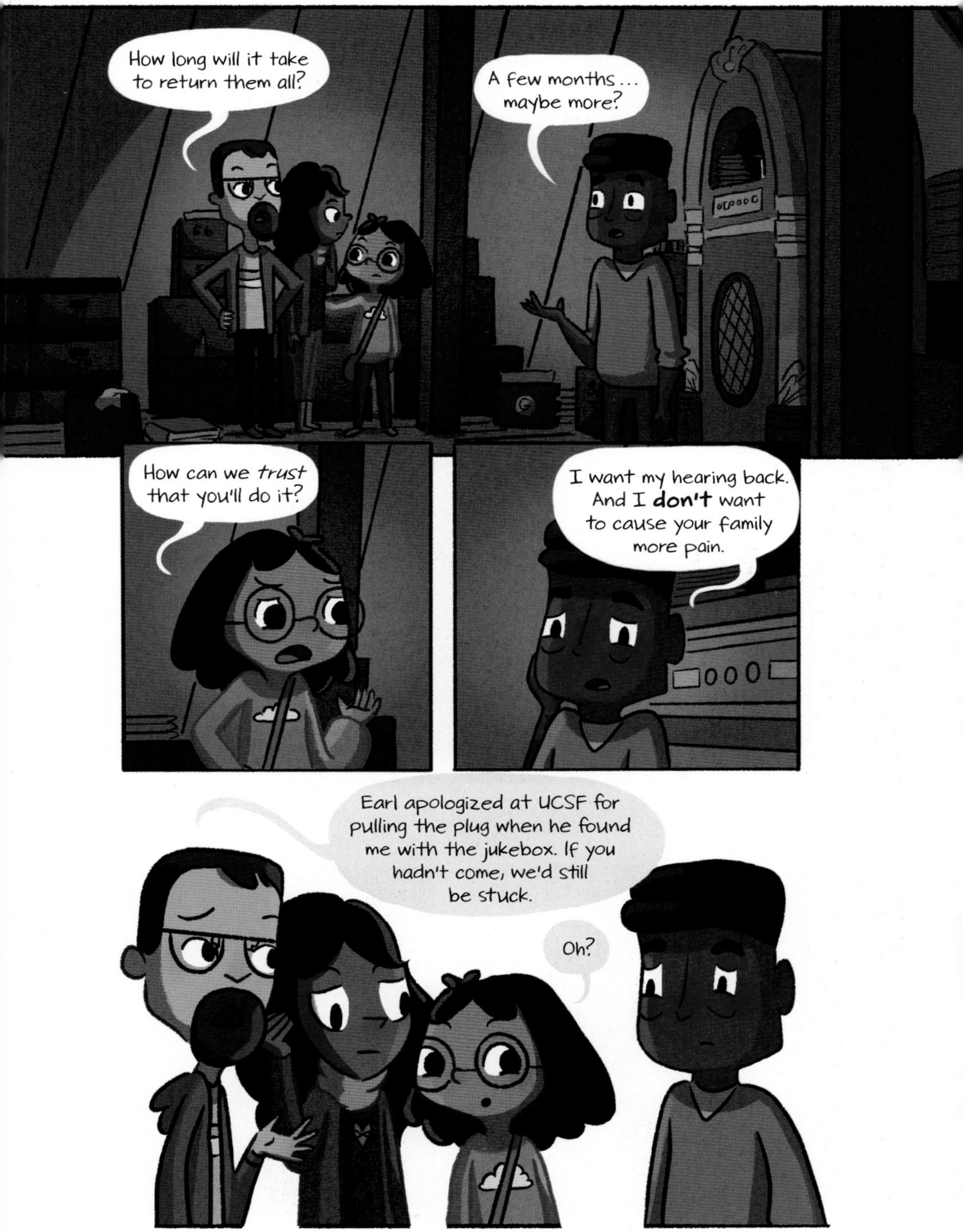
How long will it take to return them all?
A few months... maybe more?
How can we *trust* that you'll do it?
I want my hearing back. And I **don't** want to cause your family more pain.
Earl apologized at UCSF for pulling the plug when he found me with the jukebox. If you hadn't come, we'd still be stuck.
Oh?

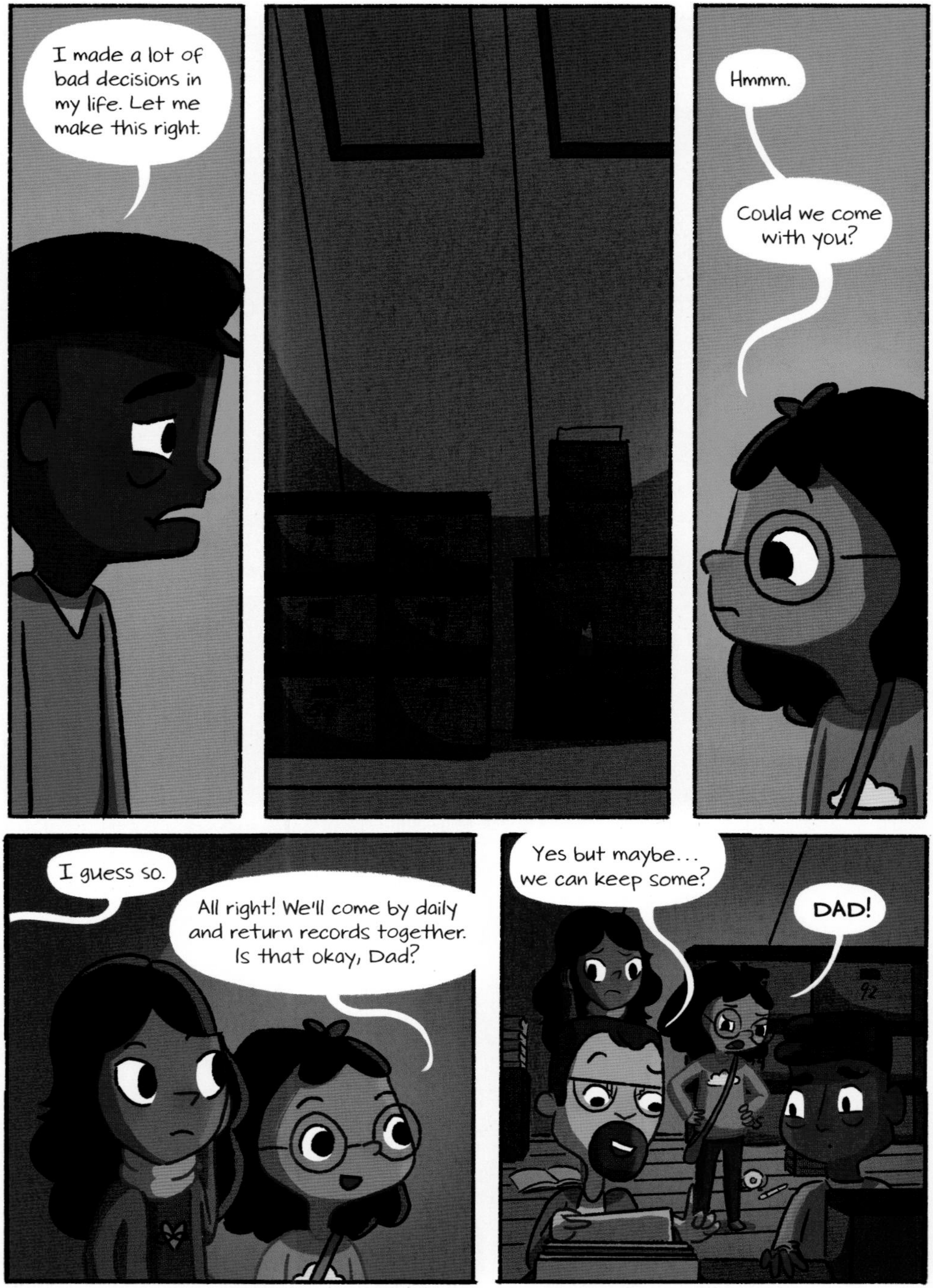

I made a lot of bad decisions in my life. Let me make this right.
Hmmm.
Could we come with you?
I guess so.
All right! We'll come by daily and return records together. Is that okay, Dad?
Yes but maybe... we can keep some?
DAD!

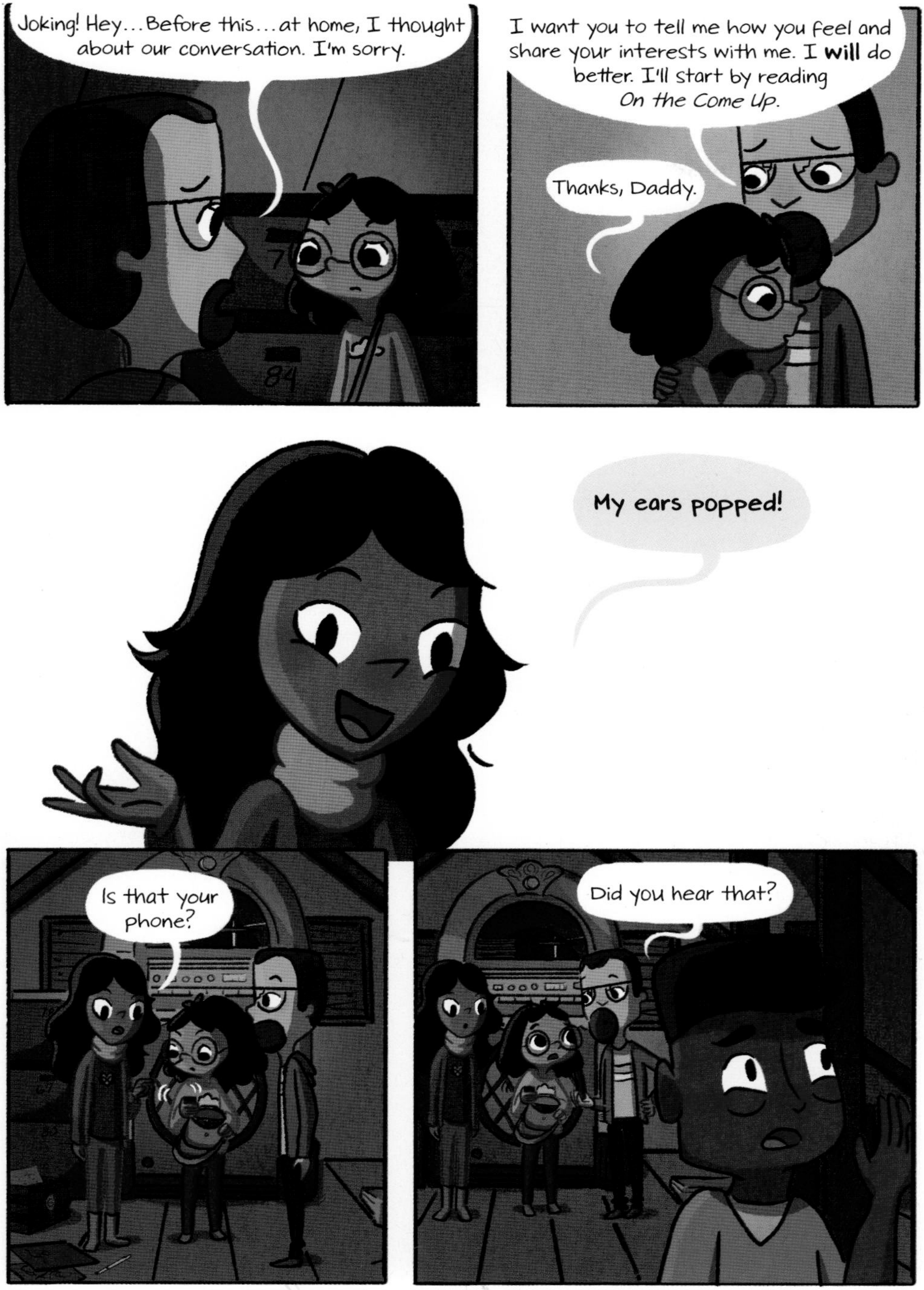
Joking! Hey... Before this... at home, I thought about our conversation. I'm sorry.
I want you to tell me how you feel and share your interests with me. I **will** do better. I'll start by reading *On the Come Up*.
Thanks, Daddy.
My ears popped!
Is that your phone?
Did you hear that?

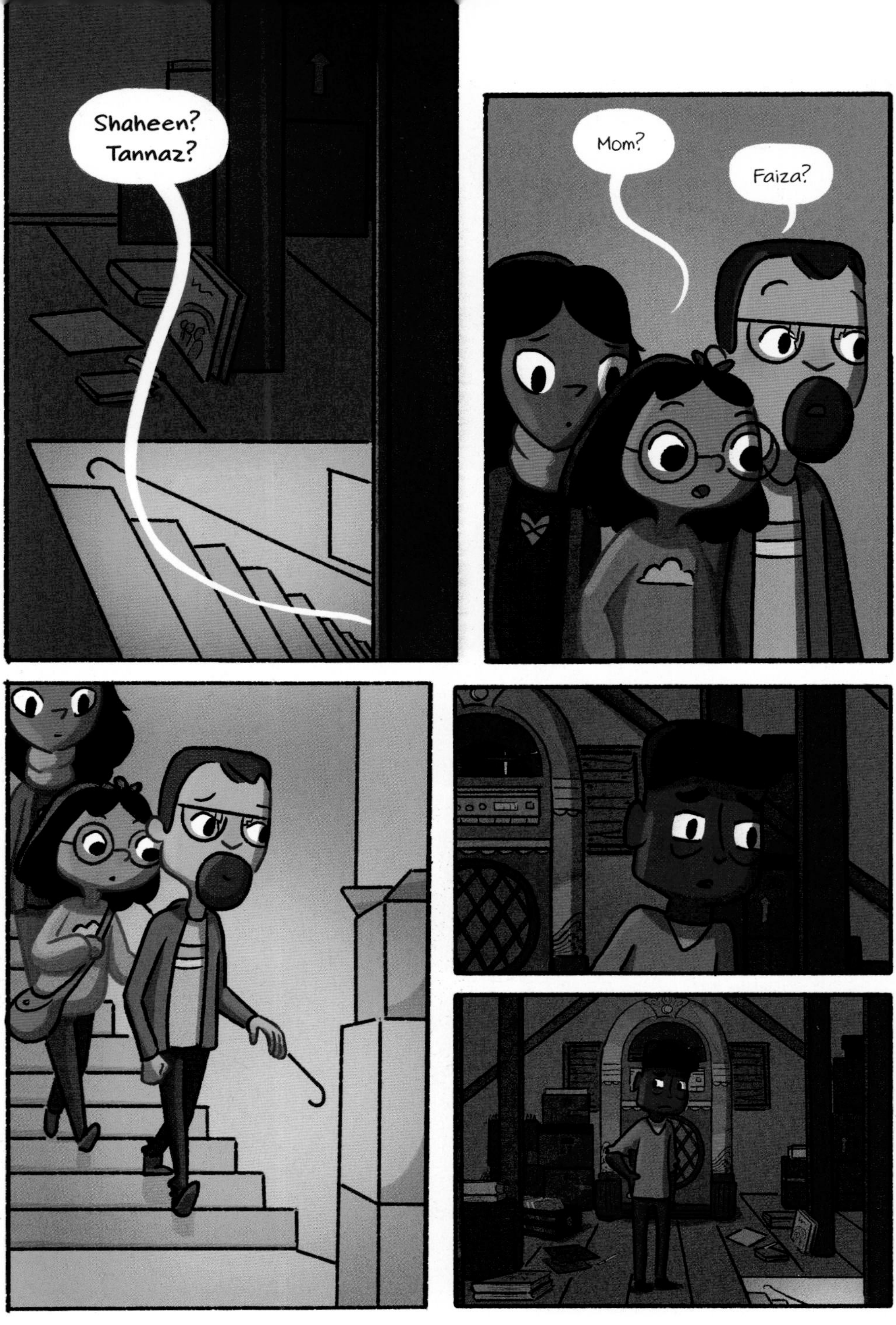
Shaheen? Tannaz?
Mom?
Faiza?

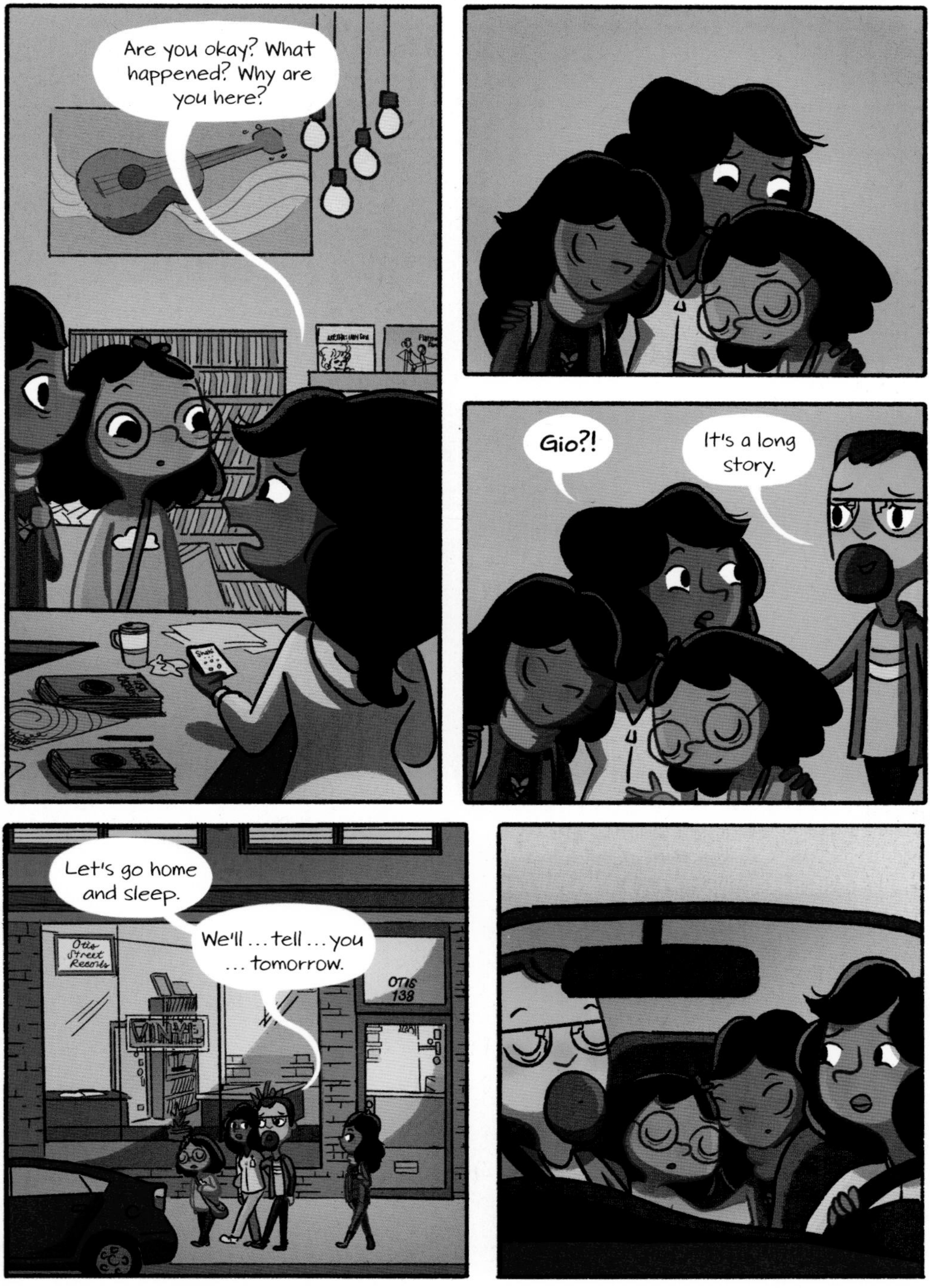

Are you okay? What happened? Why are you here?
Gio?!
It's a long story.
Let's go home and sleep.
We'll ... tell ... you ... tomorrow.
Otis Street Records
OTIS 138

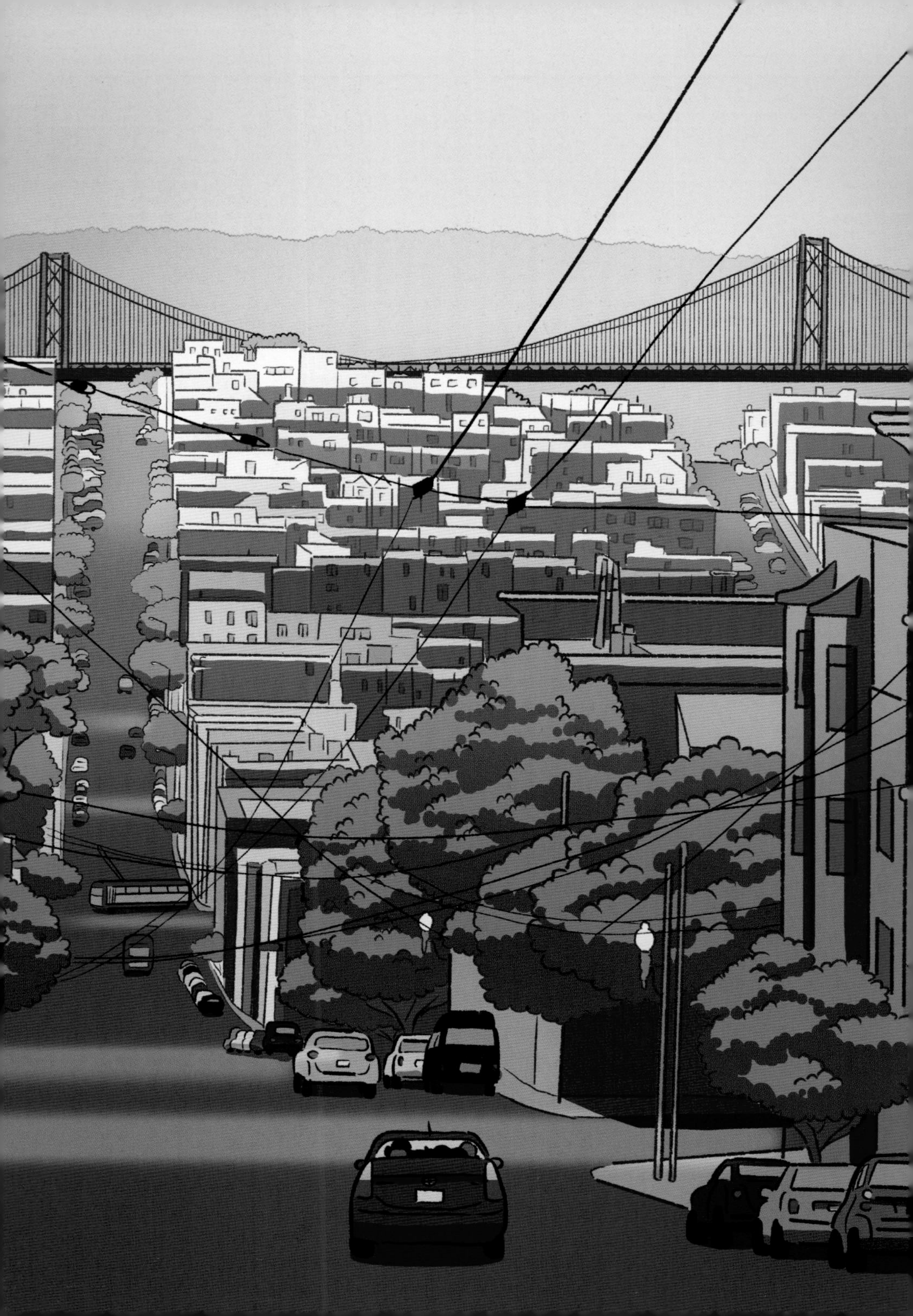

Eight months later

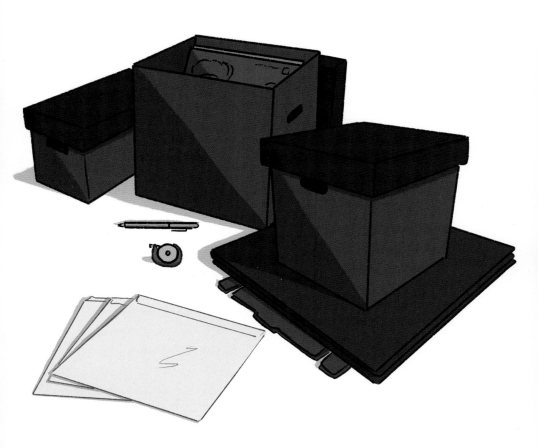

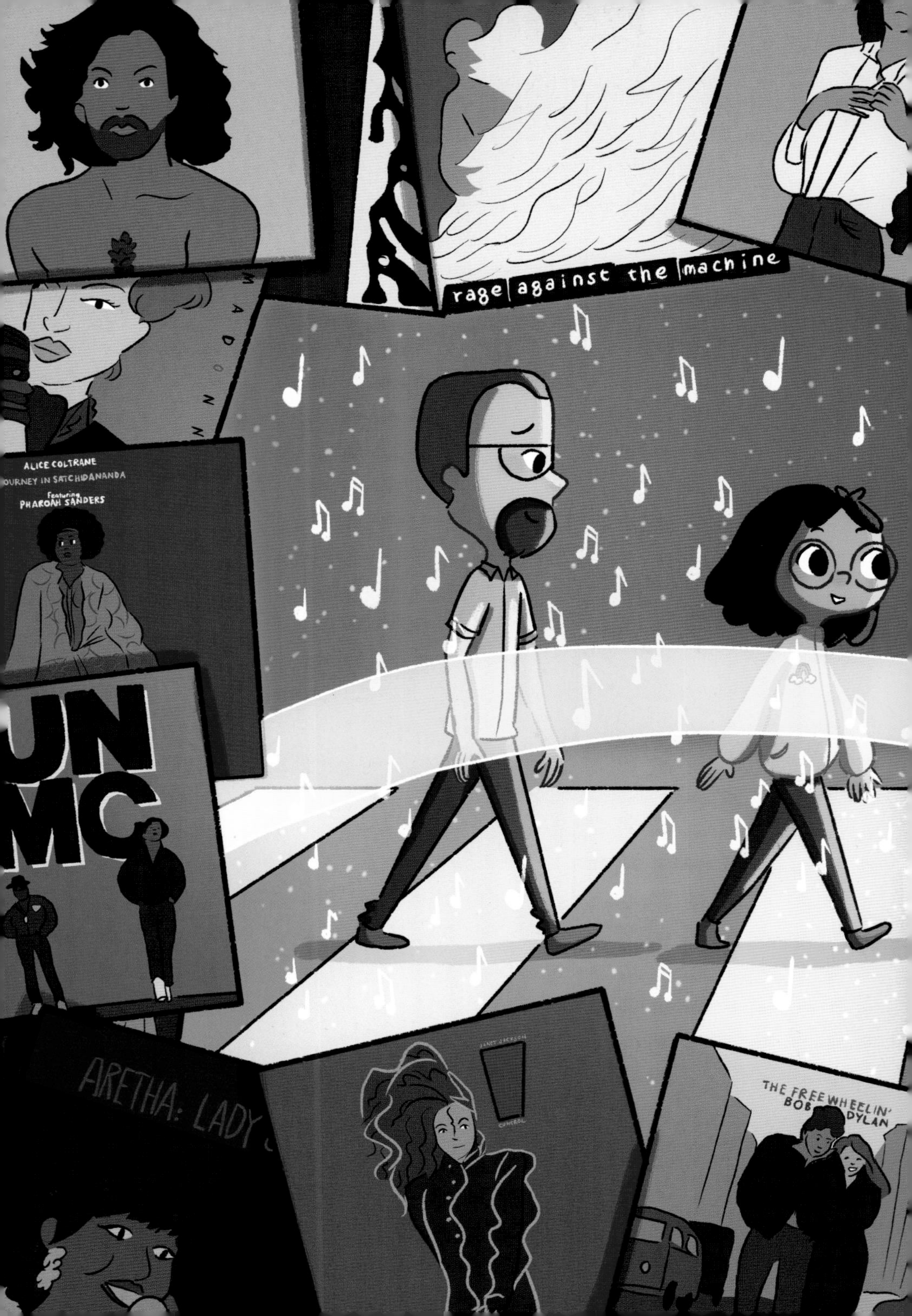
rage against the machine
MADONN
ALICE COLTRANE
OURNEY IN SATCHIDANANDA
Featuring PHAROAH SANDERS
UN
MC
ARETHA: LADY
THE FREEWHEELIN' BOB DYLAN

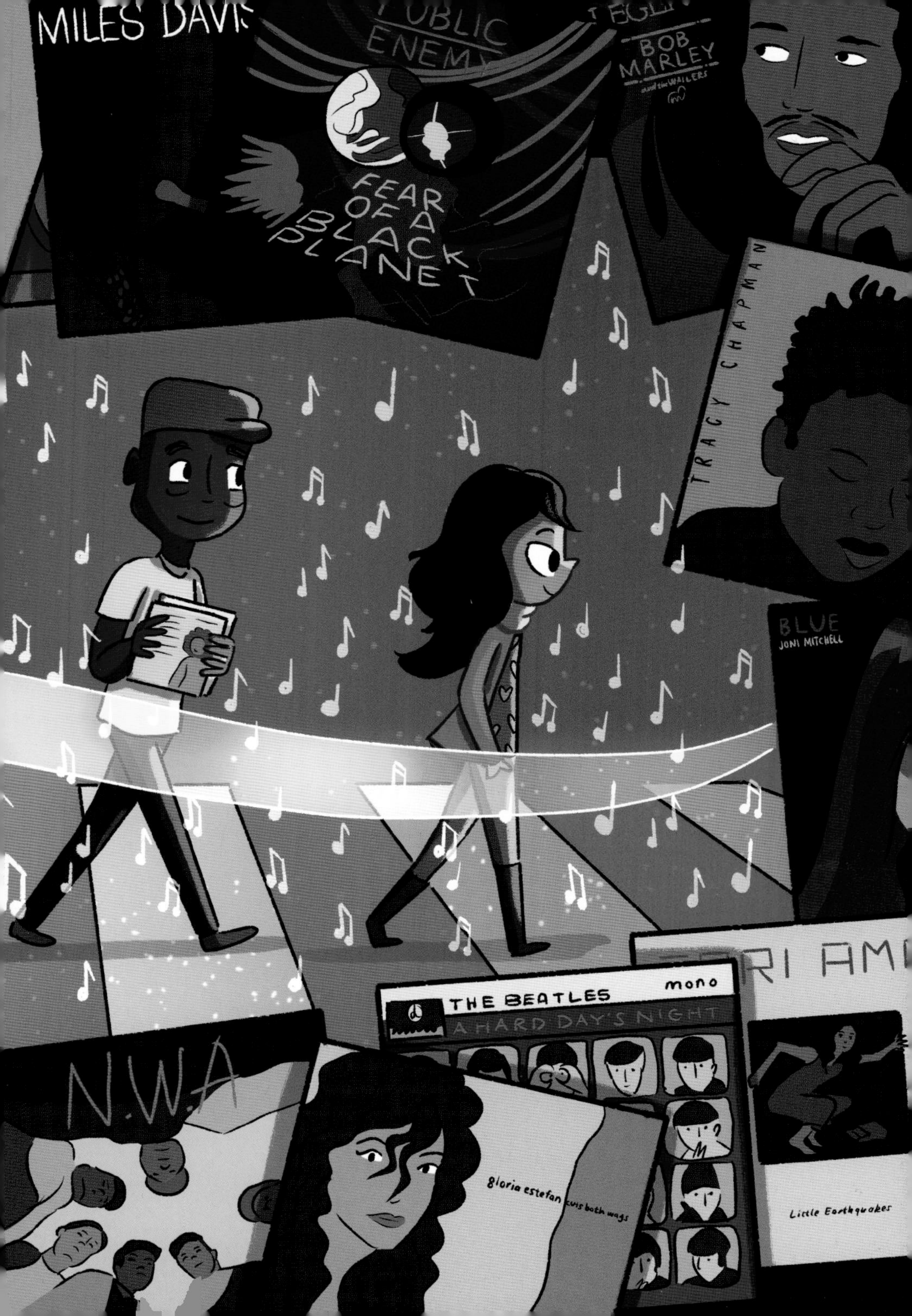
MILES DAVIS
PUBLIC ENEMY
FEAR OF A BLACK PLANET
BOB MARLEY
and the WAILERS
TRACY CHAPMAN
BLUE
JONI MITCHELL
THE BEATLES
mono
A HARD DAY'S NIGHT
N.W.A
gloria estefan cuts both ways
Little Earthquakes

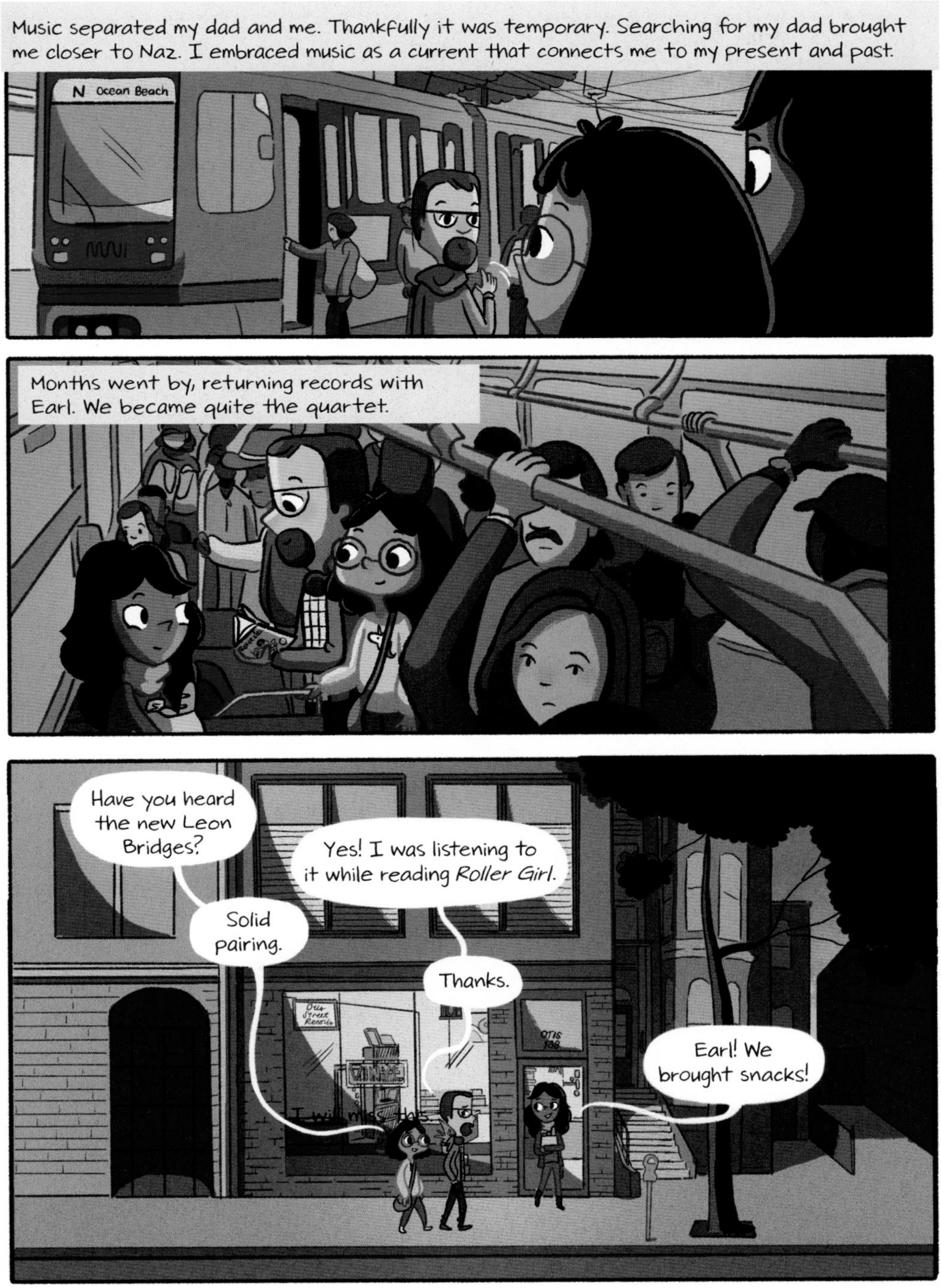
Music separated my dad and me. Thankfully it was temporary. Searching for my dad brought me closer to Naz. I embraced music as a current that connects me to my present and past.
N Ocean Beach
Months went by, returning records with Earl. We became quite the quartet.
Have you heard the new Leon Bridges?
Solid pairing.
Yes! I was listening to it while reading *Roller Girl*.
Thanks.
OTIS 138
Earl! We brought snacks!

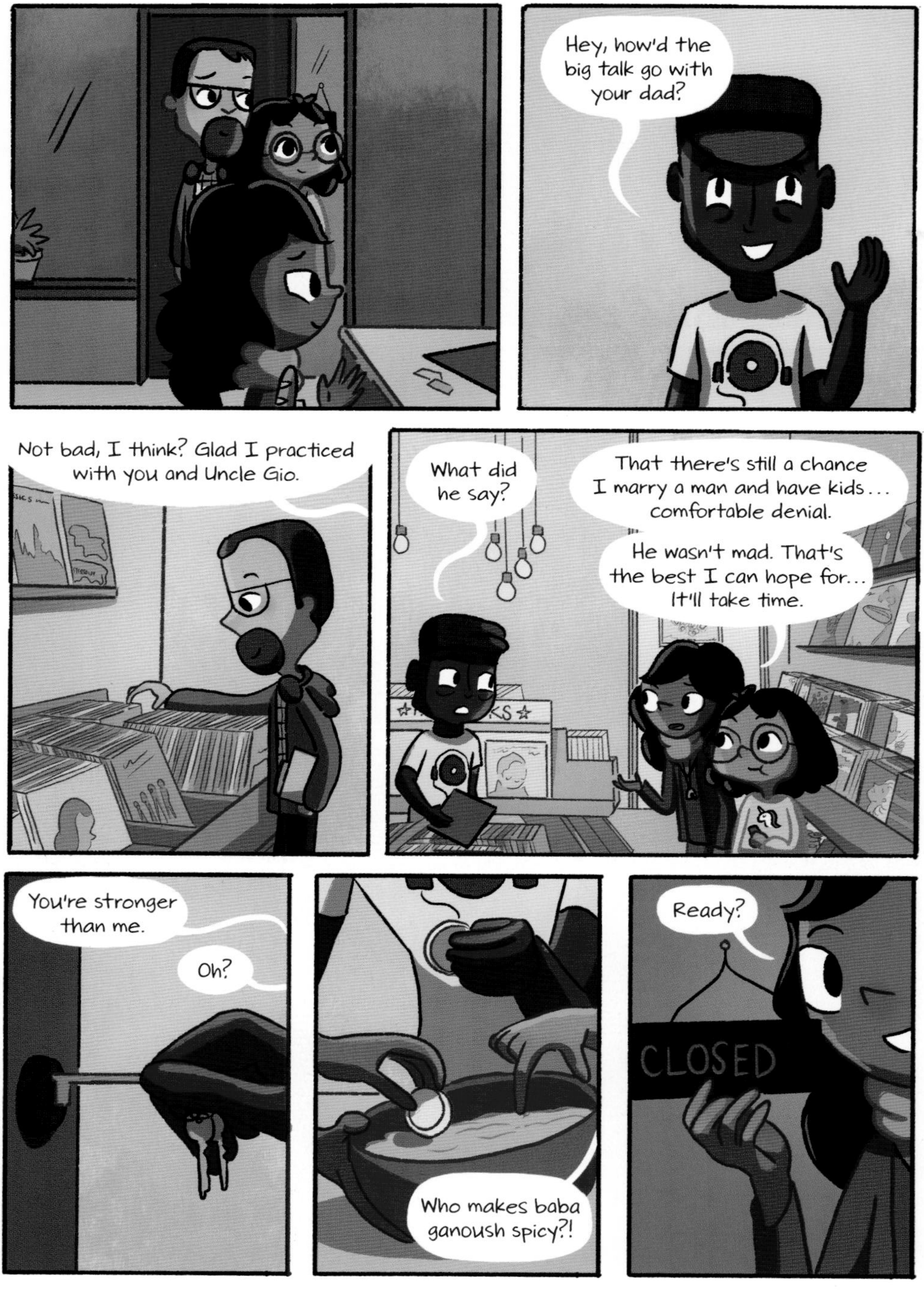

Hey, how'd the big talk go with your dad?
Not bad, I think? Glad I practiced with you and Uncle Gio.
What did he say?
That there's still a chance I marry a man and have kids... comfortable denial.
He wasn't mad. That's the best I can hope for... It'll take time.
You're stronger than me.
Oh?
Who makes baba ganoush spicy?!
Ready?
CLOSED

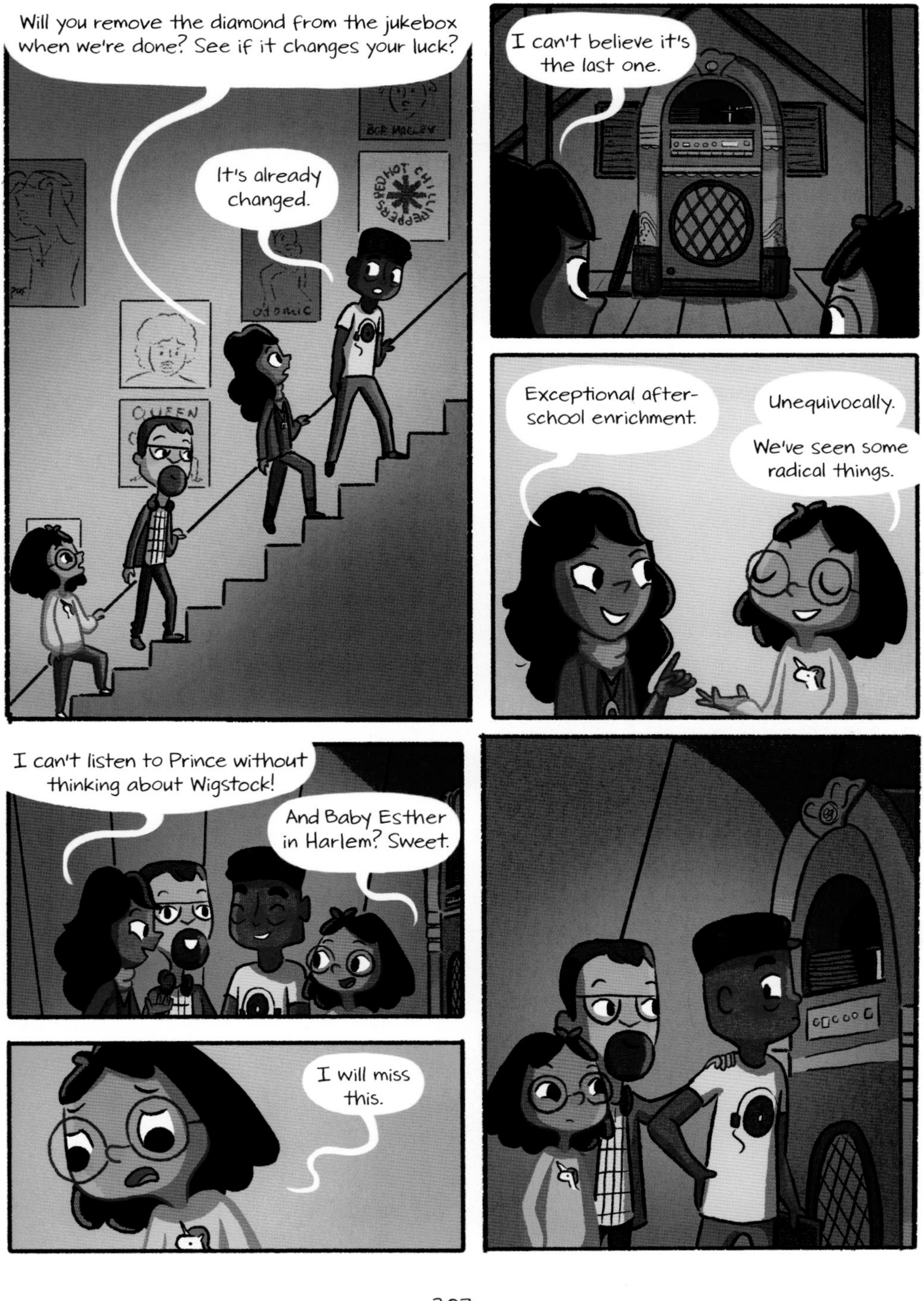
Will you remove the diamond from the jukebox when we're done? See if it changes your luck?
It's already changed.
BOB MARLEY
RED HOT CHILI PEPPERS
QUEEN
I can't believe it's the last one.
Exceptional after-school enrichment.
Unequivocally.
We've seen some radical things.
I can't listen to Prince without thinking about Wigstock!
And Baby Esther in Harlem? Sweet.
I will miss this.

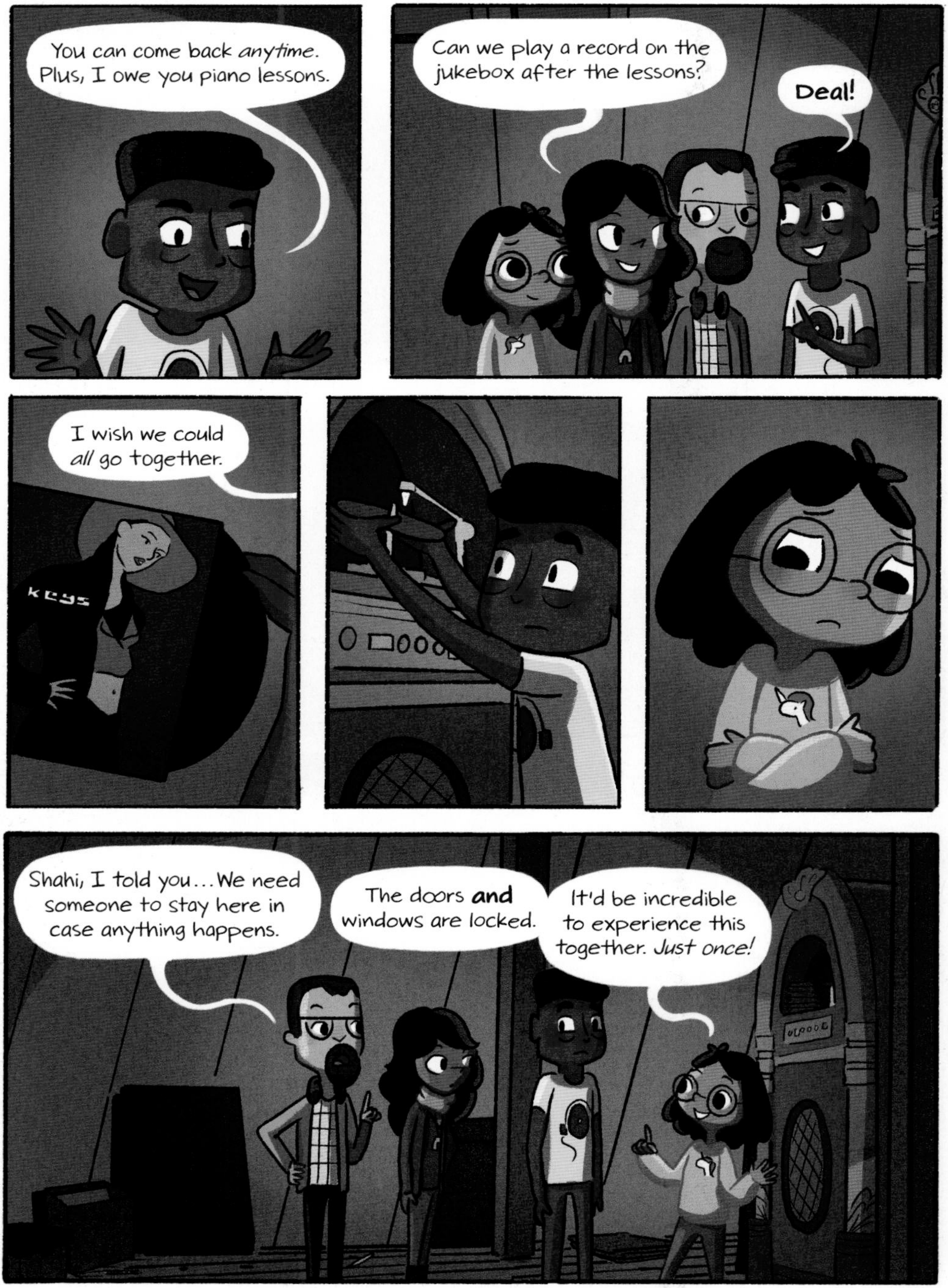
You can come back *anytime*. Plus, I owe you piano lessons.
Can we play a record on the jukebox after the lessons?
Deal!
I wish we could *all* go together.
KEYS
Shahi, I told you... We need someone to stay here in case anything happens.
The doors **and** windows are locked.
It'd be incredible to experience this together. *Just once!*

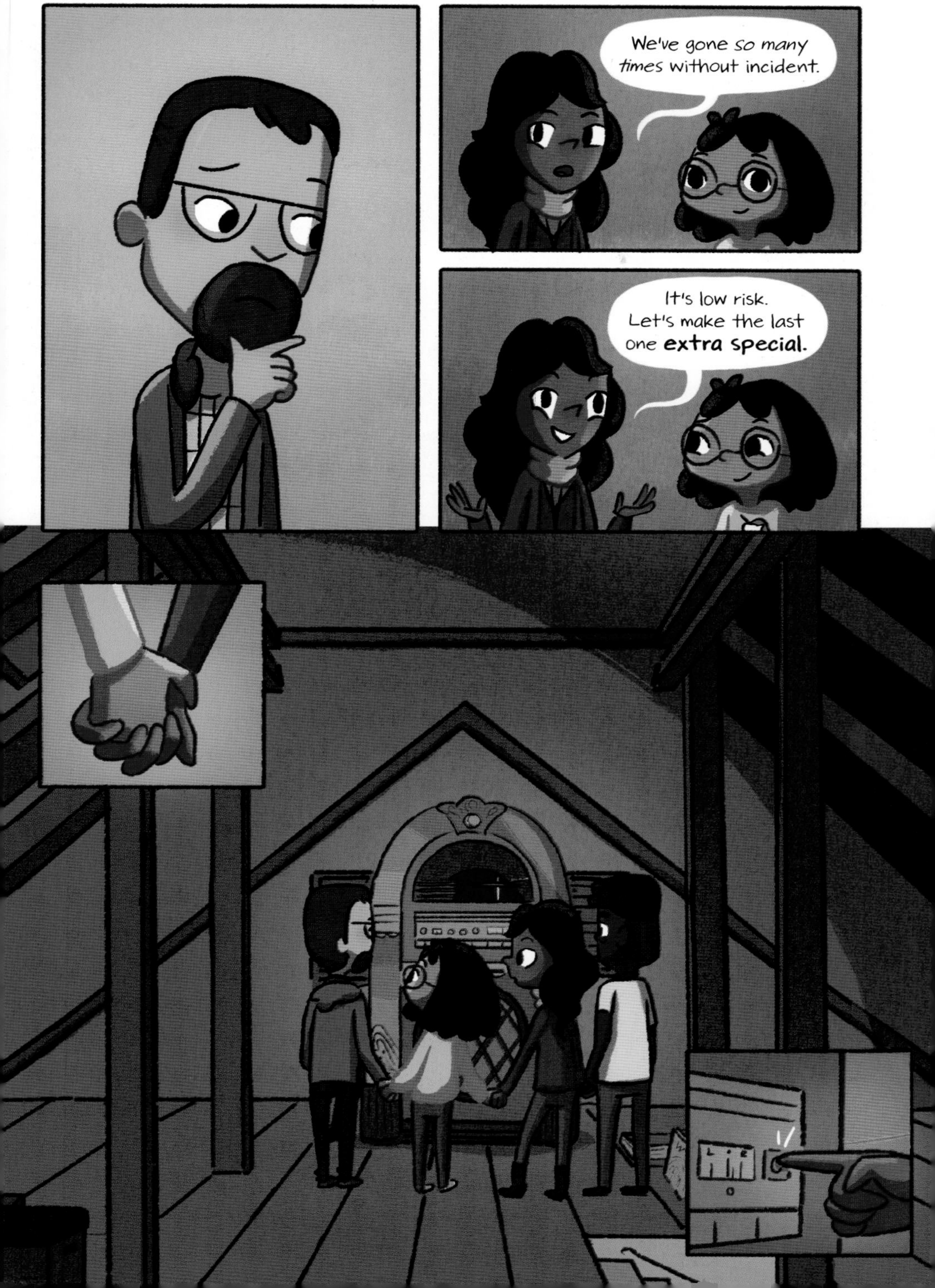

We've gone so many times without incident.
It's low risk. Let's make the last one **extra special.**

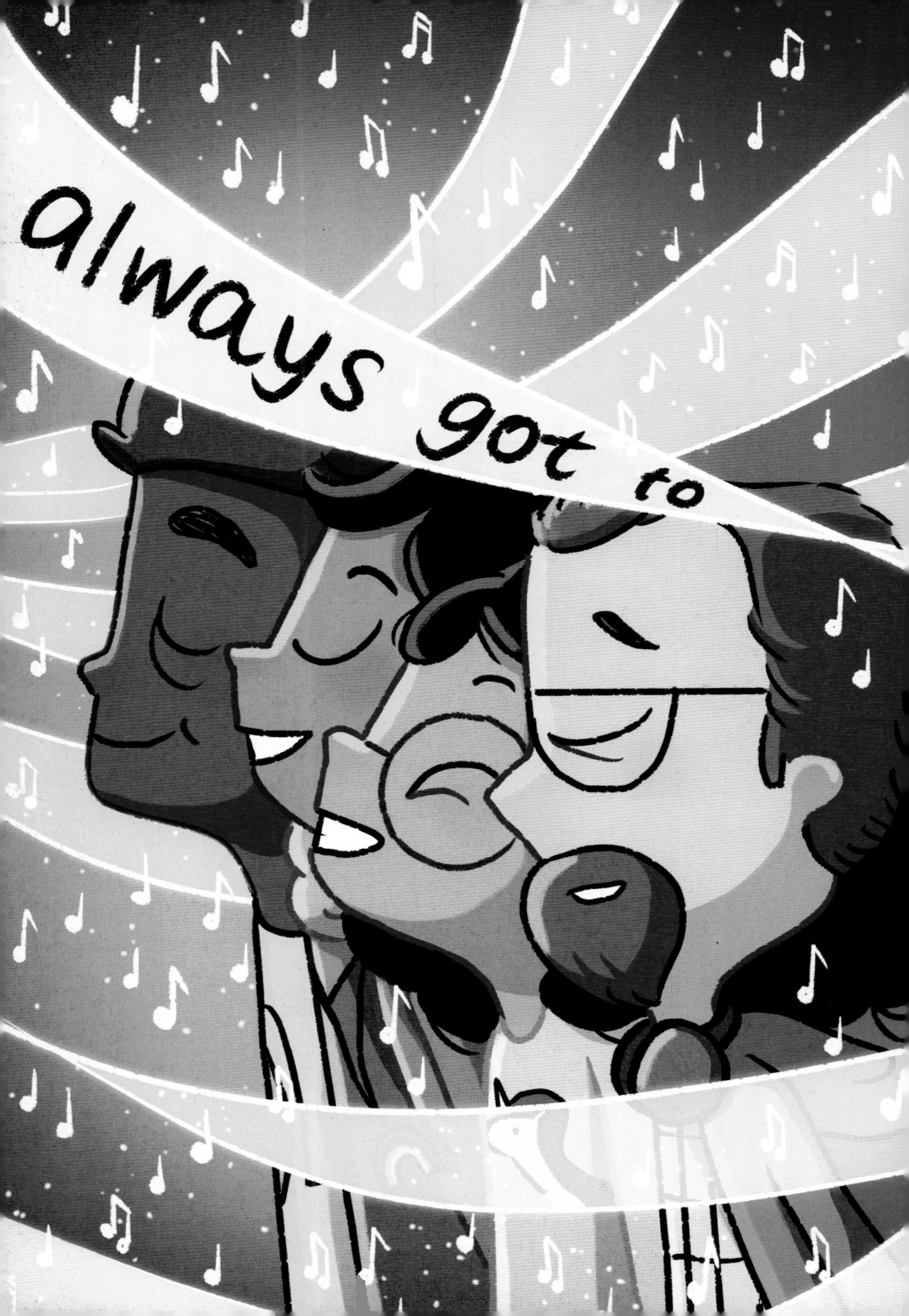
always got to

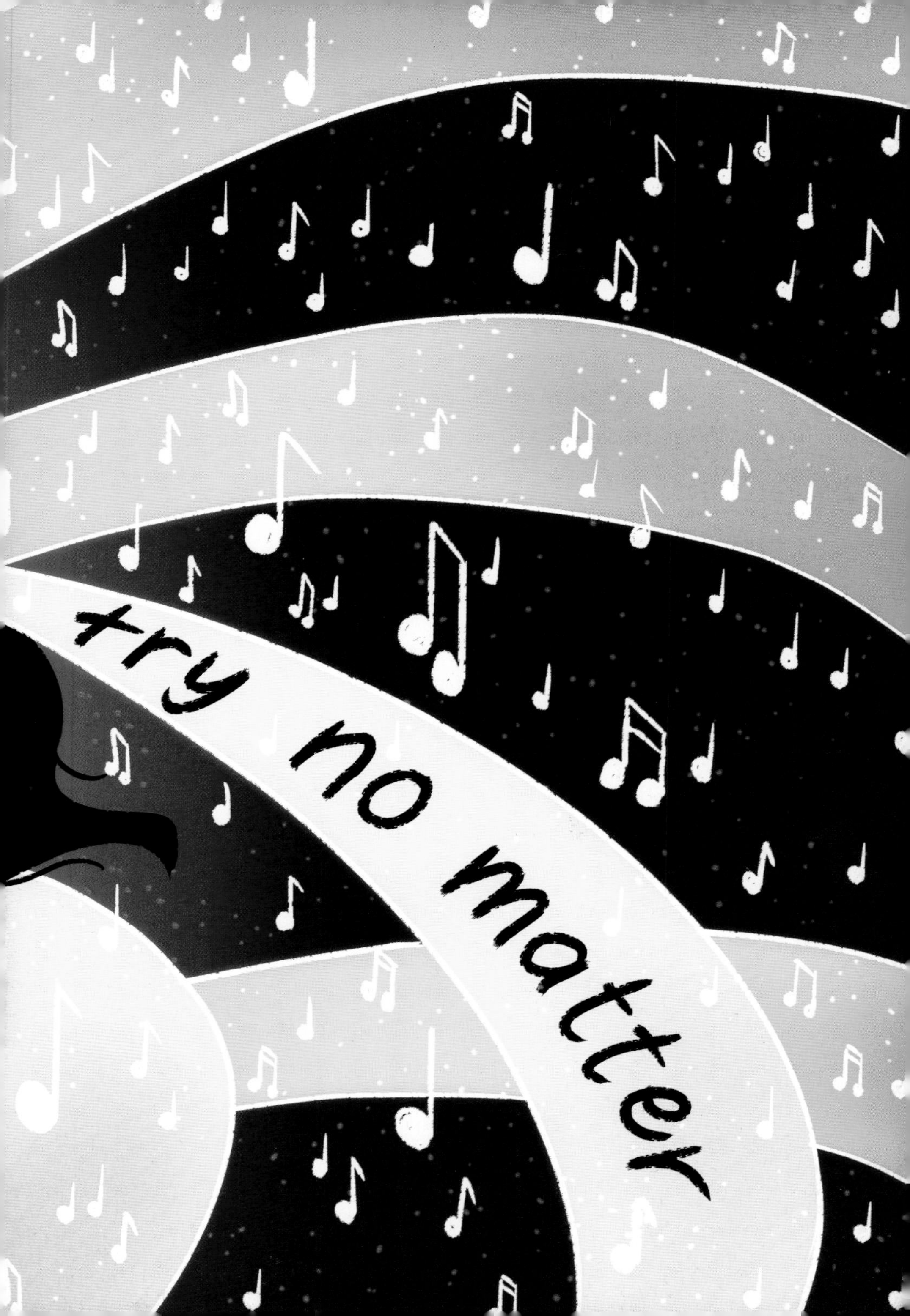
try no matter

PLAYLIST

Rock Me - **Sister Rosetta Tharpe**
Lean on Me - **Bill Withers**
Dance or Die - **Janelle Monáe**
Nobody Knows You When You're Down and Out - **Bessie Smith**
'Deed I Do - **Ruth Etting**
The Assignment Sequence - **Nina Simone**
I Got the Feelin' - **James Brown**
What's Going On - **Marvin Gaye**
The Message - **Grandmaster Flash
and the Furious Five**
I Would Die 4 U - **Prince**
You Send Me - **Aretha Franklin**
Baby Can I Hold You - **Tracy Chapman**
Journey in Satchidananda - **Alice Coltrane**
Three Little Birds - **Bob Marley**
California - **Joni Mitchell**
So What - **Miles Davis**
The Sound of Sunshine - **Michael Franti & Spearhead**
Coming Home - **Leon Bridges**
Blowin' in the Wind - **Bob Dylan**
A Woman's Worth - **Alicia Keys**

A note from Nidhi

*"Music, at its essence, is what gives us memories. And the longer
a song has existed in our lives, the more memories we have of it."*
—Stevie Wonder

My road to adulthood was paved with books. Without stories, I wouldn't have
survived my childhood. Music was equally important. I can name a song or
musician for each milestone moment in my life. One of them is the day I met
my husband, Nick, at the University of California at Santa Cruz. We were
sophomores in the year 2000. His roommate toured me through their
apartment and I stopped in Nick's room, which was covered in music posters.
His Ani DiFranco poster sparked our first hug and conversation.

Throughout our years together, we experienced great happiness and loss.
His brother, Joe, passed away suddenly in the early years of our relationship.
Music connected Nick and Joe. The last time they were together was at a
concert. Many years later, in our first pregnancy, we had a stillbirth. I remember
the Mason Jennings song that was our only comfort. Music helped us celebrate as
well. We walked down the aisle to a Red Hot Chili Peppers song.

Nick is a vinyl collector. We have 1,700 albums in our home. It's no stretch to
say that this book wouldn't exist without him. Nick regularly shares facts and
stories about music, and I feel fortunate to learn from him. One that I found
fascinating was when a James Brown concert was broadcast in Boston.
The country was mourning and upset about the assassination of MLK. There
were protests in most major cities. Boston was quiet because James Brown
shared his music with that community.

Once, I asked Nick why jukeboxes don't play full albums. They do, but they're
very rare. We discussed the enormous size and impracticality of a jukebox
that plays a twelve-inch record. As we spoke, I connected the notes of music,
history, and memory. I went to the drawing table and sketched this:

That was 2014. I continued writing pieces of *Jukebox* while finishing *Pashmina*. I recalled a promise made to my friend Faheema to feature a Bangladeshi-Muslim character in one of my books. Faheema isn't Shahi, but she definitely inspired her.

I spent years talking about Shahi, Naz, Gio, and Earl. Selecting albums. Researching history. Reading. Listening. Then I spent years drawing. These characters feel more like family than fiction. These pages are inspired by people in my life and songs that I love.

And now, they're no longer mine.

They're yours.

Thank you for spending time with them.

July 2020

At conventions and events Nick often introduces himself as my inspiration. He's correct. This is a small selection of art he's inspired.

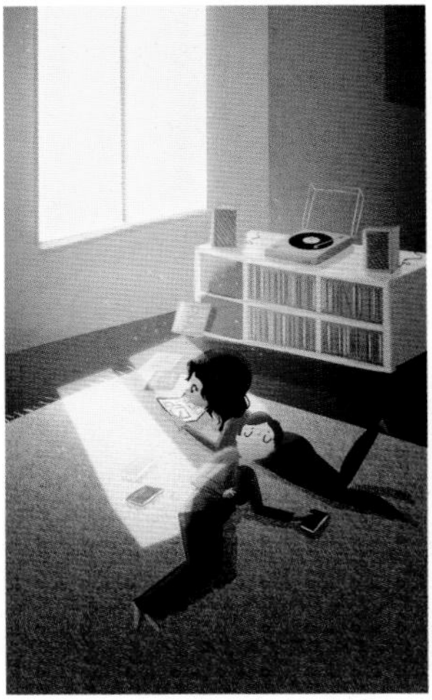

Comics & vinyl, 2012

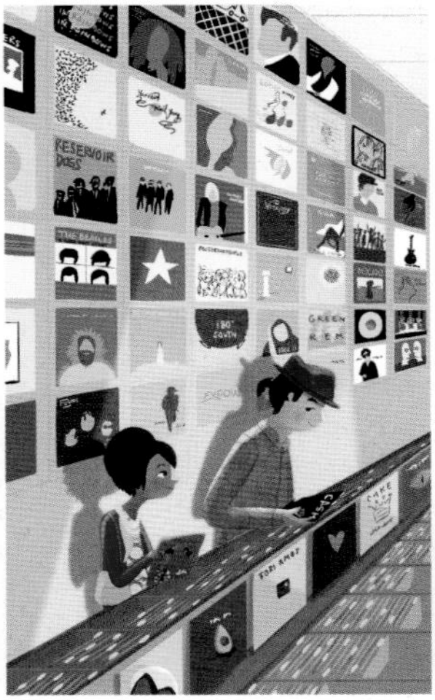
RESERVOIR DOGS

Audiophiles, 2013

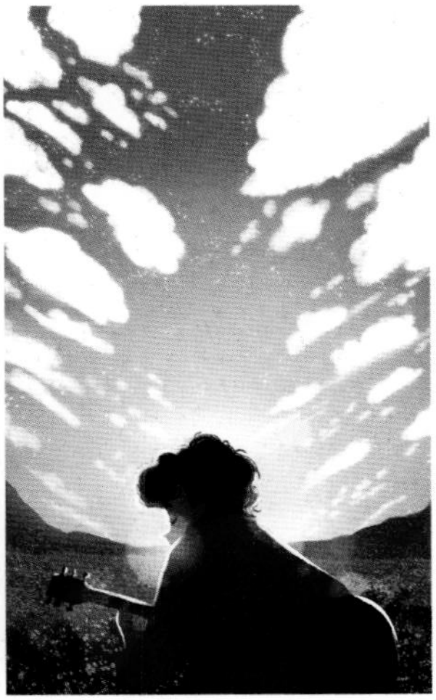

Music in you, 2017

Original
character
sketches

Refined character turnarounds

Shahi

Naz

Gio

Earl

Thumbnails

Page 1

1. Music connected me to my dad like rhythm and melody. Every moment of our lives from arguments to celebrations to our boring routines were more lively because of music.

2. But I grew weary of its perpetual place in our conversations.

3. What I didn't know was that music would be the cause of separation.

Page 2

1. Oh, I like this song.
("*Rock Me*" by Sister Rosetta Tharpe)

Page 3

1. Not surprising, you have a great ear, Shaheen.
2. Thanks, Daddy.
3. That's Sister Rosetta Tharpe. She really started rock and roll. She influenced all these men who took credit.
4. No one saw her for what she was because she couldn't sell as many records.
5. Blahblahblahgodmothersblahblahriffs...
6. Cool, so...
7. Yeah?

Page 4

1. Did you read *Ghost* yet? I left it on your nightstand.
2. Wait, Rosetta was also interesting because...
3. Blahblahradicalblah

Page 5

1. Blahblahgospelblahblah
2. Blahblahblahmarieblahblah
3. Blahblahtrailblazerblahblah
4. Mom says these days Dad's collection has become an obsession. He's constantly talking about vinyl thieves. Frequenting the same, tired record shop, asking endless questions.
5. And he hasn't told Mom yet, but he's been going on and on about a...

Page 6

Page 7

Process

Inks

Flat color

Final colors
with lighting and shading

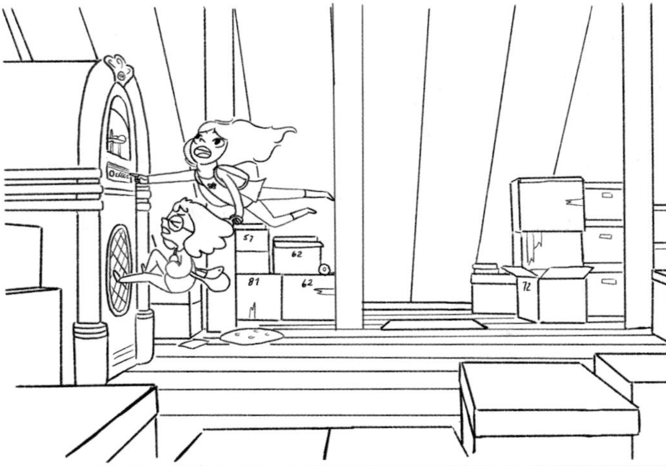
57
62
81
62
72
71

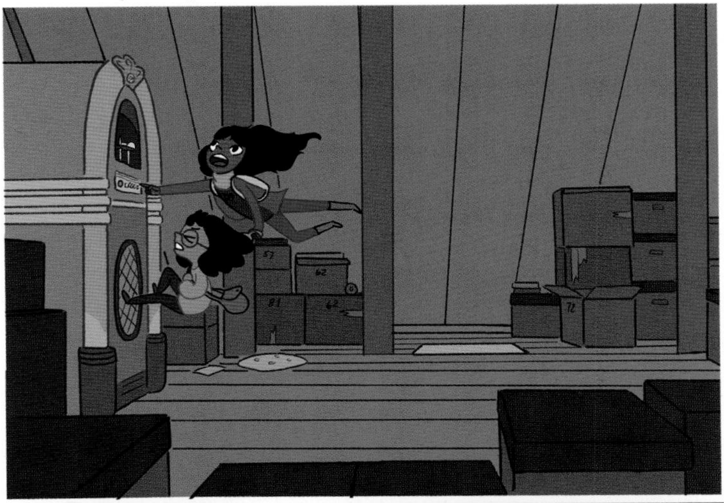
57
62
81
62
72

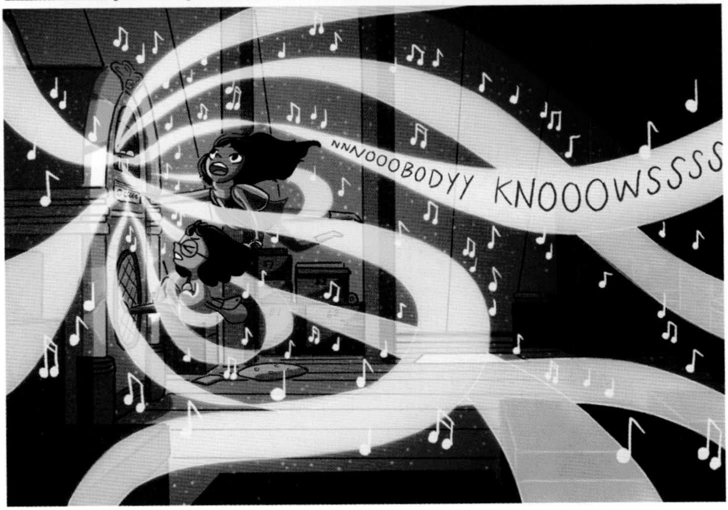
NNNOOOBODYY KNOOOWSSSS

Cover explorations

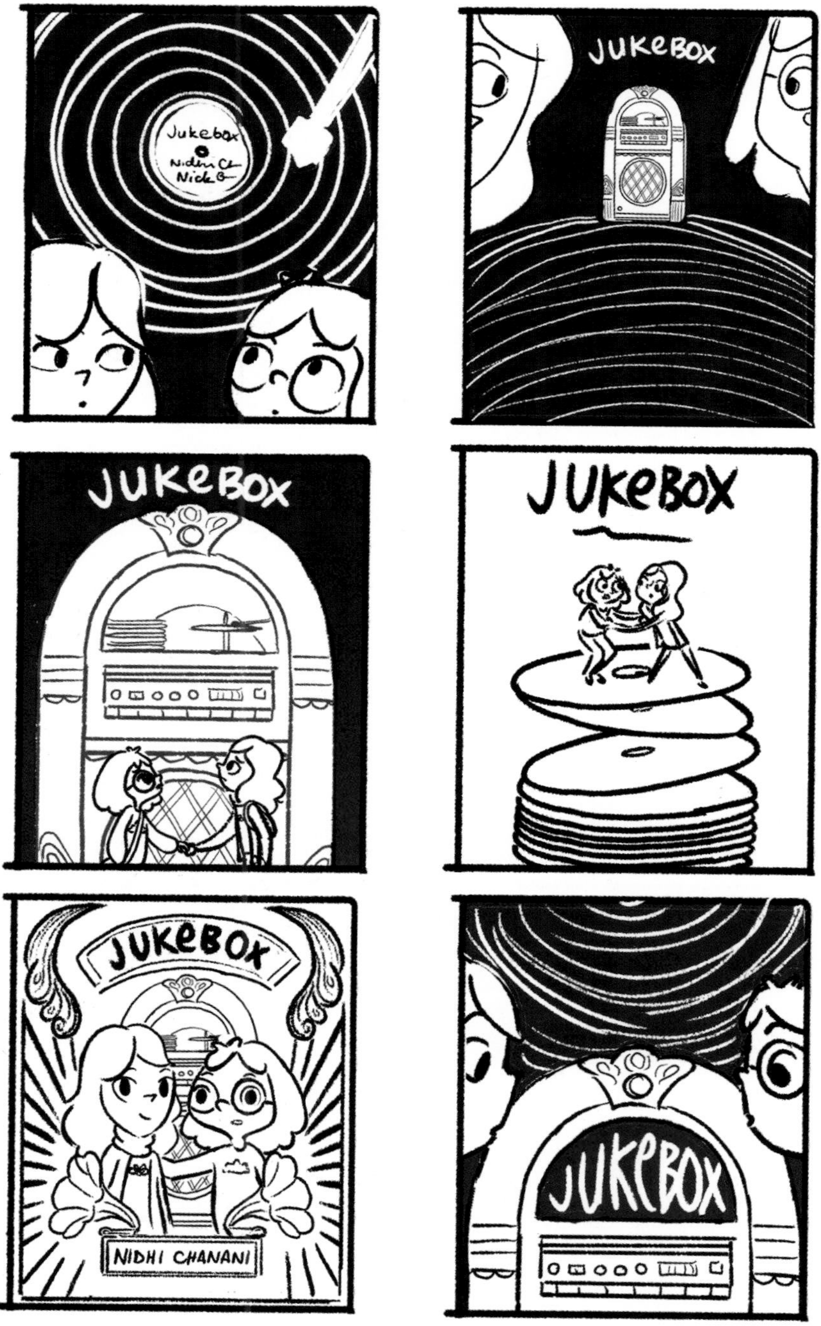
Jukebox
JUKEBOX
JUKEBOX
JUKEBOX
JUKEBOX
NIDHI CHANANI
JUKEBOX

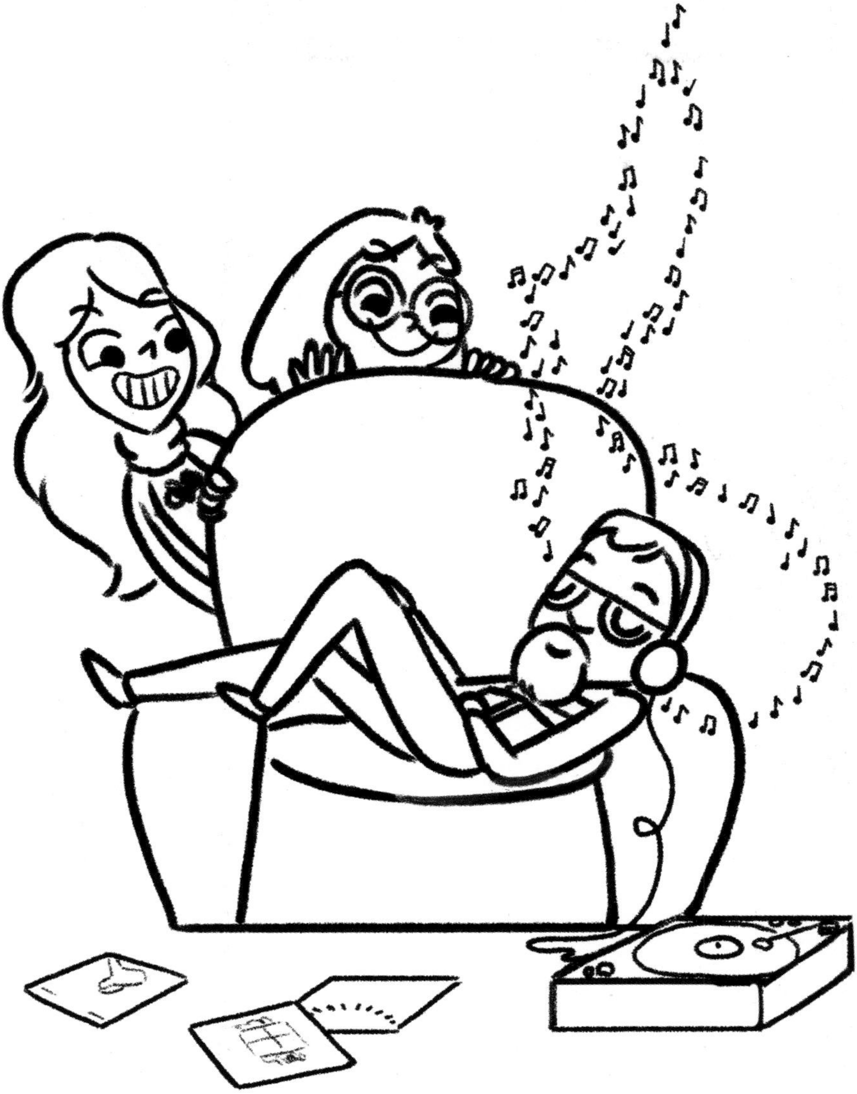

ACKNOWLEDGMENTS

Thank you to Mark Siegel for believing in my stories and the entire team at First Second for their hard work.

Thank you to my friend-editors Teresa Huang, Sunila Rao, and Lyla Warren. Your loving and critical eye helped from pitch to final art. I am so very grateful for all of you.

Thank you to Nickole Caimol, who has worked with me for years providing important and unseen support. I am forever grateful to your kind and thoughtful feedback and encouragement.

Thank you to Elizabeth Kramer for your quick, keen eye and dedication to color. We made a beautiful team.

Thank you to Faheema Chaudhury for your sugar-sweet brightness and inspiration. I know you will inspire many characters.

Thank you to the early readers: Tillie Walden, Matt Silady, Saadia Faruqi, Sherri L. Smith, Laura Ruby, and Kip Wilson. Your feedback made the story stronger.

Thank you to Maneesh Yadav, Sheetal Jain, Evan Hamilton, Mariko Tamaki, Praveena Gummadam, and Sean Leo for your excitement and encouragement through the many years it takes to complete a book.

Thank you to Leela, Nick, Bernie, Harold, and my mom for brightening my days.

Thank you to the teachers and librarians who share and teach graphic novels.

Thank you to the folks who read, share, buy, send messages, and support my work. You made this possible.

PRAISE FOR *PASHMINA*

"Colorful and deeply personal, *Pashmina* illuminates the experience of an Indian American teenager and invites us to contemplate the power of our choices."
—**Gene Luen Yang,** national bestselling author of *American Born Chinese*

"*Pashmina* is filled to the brim with magic and heart."
—**Victoria Jamieson,** author of *Roller Girl*

"Chanani masterfully turns the complex immigrant narrative into a magical and captivating work of art."
—*New York Times*

"Chanani's debut graphic novel is a charming blend of fantasy and reality with a feminist twist."
—*Washington Post*

"In this spectacular debut graphic novel, a young woman searches for the truths of her past."
—*Teen Vogue*

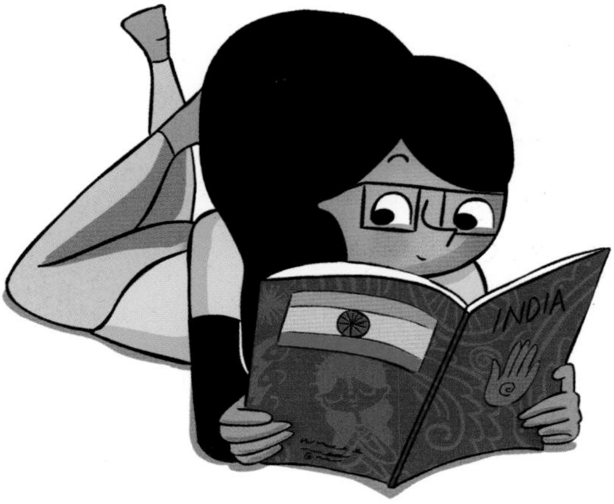
INDIA

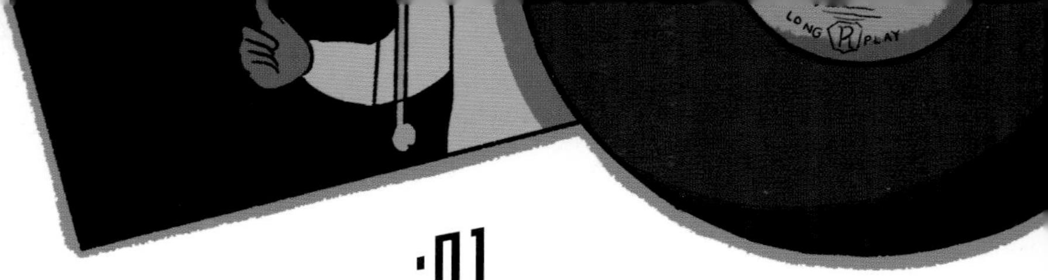
LONG PLAY

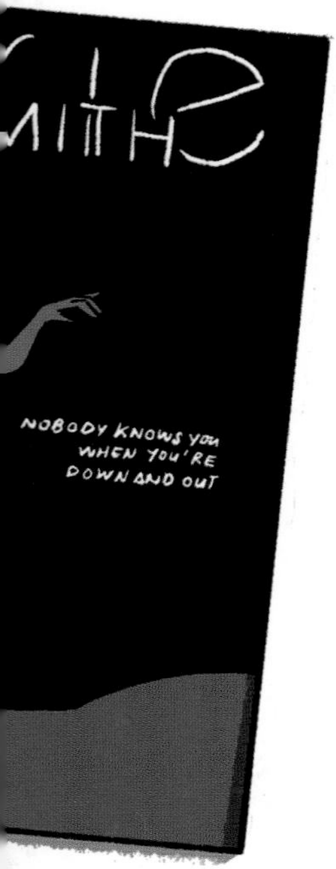
NOBODY KNOWS YOU
WHEN YOU'RE
DOWN AND OUT

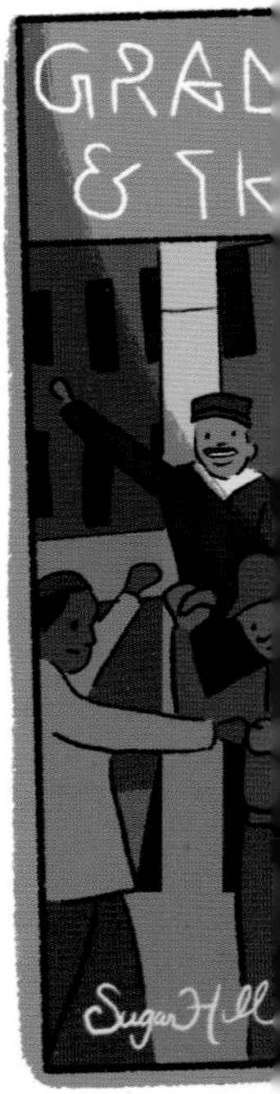

:01
First Second

Published by First Second
First Second is an imprint of Roaring Brook Press, a division of Holtzbrinck Publishing Holdings Limited Partnership
120 Broadway, New York, NY 10271

Don't miss your next favorite book from First Second!
For the latest updates go to firstsecondnewsletter.com and sign up for our enewsletter.

Library of Congress Control Number: 2020919556

Paperback ISBN: 978-1-250-15637-2
Hardcover ISBN: 978-1-250-15636-5

Our books may be purchased in bulk for promotional, educational, or business use. Please contact your local bookseller or the Macmillan Corporate and Premium Sales Department at (800) 221-7945 ext. 5442 or by email at MacmillanSpecialMarkets@macmillan.com.

FIRST EDITION

Edited by Mark Siegel and Samia Fakih
Cover and interior book design by Sunny Lee
Color by Nidhi Chanani and Elizabeth Kramer
Color flats by Nickole Caimol, RobtLSnyder, K Uvick, and Holley McKend
Lettering by Aditya Bidikar

Inked in Clip Studio Paint and digitally colored with handmade texture brushes.

Printed in China by Toppan Leefung Printing Ltd., Dongguan City, Guangdong Province

Paperback: 10 9 8 7 6 5 4 3 2 1
Hardcover: 10 9 8 7 6 5 4 3 2 1

BY ART WE LIVE

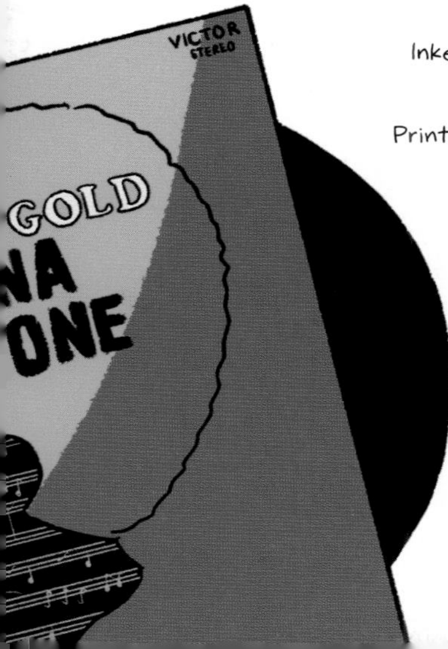
VICTOR
STEREO
GOLD

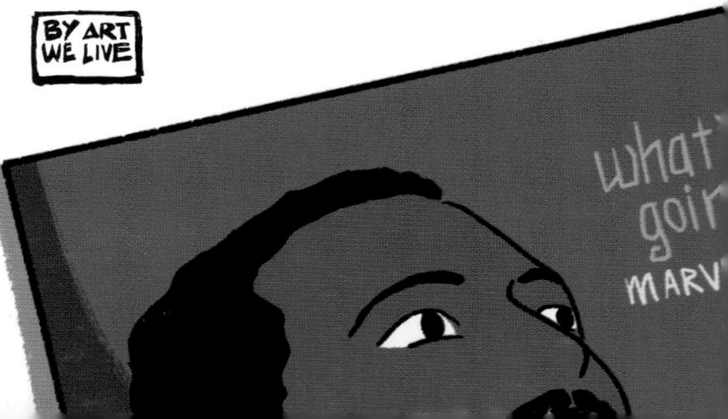